# The Apothecary

A novel by

**Dereck Hucklesby**

In memory of my parents

William and Lily Hucklesby

Visit us online at www.authorsonline.co.uk

An Authors OnLine Book

Text Copyright © Dereck Hucklesby 2007

Cover design by Dereck Hucklesby ©
The cover design includes Le Docteur Alchimiste by Nicholas Tardieu, an engraving reproduced by permission of the Science Museum.

All rights reserved. No part of this publication may be reproduced, stored in a retrieval system, or transmitted in any form or by any means, electronic, mechanical, photocopy, recording or otherwise, without prior written permission of the copyright owner. Nor can it be circulated in any form of binding or cover other than that in which it is published and without similar condition including this condition being imposed on a subsequent purchaser.

ISBN 978-0-755203-97-0

Authors OnLine Ltd
19 The Cinques
Gamlingay, Sandy
Bedfordshire SG19 3NU
England

This book is also available in e-book format, details of which are available at
www.authorsonline.co.uk

# ABOUT THE AUTHOR

Dereck Hucklesby was born in Harpenden, Hertfordshire UK, and was educated at St Albans County Grammar School and at Kings College London. He is the co-author of some forty papers in Plant Biochemistry, working mostly in Bristol, with a long period abroad in the USA, and shorter periods in Australia, South Africa and Germany. He is a devoted amateur performer of early music. His interest in history, especially in the history of science and of ideas in general, resulted in this book, his first novel.

*With best wishes*

*D. P. Hucklesby*

# CHAPTER 1

*If a lot of cures are suggested for a disease, it means that the disease is incurable.*
    Chekhov


The stench of brimstone rose to meet Celia Albright from the depths below, but she had no intention of abandoning hope. It was not her style. Crossing herself, she began a cautious descent of the stairs, trying to recall which was the crumbling step. Ahead of her the reek of hot sulphur welled up, co-operating pungently with the following wind of garlic from her interrupted cooking. The house smelled like the Devil's kitchen. Since it was the middle of the day, no candles were lit, and she had, in her anger, set off without preparation into the darkness of the basement stairs, overlooking the hazards of the journey into the bowels of the building.

At some time in the past the cellar had been a workshop, but was now used by an apothecary as a storage place – so he had said – for the apparatus and medicines of his calling. She had agreed to let for a generous rent. Generosity was a quality so rare among her tenants that she should have been suspicious. Why had she not asked more questions?

Devising in her mind unpleasant deaths for the apothecary, one of which was poisoning him slowly with his own malodorous vapours, almost accelerated her own extinction. The firmness of the ground to her heel was suddenly unmatched by the experience of her toes, and she pitched forward momentarily before managing, with the help of a vigorous push of her hand against the wall, to save herself. Instead of falling she accelerated, upright and on her feet but unbalanced and out of control, down the remaining steps. Arriving precipitately at the blank wall at the bottom of the stairs, she buffered herself with her hands, and then sat down heavily against the door that led into the room on the right. Its hinges and catch were severely tested by the unexpected visit, but they – like her substantial frame – had been built to last. Celia Albright's arrival was announced by a prolonged clatter followed by a crash. For some seconds she sat there, exploring the descriptive possibilities of the English language. Then she crossed herself again. It did little good.

'I'll serve his bollocks for supper,' she muttered.

\* \* \* \* \*

'What is the Green Lion, father?' asked the flaxen-haired boy.

At first the apothecary paid no attention to the question. He was deep in thought. His spirits were rising a little, but they had started the day lower than the dark basement in which he now stood. Concentration on practical matters he found was helpful to dispel such moods. Work was already in progress in this unsuitable cellar into which he had recently moved, but there was much sorting and setting-up still to be done. The words of Paracelsus came suddenly to his mind:

*'Their shops are nothing but foul sculleries, from which comes nothing but foul brews.'*

Paracelsus had been referring, alas, to apothecaries. He looked around him guiltily. The great philosopher and healer was his guiding light. How could anyone fail to be great having been given the name Philippus Theophrastus Bombastus von Hohenheim? The apothecary quoted him frequently – to himself and to others, but these words, which he had not known to be lodged in his memory, were neither comfortable nor supportive. He paused in his task of organising the workshop. Ideally this work should be done in the open air, well away from human habitation. Nothing could be said in favour of a basement. A few things could be said in favour of this particular basement – it was large and it had an old grate with a chimney, and had apparently been used for a commercial purpose at some time in the past. At least the greater part of the smoke from his furnaces could be vented in this way. At the first attempt he had wondered – when he had extinguished the flames and recovered from a choking fit – whether the chimney actually led anywhere. Subsequent exploration with the reverse end of a broom added to his treasures some disintegrating stonework, an amorphous conglomerate of unidentifiable material, an all too recognisable dead starling complete with nest; also the skeleton of a rat.

He turned over the letter that he had received yesterday from James Fisher, a friend who had a position in London where he was well-placed for news – or if not news, rumours – of new arrivals in the capital from foreign lands. So, Roche was in England – or might be. The hunt continued, and the apothecary had no doubt that he himself was the quarry. The list of the countries, from which he had been fugitive, grew as certainly as the hairs on his chin – France, Italy, Germany several times, Spain – there seemed to be no haven where he could settle and be free of the unfortunate legacy from his revered master, Michael.

Yesterday's order from Dr Fortune contributed to his black mood. The physician had been called to the bedside of the young son of Sir Robert Pelham, who had been appointed Deputy Lieutenant of the Shire by King Charles a few years previously. The nobleman had heard somewhere of the efficacious properties of Oil of Swallows in such cases. The physician had bowed, praised the nobleman's breadth of learning, matched only by his sharpness of perception, and promised to provide a medicine containing the

Oil if possible, although it was hard to find, *very* expensive, even if obtainable from stock – and if not so obtainable it was certainly rather early in the season for collection and manufacture. The actual task of supply had of course fallen to the apothecary. There was none on his shelves. And he was sceptical of its efficacy against the boy's illness – the swallow, with its swift flight and hectic activity, its mysterious appearances and departures, was presumably under the auspices of Mercury, and probably offered the worst possible treatment for a fever. Was Mercury retrograde at the moment? That would have an important influence. He must consult the tables.

The prospect of a day of long ladders and vertigo followed by the ritual murder and disgusting pulverisation in fresh herbs and butter of tiny creatures against whom he had no grudge, filled him with gloom. He might need to solve the problem with a vegetable oil of some kind, which he would disguise by an unusual colour and scent, and would dignify by a suitably elegant and equivocal label.

Deception! His life seemed full of it. He prayed frequently to the Lord God that this particular cup might be taken from him. But the circumstances of his birth and upbringing had determined otherwise. And one deception seemed always to lead to another, often with multiplication. He was painfully reminded of the predicament even in the simple act of signing his name – or rather signing whichever name he was currently using.

What he had told Celia Albright was indeed truthful, as far as it went. His room in the centre of the small town was small and overcrowded. He needed storage space for the herbs and medicines and the apparatus of his profession. The floors and shelving space available were lined with bottles, boxes and packages labelled by the supplier or his own neat handwriting. The physicians operated by attempting to clear out the patient's system, and if bleeding was not considered sufficient, a whole arsenal of products was available. Disease must be expelled, violently if necessary, from the body. There were four routes for expulsion, and the contents of his shelves mapped these. Here were the vomitives. The purges came next – the gentle manna, tamarind and rhubarb, and the furious scammony, vigorous to the point of homicide, of which a young man, called Culpeper or some such name, whom he had met in Cambridge, wrote 'it will gnaw their bodies as fast as doctors gnaw their purses.' The need for careful use of purgatives was underlined by the sudden demise of a lady-in-waiting at Versailles who responded enthusiastically to her physician's treatment with the expected expulsion together with several yards of intestine. Next on the apothecary's shelves came a line of diuretics – extracts of clivers, butcher's broom, horsetail, pimpernel... and then the diaphoretics. The body's problems were to be sicked, shat, pissed, or sweated out.

He must also be ready to provide medicines against specific diseases. Guaiac from the Caribbean, sarsaparilla from Mexico, China root from the Orient, all considered effective against the pox. And garlic, useful against infections and one of the few hopes of protection, slender enough, against the plague ('No danger in this house,' he muttered to himself, sniffing the air). Theriac was considered effective but impossibly expensive. Luckily it was possible to make the latter in versions cheaper than those prepared by Galen.

Several jars of a dark brown substance, apparently indigestible, which appeared totally unlikely as a medicine, provided in fact one of the few cures in which he had some confidence. It looked suspiciously like wood and was in fact obtained from a tree. It was known as Peruvian Bark or Jesuits' Bark from the name of one of its most enthusiastic importers, and was effective against the ague.

In London he might be asked to supply at short notice, vipers' flesh or crushed deer antlers or goat urine. Sometimes the apothecary hated his work. He had not personally been required to provide rhinoceros or unicorn's horn, nor Bezoar stone from the gut of a wild Persian goat, but other apothecaries of his acquaintance did so. They were men with a richer clientèle than he had ever been able to accumulate. The noble especially, presumed that their sickness demanded noble cures, and a few apothecaries might receive orders for medicines which included powdered pearl or red coral, ground emeralds or gold or silver. The latter conferred a mystical but permanent blue colour to the skin. In this country practice the people were very poor. They could not afford expensive remedies and he was in little danger of having to stretch his mind as to where he could acquire lapis lazuli, raw silk, musk or oil of scorpions, nor indeed was he in danger of making a rich income from providing such cures.

The apothecary was a man of about thirty, not quite bulky enough for his height, with a slight boniness, which suggested that he might be uncomfortable to lie on, although this had not led to serious deprivation. His complexion revealed his trade, with its indoor situation and stuffy, often foetid, atmosphere. His profession, or rather his unofficial profession, was further indicated by what Michael had referred to as their badge or seal, in this case a scar near his left ear which was the only tangible result of an experiment which had ended abruptly and yielded no information other than the highly combustible nature of its products. Occasionally he would look in a mirror and reflect that a few fortunate individuals possessed faces that seemed to have been designed, while most – including himself – had to be content with an arbitrary selection of features. He had his father's nose and his mother's mouth but his chin and brow came from God knows where, and, although these features were in themselves unexceptionable, he had the impression, whenever he saw them, that they had just been introduced to each other for the first time.

Not all of the materials on his shelves were of plant or animal origin. Paracelsus had brought quicksilver to the aid of sufferers from the pox and, more generally, brought chymistry to the aid of medicine. In his youth the apothecary had used these remedies enthusiastically – too enthusiastically he now suspected. Quicksilver and antimony were the miraculous new treatments for many diseases, or judging by the dispensing habits of some physicians, for *all* diseases. One cause of his present disquiet was the growing conviction that Paracelsus, the hero of his youth and his continuing inspiration, had insufficient reason for the advocacy of some of his cures, and in particular that he had been ignorant of, or had ignored, the collateral damage to the patient. Quicksilver was administered sometimes in its own remarkable form as glistening globules which seemed to have a life of their own. More usually it was prescribed as Mercurius Dulcis, prepared with vitriol, in which according to Croll, 'there may be killed the destructive spirit of vitriol and salt in mercury sublimate.' This powder, tasteless, and innocuous enough in appearance, was not in the apothecary's opinion as harmless as the physicians maintained, but they knew better than he – the law said so – and his task was to prepare and supply this substance which, among other effects, stimulated copious salivation, thus providing a fifth route for evacuation.

Mercury and antimony, the former in particular, were central to his interests. But not strictly to his medical interests. They were the gateway to the incorruptible and eternal city, and it was towards this place that he was this morning again turning his thoughts, as his predecessors had done for many centuries.

'What is the Green Lion, Papa?' asked the flaxen-haired boy again, this time more impatiently.

He glanced down. The boy's question had been prompted by a much-travelled piece of paper decorated with chemical splashes of diverse colours, one of which had worn into a hole. The apothecary carried the paper over to the grating and, squinting in the slightly improved light, read again the text, which was headed *Invitation to the Wedding*.

*Some have called him the Green Lion; to others he is the Babylonian Dragon. We speak no more of his person, for a Word to the Wise is as a Book to the Foolish. Confine him in his lair, but treat him not over-harshly, that it to say sufficient only for the fusion of Saturn. When he is cooled, add then an equal part of volatile Venus and a third part of argente vive, seven times washed with water from a font used for the Baptism of a female child. Grind carefully and heat in a crucible. This is the hope of Neptune and in it you may discern, as the days pass, the Beak of the Crow and the Doves of Diana...*

The sentence would have done credit to the King's Security Service. On another day, he might have expanded his chest and begun 'Well, my boy. This is how it is.' But he caught the look in the lad's eye. He was in one of his awkward moods. He answered with caution.

'I am defeated by "Neptune". It suggests water of course but seems to refer to a mineral. The metals are named after the planets whose properties they share, which in turn reflect the glory of the gods. Mars is iron, for example, Jupiter tin. Saturn, to which he refers, is lead. Diana is associated with the moon, whose light is silvery, and which indeed is used as a symbol for silver. Diana's Doves probably means silver in one of its forms. But there is no planet called Neptune. He cannot mean a metal. Venus I understand – that is cyprium or copper but which is the *volatile* Venus?' The term diverted his mind into an unrelated channel bringing the first smile of the day to his face. To himself he muttered. 'True. I was with a volatile Venus very recently – yesterday in fact, but the text can hardly be referring to her.' He felt a familiar twitch from somewhere in his groin. 'Down Nimrod,' he muttered, 'back to your kennel!' To the boy he said, 'Venus, in the author's vocabulary, is copper. The Green Lion, I cannot identify.'

The flaxen-haired boy was not satisfied yet.

'If Venus is copper, Father, why doesn't he just say so?'

'It is an ancient association. Alchemists have created a language for their own particular (but unofficial, not to mention illegal) Guild and it serves the same purpose as those of other professions and trades, that is, of course to ensure that its practitioners can be understood by others in the same occupation, while remaining incomprehensible to those outside it. To maintain an impressive obscurity is good business for any trade.'

'But, Papa, you do the same job and still don't know what he's talking about.'

He glanced at the boy but did not see him. The boy became so real at times that he almost believed him to be by his side.

'He wishes to impress of course. He wants to kidnap attention. It is a kind of violence. Colourful names of any sort will do. No, not of any sort – they must convey the atmosphere of learning, imply that the author is intimate with the classics, that he lives day and night with Aristotle, Plato and Hermes.'

He smiled suddenly to himself. The last thought was bizarre, presumptuous and possibly immoral. It reminded him also of his own characteristics, one of which had survived fifteen years of good resolutions – his habit of using resplendent language. It was part of his training. It was not without merit in his apothecary's shop. He had cured all manner of ailments with a medicine and a resounding phrase. The medicine usually needed all the help it could get. And distaste towards the extravagances of the authors of the Green Lion and the Babylonian Dragon came ill from one who had extracted a shining white salt from pigs' urine and named it Star of the East. He fell back on the usual expedient – quoting an Authority.

'Albertus Magnus put it well: *But I the least of philosophers, intend to describe to my associates and friends the true art easy and infallible; nevertheless so that seeing they shall not see, and hearing they shall not understand.*'

The flaxen-haired boy would not let go.

'I can see that he wants us to be impressed. I don't mind that. That's all right with me. Or it would be if we could understand. If we don't, he might as well not bother and we could all play football instead.'

'I keep telling you not to play that dangerous game, you scamp. Several hundred oafs kicking a pig skin about the street... But you are correct. Why, if the author is confident that he can do what he says he can do, does he offer his jewels in such impenetrable wrappings? Clearly he wishes to arrest our attention, to amaze us...' His peroration was interrupted by a loud crack like musket shot issuing from a crucible which was heating on the sand bath. The solution which he was evaporating was dry, leaving a residue of crystals. There was no danger, no explosion, no imminent fire. The crystal structure in parts of the residue modified suddenly in the heat – a phenomenon which he called 'crepitation', and had sometimes referred to as the Guns of Calais. When the process was complete the crystals might form a regulus. They might. Was it likely? No. But Michael had told him 'creative work is for optimists only'. Nevertheless a regulus was more than he dared hope.

The sharp report reminded him that he had several ventures running simultaneously. This was a dangerous habit, he admitted, but life was short and many of the processes were of long duration. He must pack as much in as possible. If he did not remain alert, though, the policy could make life abruptly shorter. He walked across to a corner where another longer term project was heating, or rather, maturing. One way of exposing material to a moderate heat over a period of time, was to place it in a glass vessel and hang this in the steam of boiling water. This needed constant attention. Better was to use a mixture of brewer's grain, wheat bran, sawdust, chopped hay or straw, moistened and pressed together. This was then packed around the vessel containing the substances and by some mysterious natural process produced heat. For really long periods of warming it was customary to enclose the mixture in an egg shell and victimise a broody and unsuspecting hen, under whose body it was placed. On this occasion, though, he had chosen a fourth method. This was called *venter equinus* and required the vessel to be packed in horse dung. The unique ambience of his laboratory owed most to hot sulphur but the *venter equinus* added an interesting frisson.

The boy was gazing around the room at the various pieces of apparatus, a collection of grotesque shapes that might have come from a painting by Bosch. Joseph loved not only his Art, but its apparatus also. Even the names of the furnaces and vessels – the athanor, cucurbit, ampulla, scutella, cassola, cincritium – were a kind of music.

'Is it really possible to make gold from lead, Papa?'

'Making gold is not our purpose.'

'I know that', said the boy. 'At least that's what you say. I just asked if it is possible.'

'Many believe so. Many have tried. Some claim to have achieved it.'

'I don't believe them. They just say that they did.'

The boy was the lead actor in the *dramatis personæ* who occupied the apothecary's imagination. At the head of the cast was the apothecary himself. He had been known to hesitate for a moment when asked for his name – not because of any memory defect but through having had too many names, too frequently changed. These tended to overlay the one – Joseph Skledowski – which his family had provided. He had been at other times Johannes

Ledermann, Thomas Schmidt or Zdzislaw Drohobycz, the latter eventually failing the test of enunciation when he crossed borders. Once, very briefly – until he opened his mouth and everyone giggled at the brand of English that emerged – he had become Thomas Smithson. At present, in the village, he was known as Michael Muller although Michael Müller had been his intention.

The flaxen-haired boy was the imaginary son that the apothecary would have liked to have in real form, although he never admitted the desire. He was the creation of a lonely man who had been hunted from country to country. The lad provided him, in some measure, with a feeling of comfort and normality. Joseph had become accustomed to casting his thoughts into a kind of Socratic dialogue with the flaxen-haired boy as a sceptical opponent who expressed himself with an insouciance that a flesh-and-blood boy would not have dared, and that might have earned a clip around the ear rather than immortalization in a philosophical treatise. Preparing himself for further intermittent evidence of crepitation, he tried to answer the lad's question.

'Many claim to have made gold, but few have become rich. Mostly they try unsuccessfully to deceive us, or successfully to deceive themselves. But I believe with many others that it can be done. And that is because there exists a common ground to everything God has made. Empedocles realised that there are four elements only – a wisdom that was confirmed by Aristotle and Plato. Because these provide a common ground to everything that exists, it follows that interconversion of substances occurs by adjustment of their content of the four – earth, air, fire and water. Such mutability we see all around us, not only in Nature but also in those changes that result from our own promptings. In spite of their diverse appearance and behaviour it is only in the proportion of these elements that our metals, although of such diverse qualities, differ. Because of this they may be converted one to another, and indeed, their nature changes gradually as they lie in the darkness of the ground. Each metal may in time pass into another by a natural process of growth and renewal, seeking always its own ultimate perfection. We see this in many cases. For example the precious metal silver is always found with lead from which it has been transformed by a process of growth and differentiation, almost like a plant, a kind of quest for perfection and release, conducted deep within the earth. We do not wholly understand it. But this transmutation is a fundamental thing, created by God, which may perhaps be rediscovered and repeated.'

'Why,' he asked himself, 'am I telling the lad all this again?' The unease that he felt was becoming too familiar. Nor was it provoked by the footsteps descending the stairs, which were drowned by the intensity of his thoughts. Lecturing the boy on the rationale of transmutation was becoming a daily occurrence. More alarming still was the realisation that this was the second time this morning. Could it be that there was a doubt in his mind that he was trying to ignore or dispel? – a fear somewhere deep within him, not yet confronted? He had grown up with two faiths. One concerned the nature and purpose of man and his relationship with God, which was embodied in the Christian religion. The other related to the structure of the world and of the stuff from which it was made. The two faiths were not entirely separate. The structure of the world had been created by God. The Christian faith was beyond question. It had the authority of God's Word, which he could – and did – read every day. But the Bible had little to say about the metals, elements, substances... There were other authorities for these, revered by countless generations. They were not God however. So far he had not gone beyond this point.

He sought reassurance by repeating to himself the opening words of the *Fama fraternitatis,* which carried the force and dignity of a movement, founded by Christian Rosenkreutz, already two hundred and fifty years old. He had read the Rosicrucian manifesto so many times that he knew much of it by heart:

*Seeing the only wise and merciful God in these latter days hath poured out so richly his mercy and goodness to mankind, whereby we do attain more to the perfect knowledge of his son Jesus Christ and Nature, that justly we may boast of the happy time, wherein there is not only discovered unto us the half part of the world, which was heretofore unknown and hidden, but he hath also made manifest unto us many wonderful, and never heretofore seen, works and creatures of Nature, and moreover hath raised men, imbued with great wisdom, who might partly renew and reduce all arts (in this our age spotted and imperfect) to perfection; so that finally man might thereby understand his own nobleness and worth, and why he is called Microcosmus, and how far his knowledge extendeth into Nature.*

This was the point – to understand and master the external world. And in mastering it, to improve or even to perfect it. The Stone was known also as the Medicine.

'Very nice,' said the boy. 'But what has it got to do with this?' He indicated the crucible, which was making a creditable effort to simulate cannon fire.

'We are attempting to make the Philosopher's Stone. When this is done all things are possible, not merely the trivial transmutation of base metals. First we have to make the Universal Solvent. This we are preparing from the Volatile Salt and the Fixed Salt and Spirits of Nitre.'

A sudden clatter from the stairway outside was this time too dramatic to allow further explanation. There followed the sound of footsteps accelerating out of control down the last few steps of the staircase, then a muffled thump as of a soft but heavy object striking a wall and finally an ear-threatening crash from the door of the room. The door vibrated for several seconds as its catch was visibly under siege and for several seconds seemed likely to surrender. The percussive noises were succeeded by the cussive; a volley of vivid language was evidence that the victim of the accident was not seriously injured. Her bones and her powers of invention were still intact. Joseph recognised Celia Albright's voice and vocabulary. A Christian mission was required, even if she was a closet-Catholic. Hastening across to the door, he pulled it open. The unfortunate woman, who had ended her adventure sitting on the floor with her back leaning against the door, was halfway through the process of heaving herself to her feet by pressing against it as a support. The apothecary's well-meant mission ended with Celia Albright entering his domain by rolling in backwards.

# CHAPTER 2

*And ruled by dead men never met,*
*By pious guess deluded...*
        W.H.Auden.


Celia Albright hauled herself heavily to her feet, attempting to adjust her skirts to some degree of decency, while the apothecary tried to give the impression that he was looking the other way. Somehow she managed to dust herself down and stand, while at the same time fixing Joseph with an unwavering glare. This was not the Babylonian Dragon but it was likely to be sufficient. There was certainly fire on its breath. He instinctively took one step back, but then checked himself. It was better to stand his ground. A casual civility was his best hope.

'Good morning Celia. I think you have found the step that needs repair. I hope you are not hurt.'

His greeting inhibited Celia Albright for a few useful seconds. At last she found her voice.

'What is that terrible smell?!'

Of all the openings that Celia Albright might have chosen, she had hit upon the one most certain to enrage him. He had been asked this question with such maddening frequency through so many years that he was no longer capable of a rational response. Instead of being inured by repetition, he had became increasingly sensitised and infuriated. His rages were usually cool-headed, however.

'I think it may be your soup. Possibly burning. Perhaps you should take a look?'

'It's your muck that stinks! It's what you're doing here! What *are* you doing here? It's that thing over there. What *is* that thing?'

She pointed an accusing and still trembling finger at the crucible. The crucible responded with another example of crepitation. The loud and unfortunately timed report made them both jump.

'Mother of God,' she exclaimed. 'You will kill us all before you've finished. You'll kill us all before the day is through. The whole house will be in flames and we'll be roasted in our beds. You said you wanted to store your medicines here. And I was fool enough to believe you. I should never have trusted a man from Poland. What do you think you're trying to do? Apart from killing us all?'

'There is no danger. I am truly sorry about the smell…'

'A liar. You said you were storing medicines.'

'I am storing medicines. What I said was true. There is little room in my shop. Storing, certainly. But I have to manufacture medicines too. Perhaps I did not explain clearly enough.'

'You didn't explain at all,' said the still furious woman. 'You didn't even try and didn't intend to.'

'Preparing medicines is an essential part of the apothecary's work. Sometimes I can buy them, but often must prepare them. I mix them or even have to make them from the basic ingredients sent to me. It is what we do as apothecaries.'

'Well you get out of here. I can't have this in my house. Find somewhere else to burn down.' She broke off suddenly. In making an eloquent gesture of dismissal, she had shifted position slightly and in the changing perspective, a small but brilliant flash of light like a passing ray of sunlight winked at her from Joseph's crowded table. Her world was constructed from iron and lead, but she knew value when she saw it.

'Is that gold?'

Joseph cursed his luck. A bad day was getting worse. But he answered casually.

'It is. A metal of great beauty.'

'It certainly is. And it buys beautiful things. I wouldn't mind getting some. A lot even!'

'I wish you the luck you deserve. But it is beautiful in its own self. Rarer still than silver – it does not tarnish or rust. It never changes. No liquids can corrode it.' Joseph knew that this was not strictly correct, but his poetic sensibilities were beginning to take control again. 'It is of the sun. Its seeds must be nurtured by the sun. It is the noble metal. It is the metal that the great Italian painters used to depict the Holiness of Mary, of Christ and of the saints. It is the metal of kings and of God.'

Celia Albright picked up the small piece of metal and examined it thoughtfully, turning it around in her fingers. Her expression gradually passed from curious to disdainful.

'It's a shapeless lump. It should have been made into a ring or brooch. It's no use to anyone like this – except for you to admire alone in a dark cellar. It's still raw. It wants cooking!'

The last phrase was spoken with her derisive but attractive laugh. The woman's customary good nature and high spirits were taking command again. Joseph attempted to reply casually but could not wholly keep the tones of reverence from his voice.

'I prefer that it should remain in the form in which it was given to me. It was a gift from my friend and mentor in the last days of his life. It is a treasured possession because of those circumstances and because he honoured me, far beyond my expectations or remotest thoughts, with a gift loaded with such profound meaning.'

'Your Master must have thought highly of you to make such a present. But it would have been better to make it into something sensible.'

'He wished to remind me of its unique origin. It is no ordinary piece of gold. It was not dug out of the earth, but was made by conversion from copper and silver. It represents one of the great achievements of human effort.'

Before he had wholly finished this sentence, he knew that it was a mistake. Celia Albright, as the offspring of an innkeeper, and especially as a woman, was not considered to merit education except in a few severely practical subjects. Her finishing school lacked special buildings. Her Colleges – the kitchens of the gentry's houses and the rooms that doubled as offices in seedy taverns – had equipped her with an impressive acumen. She had survived by sharpening her mind on a range of bizarre tenants, of whom Joseph was merely the latest, although admittedly belonging to a superior breed. Her intuitions, which had saved her on many occasions, sprang into action.

God preserve us,' exclaimed the good lady. 'He must have been an alchemist. A black-faced cauldron stirrer, brother to a bandit, first cousin to a witch.'

Joseph inwardly cursed his own folly. As usual he had said too much. He was desperately working out a response.

'Certainly not,' he exclaimed, rather too quickly. He regarded Celia Albright as a friend and had no wish to lie. The alternative was to give an erroneous impression. 'He was a seeker of that mystery that lies in the nature of things. He knew alchemists though, and the gold was given to him by an alchemist in gratitude after my master, who was an outstanding scholar and a healer of great wisdom, had cured him of a life-threatening disease.'

'Hoo,' she said, 'Don't tell me. I've met them, had them staying here in fact. They're all the same. Every sort.' Realising that the conjunction of these statements might be confusing she added, 'every sort of rogue. They are all the same when it comes to paying. The last one still owes me for six weeks. And they are all going to be boundlessly rich next week. Not this week. Next week. And a seedy, sick-looking lot too. Never go out in the air. Always poisoning themselves with some terrible muck or suffocating themselves with a dreadful smell. Come to think of it, you don't look too good! You're not one, are you?'

The last was a jocular suggestion. Or was it? The woman was getting too warm for comfort. 'No,' he said, 'certainly not. No.' He needed to start talking, and soon. 'My Master was a man of outstanding intellect and wisdom who wrote many books which are read and respected throughout Europe. Wherever I go they travel with me.' He indicated a small pile of books on the table.

Celia Albright was visibly impressed in spite of herself. Books always impressed her. She could not encompass in her imagination the writing of a book. She reached out a reverent hand towards the pile, with an apprehensive 'May I?' glance towards Joseph. She touched the uppermost book carefully, as though it might still be hot from the author's thought processes.

'How can anyone know enough to write all this? What was the writer's name?'

'I know his true name of course, but I speak of him only by the name by which he himself liked to be known, the name he used in his writings. Those he signed as the Cosmopolite.'

Celia sniffed her eloquent sniff. She was a virtuoso sniffer. This particular version suggested suspicion tending to, but some way short of, contempt.

'That must have been useful in concealing himself from the authorities! God save me,' she added. 'This isn't English. It's in some heathen language.' She was suddenly overtaken by the thought that she might be giving offence. 'It's not Polish, is it?' she asked anxiously.

'Latin.'

'Like the Mass. Come to think of it, I don't understand much of that either. What's the title of this one?' She indicated the book at the top of the pile. With some difficulty she answered the question herself.

'Treatise on the Philosopher's Stone. That has to do with making gold. I know that. The other scoundrels told me that.'

'Transmutation of metals to gold is only one of the many possibilities. The Philosopher's Stone will transform Man and the World in which he lives.'

The point did not seem to register with Celia Albright.

'I've been wasting my life. What a way to try and earn a living! Eighteen hours a day, seven days a week, providing food and shelter for people who are generous with their complaints and demands, but stingy and late with their payments. How should I set about making some gold? I've plenty of old metal in my sheds.'

'I am not an authority on the subject. I can only tell you what I have read. In theory it can be formed from other substances by transmutation. But the best is to begin with a small amount of gold as a seed and to create the conditions for it to grow of its own accord – to multiply. This reflects the process by which Almighty God has caused gold and all other metals and substances to grow in the earth. In order to obtain the Stone, and with this to command the way to transmutation of base metals, it was necessary to have a small amount of gold to begin with. Long ago, I dared to think this an injustice of God. But my great teacher reminded me of Christ's story of the master who had left money with his servants, that they might use it. This parable embodies the principle of multiplication. From nothing came nothing. Only God can truly create. Every year, at harvest, the farmer must put aside some small part of the gathered corn as seed for the next year's sowing.'

'And an even larger portion for the Church and Crown,' added his formidable landlady. 'But that is it. You have said it yourself. Only God should do this. It is a sin against God to attempt to make gold. He has created in our world all the gold it needs. It is not proper to try to make more than He in his wisdom has already provided. It is against Nature and against God. And we should be satisfied with what we have. Not be greedy for more.'

'Gold is not always the purpose of the alchemists' work, believe me...'

'Of course not! And I'm the Queen of Spain! Rubbish! They want to become rich, get land and big houses, wives and children all in beautiful clothes, all eating out of golden bowls with jewelled spoons.'

Joseph smiled faintly. 'The purpose of such work is not primarily to make gold. Its purpose is to prepare the Philosopher's Stone. When this is done, all things are possible. The world will be redeemed from the penalties of disease and death brought upon it by the transgressions of Adam. It is the Great Work, the release of mankind from the bondage of misery.'

'You mean, cure the plague and the pox?'

'Yes – the plague and the pox, and the many other afflictions from which we all suffer. Even Death itself. But not cure these things only – to dismiss them, deny them existence.'

The thought struck some chord in the housekeeper's under-used intelligence. 'But that is the greatest thing of all. To be a Healer. To understand why God has brought these afflictions upon us. How I wish that I could have done something like that, however small. With the knowledge your Master has gained, he must be very healthy. One should seek him out and learn from him. Which country does he live in?'

'He is dead,' admitted Joseph.

The landlady laughed – a surprisingly tinkling teen-age laugh for such a large middle-aged woman – then stopped suddenly and crossed herself. 'God rest his soul. Poor man,' she said sincerely, but could not suppress a final little tinkle.

'He lived to a great age,' said Joseph irritably. 'About seventy. No work is ever complete, of course. To understand the works of the Lord entirely is not possible or even desirable.'

'Amen to that. But where does the gold come in?' asked Celia Albright suspiciously. 'If these people are so high-minded, why bother with the gold part of it? They just want more money like the rest of us.'

'How,' thought Joseph irritably, 'did this plain woman become so smart?' Her earthy cynicism had considerable appeal to Joseph, as did her views on Authority. He just wished that she were using her talents on someone else.

Celia wrinkled up her nose, not entirely because of the atmosphere, which was worsening by the minute. Another report from the crucible elicited a little scream from the landlady and gave Joseph a breathing space in which to rally his arguments. He felt suddenly desperately alone. The fantastical flaxen-haired boy had disappeared at the first cry from outside the door. He had been replaced by this very real woman, fat and nearly fifty with a smallpox scar on her upper lip. It was true that there was much to be said for a bulky housekeeper. 'Never eat a meal prepared by a thin cook', Michael had told him. Nimrod had opened one eye and then pointedly gone back to sleep in his kennel.

Before he could reply, she had picked up the many-coloured sheet of paper from the table. Celia Albright might not be Queen of Spain but she was Queen in the country of the Illiterate – unlike most of her friends she could half-read. It was a laborious process. She peered at the paper, her lips moving.

'What is the Green Lion?' she asked.

'It may refer to the green deposit which forms on copper when exposed to the weather. But there are other possibilities. I was trying to work that out when you decided to fall down the stairs. It may be part of an instruction sheet for chymical preparation. It is entirely useless. You can have it. Perhaps it's a kitchen recipe. Take it away and cook it. It might be an improvement on your stews.'

'You needn't eat them. Get out of here anyway and take your smells with you. And if I were you, I would hide all this stuff' – she inventoried his treasured equipment with a dismissive sweep of her arm – 'the Sheriff's men are coming. Not that you have anything to hide of course,' she added with a hint of what could have been amusement, could have been menace.

'My God! When?' was Joseph's involuntary response. He knew immediately that this reaction had better be modified. 'You never know with those people – they can pick on you on some pernickety point, although you are working absolutely within the law. They act from personal animosities – and they just love to persecute foreigners.'

'Hmm. You don't need to tell me. They will be snooping about hoping to catch me brewing beer without a licence. Or worse – it may be another round of harassment of Catholics.' She added innocently, 'I suppose you will be leaving then.'

'No. Certainly not. Why should I? I am not a Catholic, as you know. I have nothing to hide – nothing, that is, except the tools of my profession as an apothecary. Those might be misinterpreted by someone who wanted to make mischief or had a grudge against Poles. Or who was simply looking for favours from his superiors. No, I shall certainly stay.'

'Well,' said this awkward woman, 'don't leave too soon. And by the way, two men came to the inn yesterday. They were asking after someone called Thomas Shermit or some such name. We told them that there was no one of that name in the village. I would not have bothered to tell you but they mentioned that the person they were looking for spoke like a foreigner, possibly Polish. Is anything wrong?'

The last question was prompted by Joseph's complexion, which had become even less healthy than usual. His hesitation in replying did nothing to convince her.

'No,' he said at last, 'I'm not expecting visitors, not the Sheriff or any one else. And I'm not running away.'

'Good. Because I hoped that you might give me some advice. I wanted to speak to you about my daughter.'

Nimrod had opened his eyes and flapped both ears. He was preparing to heave himself to his feet.

'Your daughter! Ah yes – Caroline – how is she? A charming and beautiful girl. You must be very proud of her.'

'Hmm. Charming and beautiful certainly. You didn't mention virtuous, though.'

'I am sure that she is that too.'

'Well, I'm not. Frankly I am worried. Her habits have changed of late. Until recently I always knew where she was and what she was doing. Now she disappears quite often and resents me asking where she has been.'

'But that is normal surely. She is becoming her own person. Many young women are married by her age.'

'I would not mind that, although it is too soon. My fear is that she is meeting someone secretly.'

'Surely not? I expect that there is some simple explanation. And why ask me for advice? I have no experience in counselling. I have a number of skills but they have no bearing upon the young human heart and all its difficulties and vagaries. That is much more complex even than medicines. You must go to a priest.'

'Father James,' said Celia Albright contemptuously. 'We all know about him! The only thing to be said for talking to him about secret lovers is that he has had plenty himself. He must be an expert in the subject.'

'Doctor Fortune would help you.'

'I can never get hold of him. He's always out killing someone. Besides he's too old. He must be nearly seventy. He's forgotten what he never even knew. I need to talk to you. You are one of the few educated men in the district. You are intelligent. At least I thought so until this morning. You have travelled and have a lot of experience – God knows where and of what – but you often give sound advice along with your medicines – I have heard you. Others say so, too.'

Joseph was about to devise another objection, but the crucible saved him the trouble. It was getting into its stride. It discharged a fusillade of shots. Celia Albright could face out most things, but the apothecary's cellar was outside her experience. She gave a little shriek and rushed for the exit, pausing only to lean back into the room, from a position of comparative safety, protecting most of herself with the bulky door.

'Friday afternoon,' she said. 'I'll come to your shop.'

# CHAPTER 3

*For nothing can be sole or whole*
*That has not been rent.*
      Yeats.


Joseph groaned as the sound of the footsteps receded, punctuated at one point by a slight clatter and a muffled oath as Celia Albright rediscovered the faulty step, fortunately with less drama this time. His mentor and surrogate father, the renowned alchemist, Michael Sendivogius, who was of noble descent and a professional diplomat, had told him that a prince who received only two pieces of bad news in one day was on holiday. For the first time in his life he began to feel sorry for monarchs and their ministers. He had suffered three items of bad news in as many minutes. The sheriff's men were on the road. What was that about? In pursuit of petty crimes no doubt – tax evasion, failure to have a licence for this and that; they were not pursuing criminals but harrying people who were short of bread and forced to take short cuts.

But worse than that, there were men on his track again. Michael, whom he had described rather disingenuously as a Healer, had indeed been an advocate of Paracelsus's view of the human body and its ailments, but had spent much of his life studying many aspects of alchemy, not only its medical content, trying to make some sense of the structure of the World. His studies included the preparation of the Stone; he had suffered one abduction and several attempted abductions by those who coveted his knowledge and were prepared to get it by any means. 'Gold is the greatest seducer in history – not even Zeus does it better,' said Joseph to himself. Now it was he, Michael's pupil, who was at risk, the supposed heir to his master's secrets. It was not murder that he feared – killing him would defeat their purpose. The probable abduction and torture was a worse prospect still. Why had he not asked Celia Albright to describe the strange visitors? He had buttoned up too quickly. It might be worth introducing the subject again, tactfully, when he next met Celia, to get a description of the visitors.

The prospect of an afternoon of the well-armed woman laying her bombards and ladders to the walls of her daughter's problems filled him with horror. Fortunately he was not going to be here on Friday – he would be attending a meeting many miles away, a fact that he had deceitfully failed to convey to her. And worst of all, he might be forced to move his home yet again, just at the point when he thought that he was at last settling down to the penultimate but lengthy process of the Great Endeavour. The great Philosophers generally agreed – on this, if little else – that manufacture of the Stone required long periods of time. Nature's final citadel could only be taken by a lengthy siege. According to the instructions that he had, ninety days were needed for the manufacture of the Stone. Fool! To have been trying to prepare the regulus in this place – what stupidity! The process was certain to emit sulphurous fumes and draw attention to his activities, to bring objections straight to his door. He might as well have spent the whole night playing a sackbut.

He stepped across to the corner of the room where a green cloth, bearing a crude but dramatic representation of Cassandra foreseeing the destruction of Troy, covered a round object some six inches in diameter. He picked this up and brought it over to the better light. Removal of the cloth revealed a small globe of some crystalline material. This too was a legacy from Michael, who had also taught him how to use it. He did so only in moments of distress or doubt or when crucial decisions had to be made. He spent a minute or so uttering quietly what seemed to be a prayer for illumination, then bent reverently over the sphere. At first he could see little, but gradually the swirling shapes resolved into his own features, distorted and indistinct. Behind the caricature of his face, somewhere beyond the pinched cheeks and the swollen nose, were various indefinite and moving shapes, a black triangle perhaps, certainly a symmetrical figure that could have been a geometric demonstration, a flying bird, a witch's hat or almost anything else. Was that a girl's face? It was difficult to say. More fog swirled about the images, creating amorphous blots that slowly elongated and gathered together, end to end. Were those bones? A skeleton?

He hastily covered the globe with the green cloth. He tried to stopper the fountain of panic that was rising within him. Crisis management was the key – he was the expert. His friends came to him from all sources of the wind for advice. He had evolved, over many years, the four Laws of Crisis Management. It was worth a small book when he could find time.

**First Law or the Remove the Pan Strategy.** Attend to whatever small practical matter has any degree of urgency. If there are many urgent matters, deal with them in descending order of urgency. Avoid catastrophic consequences by bearing in mind the severity of the ultimate damage. No good jumping out of the kitchen window because there is a tax collector at the door if the fat-pan burns the house down. Of course, one is not always afforded time in which to attend to the smaller practical difficulties. The principal problems may be too exigent. In that case, proceed directly to Law Three. Otherwise the Second Law may be useful.

**Second Law or Drake and the Armada Strategy.** If there are difficult decisions impending that do not require immediate attention, deal with some small, unconnected matters first. Complete the action in which you are engaged, even if this is recreational. Play bowls if available. This has a calming effect and clears the mind, allowing one to consider coolly the principal problem or problems.

**Third Law or the Thermopylæ Strategy.** When faced with a number of problems simultaneously, confront them in the narrow pass. Do not attempt to vanquish them all at once. Analyse them and recognise the order in which they must be approached. The actions required when facing more than one problem will usually overlap in time. Make a plan that addresses items in the appropriate chronological order, irrespective of the problem to which it belongs. If the plan gets too complicated for the mind, write it down.

**Fourth Law, also called the Fast Horse.** (This has inferior status compared with the first two laws and should not – tactfully – be included in the book when published.) Unfortunately, in an imperfect world containing even more imperfect human beings, not every problem can be solved. Joseph thought of this as Eve's pip – the remnant of the original apple given by Eve, which obstinately persists and has somehow been built into the World structure. If no solution can be found, then the sufferer should remove the problem from his presence – or more probably, since the sufferer is likely to be more mobile than the problem – the sufferer should remove his or her presence from the problem. A graceful retreat is recommended, but do not entirely scorn an undignified gallop.

Joseph began the attempt to put into practice his own guiding principles. The First Law first. The crucible, which was becoming increasingly obstreperous, was the place to begin. With the aid of a large pair of tongs he took this from the fire and placed it in one of the many draughty corners of the basement where it would cool quicker. As he passed the grating the light from outside fell on it. He stopped suddenly and for several minutes stood looking in amazement at the residue in the crucible. This had assumed a fascinating shape. He fetched his notebook and made a drawing and some notes, trying with only partial success to convey the beauty and mystery of the crust that had formed. It was in the shape of a seven-pointed star that was constructed entirely of granules arranged concentrically around the centre of the star. The arms of the star, as well as its central body, were constructed from the circles and it was easy for the eye and the mind to extrapolate the circles into the spaces between the arms. Certainly it was the regulus described by various authors. It was indeed a thing of beauty and mystery. The cautionary words of the pseudonymous 'Basil Valentine' came to mind concerning the regulus, '[many] have spared neither labour or expense to bring about its preparation. But very few have succeeded in realising their wishes. Some have thought that this star is the true substance of the Philosophers' Stone. But this is a mistaken notion, and those who entertain it stray far afield from the straight and royal road'. Well, the apothecary congratulated himself on being one of the few. But the doubts that had afflicted him at waking were still with him. Perhaps there was a 'royal road.' If it existed at all, it was definitely not 'straight'.

Joseph stood for a while gazing in awe, bewilderment and excitement at the residue in the crucible. His reverie was interrupted by a cracking sound from the far end of the room, where the Universal Solvent and its dissolving metals were still heating. For a moment his mind leapt to crepitation and the earlier displays of gunnery from the crucible. But the crucible was quite cool now, and in any case was right beneath his nose. He began to walk cautiously towards the sound, peering closely at the furnace in which the refluxing was still continuing. When he had reached a point about five feet away, he picked out what appeared to be a long black hair straddling the surface of the retort in the vertical direction and extending almost from the top to bottom of the flask. Experience told him immediately that this was no hair – his hard-won and expensive vessel had cracked. The probable implications of its mechanical failure rushed immediately into his mind. He had heard from several alchemists already about the danger of the inflammable airs generated by metals as they dissolved. A particularly graphic account had been related by Raymond Norris who still carried marks in his face like smallpox scars, but too angular to be the residue of that horrible disease. Joseph threw himself to the ground, buried his nose in the earth floor and covered his head with his arms. It was a wise move, made just in time. A huge bang, short and sharp but very loud, was followed seamlessly by a hailstorm of smaller reports as the shattered remnants of the retort struck the walls and floor of the cellar. These were counterpointed with a street-band of percussions and tintinnabulations generated by the shards of flying earthenware striking or passing straight through the metalwork, pottery and glassware of his expensive collection of equipment. The final sounds, gradually dying away, were of pieces of apparatus, which had been unbalanced by shrapnel, bending or smashing as they struck the floor. When the tumult had died down, he heaved himself to his feet. Apart from one cut on a part of his head which he had not managed to cover and several on the backs of his hand, he was unhurt. His vessels – alembic, paropsis, testum and the rest – were distributed all over the floor, like a shredded dictionary.

As the sounds of the explosion died away they were replaced by indicators of panic from above – a confusion of pounding footsteps, distant cries and oaths and the slamming of doors, most clearly of the door into the street. After the last of these noises, there was an eerie silence. The occupants of the house had ignored the first three Laws and voted unanimously for Law Four.

Joseph began to wonder what was needed to complete the day. It had begun with a possible ill-omen. On his way to his basement laboratory, he had met Celia Albright's mother, widely regarded in the locality as possessing evil powers. Personally he found her an interesting if rather disagreeable woman, astringent but exceptionally intelligent. She had nodded to him, added an enigmatic, rather sardonic smile, and wished him 'Good Day.' At the time – too early and on a drizzly morning – he had wondered whether she was offering a Good Day for him or expressing her opinion that it was a Good Day for witches. His morning had begun indifferent, proceeded to bad, threatened awful and then plummeted to disastrous. He supposed that 'catastrophic' must be the next category. Time rolled inexorably on. He would find out in due course, no doubt. In the meantime, the only feasible course of action was to proceed under the first law – urgent practical matters, which had multiplied considerably. The new starting point was a broom. He fetched one and began to sweep up. It was going to be a long task.

He began furthest away from the centre of devastation and worked his way gradually inwards, accumulating a growing tide-line of increasingly diverse wreckage as he went. It was not unlike decoction of a complex liquid containing many components. Among the ruins was, he was shocked to find, the pieces of the treasured globe into which he had been gazing not many minutes before. Eventually he was sweeping up pieces mostly of the retort itself. For no definable reason, he bent down and picked up one of the shards and began to examine it.

Looking back many years later, he would recognise this as one of the defining moments of his life. The piece of broken pottery was utterly ordinary. It was of an undistinguished brown colour. The external surface was slightly shiny, like many other pieces of pottery found in the laboratory or kitchen. The broken surface was of the same colour but dull and unreflective. There was a hint that it might be granular, and there were occasional flecks of lighter colour, some of a yellowish buff colour, some almost white. Its sheer ordinariness was the point. Its mundane character, its unapologetic lack of distinction began to fill his vision and overwhelm his mind. This was not one of those spectacular substances that occupied the daily attention and nightly dreams of those who practised his craft. It was not gold, the exquisite metal of many endeavours, nor even silver. It was not the remarkable red ore, cinnabar, which could be changed into insubordinate, running, glittering, magical globules and a strange brilliant yellow powder – and from them recomposed. It was massively commonplace. And he had no idea what it was made of. It seemed to gaze back at him ironically, nudging him, saying 'go on then, name me, tell me what I am: you've been studying me for centuries, tell me something about myself – nothing advanced, just tell me one simple thing, the first thing, anything.' Joseph continued to gaze at the shard, for some minutes, horrified. At last he looked up and saw the rest of the room. But there was no escape there either. Everywhere he saw materials about which he knew nothing. Wood, metals, brickwork, glass, stone, earthenware, soil. He knew nothing of their composition nor of their relationship with each other, what they shared or how they differed. He was standing in the centre of a huge mystery – not the World or Universe on which he often liked to have big thoughts or scare himself, not the beauty and grandeur of the night sky, nor the fecundity and endlessly subtle colours and textures of his adoptive landscapes. Just a rather squalid basement, among hundreds of similar basements, made of everyday materials. He was an ignorant man among ignorant men.

After some minutes more, he resumed clearing-up and then began to pack the undamaged remains of his laboratory into boxes.

# CHAPTER 4

The sun was warm on the apothecary's back. For the moment the problems and complexities of his two professions were being ignored. It was the first day this year in which the sun had reminded the people of Northern Europe, who had become accustomed to the welcome but inhibited sunlight of winter, of its true intensity. It was a day for celebration and renewal. In the place among the trees where Joseph was lying, the ground was rough, but for the time being he was comfortably cushioned. The wood was expressing itself in a variety of shades of green, shades of an almost absurd freshness, which it would not match again for the rest of the year. A triumphal chorus of voices greeted it. The robin, which had bravely sung all through the dark days of winter, now performed with restored conviction and was joined by the renegades – those like the thrush and blackbird who had mostly rested their voices through the uncomfortable seasons and could now burst into song so glorious that it carried for a quarter of a mile – and others – the blackcap and nightingale – who had actually fled the country, but had now returned and retuned, adding an exotic flavour to the symphony of sound. Even the jay contributed, possibly with good intentions and certainly to the best of its abilities, with a sound like tearing petticoats. Close by, a wren, the most remarkable of all the performers, was amazing the forest with the volume and sweetness of sound, which it could produce from a body so small that it seemed hardly worth possessing. It was one of the many miracles happening all around him. God was in Heaven, undoubtedly, and here on Earth too.

At this particular moment Joseph fervently hoped that God was preoccupied with the more pressing problems of Earth – and of Heaven, if any were allowed there. Joseph would have felt embarrassed to say the least to have been noticed by the Deity just now. A voice as charming to him as that of the birds spoke from somewhere beneath him.

'Please, I want to come on top now!'

Joseph began a retrograde motion, like Mars.

'No, don't leave me! We can turn over like this.'

This was new, even to Joseph, but bold experimentation was his *métier*. The strange eight-legged creature began slowly and tentatively to rotate with all the dignity of an inverted tortoise trying to right itself. The manœuvre was possible but difficult. It was almost complete when a sudden sharp pain stabbed Joseph in the lower back. The discomfort subtracted from, but did not entirely negate, the satisfaction of the remainder of the morning.

Later they were walking back through the wood.

'I am coming with you,' said Caroline Albright.

'I'm afraid that you can't, my Dear, much as I would love to have you with me. A conference of natural philosophers is the most boring thing on Earth, except to natural philosophers, and often to them also.'

'I don't mind being bored.'

'You would not understand a word. And there is nowhere else to go. Nothing else to do.'

'It wouldn't be boring anyway. Not with you there. It's never been boring yet!'

'In any case they would not let you in. The Society has extremely strict rules. Even marriage partners are not allowed to attend. The generally held view is that success in the Great Enterprise will depend not only on the skill of the operator but upon the purity of his motives and the rigour and virtue of the life which he leads.'

Joseph realised immediately that he had said the wrong thing. Some things are true but ridiculous. He was surprised to find the blood rising to his face as he spoke. He thought that he had given up such responses in his youth. In his frequent self-examinations his motivation, idealism and energy directed both towards his official and unofficial professions passed with distinction, but virtue was a lamentably failed candidate, one who resat the examination every year but always with the same result. What passed across his face was something like a blush.

Caroline answered with something like a snort, which transmuted into something that was definitely a scornful laugh.

'No wonder that you haven't been successful yet! And I doubt whether the others stand much chance.'

Her tone changed suddenly. She had suddenly noticed Joseph's grimace. 'Have you hurt your back?'

'It sometimes happens in moments of stress or misbehaviour. It's nothing much. It will soon pass.'

'Well at the least I can join you for your journey to Cambridge.'

'I am really sorry, but that is not possible either. The College will not admit women. You may regard this as unjust, but it is the way of the world in which we live.'

'I can stay somewhere else.'

'I cannot afford that. And neither can you. And the scandal that would ensue if we were seen together would ruin immediately the whole purpose of my visit there to learn what I must learn from the few people who are in possession of that knowledge.'

Joseph did not mention a more potent argument for Caroline not travelling with him to Cambridge. He was not going to Cambridge. He was going to stay temporarily with James Fisher in London, but attending first a meeting with others of his persuasion at the home of the Baron Mixford in Lincolnshire. His few possessions would be sent after him in due course, and there he would stay with James until he could find some more satisfactory permanent arrangement.

'We could be married first.'

'My Dear, you forget that I am married already. I have a wife and a young daughter.'

'I didn't forget. I am only trying to forget. You married in a foreign country – thousands of miles away. It doesn't count! And anyway no one would know.'

'Hundreds of miles. And news travels eventually. Especially if you don't want it to. Especially if it is scandalous.'

'Well, I don't believe it and I don't care. Hardly anyone goes to Poland or comes from there. Except Lord This and the Marquis of That who are trying to arrange a war or to avoid one according to what the King ate for breakfast. And we don't keep such company anyway.'

'That is an over-simple view, I am afraid. I have already attracted too much interest. I believe that the Crown's agents are already interested in my movements.'

'But why? You haven't done anything wrong.'

'Only attempted to improve the human condition. And spoken with a foreign accent, which immediately arouses suspicion.' He turned to her and took her by the shoulders. 'Look, my dear, I shall be away for two weeks only. After which I have no more journeys to make. We shall be together for a long time. We shall have many happy times.'

'You will soon think of somewhere else to go,' said the disgruntled Caroline.

As they parted – tactfully before reaching the open ground near the village – Joseph booked himself a whole abbey of prayers and penances. But his choice was made. He was leaving. He would not, could not, change his mind. Lincolnshire was his next destination.

# CHAPTER 5

'And so, O Asclepius, man is a great miracle...'

The sublime words of the thrice-great Hermes were interrupted as Joseph's horse put its foot into another hole in the road – a road that was barely distinguishable from the fields through which it was passing. It was time for a further intermission in his torturous progress.

Joseph dismounted his horse with extreme care. His bizarre angular movements, with his right leg held straight and stiff as he swung it over the horse's back, like a dog cocking its leg, and the grimaces he made as he did so, were unmistakable evidence of a bad back. The journey had been a nightmare. Sitting, he realised, is the worst position possible for a man with an injured back – better to stand or lie down. Sitting on a horse in motion was a torture that the King's agents would have been proud of if they had devised it. Several times he had dismounted and walked for a while, and would have done so more often had the changes between the two modes of progress not been so agonising. Also, he might have arrived several days late.

He plunged his hand into his pocket, searching for a small phial of anodyne that he had himself prepared. He must find relief somehow. What his hand encountered first was a small metallic object. Puzzled he pulled it out and examined it. It was an amulet bearing the insignia of the lamb and flag. He was familiar with such amulets and their symbolism. The lamb was the Lamb of God and the flag bore a cross – not the cross only of St.George of England – but the cross as an early Christian symbol representing Christ's victory. On an expensive piece of jewellery the Cross would have been rendered in red on a white background. This amulet was a poor object, of common metals crudely soldered together, but glittering quite nicely. It was trying to pass as gold with a silver inset, but lacked conviction. On the reverse side in tiny script were the words: '*And deliver us from evil*'. It was clearly intended to ward off evil spirits.

The people of the village would often carry amulets or charms of various sorts. Sometimes their purpose would be defence against various sicknesses – almost any kind of object might be found, from gold rings to snake skins or hare's feet – competing with his medicines. Or they might be religious in nature like this one, an example of a kind that were still popular; less so now, since the Protestants – and especially the Puritan element – often viewed them as examples of Roman superstition, regrettable but only to be expected. The most common kind had been the *agnus dei*, made from the wax of Paschal candles that had been blessed by the Pope ('Hallow Tallow', Joseph liked to call this act). This amulet belonged to the same family. It was a cheap article which may have been blessed, but certainly not by the Pope, more likely by the local priest, or failing that the village Cunning Man. For a few seconds he was puzzled as to how it came to be in his pocket. He himself carried an amulet but this was suspended on a chain around his neck. He recalled suddenly and with irritation that it belonged to Thomas Tatt and that he had been about to return it to him but the sudden eruption of his life in the last days had driven the incident from his mind.

Tatt was an occasional visitor to Joseph's shop and not on the Most-Welcome list. He came when he had an insufficiency of work and an excess of malevolence. On this occasion he had been showing off the amulet, which evidently possessed skills in both the religious and the medical fields. He extolled its virtues and emphasised the superiority of its prophylactic talents to anything that Joseph could produce. When Joseph had suffered enough – a short process on this occasion – he had asked Tatt whether he had heard about the Red Blot, a new scourge, *very* nasty, *very* deadly and distinguished especially by its extreme infectivity, much greater even than that of the pest. Tatt, already showing signs of alarm had asked how Joseph knew about the new sickness. Joseph replied, with no indication at all that he was fabricating, that he had just attended a patient suffering from the disease and was seriously worried about his own safety.

'Did you say *very* infectious?' Tatt had asked.

'Very. It is spreading like a forest fire in Hertfordshire and may soon…'

It had been unnecessary to complete the sentence. It was only some hours afterwards that he discovered that the fleeing Tatt had left his first line of defence against Red Blot lying on the table. Joseph laughed and pocketed it, with the intention of returning it next time he met Tatt or one of Tatt's neighbours.

Joseph's discomfort was not the result only of physical pain. The first impact of his vision in the laboratory after the explosion, had dimmed, leaving him with the preconceptions of his upbringing. He was confused. The certainties of his childhood and early training were still there, but somehow would not sit still. They wavered and shimmered as though seen through a heat haze. As he rode, he sought reassurance by repeating to himself the opening words of the great Egyptian magus, Hermes – words older perhaps than the Ten Commandments:

*'And so, O Asclepius, man is a magnum miraculum, a being worthy of reverence and honour. For he goes into the nature of a god as though he were himself a god: he has familiarity with the race of demons, knowing that he is of the same origin; he despises that part of his nature which is only human for he has put his hope in the divinity of the other part'.*

The magnificent thoughts failed to bring their usual excitement and comfort to him. 'There is something wrong with me,' Joseph thought. 'Not my back only. Something is awry in my soul or my thinking or both. Perhaps I am becoming too critical. Certainly the account of the Creation given in Genesis and that described by Hermes cannot both be literally true. But I have assumed that, in essence, they find accord. They set out the relationship between God and Man. But Hermes seems much clearer than Genesis on the divinity within ourselves. *For he goes into the nature of a god as though he were himself a god* – an altogether more cheerful view of the human being than the miserable sinner ministered to by the Christian churches. Perhaps priests have a personal interest in promoting this gloomy view. It might be good business, like vomitives or bleeding – or that stuff from Galen about adjusting the humours, which, thankfully, Paracelsus has swept away. What did the Old Testament actually say on the subject? *And God said, Let us make man in our own image.* Put aside the difficult theological question – to whom was God talking? – and pass on to the next verse. *So God created man in His own image, in the image of God created he him.'*

Joseph mounted again and rode on. '*In his own image.* But what did that mean? Head, legs, heart, liver, penis? No. It must refer to man's spiritual qualities. So Adam must have been God's equal until the Fall. That makes two gods at least.' His thoughts were certainly becoming heretical.

And Hermes was not particularly consistent either. In other passages, he seemed to share the more pessimistic view of Christianity – that flesh, and indeed all features of the World, were lamentable and to be shed thankfully in return for the life of the spirit and the eventual rejoicings of a higher existence.

The wisdom of the Ancients could not be dispelled in a day or a moment. And he was on his way to confer with others, who – in spite of their many differences of opinion – would be unlikely to have embraced any radical thinking since he last met them. He must switch into debate mood, especially as he would be expected to speak. He had chosen his subject some weeks previously. He would address himself to problems of communication and his text would be '*so that seeing they shall not see, and hearing they shall not understand'*. His criticism of such an eminent authority should start the hive buzzing.

This was his first visit to the home of the Baroness. The manor house was an imposing building, large but slightly austere, in wooded country not far from Grantham. The present owner, William Richmond, Baron Mixford, had inherited the manor and the title from his father, Edmund Richmond, who was largely responsible for the present scale of development of the estate. Although a peer of the realm, Edmund had preferred the life away from Court, being by nature a farmer and land-owner, devoted to the life of a country gentleman, skilled in the management of crops. An intelligent man, who had treated the labourers and craftsmen of the estate with a sensitivity unusual for the age, he had nonetheless tended to sympathise with an earlier peer, the Duke of Norfolk, who had expressed the sentiment that 'it was Merry England before this new learning came.' That had been said nearly a century earlier when the 'new learning' had been a revised Latin and an eruption of humanist literature. In the meantime, England had become arguably even less merry and the learning was becoming ever newer. Edmund Richmond preferred to acquire his wisdom and the knowledge he required by word of mouth from his many contacts, high and low, and was predictably alarmed when he realised that his son William was seriously addicted to the reading of books. When the time came for the young man to take over the running of the estate, he had already become a well-respected figure in public life, and because of his administrative skills was being processed through a number of appointments, first at Court and then in Parliament as a preparation for probable high office. He solved the problem of a dual life in a sensible way by appointing a capable farm manager, so that the estate, while not growing in size and scope as it had under his father, continued to prosper.

The efficient handling of the estate was promoted by his choice of a wife. William reached that age when a man wakes in the early hours of the morning and, against his wishes or expectations, finds that he is troubled by the thought that he has attained what for him seems to be nearly middle-age and that he has neither a wife nor heirs. He was a mere twenty-eight years old and in the clear light of day told himself not to be so stupid, but the disturbance of his small-hours' sleep happened again and continued to happen. He had for years been plagued by the hints, offers and sometimes threats, of nobles, courtiers and magnates with daughters to spare. The problem with which he was familiar was not how to enter the marriage market, but how to avoid it. His change of attitude was welcomed in many quarters, and eventually he found himself a guest of an eminent Marquis, who was blessed with no fewer than three daughters, and rather less than blessed with the desirability of finding husbands for them. The Marquis's first thought in connection with William, concerned the eldest, Viola, a noted beauty. The parents were startled, and Viola intensely irritated, when conversations, tactlessly long and intense, developed between William and the second daughter, Penelope. Since this was, in the matrimonial sense, their problem daughter, physically less well-endowed than the eldest, and with a disinclination to follow schedules prescribed for young females, any feeling that the parents had concerning possible discourtesy on the part of William Richmond was quickly consumed in the realisation that their second thoughts were better than their first.

\* \* \* \* \*

Edmund Richmond would have sniffed scornfully at Penelope's reading habits. She had from an early age access to the library of her uncle, an ardent collector of books. One of the formative events in her life was reading Galileo's *Dialogue Concerning the Two Chief World Systems*. After this she read astronomy voraciously, going back to the original revolutionary work of Copernicus, *On the Revolution of the Heavenly Bodies* and to the few commentaries upon it, mostly adverse. Eventually she came to, and was defeated by, Kepler's enigmatic but compelling books *Mystery of the Cosmos, New Astronomy* and *Harmony of the World* – mysterious from their Pythagorean and Platonic thinking, from their difficult Latin style, and their mathematics, a subject which was not been considered appropriate for a girl's education. They seemed to be making propositions of great importance, but she was not able to assess their significance with any confidence. And why had Galileo not become an advocate for Kepler in the way that he had for Copernicus? Surely it would have provided a crucial weapon in his fight with the Vatican? From the obscurities of Kepler's astronomy, she passed on to the lucidity and eloquence of Francis Bacon's thoughts on scientific method, and then began to ponder the status of other sciences. Astronomy and mathematics had been proper activities for philosophers for at least eighteen centuries and a vast and complex literature had accumulated. Aristotle and Theophrastus had studied living creatures and plants and made an attempt to classify them. Who had made further studies? Surely these admirable Greeks had not exhausted the subject. Many of her teachers seemed to consider that Aristotle had exhausted *every* subject. There were indications that a new attitude was developing towards studies of the functioning of the human body, but what was happening in alchemy? Was alchemy a subject that could be studied with the methods recommended by Bacon? How did it relate to the making of inks, paints, paper, to the smelting of copper and iron, to the manufacture of gunpowder?

It was, however, Kepler who struck the first spark in her first meeting with William Richmond. After the usual introductions, courtesies and tentative biographical explorations, she realised that she had, for the first time in her life, met a man with real mathematical knowledge. Eventually she manœuvred him sufficiently aside from the family conversations to surprise him with topics he had certainly not anticipated. She began by asking him whether he had read Kepler and if so if he had understood him. He had and he thought that he did. He was also delighted to explain. From this point the conversation ascended into the firmament and never really returned. The meeting of minds was reciprocal. In addition, there was something exciting about the shape and strength of William's back, and she was fascinated by the way in which his slightly too prominent Adam's apple made swift little journeys up and down when his conversation became animated.

'Isn't it wonderful, Mama?' said the youngest daughter who already knew what was going to happen, but was sternly shushed by her mother, 'Penelope has found another bighead.'

They were married a few months later. They passed through the perilous door of matrimony a little changed, as is customary and necessary, but largely undamaged. The intellectual interests that had first focused their attentions, continued and grew into a major industry. They were helped by William's contacts at Trinity College, which although not exactly a powder keg of new thinking, was home to a few scholars with interests in mathematics and the sciences. Gresham College in London was another source of information and discussion. There was plenty for the couple to discuss. Sometimes discussions became arguments, and occasionally arguments became quarrels. At such moments, Penelope usually backed down and concentrated on the journeys of the Adam's apple, which still fascinated her and filled her with a desire to kiss it. Alchemy was the most usual topic of dissension. William could not come to terms with a subject that included Green Lions and Diana's Doves. 'A monstrous menagerie,' was his grumble. In vain Penelope pointed out that this was the only chymical literature in existence and that its terminology had to be accepted until it could be replaced by something better, and if possible translated into more normal language. They liked to invite to the house people engaged in new ways of thinking, to discuss and to give papers on their thoughts, reading or experiments. Travel was slow and the distances from London and other centres great, so guests would stay for some days and these meetings became major events in the year's diary and in the gossip of the couple's aristocratic neighbours. Alchemists were not entirely forbidden but William allowed them hospitality only when he was absent on affairs of State ('menagerie attendants,' he muttered), and the Baroness hosted these occasions.

 The dreadful journey was finished. Joseph had arrived, although late. He handed his horse to a groom who had appeared with unostentatious efficiency. As he turned stiffly away towards the main door he saw that he was separated from the entrance by an elderly man, distinguished, in spite of his age, by upright carriage and easy movements. It was a man he had not seen for some years but he was instantly recognisable as the Rev Alistair Douglas, Vicar of Cranford. Priests were not supposed to study alchemy. Nor were sovereigns of England for that matter, but the fact had not deterred either Queen Elizabeth or King James from employing its practitioners. Such studies were against the law of the land and scowled upon by the Church. Some of its priests were adepts, nevertheless. This priest was an alchemist and reputed to be a Rosicrucian. He shared Joseph's lofty view of the aims of their subject and his belief in the need for the alchemist, if he were to be successful, to follow principles of austerity and chastity. Joseph could only admire his ability to put these ideals into practice. This discrepancy in performance made him uneasy in the priest's presence and he needed to be physically and spiritually at his best to converse with Douglas profitably. This was not such a moment, but there was no escape. The priest avoided addressing him as Michael Müller. He was one of the few people at the meeting who would know Joseph's real identity.

'Brother Apothecary,' exclaimed the priest, 'Welcome, and how splendid to see you again – but, poor fellow, you have been struck by flying fragments of pottery – I recognise that shape of scar immediately.'

'Greetings, Father,' replied Joseph. 'Yes, pursuit of our great endeavour led to an explosion. But I was fortunate. My injuries were slight, by God's grace.'

'But your back was hurt also. I saw you dismounting in obvious pain.'

'Yes, I found myself on the ground in a strained position,' muttered Joseph, mentally imposing several more penances upon himself. In the short term a change of subject would be desirable. 'Has anyone else arrived yet?'

Douglas looked at him in the way that always made people feel uncomfortable. It combined tact with understanding. Perception was greatly to be admired, thought Joseph. It would be especially admirable if one's friends and colleagues would be more selective in its use.

'You are the last to come. You must have had a difficult and painful journey. The others have all arrived from near and far.'

Joseph needed to begin the identification of those who would be present. It was not impossible that the confederates of Roche might be in attendance. 'There is danger in what we attempt,' he said, 'in its intrinsic difficulties as well as in the attitude of the authorities. Are we safe here?'

'No doubt of it. The houses of the aristocracy are the safest places for meetings of this kind. The church-wardens menace only persons of lowly status. The secular authorities will think, not twice, but many times, before they confront a viscount or baron. It is an unfair world but we must not allow the Devil to monopolise the benefits of its injustice.'

'I suppose not.' Ethical discussions tended to bemuse Joseph, giving him a headache. 'I saw troops during my journey – lots of troops – too many for comfort. Trouble is brewing for someone, somewhere.'

'The King and Parliament are continuing their disastrous struggle for power. They have no conception of where true power lies. They are concerned only with the trivial powers of nations. They are tennis balls dispatched from end to end of a court, back and forth, back and forth, by hands that they do not even see. The King, perforce, has his headquarters in Oxford. Even in happier times the King and all his ministers, their officials and the squalid team of favourites and hangers-on leave London in the summer for the provinces, as do the supporters of Parliament. But not from choice. They are driven out every year by fear of the pest. About disease, ageing and death they can do nothing. We who are gathered here have the key. The day is on hand when that golden key can be at last be turned.'

'Yes, maybe,' answered Joseph.

The priest looked at him searchingly again. 'But you are exhausted and in pain,' he said. 'It is inconsiderate of me to keep you talking here. I beg your pardon. Go and get some rest and, if you are able, join our discussion this afternoon. A few of us will be considering the significance of Drebbel's voyage underwater from Westminster to Greenwich.'

Joseph stared at him uncomprehendingly. 'What is that to us? That has nothing to do with the great endeavour.'

'Ah, but the occupants of this sub-aquatic vessel did not suffocate during the course of such a long journey. They were sustained by a Philosopher's Stone of the atmosphere. Come and hear about it if you can.'

Alistair Douglas turned to continue his exploration of the grounds and within a few minutes Joseph's needs were smoothly provided by the wealth and efficiency of a great house.

# CHAPTER 6

*Oh! Let us never, never doubt*
*What nobody is sure about!*
    Hilaire Belloc.


The speaker was from that island in the ocean to the West of Britain, a land of which Joseph knew rather little. Like the other listeners he was working hard on the young man's brand of the English language.

'A man entered the city of Seville with great ceremony. No one had heard of him before, nor could tell easily whence he came. His complexion suggested an origin in one of those lands that border the Eastern end of the Mediterranean Sea but he might have been born perhaps in the farthest lands of Alexander's conquests. Any prejudice which the people of the city might have felt on account of his race and religion – neither of which they could confidently determine – was put aside willingly on the highest ethical considerations. That is to say, he was clearly very rich. With him came a retinue of servants who attended instantly to his every requirement. Although his servants were dressed in the smartest livery, his own dress was always simple, and, although of the best material, consisted of long white robes only, so that he carried with him a subtle suggestion of the New Testament. On account of his generosity to those he met and the feasts that he held, he initially became known as the Sultan. But some began to refer to him as Balthazar, and this is how he eventually became known. Those more observant noticed that he had hired a workshop and that the vapours issuing from it did not suggest that carpentry was its purpose, nor any of the common crafts. The rumour grew that he was a magus and that he had travelled from the East following some new star. Also that he owed his obvious riches to his secret knowledge of the means to transform iron or lead into precious metal. As time went on the list of substances which he could ennoble grew and came to include wood, leather, soil and even camel dung.

After some weeks Balthazar announced a great banquet to celebrate his Birthday. The nobility and the rich merchants of the town – all who appeared to have a little money – were invited to this sumptuous occasion. They were lavishly wined and dined and the atmosphere became ever more relaxed and merry. The host was himself in jovial mood, so much so that someone, the Mayor I believe, who had seen courage at the bottom of his wineglass, felt able to ask him confidentially if it was true that he could turn common metals into gold. 'No,' answered the Magus, 'that is beyond my powers, but I have learned how to multiply gold a hundred or even a thousand times. We have all of the night before us. If you wish I can arrange a demonstration.'

So the remains of the feast were cleared away and replaced by a gleaming bank of retorts, flasks and other vessels, and a small furnace was set up. The Sultan collected gold coins from all present, promising at least a hundred-fold return. Those who had no coins with them sent servants home for money or borrowed coins from friends. The preparations took several hours but the passage of time was well lubricated and slipped smoothly away. At last all was ready and the host, with great ceremony, produced an ampoule containing some dark crystals which, when he held them up, were seen to possess a lustrous red translucence, almost as though able to produce their own light. One man who tried to snatch them from the hands of the magus was apprehended and taken away for trial. The coins were placed in a large open beaker, the elixir was scattered over them like pepper over a beef steak and an enormous inverted funnel, the upper end of which was connected to a series of condensers, was lowered over the beaker. The beaker was swung into place over the already blazing furnace. For the first time during that festive evening, the revellers fell silent as they waited with eager anticipation for the event that, throughout their lives, they had heard about but had never thought they would see for themselves. Suddenly there was an enormous explosion, a sound so loud that no one could hear or be heard for several seconds. The candles and lamps blew out and clouds of fumes and choking smoke filled the room, sending the guests coughing and spluttering about in confusion and discomfort. When eventually the doors were opened to let in air and the lights were restored, the Sultan was no longer there. Nor was the elixir. And there was no sign of the pile of gold coins. From the street came the sound of galloping hooves dying rapidly away in the distance.'

It was late evening, after a relaxing supper and the Irishman's story was greeted with immoderate laughter. Only Alistair Douglas remained tight-lipped throughout. When the mirth had died away, he said politely to the story-teller, but with a bitter edge to his voice:

'You tell your tale well, but perhaps you will be kind enough to inform me when I should laugh.'

'Oh come,' said one of the company, 'I know you are a pillar of the Church, but even Almighty God must surely enjoy a joke occasionally. He must see and hear enough of them.'

'Certainly he sees them,' Douglas replied, 'but I doubt whether He enjoys many. He probably finds them as distressing – if God indeed can be distressed – as I did this one. All my life – and certainly I speak for everyone – I, you, all of us have suffered from the disgraceful activities of charlatans, fraudsters, swindlers, embezzlers and rogues of every type who masquerade as adepti. It is not difficult, as you all know, to simulate transmutation and projection – the colouring of base metals to resemble the precious is a craft dating from ancient Greece, not necessarily fraudulent. Any of us could cheat if we wished. Many have been hanged for such actions, and rightly. The wrongs that they do to their victims are done equally to us. That is why we can rarely work openly, why we must hide away in wretched inappropriate cellars, why we must proceed with extreme care in approaching those who might become patrons for the advancement of our studies. It is the reason why we are often reviled by decent people and courted by scoundrels who wish to join us to make a quick and crooked fortune. It is also the reason why we must conceal our meanings in metaphor and myth, mysticism and just plain mist.'

'Or part of the reason.' Joseph had spoken at last.

'What is the other part, Apothecary? You've been unusually quiet today.'

Before he could answer, Douglas had continued, and immediately arrested Joseph's attention. He was quoting from Sendivogius.

'"The searchers of Nature ought to be as Nature herself is, true, plain, patient, constant... and that which is chiefest of all, religious, fearing God, not injurious to their neighbour"' He went on, quoting from himself, 'the purification of substances that we attempt, the bringing to perfection of the base metals that we seek, mirror our own spiritual quest. The destruction and resurrection of the gross materials, with which we begin, is the seed that has been cast away and has putrefied in order that it may germinate and grow, as described by Christ. The alchemist and his alchemy cannot be separated. They are intimates, who work on each other to their joint and reciprocal ends. The adept and his work are like opposed mirrors, the reflections stretching away endlessly into the infinity.'

A much-travelled man from Italy was more interested in the details.

'It is a good story. Like all good stories it has different *dramatis personæ* each time that I hear it. It seems to have happened many times over. Each time in a different town, in a different country.'

'Perhaps it was the same man, moving on, to repeat his success elsewhere. It is not the kind of trick that you could perform twice in the same place. He will certainly have become exceedingly rich.'

Francis Neil – clearly from the South of England, probably from London – a young lawyer with well-chilled eyes and a nose that was too pointed for his neighbour's confidence or his wife's comfort, interrupted.

'Not so. The story creaks like a jobber's door. Just think a moment – how did he make a profit out of this business? How could those gold coins cover the cost of his venture?' The nose began to tremble triumphantly as it always did when he thought he had cornered the opposition. 'Pay for the servants, the livery, the feasts, the workshop? What happened to the servants when their master was galloping away? Did he take them with him, pay them off? He donated an expensive laboratory to the town? How did he extract himself from this darkened smoke-filled room with rich men milling about in a panic, carrying a heavy tray of gold coins?'

An Italian replied. 'Well, he stood a better chance of making money than we do – or any of our predecessors or successors. All alchemical gold is Fool's gold. The swindlers are the only ones who will ever benefit from our studies.'

'Mon Dieu,' exclaimed a Frenchman. It is as cheerful here this evening as a donkey's funeral wake. Clearly we have run out of wine. We should seek a restitution immediately.'

The cure was attended to at once, but as with most remedies was not entirely effective. The man with the pointed nose who had dissected the story of the Sultan with such scepticism still had more iced water to throw about.

'You are right to presume that projection will never be possible. It is possible in principle but too difficult in practice. And even if it were, it would ultimately not be of use. Oh yes, the man who achieves it may gain an advantage, may become very rich. But I assume from the elevated sentiments I have heard from all around me that such a desire is far away from the thoughts of anyone here. Consider, if you are able to see beyond your noses' – here he was on dangerous ground but no one dared to take advantage – 'when it becomes possible freely to convert lead into gold – what will be the value of gold? The answer is inescapable. It will be the value of lead. Or little more. With what will the streets of the city be paved? They will be paved with lead or might as well be so. The streets will look well. They will sparkle bravely in the morning sun. They will be of the same value as the Duchess' resplendent necklace. The value of lead.'

'But at least the woodcutter's wife would be able to enjoy the privileges of wealth which are presently denied. There would be a true democracy of riches.' The man who spoke had a deep voice and an eloquent, persuasive manner. Those present knew him well – that is to say they knew a lot about his present life; his past, though, remained mysterious. He was obviously highly educated, but made his living from various rather dubious enterprises. Rumour suggested that he was an unfrocked priest or a disgraced lawyer. One of his skills was the telling of fortunes from significant facial and cranial characteristics – authorised and proven by the most eminent philosophers, of course – for which he charged a small coin, or a larger one if the subject looked capable of parting with it. His name, Robert Surtees, was rarely used by the alchemists in his absence. They alluded to him by a less flattering title, Bob Nob Job, relating to his way of making a living. The caustic Francis Neil replied:

'Yes. A democracy. A universal equality. We would all be poor. Value is the daughter of rarity. When there is nothing of rarity there will be no wealth – not for anyone.' The nose began to tremble again. 'No father, no daughter. And I am not talking solely about great riches, not worrying over the destitution of the nobility or the suicide of rich merchants. I am talking about prosperity of the whole community, prosperity as it sifts down – or should – a prosperity which has to be related to something of which little exists, which is difficult or dangerous to obtain.'

'Diamonds would do,' said the Italian, thoughtfully. 'Perhaps we should find out how to make diamonds. They are brilliant also and similarly incorruptible. Extremely hard. Harder than anything else which God has made. In this contest, gold is easily defeated.'

'Not incorruptible', said the Frenchman. 'I have proved this by placing one under a burning glass. My wife would not speak to me for a whole month.'

'I am glad to hear that some good came of it.' Joseph had spoken at last. 'Occasionally we are asked to provide powdered diamond as a medicine.'

'And is that effective?'

'It disappears without trace. I have a theory as to where it re-emerges, but will not trouble you with it while you are digesting supper. Certainly it gives excellent support to the vanity, and that in itself may contribute to good health.'

'Vanity is pride, one of the seven deadly sins. It contributes not to our health but to our eternal damnation.' The comment came from Benjamin Green, whose ingratiating manner had immediately irritated Joseph when he had been introduced to him on the previous day. Benjamin had greeted him as if they were old comrades-in-arms who had saved each other's lives, possibly several times.

'Even so,' said Alistair Douglas, 'but nonetheless, our Brother Apothecary has a point. Certainly we must love ourselves if we are ever to love others.'

Joseph was too surprised at this comment to respond. 'Why has no one ever pointed that out to me before?' he thought. He was about to say, 'Yes, true. We must begin by loving ourselves. But how much?' He was too late, though. By now the action was elsewhere. A lanky, pale-faced man had moved the subject on.

'There is no sense in discussing the problems of wealth, or even in talking about projection and the manufacture of gold. First we must make the Philosopher's Stone. I take it that we are here to exchange ideas as to how close we are to this achievement, and what remains still to be done.'

'The Philosopher's Stone.' A young Englishman, James Fisher – Joseph's close friend – spoke almost to himself. But his musing tones arrested the company's attention. 'That I have never understood. Transmutation I accept. It is possible because all metals have a common ground. Indeed it happens continually deep in the earth – Nature's processes taking the best course possible, as Aristotle has told us, journeying towards perfection – and our task is to understand those processes and to repeat them. *Art is Nature, with men to help*. All things partake of the four elements. In the metals, as we know from the wisdom of the Arabs, these elements are in turn expressed as Mercury and Sulphur – not the common mercury and sulphur, but purer, nobler and more potent forms which we call the Mercury and Sulphur of the Philosophers. But the Stone, the Elixir, the Medicine – it has many names… what reason can we have for believing that Projection is possible – that it is possible to take a tiny amount of something that we have prepared laboriously from common materials, and then project those few crystals upon great masses of some crude material like lead, transforming the mundane into beauty and worth?'

'David smote Goliath.'

It was a new voice. The speaker was the most colourful of the participants. The dress code at the meeting was uncertain – uneasy even. Because of the rarity of such an event, there was no tradition or norm. Some had dressed as though making a personal statement. Others had adopted a more cautious approach, dressing soberly in a non-confrontational manner designed not to refer to any particular allegiance. And this again was difficult – and important – because of the divergence of dress codes between dissenters and those who supported the established Church and of the powerful political and military forces that stood in the shadows behind them. The international flavour of the meeting further confused the scene. Don Hidalgo had no doubts. He was presumably unconcerned with little local squabbles in England. His attire was speaking up for himself and for Spain. But not for modern Spain. For Spain some fifty years ago. Instead of the pants and almost knee-length boots of most of those present, he wore hose and a doublet with knee-length skirt. The doublet opened at the front to reveal a richly decorated silk shirt, which was also exposed in long full sleeves. The shirt carried a mass of symbols among which could be seen instantly the Christian Cross, the Muslim crescent, the red cross and roses, mandalas, hexagrams, symbols of the planets and a multitude more, clamouring for recognition. The shirt itself was worth an evening's study. He wore a small beard and his hair was cropped short, unlike the Cavalier fashion of flowing shoulder-length hair sported by several of those present. Hair styles had been more difficult to conceal. His intervention produced a hiatus in the discussion.

'I beg your pardon,' asked Alistair Douglas.

'David smote Goliath,' repeated Don Hidalgo in solemn tones. 'But we need not quarry the Bible for understanding on this point. We have only to look around us. It is possible because that is how God has ordained it. It is possible because it is the way in which Nature works. Who has not seen his cook (here there were glances exchanged in the company among those who had barely set eyes on a cook, let alone employed one) – add a small sachet of rennet to an urn of milk. Or in his bakery – (further glances were exchanged) has not seen a crumb of yeast mixed into a bowl of dough to enlighten and enliven the flour and water. Or in his brewery has not watched as a handful of yeast, cast into a vat of juice of the barley, transmutes it in the course of time into the refreshing and animating liquid that we know.'

Don Hidalgo now had his listeners' total attention, especially after the last example.

'But do you conceive how this to projection relate might?' This was a German representative speaking.

'Spagyria,' answered Don mysteriously. 'Spagyria is the answer.'

There was a hiss of whispering all around the room as 'spagyria' was discussed and eventually elucidated.

'But what is to be taken apart and with what put together again?' asked Francis Neil.

Don Hidalgo spoke in hushed reverential tones that were easily audible all over the room. The capitalised words in his sentences were as clear as if they were printed in a book.

'The Sun has a little Sister. A very little Sister who never moves far from the side of the Golden One, but has powers utterly beyond her stature. In due time she must be married to the Brother of Jupiter, who is the Keeper of the Key. Their union will be blessed by Queen Jezebel but must be honoured on the Third day of the Moon. Then Apollo's Sister will achieve her full powers reflecting the Sun's heat though not her glory. But in this state she becomes the anointer of Kings.'

Alistair Douglas was as courteous and to the point as ever. 'I fear that my slow mind has not followed you entirely. What you have said suggests that you have learned some part of the secret of the Ancients. Would you be able to explain further?'

'Tomorrow. Tomorrow I will explain All. Today is the Day of Thor and is not auspicious. Do not attempt the work of the Magus on Thor's Day.'

'Very well. We will commit some time tomorrow. Perhaps Freya will be more amenable.'

'Freya smiles more kindly upon these enterprises,' the Spaniard replied. 'And then I will tell you. Not only will I tell you... I will show you.'

There was a great murmur among the company. A man bold enough to demonstrate – presumably – a transformation of base metal to gold. Many claimed such achievements. Few were prepared to show how, even in private. The buzz was brought to an end by the Irishman:

'I trust that we are not required to contribute gold coins!'

There was general laughter.

'Tomorrow evening then,' said Alistair Douglas, 'after the discussion.'

\* \* \* \* \*

Joseph was talking to his best friend James Fisher after the promise of transmutation.

'Will our Spanish friend deliver his treasure tomorrow? How much did you understand of his peroration?'

'Rather little. "The Sun's little sister who moves not far from her side" is of course Mercury.'

'Yes, that was obvious. But I presume that he is referring to the vulgar mercury as it is prepared or mined, rather than to that ineffable and fugitive essence, Our Mercury, the Mercury of the Philosophers.'

'Yes, I believe that he means the common mercury, and I think the process he describes is intended to release the Philosophic Mercury from it.'

'But who is the lesser brother of Jupiter?'

'I don't know. Jupiter usually symbolises tin. Perhaps the brother is zinc or antimony which were often prepared accidentally in the smelting of tin and confused with it.'

'Of course.' Joseph had made the Biblical connection. 'Antimony. Jezebel used stibnite to blacken her eyebrows.'

'Well done. But how about the moon? Silver presumably.'

'Yes. And the third day is three parts in twenty-nine of the moon's cycle. The proportion in which the silver must be added. But the mercury then attains the sun's heat but not its glory.'

'I think that may refer to a few reports I have heard,' said James. 'That when the True Mercury is released from the common mercury, great heat is generated. I have tried myself to study such incalation, as it has been called, but was unable to reproduce it.'

'We can congratulate ourselves. Perhaps we should away to a laboratory and forestall the learned Spaniard! The prize might be a great one.'

'And might not. I am too tired. Anyway, it is Thor's day and inauspicious!'

James was worried on his friend's behalf.

'You were quiet today. And not well?'

'I am well enough. Just not sure that I should be here,' said Joseph.

'Why? You have not had an accident, I hope?'

'Only inside my head.'

'That may be the worst accident of all.'

'I have tried hard all day to take the discussions I have heard seriously. They have seemed like the twittering of birds in a wood. Sometimes charming, sometimes raucous, always foreign, always going on somewhere else, carrying no meaning to my mind. *Irrelevant*. That is the word I was groping for. Even the best of those here seem somehow irrelevant. Talking a language which I no longer understand – or understand but no longer wish to speak.'

And he went on to describe the explosion in his laboratory – 'trivial really as these things go' – and the revelation presented to him by the pottery shard.

'Since when I have been circulating idly, without purpose, on a listless wind, like the Ancients in the Uppermost Circle of the Underworld.'

'Shock. The explosion was worse than you realise. You will soon return to normal. And you are still in pain. That is obvious. You damaged your back at the same time.'

Joseph, who was a private person, secretive even, examined his friend thoughtfully. He did not release information about himself easily. And he did not relish his personal adventures becoming public property. But a close personal friend could be trusted not to pass on his embarrassments.

'That was a different – and pleasanter – incident.'

To his friend's enquiring eyebrows, he replied, after a few more moments' hesitation,

'Venus was in the ascendant.'

\* \* \* \* \*

The excellent and austere Vicar of Cranford was introducing a topic informally to a small, sub-group of the conference.

'Cornelius Drebbel was born, I think, in Alkmar, in 1572. He died twelve years ago in London. He was a chemist and engineer of great ingenuity with diverse inventions and processes to his credit. In 1604 we know that he was brought to London by James the First to work on the construction of a boat able to travel under water. Presumably the good King was interested in the possibility of puncturing enemy galleons below the water line and without the galleon's crew being aware of their imminent peril. Inventors become especially popular if their inventions have possible military use. Such a device, if he had been wholly successful, might now be turned against his own countrymen. This irony, which could provide a kernel for ethical discussion, is not my subject today. I want to draw your attention to his achievement. In 1621, a boat constructed as Drebbel directed, made a passage under water, at a depth of twelve to fifteen feet, from Westminster to Greenwich. The boat was waterproofed by greased leather and was propelled by twelve oarsmen. The journey in itself is remarkable – '

'Remarkable indeed, incredible even.' The interjection was made by Francis Neil.

'And,' added Alistair Douglas, with a reproving glance in the direction of the interruption, 'is well attested by reliable witnesses, including King James himself. But now I come to the matter that concerns us all. To refresh the atmosphere in the boat, which might well have stifled the unfortunate crew with the foulness that accumulates in such closed and cramped quarters, a bottle was opened, releasing some essence into the air, bringing immediate relief to all present. I do not need to explain to you the importance of this eventuality. Various interpretations might be possible, but I am going to suggest to you that the active principle released from the bottle was in some way related to the Philosopher's Stone – that the air which gave such instant relief may have been an evanescent part or emanation from the substance which we believe will one day impart health to, and relieve the sickness of, mankind.'

'May I ask from where you have acquired this information regarding Cornelius Drebbel's voyage?' Francis Neil had spoken in his most courteous and polished manner, which usually presaged trouble.

'I spoke of it to an excellent and reliable physician, who had authority in the matter.'

'Had the physician himself witnessed Drebbel's voyage?' The question was put by Joseph's friend, James Fisher.

'No. He had not himself been present, but he was, so to speak, one tier back from the riverside. He knew Drebbel intimately and had the account directly from him. He was married to Drebbel's daughter. A written account from the same source was made in 1625 by Johannes Faber.'

'Ah,' exclaimed Dr Neil vindictively. 'The source was a close member of Drebbel's family. Then we may disbelieve it, or at least presume that the account will include distortions or exaggerations which direct a more glorious light upon Cornelius Drebbel and, by reflection, upon his relatives.' The point he was making scored two twitches of the nose.

'I am, I think, after many years of pastoral work, able to make a good assessment of a man's character, and of the veracity of what I am told. I can only assure you of the total integrity of Drebbel's son-in-law and the confidence I have in his account.'

'Do we have to disbelieve everything now?' Tom Stowe had spoken, a man whose face, always ruddy, was now beginning to glow like the coals in the fire. 'People are trying to discredit everything. Some of them. They will be disbelieving Aristotle and the ancient philosophers soon, and after that God's Word as given to us in the Bible.'

'Reliability of sources is never easy to determine,' said James Fisher. 'Best perhaps to examine the story on its internal evidence. I have made the journey by water along the Thames from Westminster to Greenwich and I know it to be a treacherous and dangerous passage. Care is required in a boat above the river. How could it possibly be made underwater with all the difficulties of navigation which that inevitably brings?'

Tom Stowe had the answer. 'Mirrors. By mirrors. They have been in use in land battles for hundreds of years. They enable the soldier to see what the enemy is doing without exposing his body to harm.'

Francis still had cold water to throw. 'More likely that there was an escort boat on the surface, probably with a rope attached to Drebbel's boat.'

Alistair Douglas was determined to direct the discussion. 'But the putrid atmosphere and its purification – that is what really concerns us. What was in the bottle that was opened to relieve their breathing? Could it not have been the long sought-after, long desired elixir?'

'It might be so.' Joseph joined the discussion for the first time. 'I believe that the air around us possesses, not only the substantial, palpable part which we sense as wind and which may be of such force that it can capsize a large ship, but also an insubstantial or spirituous part of great virtue that brings life to all living things. And that this may indeed be an aspect of the great elixir for which we have long searched.' Tom Stowe intervened again:

'To all living things? Do you include the mean animals and plant life too?'

Joseph replied. 'All require it. And I believe that this evanescent part of the air can in some circumstances pass into substances such as nitre and from there pass in turn into an ailing plant – into a stricken plant, yellow and stunted – to renew its breathing and donate to it new colour, life and vigour.'

'Tell me Apothecary' – Francis Neil was speaking with dangerous politeness again. 'I know you to be a master of your excellent and indispensable profession. But – such is the necessarily imperfect state of our knowledge, there must be some medicines which the physicians require you to prepare in which you have little confidence?'

'All too many.'

'And yet sometimes, when these are given against, perhaps, your better judgement, do they not cure the patient's affliction?'

'Yes, sometimes that is so, although I suspect that in the case of serious sickness the beneficial effects are temporary only.'

'Then I am going to suggest that the relief which these underwater sailors experienced was a simple consequence of the opening of a bottle, of any bottle, containing something or anything or nothing. That the opening of the bottle fulfilled the expectations which had been previously given to them by the captain of the boat and that this was effective as the workings of some prepared medicine.'

Alistair Douglas was offended. 'You mean that Drebbel played a trick on them, made fools of them. That is a disgraceful idea, a slander against an honourable man.'

'Not at all. He relieved their respiration. He made them feel better. That is what apothecaries and physicians do. As they should. And clergymen do it too,' he added with a just-discernible sniff and an all-too conspicuous twitch.

Discussion continued for some time. There was general agreement that the Vicar of Cranford had drawn attention to an important matter, worth further thought and investigation. The opinion was not quite unanimous.

'I believe it to the same extent that I believe in flying witches.' Francis Neil dismissed airborne hags and Cornelius' Drebbel's feat with a single twitch of his nose.

\* \* \* \* \*

'Benjamin Green', said James Fisher in a low voice, almost a whisper. 'I suddenly recognised him when he made that comment about vanity the other evening. He was called something different last time I heard about him. He has too many names for my liking. They are designed to confuse us, and by now may well confuse him.'

Joseph laughed. 'I know the feeling.'

'Your changes of name have been forced upon you by circumstance. So have his, I suppose, in a manner of speaking. One of the circumstances was a prison in York, seven years ago. He is also Anthony Long and George Park and, I suspect, several more people. I do not know which name he was born with.'

'I have almost forgotten mine', said Joseph.

\* \* \* \* \*

The company settled down into chairs for the discussion. The start of the meeting was delayed because of the absence of the Baroness. Eventually a servant was located and sent to make tactful enquiries of her intentions. He returned with her apologies, excusing herself on account of serious news that she had just received. The discussion was to be led by Joseph. He and Alistair Douglas remained standing, the latter only while he introduced the subject and the discussion leader. He made the usual courteous compliments to the members of the Society gathered there, and then to the speaker.

'Many of you are already familiar with the distinguished first speaker, if not by personal acquaintance, then certainly by reputation, and will know that although young, he has achievements and wisdom beyond his years.' More followed in the same vein, but avoiding any allusion to Joseph's early association with Sendivogius.

'He has chosen, and will introduce, as this afternoon's subject for the Society's consideration, 'communication in chymistry.' We thank him particularly for speaking today in spite of being in some pain due to an injured back. He asks you to excuse him if he remains standing throughout, implying no discourtesy to whoever is speaking at the time.'

This concluding remark evoked a response which neither Joseph nor perhaps the Reverend Douglas had anticipated. A ripple of inadequately suppressed laughter travelled around the room, washing here and there past individuals whose lips tightened visibly, like a wave shifting sand, but breaking over undisturbed stones. An unofficial, wholly informal but reliable vote had been taken concerning the status of moral purity among the adepti. Joseph scowled and glanced sidelong at Alistair Douglas, who looked puzzled, although Joseph was not so sure that he really was. Clearly his best friend, James, had been less than discrete. Probably he had told only one other person, another close friend who could be relied upon not to chatter. At least James had the decency to look embarrassed when the Joseph glared across the room at him. But there was nothing to be done other than proceed with his speech.

'You will all know of the writings of the Cosmopolite, who for many years sought for a way to enhance the health and wealth of men, of their families, their children and the whole community. And as most of those present today *are* – and the remainder *should be* – he was puzzled. This shows clearly in his books. I shall quote two short passages that will bring the difficulty before us to examine. The first is from a book titled *Process on the Central Salt.*

"Caution. You should, at any rate, not put in more than six pounds at a time i.e. mix 1.5 pounds of nitre with 3.5 pounds of soil. Distil this into a receiver as with aqua regia. Into the receiver add about two pounds of distilled rainwater, so that the dark red spirit which is produced will enter and settle there. When the distillation is thus properly accomplished, cool the furnace each time, take the product out carefully and store it... The distillation ought to stop when the spirits have been removed from the liquor on the water-bath... This will be apparent as soon as colourless spirits cease to be evolved."

I invite you to contrast this with the Cosmopolite's thoughts on the Salts, expressed in the same book.

"The first is a Central Salt, which the Spirit of the World begets without any Discontinuation in the centre of the Elements by the Influences of the Stars, and is governed by the rays of the Sun and of the Moon in our Philosophical Sea. The second is a Spermatic Salt, which is the Domicile or Seat of the Invisible Seed, and which in a gentle natural Heat, by the means of Putrefaction gives of itself the Form and Vegetable Vertue... The third Salt, is the last Matter of all Things, which is to be found in them, and which remains in them even after their Destruction."

Here we have, within the same book and the same subject, by one author, two languages. The first is the language of instruction. It has a simple clarity so that I am confident that I could at any time walk into my laboratory and follow exactly what was done, and I would have no difficulty in achieving the same result. The second is the language of metaphysics or philosophy. In this passage I sense that important things are being said – not least about the relations between light, air, putrefaction and vegetable form, but the ideas are too general and the thinking too personal for me to grasp the author's meaning. I emerge with no better understanding of the substance of the world. It is not the philosophical language of Socrates or Aristotle that was designed for challenge and counter-challenge. It is a language where no counter-argument is possible or expected, where the only response which can be made is a different set of equally unchallengeable statements.

Perhaps I should apologise for bringing my half-formed thoughts before such a distinguished gathering this afternoon. Perhaps I should not be speaking at this meeting. But the opportunities are few, and it may be that someone here has suffered the same doubts and can resolve my dilemma, or can in some way correct the error in my thinking. I am coming to believe that we cannot hope to make further progress until we have unified our ways of discussing the subject in which we are all deeply concerned.'

'Excuse me, sir.' Tom Stowe, his face resembling a blood orange even more closely than usual, had risen to his feet, giving a tardy and half-hearted request for permission in the direction of Alistair Douglas. 'I hope you will not mind me speaking at this point. You are not I hope suggesting that we confuse the terminology of the workshop with that of philosophical argument.'

'I am suggesting that we apply to the discussion of philosophical principles the clarity in description which we use – or, more accurately, some of us use – in giving account of our daily work with chymical processes.'

'But that is to confuse base mechanics – I mean no disrespect', he added hastily, 'to the distinguished work of the company here – with the powers of the philosopher who can, by the devotion of many years of study of the First Principles, move us gradually towards an understanding of the world which God has provided us with. Something I have always tried to do in my writings.'

'We have read some of them.' This time, Francis Neil had spoken. 'They read like Paracelsus after a bad night in the tavern. Have you read Descartes's *Discourse on Method*, Apothecary?'

'I regret that I have not been able to do so.'

Francis Neil's nose gave a victorious tremble. He had scored another hit. 'An apothecary is committed to our good health and we thank God for it. But understandably he has limited time in which to develop a proper competence in philosophical matters. You should read him. He has attempted what you have suggested, but with curious results. And only in mathematics, not chymistry.'

Tom Stowe was almost shouting. 'Descartes! A joke. He has started from the wrong end of God's Creation. From his miserable self and his mundane surroundings. The author was correct in his writings about the Central Salt – not of course in detail, but in approach. He is attempting at least to relate what we see here in our limited existence, with our limited vision with the First Causes, with the Sun, Moon and Stars in their Higher Spheres.'

'I feel that I have not made my point sufficiently. Here is a further example. An anonymous extract which I came across recently. Joseph picked up another paper and began to read;

'Leda must be white and pure, for her lineage is noble. Her essence is of the finest, thrice-distilled. Therefore she shall bathe only in the purest of waters. Ensure that these are free of all sediment or discolouration, for her sweetness must remain unsullied. Two handmaidens shall accompany her to the shore, one robed like the sun, the other with apparel blue as the sky, for she permits the presence only of those who have the greatest faith. There she shall await the rush of wings and the thrust of Jupiter, who must be presented in the finest...'

He had no time to read further. Tom Stowe had risen to his feet again, more vivid than ever. To Joseph he seemed about to suffer some kind of seizure.

'The meaning of the script is perfectly clear to me. And to anyone of our persuasion who has taken the trouble to master the terminology...'

'Of course you understand it.' A dark-haired man with a stutter had spoken. 'You wr-wr-wrote it!'

This insight provoked a general uproar, mostly laughter. Joseph was genuinely taken aback. He had no idea that the author of his example was among the company, and was attempting to apologise for the unhappy choice. His efforts to retrieve the situation were lost in the developing furore. The red-faced man was still shouting explanations about the insemination of Leda. His critic was pointing at him, mocking him. The Reverend Douglas was shouting in vain for order. Finally the red-faced man snatched the paper from Joseph's hand and whirling around again to confront his critic, collided with him. The critic pushed him away roughly, causing him to trip over an expensive chair, which shattered. By the time he had extricated himself from the remains of the unfortunate piece of furniture, he was beyond all control, either by himself or anyone else. He threw a punch at his critic, which fortunately missed, and received another in return which unfortunately did not. His bulky friend seemed to relish the opportunity for some physical involvement after sitting about for several days and came to his friend's aid with a blow that balanced the budget nicely. Another joined in on the side of the man with the stutter, and any further hopes at audit were quickly lost as the four traded hostilities rapidly and with varying efficiency. The remainder of the company abandoned philosophy for the moment and some of them were sucked into the whirlpool swirling about the middle of the room as they tried to separate the combatants and received various samples of the goods on offer for their own consumption. The table that Joseph had been using was thrown against the wall and several more chairs were dispatched across the room. The noise and confusion were such that the opening of the door into the room was not heard, and the bartering of blows continued, only gradually subsiding as progressively more of the company became aware of a figure standing as still as one of her statues in the doorway. The noise died away into a general embarrassment as the silent figure of the Baroness was recognised.

The combatants tried, not very successfully, to imitate respectable humans and to melt away into the throng as though they had played no leading part in the action.

Joseph presumed that the Society's proceedings had come to a sudden end. They would be shown the door. Penelope Richmond was more than capable of handling this scene in a dignified manner. She simply stood and stared with disdain at the disgraceful scene that she had encountered. The room began to empty. Tom Stowe was trying to conceal himself behind the man with the stutter, who was slinking towards the second door of the room – a better choice of hiding place would have been behind the bulky man, who must have weighed twenty stone at least, but he was busy; he seemed to be engaged in practising the improbable art of Invisibility. The participants gradually disappeared in a kind of act of distillation, presumably reappearing in some other place where the temperature was lower. The Reverend Alistair Douglas, with a moral courage notably lacking in the others, lingered to attempt an apology. Penelope answered with a contemptuous glance and turned away to call a servant who would restore whatever was restorable and remove the rest for repair.

Douglas was only a few paces along the corridor leading away from the devastation when the Baroness called him back. She had had second thoughts.

'Obviously this was no fault of yours Reverend. I would be glad if you would oblige me by rounding up these people. You may borrow the dogs from the farm if you wish! I have received serious news, which I was about to divulge. It affects them all. They are in some danger. On further reflection, I would prefer that they do not get what they deserve. I believe that Royalist troops are approaching the house. Tell the fools to assemble here immediately and prepare for a quick end to our meeting.'

# CHAPTER 7

After the stress of a lecture and discussion that had gone so awry, Joseph needed fresh air and some gentle exercise. A stroll around the estate seemed a suitable therapy. In the preceding days he had been too occupied with discussion, and the rare chance of meeting others who shared his interests, to have explored the grounds. In most respects, these proved to be as anticipated: here were the expected buildings, the necessary adjuncts to the house of an aristocratic family – stables, coach houses, stores for equipment used in hunting and the sports of the upper classes (although – if Joseph had been correctly informed – not of William Richmond) mostly dedicated to faunicide. In the distance he could see the farm buildings, dairies, tool-sheds, and the many acres of land, which supplied some of the Richmond family's income. Everything was as usual for a rich estate, remarkable only for its tidiness and modernity, but quite close to the house, and hidden from it by a line of trees, was a building whose function was not apparent. It was a long and low, obviously quite new, but unexceptional apart from an excessive array of chimneys, from one of which smoke was rising. A blacksmith's forge perhaps? – but there was no evidence of horses, no hoof marks, nor any place where they might be tended. His curiosity was aroused.

He pushed open the door, expecting to find a workman of some sort inside. There was no one. The first thing he saw was a portable furnace, still hot, standing in one of the chimney recesses. People had been engaged in work of some kind here very recently. As he stepped forward, bottles, long lines of them, neatly labelled and arranged, winked at him in various colours in the late afternoon light. His perplexity lasted only a few seconds more and was replaced with astonishment. That object in the corner was an old friend – nothing less than a *bain-marie*, an invention attributed to the mysterious Mary the Jew. And there were furnaces of many types, covering every possible requirement. Here was the explanation for the chimneys. Apparatus for filtration, calcination, sublimation, assation, ablution, cibation, inceration and mundification – of a quality and variety which he had never been able to afford and probably never would – stood all around the room begging to be used. So, the Baroness not only hosted congresses of alchemists, but she owned also a beautifully equipped laboratory. Was she then a true adept? Did she personally expose herself to the fumes and hazards of the seekers after wealth, health and immortality? Joseph wandered around the room in continuing astonishment. Here were the standard alchemic substances to be expected in most laboratories. These gave way to dyes and herbal remedies from all over the world. On another shelf were rare and costly items, familiar to him only from books or hearsay.

Next to the main laboratory was a storeroom, in which there were alchemic substances too, but in large tubs and boxes, in almost factory-scale quantities. He noted a large bin of nitre and another of sulphur. There were several large bags of charcoal, presumably to fuel the furnaces.

Pushing open another door, he found a library – not a repository of the classics, such as he had seen in the Richmond mansion, with elegant tables and chairs at which to work, or deep armchairs in which to read or nod off to sleep, but a huge collection of books on natural philosophy including all of the standard text books on alchemy and industrial chymistry; the furnishings were a business-like collection of hard-backed chairs and benches.

'When are we going to have a place like this?' asked the flaxen-haired boy.

'When we've made gold, I should think', answered Joseph. 'It's our only hope.'

'But we can't find out how to make gold or anything else until we've got a place like this', said the boy.

'Too true', agreed Joseph, who was by turns, envious, elated and depressed. 'Perhaps we had better give up and study something else.'

As he was about to leave, he caught sight of a notebook lying open on a bench near the door to the exterior. Here perhaps was the answer to Penelope Richmond's mysterious activities. A temptation to such an insight as this was not to be resisted, any more than a temptation to almost anything else. He began to read and was soon thoroughly absorbed in his detective work. The Lady was interested in the clarification of the language of their subject, reinforcing his own developing view. He turned more pages.

She had become interested in alchemy and plant growth, feeding common substances to radish plants and recording heights and weights during growth. Why choose such a humble plant? Judging by the records she had made, most of the plants had expired miserably, mercifully preventing any unfortunate person from eating them. With nitre the plants had flourished splendidly, a fact that he already knew and over which he and Michael had puzzled many times. And here was a strange experiment where she had been calcining copper in an open crucible, weighing the metal before, and the calx after, heating. What was to be gained he wondered, by such a simple-minded trial? And she had got the result wrong anyway – she had recorded an impossible gain in weight.

He was thoroughly absorbed in studying the fascinating subject matter when a shadow fell across the book – a rapidly moving shadow, elongated in shape, and moving in an arc towards him. It was about to merge with the vague shadow of his head, thrown on the pages before him by the setting sun that was shining almost parallel to the earth in the last splendour of the day.

Intuitively he leaned sideways. A hard object brushed his ear and a searing pain invaded his shoulder. He staggered and would have fallen, but his arms had already been imprisoned by two men. He began to struggle desperately, but the men, neither of whom he knew, had been chosen well for their task and were altogether stronger. One of them twisted his arm behind his back and clamped his neck in the crook of the other arm, immobilising his head. Now Joseph saw a third man whom he recognised immediately as he-of-too-many-names – Benjamin Anthony Park Green, or whatever – the graduate of York Prison. This time there was no false bonhomie. The man merely smiled grimly, grasped a handful of Joseph's hair with one hand and, with the other, clamped a wad of material over his nose and mouth.

Joseph struggled all the more desperately but his head was completely immobilised. The smell was of many times distilled liquor with a tinge of something else, nepenthe or curare or some such extract. The rows of bottles, glinting in the last rays of the sun, started to flicker, then to process like a macabre torchlight pageant, and finally to race erratically back and forth flashing hysterically, while the benches, shelves and ceiling began to waver and wallow in a drunken fashion. His knees seemed to have chosen apostasy, and were threatening a campaign of non-co-operation. The sights and sounds in the swaying laboratory were unnaturally magnified and distorted. Among them he heard what he thought was a distant pistol shot.

## CHAPTER 8

Celia Albright turned in at the gate of her mother's cottage, pausing for a moment to look at the garden. It was too early in the year for much to be seen. The small plot was neatly set out, the earth laid fresh and bare. The soil echoed the surrounding countryside. It was newly swept clean, looking much as it had in the late winter but carrying the latent promise of spring. A few points of green heralded another year of vegetables that would form the basis for the old woman's meagre existence, or perhaps indicated a resumption of the annual contest with the armies of the weed kingdom. Celia was carrying under a cloth a succulent addition to her mother's diet, a plum pie prepared with the last of the previous season's preserved fruit, surplus from her catering activities. As usual the garden was full of birds, congregating here as they did nowhere else in the village, chattering and chirrupping, hurrahing and moaning among the infant, but startlingly green leaves of the hawthorn bushes that fringed the property. Her mother greeted her with the perfunctory nod, which was her trademark, and a swift peck on the cheek. She lifted the corner of the cloth.

'Did you make this?'

'Who else, Mother?'

'Could have been the gardener!'

The words were uttered with a serious face, conveying no sense that she was making a joke. Fortunately Celia had grown up with her mother's rather corrosive sense of humour and understood it. The same could not be said for the other villagers. Celia laughed, and her mother broke into a quick, dry smile.

'Thank you. The birds will enjoy it. And me too, if there's any left.'

The sparrow that flew down and attempted a pre-emptive peck at the pie might have been trying to illustrate her statement. Celia responded with some angry but ill-directed swipes.

'Shoo! Get out! I didn't make it for you, you little scoundrel.'

'Don't do that to him,' said the old woman. 'I always give them half anyway.'

'I made it all for you. Not just half. And that brings me to another point. We've got to talk seriously. People in the village are talking about you –'

'Look!' exclaimed the old lady. 'A swallow! I saw the first of the year this morning. That's the second.'

Celia sighed in exasperation. She decided to try again later.

'So it is. Or a swift perhaps.'

Her mother answered with a contemptuous hiss.

'Swift indeed. Can't you tell the difference? Swifts don't come till May anyway.'

'Where do they all go in the winter?'

'Africa.'

The dormant intellect of the pragmatic Celia was aroused.

'It's amazing how they find there way there. And back.'

'It is amazing. Wonderful.' The old woman agreed, adding mysteriously, 'they have magnets in their heads.'

It was Celia's turn to sound scornful. 'Magnets!' she said. The scorn turned to a laugh. 'What nonsense you talk. What do you know about magnets anyway?'

'Quite a bit. One of your customers told me about them. You should try talking to them sometimes. You might learn something.'

'I do talk to them. It's usually about when are they going to pay.'

'This one was from a place called Gresham College in London. They give free lectures there for ordinary people, people who want to know, like us – like me,' she corrected nastily. 'He told me that the compass needle is a magnet. Not only does it point almost to the North Star, but it points down a bit too, sometimes more, sometimes less – according to how far you are from the Pole. Birds must have them. Stands to reason.'

'It's all too much for me. There can't be room for a magnet in that little head anyway,' protested Celia as the bird obligingly flew by again.

'There's more room there than in yours!'

'I remember the man who told you about magnets. He liked my food and left a handsome tip.'

'You should make more use of these people. You might learn a lot. There's that apothecary fellow there now. The most intelligent man I ever met. He told me about mercury and antimony and some of the other things they use as cures these days. Try talking to him.'

'I can't. You're out of date. He left suddenly, without telling me.'

'Oh my God. I misjudged him then. I didn't think that he was the sort to hook it without paying.'

'He did pay. He left the money and a note saying that he had been called away to his sick mother. I don't believe the last bit. I found afterwards that he had gone for good. Cleared his shop too.'

Alice Selworthy looked thoughtful. 'Hmm. Caroline will be disappointed!'

'Caroline! What has it to do with Caroline?'

'She liked him. A lot, I shouldn't wonder. Don't know how far it went. You were too busy to notice. And too stupid!' she added for good measure, continuing, 'you'd better watch her. It's the mating season. Look, I'll show you.'

She stepped into the garden and began an astonishingly accurate rendition of the thrush's song. Almost immediately a confusion of thrush sound poured in upon them from the surrounding trees.

'I can do blackbirds too,' she said. The equally eloquent but less formal song of the blackbird burst from her lips. She was soon answered from the trees. She responded with more song, alternating with shorter and more specific call-notes. The calls of the blackbird sounded from the bushes, closer than before. She continued, issuing song and calls repeatedly, then waiting to listen. The sounds from the bushes came nearer, until at last a blackbird appeared on a post at the bottom of the garden, its head turning first to one side, then the other, scanning for the interloper and ready to act appropriately according to its sex. Celia could have sworn that it wore a puzzled look. Alice's next production was a blackbird's brief scatter of alarm calls. The bird immediately turned tail and fled for the safety of the undergrowth in the wood.

Alice laughed and immediately began the song of the robin. This time there was no caution or hesitation. A robin seemed to materialise from nowhere at all and settled immediately on her outstretched finger. It was rewarded with some crumbs of pie.

'Mother. Listen to me.' Celia's voice betrayed amusement, admiration and fear. 'You must listen to me. It's wonderful and I love it. I love you too. But you have to stop.'

'Why? Because of a crowd of ignorant pigs? No, not pigs. Pigs are intelligent. Donkeys. Sheep.'

'They're not all stupid. And they are the people we live with. The people in our village and the other villages around. They matter.'

'I suppose *you* think I'm a witch too.'

'Certainly not. I *know* that you are not. But what I think may not count for much.'

'Witches don't exist,' muttered the old woman. 'Some day they will realise it. Not in my lifetime though.'

The daughter paused.

'I don't know whether they exist or not. There are many bad things that we can't account for. But I know that you are not one. You are just too clever for your own good. And a bit weird. And definitely too rude.'

'I just speak my mind.'

'I know. But you speak it too often, and too harsh. And with sarcastic jokes which people don't understand and take in the wrong sense.'

'They should learn. Anyway, I'm what I am. It's too late to change now.'

'It's never too late. Soon it may be too late not to have changed.'

'Meaning what?'

'The rumour is going around that they will put you on trial. As a witch.'

For once the old woman's assurance was shaken. She was of pale complexion anyway, but became visibly paler. She stood in silence, looking into the garden where a bullfinch was exploring the boughs of her apple tree. At last she said, 'they can't. They have no evidence. They have no reason.'

'I am frightened. Terrified for you. People will come forward with evidence. They always do. If they don't have it, they will make it.'

'Well,' muttered Alice, half to herself, 'I am a woman. And old.'
'What do you mean by that?'
Her mother turned to her fiercely.
'Haven't you noticed? Witches are always women. Nearly always. And the courts who condemn them are men. Nearly always. And the women are mostly old. Men resent women becoming old. It injures and angers them. When did you last hear of the trial of a young man as a witch? He is more likely to be consulted as a Cunning Man, asked to advise on the recovery of lost property, or asked to advise on the prevention of falling milk yields, not blamed for their deterioration.'

'Don't glower at me, ma. I'm on your side. Remember? What you say may be true. But it's often the women who accuse them at trials. They're the ones who'll stand up in court and accuse you.'

'The silly bitches have nothing better to think about. Nothing else to do but prattle. What are they saying about me anyway? You seem to know what's going on. You must be talking to them too.'

Celia's lips compressed but she decided to ignore the implications of the last remark.

'It's common knowledge in the village now. Everyone knows what is being said and what is likely to happen. You must do something before it is too late.'

'What am I supposed to do. Make them a plum pie I suppose.'

Celia's hands were clenching and unclenching but she managed to speak calmly.

'They would not eat it. They would be too scared. They would think that it would put them under your control. You need to be pleasant to them and speak some kind words. Show some sympathy.' She added, 'And get rid of the birds.'

'The birds!' Alice's astonishment was genuine. 'Certainly not! Why would I get rid of the birds?'

'They think that the birds are in league with you. That they are your spies. Your helpers. Your instruments.'

'My familiars. Birds as familiars! That's rich. Cats, dogs, mice, moles, rats I have heard of, but birds! – that's new.' The news brought the old woman a kind of grim hilarity. 'Good,' she said. 'Perhaps they'll stop eating them next, in case they carry something evil from me.'

'They already have. A few of them. The rest are tucking in as usual.'

'But why birds as a witch's agents? Birds are the most, innocent, the most light-hearted, the most beautiful of God's Creation.'

'Maybe. But they go everywhere. Nothing is private from them. Nothing secret. They have wings and eyes. They peer in at windows. And some of them steal. Which brings me to another point.'

'Oh dear! Not another point. Has someone died of chicken plague?'

'Fred Willis says he saw a blackbird stealing a ring which his wife had put down.'

'Blackbirds don't steal rings. Jackdaws and magpies steal bright objects. It must have been a jackdaw. If it happened at all,' she added.

Celia choked down her exasperation once more. 'I don't know or care what kind of bird it was. The bird was black. Or so they say. The trouble is they are saying that it flew away in this direction. They say it was heading towards your house. They are saying that you sent it. That it was acting under your commands. And that idiot, Tatt, has some nonsense about a piece of jewellery. As if the fool ever owned any!'

'Sometimes I wish I had such powers. I would give them a few bad moments.'

'That kind of talk will get you into real trouble and no one will be able to help you,' said Celia angrily.

'Well maybe. But I shall coo like a turtle dove if they ask. I promise. They can search the house if they want. There's no ring here. The ninny probably dropped it in her own garden anyway.'

'I am worried, said Celia. 'Say the bird had taken it and had dropped it in *your* garden. That would sound terrible in a law court. And I can't imagine you cooing like a dove.'

'If a bird had taken it, it would be in the bird's nest. That's what they do. They seem to like decoration. No use to me up there even if I had caused the bird to take it. And I can't climb trees.'

'The thing is ridiculous, of course. And Tatt is a well-known ninny, anyway. And everyone knows that. But they will listen to him if they want to. And that is just the point. You must give them no chance. Get rid of the birds. Stop feeding them. Drive them away. Put up scarecrows, nets, gongs, anything which will frighten them away.'

'Certainly not.' Alice smiled her sudden charming smile that flashed out occasionally like January sunshine. 'What would they say, those birds? Who would I have to talk to?'

'Luckily they don't talk.'

'Oh yes they do. Not to me though, just to one another. I am trying to understand their language.'

Celia's mood lightened in response. She laughed. 'You really are preposterous. I don't know how you think it all up.'

'I'm serious. I've listened intently for years to what they are saying. They don't speak to me. They talk to each other. It doesn't take long to notice that the great tit has a whole collection of call notes that mean different things. And you may think that the song of wren is always the same –'

'I don't even know the wren's song!' interrupted Celia.

'How can you live all your life in the country and not know the wren's song? It sounds the same always, until you listen very carefully. Then you realise that it's fashioned to the occasion. It's frequently offered to another bird conveying an important message. They are building up a whole language.'

'Well, maybe. Perhaps I will begin listening too. On second thoughts it might land me in the trouble you are making for yourself. Anyway I'm likely to be too busy.'

And to emphasise the last point, she offered her apologies; she must go – there was supper to prepare for several impatient people. 'Sometimes they remind me of those pink, clamouring mouths in a nest,' she added as she prepared to leave. Departing she shouted back over her shoulder, from duty rather than in hope, 'Get rid of the birds. Be nice to your neighbours!'

'They can go piss in their ale!' said Alice.

# CHAPTER 9

The two men held Joseph in a tight grip. An arm was still flung around his neck, half-choking him and his arms were screwed painfully behind him. But Benjamin Green's grasp on his hair faltered; something had distracted him. The sound that Joseph's inflated senses had heard as a remote pistol shot was merely the lifting of the latch of the external door. Benjamin Green turned sharply away from him towards the door as it swung open. The pad fell from Joseph's face and, as he gulped in air, the world began to cease heaving about and assumed some semblance of normality. A familiar figure, with its familiar confident poise, was framed in the doorway.

'Bob Nob Job!' exclaimed Joseph.

Robert Surtees ignored the greeting, or more probably was too amazed at the scene he had encountered to notice. Presumably he had been walking in the grounds with the same restorative motive that had taken Joseph there, and had been overtaken by a similar curiosity concerning the mysterious building. For an instant his face registered astonishment, cancelled immediately by his usual relaxed urbanity. This was replaced in turn by a gentlemanly concern for Joseph, whom he now addressed.

'I greatly regret the disgraceful end to your talk, Apothecary. I trust that it has not seriously distressed you.'

It was Benjamin Green who replied. 'Müller has been taken ill. The experience was altogether too much for him. He appears to be having a fit of some kind. We have had to apply quite drastic remedies to subdue him.'

'So I see', Robert replied drily. He glanced at Joseph. 'It is most fortunate that you had these two gentlemen at hand to assist. It is very kind of them.'

Green explained. 'They were taking a short cut across the estate on their way to join the Royalists. Luckily one of them proved to be a qualified physician.' He nodded towards the man holding Joseph's left arm.

'Indeed', said Robert gravely, 'appearances are deceptive. I would have mistaken him for a sailor from a slave ship.'

Green glared momentarily, but quickly assumed his most lubricious manner. 'Brother Apothecary is in good hands. We would not wish to trouble you further or trespass on more of your time.'

'It is no trouble. And I have an evening in front of me, free of appointments. The best course would be for you and I to help Müller back to the house where we can fetch expert medical attention.'

'Get out, and do it now!' intervened the sailor from a slave ship, in wholly unphysicianly tones. Probably he had not appreciated Robert's opinion of the image he presented to the world. Green stared the man into silence, and then continued in conciliatory tones.

'There is much that you do not understand', he said. His voice dropped to a confidential whisper as he edged towards Robert. 'The situation is one of great difficulty, which I must explain to you.'

Joseph, whose faculties were recovering, shouted a warning. 'He has a knife!'

The warning was unnecessary. Robert had already correctly surmised that the surreptitious passage of Green's right hand behind his back had not been to scratch his backside. Robert Surtees's manner and way of speaking had clearly been cultivated by one of the best universities, but there were influences in his life to which he would never allude. Perhaps he had trained as an agent, or had simply been raised in a very rough street. His timing was immaculate. When Green was precisely in range but before he was close enough to strike, a long leg lashed out and Robert's foot sank into the soft flesh immediately below his breast-bone. He gasped, folded up, fighting for breath, and as his head came forwards, he received a sharp punch on the left side of the jaw, dropping him senseless to the floor.

The dramatic development distracted the other two men. Joseph, whose training was in medicine and alchemy, rather than in methods of close combat, nevertheless remembered at the right moment the rough-and-tumbles of his childhood. He kicked the man to his right, in the leg immediately behind the knee. The leg flexed and unbalanced him; he spun round and fell to the floor, threatening to drag Joseph and the second man with him. Joseph yanked his arms free and leaped across the room with one of the ruffians in pursuit. The man he had kicked was already getting up again. Joseph was cornered and needed special help. This might have been provided by the expertise of Robert Surtees but before he could assist, Joseph found another partner. His leap had taken him to the side of the furnace. He placed his foot against it and gave it a mighty push in the direction of the man who was rushing at him. The furnace collapsed, spewing red-hot coals across the floor and upon his assailant's feet. The man hopped away screaming. The second man saw that he now faced two against one and hesitated.

'Run!' said Robert Surtees.

The instruction was redundant. Joseph had reached this conclusion for himself. It was also out of date, as he was already fleeing at full speed, the decision having been confirmed by a glimpse through the door of more men approaching, none of them known to him. Together they ran towards the thick wood that bordered the field on one side. Just before they reached it Joseph looked back, expecting pursuit, but the new arrivals, who had brought several horses with them, were giving priority to the retrieval of their companions from the laboratory, from the door of which copious smoke was belching. One might have thought that Orpheus's experience was a sufficient cautionary tale concerning the dangers of looking back. Joseph's Underworld proved to be a ditch full of water. The result was a slooshing sound and a spectacular fountain of green material. Robert cursed, doubled back and hauled him out. A few seconds later they reached the comparative safety of the forest. They ran on for some way crashing through the undergrowth until they were out of breath – or more precisely until Joseph was out of breath – after which they lay down in the best cover they could find amongst the rather sparse spring foliage. For a long time they listened fearfully, anticipating that a full-scale hunt might be conducted on their account and knowing that the limited cover of the still nascent greenery might provide inadequate concealment for them. To their puzzlement and relief, there was no sound or sign whatsoever of pursuit.

As he listened to the natural sounds of the forest, Joseph began to reflect on the fate that he had just missed. By now he would have been – if it were not for Robert's intervention – strapped unconscious across the back of one of the horses that the abductors had brought, on his way to some secret place where they would attempt to extract from him the knowledge that he did not possess

A few insects, not mosquitoes or midges, but apparently some kind of tiny fly, welcomed them from the moment of their crawling into the thicket. These advance pickets seemed to have an efficient means of communication with their main force and, within a few minutes, reinforcements were swarming over the two fugitives in huge numbers. The continuing silence and the discomfort eventually persuaded them to move. They inched forward carefully through the Dog's Mercury and aspiring bluebells. After a many uncomfortable minutes they reached a place where they could peer out among the leaves and stems at the margin of the wood. Joseph crawled alongside Robert Surtees and looked across the meadows that they had recently quit in such haste. The twilight was gathering, but sufficient light remained for Joseph to see quite unexpectedly large numbers of people moving about in the field. The men who had attempted his abduction were gone. In their place were soldiers. These had obviously been there for some time, and were now gradually filtering away from the estate, shepherding some unfortunate alchemists with them.

'Ha!' said Robert in a normal voice. 'That has solved one of our problems. The Royalist soldiers came, as the Baroness feared. That is why we were not pursued by the men who attacked you. Now they are leaving. They have a number of new recruits of a quality that should ensure their army's defeat. They are being replaced by the fire-fighters, if that is not too elevated a term for them.'

Servants from the house and workers from the estate were hurrying back and forth with buckets of water and with besoms to beat out a fire. From the laboratory a thin but continuous streak of smoke was rising. It did not look especially threatening to the structure, although, even from the wood, the fire was evident to the nose, and the smell was unusually acrid. The sounds issuing from the burning hut reminded Joseph of the names of some of the alchemists he had met in Germany. Molde was plodding along steadily if unspectacularly. Krack and Poppel were very busy, although their output tended to the repetitive. It was not until Wumf joined their enterprise that things really began to progress. Joseph watched in horror as a giant fire-ball erupted suddenly from the room in which he had been reading the manuscript. Even Robert was impressed.

'Christ!' he exclaimed.

The fire-ball died down but the fire was now raging beyond all hope of control and as they watched, the roof fell in above the main laboratory. Joseph was experiencing an unprecedented mixture of anticipatory horror and excitement. The flames were spreading into the storeroom with its barrel of nitre and its copious supply of useful inflammables. Nothing much happened for a few minutes and the two men were on the point of crawling away into the wood again when a massive explosion blew out the whole of the end of the building where the storeroom was. Pieces of burning wood were blown several hundred feet into the air and gradually fell back to earth again still blazing fiercely, scorching the grass of the meadow and threatening to set fire to the hedges surrounding it. A gust of flame of a beautiful green colour edged with vermilion leaped out of the blazing storeroom. Robert's comments revealed a dispassionate interest.

'Copper,' he said. 'The place must have been a store.'

'And potash,' muttered Joseph.

A series of smaller explosions followed, each accompanied by a fresh spurt of flame. Each one glowed with a characteristic colour.

'Soda,' said Robert.

'Iron,' muttered Joseph.

The display was giving him an idea for an analytical routine – identification of substances by the colours produced in a flame. Just the thing to give to a student if he ever had one, or perhaps to the flaxen-haired boy if he maintained his present interest.

The field having gradually cleared of men, Joseph stood up for the first time for an hour or so. Water poured out of his garments. In the puddle that formed, a couple of small black objects lay wriggling. He was in no mood for studying tadpoles, interesting though they might be. Some small but malicious beast had bitten him several times, raising little irritable red lumps. He removed some water-weed from the vicinity of his knees. Something unidentified was going flip-flop inside his shirt. The rain that had appeared to be imminent all afternoon was beginning in the form of a few sporadic but large spots. Perhaps God did not approve of the fire; if so, He was acting late. The blaze was showing signs of running out of fuel, although not before it had given a nice demonstration of the presence of tin. It was time to go. The direction chosen had to be away from the house and the farm, both of which might be full of soldiers. That meant the forest and the prospect of becoming lost. An increase in the ambitions of the rain set them on their way, and for a few minutes the foliage above them absorbed the water; after that they began to get seriously wet although, after his exploration of the ditch, Joseph barely noticed. His problems were a burn on his hand, where he had used it to promote the overturning of the furnace, and a back that was making renewed protests at his running and leaping. His shoulder was very painful and his ear had been bleeding, both injuries stemming from the cudgel blow. To add to his discomfort trickles of water were running down between his shoulder blades. He tried to distract himself from the grumbles of Robert by attempting to calculate how much time must elapse before the planets conspired to a more favourable disposition.

The storm eventually lessened and stopped, having done its damage. Darkness had fallen and they were by now thoroughly lost as well as thoroughly wet. They had walked for possibly an hour and a half without the help of moon or stars to provide direction, when the trees suddenly ended and they found themselves standing at the edge of a meadow not unlike the one in which the afternoon's events had occurred. For a moment Joseph thought that they had walked in a circle, but the lack of glowing embers and the unfamiliar shapes of some buildings beyond the field's far corner, reassured him. They proceeded cautiously towards the dark shapes that gradually resolved into a farmhouse and a number of sheds and stables. Pausing, they discussed in whispers the wisdom of knocking at the farmhouse door and asking for shelter. The area, they knew, was full of military and the army's officers would possibly be billeted in the house. The sympathies of the farmer in these divided times could not be predicted and the chances of running into further trouble seemed high. The matter was settled when they found that one of the barns was easy to enter, contained no animals excepting a rat or two and offered lavish amounts of straw. Here they settled down to an uncomfortable but secure night.

Next day there was no sign of the bad weather of the preceding evening. Joseph was woken by the first rays of the sun. A fine morning promised. He had slept fitfully, his exhaustion competing with his various discomforts. He was nervous and knew that they should already have left the farm before daybreak. He woke Robert who was sleeping peacefully. Joseph felt dirty and dishevelled but Robert stepped out of his nest and immediately looked at ease. He had the gift that Joseph had occasionally met before in people, of being able to survive anything and still look confidently in command. A few friendly morning greetings of his hands towards his hair, and some shaking out and adjustments of his clothing and he was looking, if not dapper, at least respectable, and this was fortunate because he had hardly finished his rudimentary toilet when a woman appeared in the doorway of the barn. With her was a toddler, a child of two years of age or a little more, with a peculiarly intense stare. The woman gave out an exclamation that might have become a scream when it grew up.

Robert's reaction was resourceful and immediate. He took command. First he pushed Joseph firmly behind him. His thinking on this was obvious. Joseph, in addition to the signs of the wear and tear of pursuit, wettings from below and above and sleeping rough, was also still decorated with pieces of straw and occasional specimens of water-weed. His attempts to remove the remainder without the benefit of a mirror had left some patches in the region of his ears, and in various other areas of his face had thinned it but at the cost of smearing it into strange shapes. All in all, he looked like an effigy that had been devised for a particularly rancorous Skimmington Ride. Robert beamed happily at the strange woman and the stranger lad.

'Good morning Madam,' he said. 'Just the morning for a stroll in the sun with your lovely young boy.'

'I'm going to muck out the pigs,' the woman replied. 'What are you doing here? Get out before I call the dogs.'

Her pugnacious words lacked conviction however. She was already somewhat mollified by something in Robert's manner and sentiments. He had earned full marks on style, but had scored inadequately on content. It was early in the day, though, to be confronted with a sudden crisis. He hastily corrected his course.

'Ah!' he said, 'you must be the farmer's wife. It is a hard life, full of toil which does not receive its just remuneration.'

'I am not the farmer's wife. I am the farmer,' replied the woman. 'My husband died and left me to run the farm. He died before Isaac was born.' She indicated the child. 'Isaac has never known a father.'

Robert replied with evident sympathy. 'Ah, we are all hostages to Fortune, but, clearly, God has given you the strength to raise this young child in the way which your husband would have desired.'

'I do my best. But the times are hard. And no one in authority wants to know. Not the Lords of the Manor or the Members of Parliament. They go on producing new laws to make our lives as difficult as possible. Soon I shall have to sell the farm and go out of business. I would like to ask them what is supposed to happen to me and to Isaac then.'

'Indeed Madam, they have lost touch with us, the common people, and are all too intimate with their own interests. How shall the Nation thrive without those who produce our food?'

At this point the toddler suddenly spoke up.

'Don't like this man, Mummy. And why's him hiding?' He pointed at Joseph.

The child had been scrutinising Joseph with a sustained attention unusual in such a young child. He had a piping voice of a toddler just learning to speak, but his meaning was clear and there was something about him that could not be ignored. This was the very subject that Robert had been hoping to avoid.

'Yes,' said the woman. 'How did he get into that state? And what are you doing here anyway?'

'Yesterday evening,' replied Robert,' we were returning from one of the great houses where we had been conducting important business. We were riding peacefully towards our homes' – his voice became heavy with sadness and disillusionment over the human condition – 'when we were attacked by a band of robbers, who stole our horses and might well have taken our lives had we not fled into the woods. Night came, the rain fell and we were soon thoroughly lost.'

Robert had once told Joseph, 'for a plausible yarn, stick as close to the truth as possible. Don't fantasise, just make a few tactical adjustments.' He continued:

'Luckily we came upon your farm and not wishing to cause inconvenience and perhaps frighten you with our appearance, we sheltered instead in your barn confident that we were in the homestead of the Good Samaritan.'

'Got green on him's face – and red!' observed young Isaac, who was still preoccupied with Joseph.

'Yes,' agreed the woman, 'how did he get into such a mess?'

'During our flight, my unfortunate friend fell into a ditch and then a blackberry bush. He is liable to misfortunes of this kind.'

Of the three statements, the last was certainly true.

'Blackberries – at this time of the year?'

'To tell you the truth, Madam, I could not tell for certain in the darkness what kind of bush it was.'

'Well,' said the woman, 'you have had a difficult night. I don't know what things are coming to. I can remember the time when you could walk or ride anywhere here in safety. You can trust hardly anyone these days. But I realised as soon as I saw you that I was dealing with gentlemen.'

'Me saw 'em first,' said little Isaac.

'Be quiet, darling,' said his mother. 'You did not.'

'Oh yes I did.' The boy pouted stubbornly.

'Ha! Ha!' Robert laughed cheerfully and beamed at the little boy. 'I expect you and your mother spotted us at the same moment.'

'No! Me saw first!'

'What a wonderful little character,' exclaimed Robert, fortunately suppressing an impulse to clip his ear.

'Yes. He is very sweet. Most of the time.'

'But,' said Robert, 'How wrong of us. We have not introduced ourselves. I am William Brown and my friend here is John Enfold.'

'I am pleased to meet you gentlemen. I am Hannah Newton of Woolsthorpe. This is my son, Isaac.'

'Woolsthorpe. So we are in Woolsthorpe now, I presume. How may we reach the London road.'

'You are close to Woolsthorpe. Your way lies along this lane for three miles until you join a better road and then two more miles to the main London road.'

Isaac rejoined the conversation. 'Three and two. That makes thirty-two. No, six. I mean five!'

'What an intelligent young man!' exclaimed Robert, genuinely amazed. 'Madam – I have some skill and a long practice in the subject of physiognomy. Allow me to make a brief study of young Isaac, your exceptional infant. It may help you to know his likely destiny in life. It will certainly be evident in his face and the bones of his skull.'

Joseph was privileged to be present at a demonstration of metoposcopy conducted by an expert. Robert first examined Isaac's eyes, nose, mouth and ears with a silent intensity, and then began to move slowly around the child, who disobligingly turned with him at the same pace, staring at him suspiciously.

'Keep still a minute, darling,' said his mother helpfully.

'Why? What's he doing?'

'He examining your head.'

'It's him's head should be exmanned.'

The survey was eventually completed with the help of Hannah Newton gently discouraging her son Isaac's tendency to rotate. Several times in the circumnavigation Robert paused, leaned forward to view some feature more closely, whispering excitedly to himself comments that could not quite be heard. Isaac's mother was very impressed with these moments. Robert's customers always were.

'Well, Mrs Newton' he said at last, as he straightened up. 'Your son Isaac has a great career in front of him. It is clear that he has genius coupled with ambition and drive, even perhaps a touch of combativeness or asperity which will help him to pass the obstacles, which lesser men put in his path, and assist him to great heights.'

'Amazing! I had not realised that so much could be foretold from the shape of the face and head. It is too much to expect that you can predict in what field his talents may lie? He may become a great preacher, I hope?'

'It is not possible to tell with certainty in one so young. But I think that his greatness will lie in natural philosophy. In particular he will achieve eminent distinction in mathematics.'

'Oh good! He will be able to keep the farm accounts. That is a part of farming which I do not seem to be able to handle.'

'That will be well within his capacities, for sure.'

'I do not know how to thank you. Your skills certainly deserve recompense and I know that you must usually receive a substantial fee. Unfortunately I have nothing to offer anyone until after the harvest.'

'Madam, to you my services are entirely free. My friend and I are in debt to you, having been uninvited guests in your barn all night. We would not even think of receiving payment, hungry though we are.'

'I could find you some breakfast,' said the good lady doubtfully.

'You are too kind. That would be a Good Neighbourly act of the highest order,' replied Robert.

After Robert and Joseph had breakfasted on simple fare, which in their circumstances tasted like a wedding breakfast for a princess, they thanked their unwitting host and braced themselves for a long day's tramp. As they left the farm loud infantile screams followed them along the track, interleaved with alternate cajoling and threats from the mother. Young Isaac was throwing a tantrum. At one point they winced as they heard a loud slapping noise, recalling the sudden contact of a hand with tender flesh. It was followed by redoubled shrieks. The last words they heard were:

'But Mummy, I really did see 'em first!'

# CHAPTER 10

'Witches are the ruination of this country. This land, this blessed plot, this realm, this England, would be a Paradise without them, a haven where we could all prosper in peace. A haven free from pox and murrain, a haven of health for man and his sheep and cattle, a sceptred isle, a Merry England indeed.'

This was Mark Horbling speaking, eloquent by rote. There was an abstracted air about him as though he had said it all many times before. He could reproduce the same words in the dark, in his sleep, standing on his head. He had made this same speech in many a village in the South and East of England while the impressed villagers gaped, nodded or concurred in monosyllables and various local tones. His listeners today were not the village community by a duck pond, but two men, one young, one old, in a small stuffy office, which – as was obvious from its slightly tired atmosphere – functioned also as a bedroom. Mark Horbling was a short man, red-haired and with a ruddy complexion. The elder of his listeners was a man named Drover, also ruddy-faced, whose tough, tanned skin, displayed additionally as a balding skull, was that of a man frequently exposed to the sun and wind. There was something jolly about him. His words were few and usually addressed to a sheep or to his tavern companions in the evening, but he could boil over with enthusiasm on matters which affected him deeply. On this occasion he felt some kind of response was proper.

'Indeed,' he said, 'a witch is a very damnable thing.'

'You are right, sir,' said Mark. 'You are a man of perception. If they were all of your mind, we would not have the trouble we do in bringing these devilish women to justice – and indeed men too sometimes.' He hastily corrected himself on the gender of sorcerers.

'Ah, they've sold themselves to the Devil, I dare swear.'

'You are right again, sir. But that is more difficult to prove. These compacts with Beelzebub are made privately, in the dead of night, at the midnight hour with no one to witness. What we see is the child sickening and perhaps dying, the child born lame, the cattle drying up, the wheat rusting away, the sheep lying mysteriously dead in a rich pasture.'

'Ah indeed. I lost several like that last autumn. Shortly after a dog had scared them.'

'I am indeed sorry to hear it. I know the farmer cannot afford these losses. The times are hard.' He leaned forward portentously. 'This is what we are up against. We might need to take a closer look at that dog later. And to see whose dog it is. These witches have a terrible cunning and can whistle up dreadful helpers – dreadful but sometimes of a deceitful innocence of appearance.' He turned to the young man. 'Your witch,' he explained, 'often works with a familiar – usually a toad, a snake or rat, but sometimes – and these are the most cunning and devilish – sometimes with an animal we call our friend and helper, a cat or dog.'

'Or a horse?' suggested the young man helpfully.

Horbling looked at him suspiciously.

'Never a horse. At least not in my experience. But it's possible, very possible. It would help to put us off the track.'

The young man was obviously raw in this business, as his next remark confirmed.

'But with father's dead sheep – surely the dog could have done it himself, without the need for a witch?'

This turned out to be another routine argument for Mark Horbling.

'Ah, I'm glad you made that point. You are young. You do not realise yet. You are fortunate, not to have seen yet the abominable wickedness of the world. Your witch is clever, wily, resourceful, full of tricks. She – or he – will do anything to put us off the track. This county is full of sheep – aye – and dogs too. Do they usually interfere with each other?' He leaned forward conspiratorially and tapped the young man on the knee. 'I will tell you. They do not. Unless prompted by some pernicious influence which corrupts their true nature and turns them aside from the role which God has provided for their livelihood and our benefit. Or through some occasional accident, of course. But generally they must be turned aside from their purpose, must be corrupted by some malevolent intent.'

The young man looked momentarily uncomfortable but answered coolly.

'Thank you, sir, for making that plain. I realise that I have much to learn. You would find me an attentive listener and, I think, a quick learner.'

'Ah, that's it,' said the farmer. 'We didn't come to talk about my blamed sheep. It's the lad we need to chew over.'

'Indeed, tell me about him.'

'I will. As soon as I saw the notice on your door, I said to myself 'That's our Graham!' A smart lad, it said, wanted for important work for the people's benefit. And his Mum said it too. He's got brains. Not from her, I might say, certainly not! From his great-granddaddy – on my side that is. He could plough a furrow straighter than any man you ever met. And mend a cart-wheel so as you'd never know it were bust. And he invented a trap for catching mice and drowning them, which was a thing of beauty. There was nothing he couldn't do. Why I remember…'

'Yes indeed sir,' interrupted Horbling, who recalled several other interviews that he had to make during the day. 'I have heard many stories of your grandfather's feats. He had some fame in the district. But has your son inherited his talents?'

'By thunder, he has that! I should say so. Top of his class he's been. Not just once and not just. No, by George, by ten lengths every time at least. His teachers wanted him to go on to that there University at Cambridge. But I wasn't having none of they. What for? To become some fancy priest telling us what to do when we either do it already or can't ever – or a prick-nosed lawyer feathering his nest with swan's down. No, sir. I want him for one of us. To stay and do us some good here. For the people's benefit, it said. That's what I want.'

'Your thinking does you credit, sir.' Turning to the young man he said, 'Let's talk about my recent experiences. That will give us both an idea as to whether you want to do this work or not. And whether you are suited. What do you think of this? I recommend that you listen with great care.' He pulled a list from a drawer and began to read solemnly.

'Suspicious events in or near the village of Cottesthorpe. Eleven honest inhabitants of Cottesthorpe have reported the following worrying events.'

'Item 1. Death of a dozen chickens in the yard of Elijah Jones. Spring 1643.

'Item 2. A puzzling numbness in the arm of Ellen Piggott, a sudden affliction suffered in March 1643. According to the victim – "has never been right since".

'Item 3. Drying up of the milk supply 1640-41 reported in the farms of Hugh Denslow and William Brown. These were prize milkers – "best in the County".

'Item 4. Cat disappeared from the house of Annie Stowe.

'Item 5. Cottage in Green lane, abandoned after the death of Henry Mildmay, five years ago. Unexplained noises – screams and mutterings reported by several citizens. Lights sometimes seen at night although no one lives there. No one can be persuaded to do so.

'Item 6. Child born lame to Robert and Mary Gittings, September 1641.

'Item 7. Cow of Thomas Hurl developed stagger of the back legs, February 1643. Died three months later.

'Item 8. Hens almost stopped laying, June 1642. Eggs in short supply all year. Reported by Sheila Hirst.

'Item 9. Item 8 repeated the following year at another household. Reported by Audrey Tyler.

'Item 10. Failure of corn crop 1642 in the farm of James Read. Other farms with partial failure. Flour and bread of high prices all year. Many hungry.'

Here Horbling paused dramatically.

'And the final item,' he said, 'you may consider the most distressing and damaging of all the eleven.

Item 11. Birth of two children stillborn, 1642, to Henry and Margaret Hopkins and to John and Lucy Pridy. No opportunity for baptism, God rest their souls.

How do you explain all that young man?'

'Easily,' said the young man calmly. 'death of Jones's chickens due to a pestilence which afflicts fowls all over the country every year. She is lucky not to have caught it herself. Ellen Piggott had a slight stroke. Will probably suffer a more severe stroke before much more time passes. Denslow and Brown lost their milk supply due to ageing of their prize animals. Annie Stowe's cat was presumably a tom. We shouldn't worry about a creature that is off somewhere enjoying itself. The house is haunted – not by Henry Mildmay's bizarre end but by the fears of the villagers. The Gittings may be thankful that the child born was not born dead like those of the Hopkins and Pridys. These are misfortunes that have happened even to the Kings of England. Thomas Hurl's cow with the staggering back legs was allowed to run in a pasture with sheep, which are notoriously liable to such misfortunes. Perhaps the cow had consorted immorally and against nature with the sheep.'

At this point, Mark Horbling, who had been becoming more rufous by the minute as the farmer's son trivialised his carefully garnered items, could restrain himself no longer.

'A disgraceful and ridiculous suggestion, young man. You should be ashamed of yourself. And before your father too, who is working so hard to ensure your good start in this world.'

The good farmer was in fact too busy struggling with the mechanics of the suggested liaison to be shocked.

'I was only joking,' replied Graham. 'These good women Hurst and Tyler only reported what was observed in hens all over England. No one understands why. As for Farmer Read, he is agreeing with the general consensus that 1642 was a year of crop failure.'

'By Moses,' exclaimed the farmer. 'What did I tell you, Sir? How he did string all those names together. And I bet he got them right. He's his great grand-daddy all over again!'

But Horbling was looking like one of the apothecary's more dangerous ventures into chymistry. He had achieved an intensity of redness that suggested him as a potential subject of item two.

'I fear you have no feel for this work. You are too young, I expect, to appreciate the full implications of this wicked catalogue. Probably I need an assistant of more mature years, one who senses the connections which must exist between these items.'

But the young man was not finished yet. 'The items, considering them individually as I did, mean little beyond the expected misfortunes of a country town. Any town or village that you selected could relate to you single item of this kind, perhaps two or three. But eleven such incidents move us into a different field. Eleven, taken altogether, begin to point towards a shared cause, to point towards something much more sinister, perhaps to some evil influence at work in the community. The attribution of eleven such events to chance strains credulity.'

'Ha!' said Horbling, substantially mollified. 'That's exactly what I think. Strains credulity. A good phrase. I'll remember that. Some person or persons are at war with their neighbours. And Hell-bent on promoting disturbance and distress.'

'I think so.'

'Well, what would you do in my position if you were determined as I am to cleanse the town of Cottesthorpe of this foul burden?'

'Sir, I hesitate as a novice to make suggestions to one of your vast experience. But I think that I would go to these people, whom you have so efficiently itemised. I would go to them individually and privately and ask each in turn if there is anyone among their neighbours or acquaintances whom they suspect might wish them harm or whom they feel could be responsible for generating in some way the misfortunes which have come upon them. It may be that you will find they name, quite independently, some one person. Or perhaps more than one name may occur several times over.'

'Good,' exclaimed Horbling to the young man, and turning to the farmer, 'an excellent young man. I am glad you brought him here.'

'Ay,' said the farmer. 'Clever as a pig but smells better! I'm proud of 'ee.'

Mark Horbling was now ready to reveal his master-stroke to the young man.

'Now I can tell you. I have already carried out your suggestion. And with success. All but one of the victims of these terrible events mentioned the same name – Alice Selworthy of Cottesthorpe. Next Monday I leave to question further those people of whom I have told you, to gather names of more victims, who I doubt not exist, and perhaps to question Alice Selworthy. Will you accompany me?'

'I shall be glad to, sir. I thank you.'

The farmer returned to his sheep, satisfied with his day's work so far, and the two benefactors of the town of Cottesthorpe settled down to discuss details of their case against Alice, mother of Celia Albright.

# CHAPTER 11

Joseph did not know which of his crowding needs was the most urgent. He had been chased by soldiers, spent a wet night in a wood and a barn and then walked many miles to find an inn. He was desperately disappointed and depressed. He was also hungry, thirsty and exhausted. In the race for attention, thirst took an early lead. He slaked this with a draught of water, not his usual first choice of beverage. It tasted like a drink especially designed and prepared for the angelic host. Shortly after this, the race was abandoned, or rather exhaustion established such dominance that any competition from the other contestants was deferred until the next day. He fell asleep more or less where he was and as he was, and for the first part of the night slept as if in a deep cave far away from the Earth's troubled surface.

Eventually a light began to grow in one corner of his vision. At first he thought this was the dawn, but its gold was not preceded by the cold pewters and silvers of daybreak and spread too early and from too restricted a part of the horizon. The patch of gold grew in size and magnificence and seemed to be structured in some way. The vision slowly clarified. What appeared to be the bars, dots and hooks of the characters from a language not familiar to him gradually solidified into struts and joints and assembled themselves without any external help into a kind of throne. Other spars arranged themselves into a tapestry of gloriously rich colours carrying a sentence that seemed to fill the whole sky. It read;

### *A Magus is a scientist with the wrong hypothesis.*

On the throne a form, at first a mere disturbance of the glowing background, gradually grew, first by sharpening contrast to the surrounding light, and then by the accretion of shadows, until it acquired solidity and became distinguishable as a seated figure of a man, gazing down on him from the dais on which the throne was placed. Joseph threw himself to the floor in a state of terror. Here was the long-feared retribution, the day of judgement that he had been taught to fear but, as a youth, had once had the arrogance to doubt. It was too late to repent. At least, he feared so. An eternity of hell-fire and racking pains stretched out endlessly before him, consuming what had been his future.

The vision, after what seemed to be endless time, spoke to him. The voice was a normal, unremarkable human voice, slightly reassuring in its sheer ordinariness, although speaking with an accent which he had not heard before and whose geographical origin he could not begin to guess at. The figure said. 'Stand up Joseph Skledowski. You have nothing to fear.'

Joseph rose slowly to his feet, expecting to see a handsome bearded figure, clothed in long white biblical robes, having a confident nose set in a Mediterranean complexion, the head crowned with a halo of light. In fact the man possessed a competent moustache but no beard at all. By way of compensation he was able to show off a magnificent head of hair, which, although thin and receding over the brow, spread out, above and behind, in a great white frosty bush. As for the dress, this would have made Joseph giggle in more risible circumstances. This was not God or one of his apostles or saints and bore little resemblance to an angel of any order, but was perhaps an official of some lesser though important and impressive rank. He did not look particularly official either. His dress was apparently of a formal nature, since he was attired from ankle to neck in an expensive cloth, tailored as breeches and coat, with a second coat inside it, all of the same dark shade, almost as though it were a uniform. The expensive impression, although not destroyed, was definitely endangered, by some threads hanging from the middle of the outer coat, where there was clearly a button missing. And the seat was not a throne, but a chair much resembling that upon which Joseph's mentor, Michael Sendivogius, had sat when imparting wisdom concerning colic or transmutation. In fact it could have been the same chair except that, like the rest of the scene and the figure itself, it was bathed in the most glorious illuminated colours – colours he had never seen before, colours that did not exist. It was a transcendent chair and a transcendent scene.

Good morning, Apothecary,' said the visitor,' I represent the Department of Cosmogenetics.'

Joseph who had yet to stop trembling, disobeyed instructions and made obeisance again.

'Stop worrying. And do stand up. You will not have heard of me, although I was famous in my day. It is just that my day has yet to come as far as you are concerned. You may well look puzzled.'

This was an understatement of the highest order. Joseph was out of his mind with fear and bewilderment. The mysterious visitor examined him with a friendly but penetrating gaze. The eyes were brilliant, large and deep.

'The Supreme Parliament has become increasingly worried about the slow progress of knowledge in this Universe.'

'*This* Universe?' queried Joseph, looking even more shocked. 'You mean there are other – er – places?'

'Of course,' said the professor. 'You people are so conceited. Do you imagine that your crappy little universe is the only one? Their Supremacies are worried and they have decided to speed up progress on the Earth by imparting special information to one of its creatures. For some reason, which eludes me even further now that I have seen you, it is you they have chosen.'

'Indeed, my Lord. I am a miserable sinner, though often repentant. But then I sin again. I am not worthy.'

'I know that, said the professor sympathetically, 'but make the most of your luck! And don't address me as Lord. Back there they call me Bert, because they know it annoys me. Albert is the name I prefer. *You* had better call me Professor. You have now the benefit of expert tuition in the next three hundred years – some nine or ten generations – of discoveries and development in natural philosophy. My own discipline, although fundamental, is circumscribed, but I believe I am well enough informed in other fields to be able to answer any likely questions from you.'

'But my Lord Professor, I cannot do it. I must not listen. I am fearful. I remember the terrible fate of Faust. It is a mortal sin to sell one's soul for power or knowledge.'

'You do not need to sell your soul – it wouldn't buy much, anyway. I never understood why Mephistopheles was so keen on that transaction with Faust. There are no strings attached. The gain will be primarily for mankind. You will benefit too, but the Supreme Authorities have decided to put up with that.'

'Your Majesty – I mean, Professor. I hardly know where to start.'

'You might, I suggest, begin by asking me the first question which comes to mind.'

'Very well, my Lord Professor.' Joseph could still not quite digest the informality of the occasion, in spite of the professor having by now thrust an untranscendent chair to him and waved Joseph's untranscendent bottom towards it. 'I must ask you then if it is true, as Copernicus maintains, that the Earth is moving around the sun?'

For a moment the professor looked shaken and hesitant as in the nightmare of any teacher or lecturer where the first question asked him is the only one that he cannot answer. He began to mutter. 'Yes, indeed the earth moves around the sun, in a manner of speaking. But then you *could* say that the sun moves around the earth.' His manner suddenly brightened and he said confidently, 'as far as you are concerned, the earth definitely moves around the sun.'

'As far as I am concerned,' mused Joseph. 'Is knowledge then only relative, my Lord?'

The professor laughed. 'No, he said, 'many things are relative but knowledge is everywhere the same.'

'But the philosophers, sir, take so many different positions. Who among them speaks the truth?'

'None of them. They are all wrong and most of them idiots. But listen most attentively to Democritus. He may not be entirely correct, but he is the most profitably wrong from your point of view as a chemist.'

'Profitably wrong' was another shock. But Joseph managed to go on. 'Who else should I read, my Lord?'

'Bacon!' snapped the professor.

Joseph was startled by the tone of this exclamation, and assumed that the professor had uttered a favourite oath. He did indeed have a slightly Jewish appearance. Before Joseph could answer, the professor added another command that Joseph did not quite catch. He thought that the professor's words were 'and trust the Galilean.'

'I do, my Lord,' he said, quite truthfully. 'He is my daily guide in all things.'

The professor gave him a curious look as though he had expected a different response, but merely asked,

'What is you next question?'

'Sir Professor, you mention Democritus. Then substances really are made of atoms?'

'Leave out the "really". Reality is for the Supreme Parliament and even they are not too sure on certain points. But, yes, you will make great progress if you assume atoms.'

'So matter is constituted by indivisible atoms too small to be seen?'

'Who mentioned indivisibility? Why do you talk about indivisibility?' Joseph seemed to have a talent for asking questions that deeply disturbed the professor. 'I told them about it, then I warned them. And then I urged them not to do it. They heard only what suited them.' For a few seconds, the professor's moustaches showed signs of emotion, but he brought them and himself under control again. 'You do not need to bother your head about indivisibility. It would be too confusing at this stage. Chemistry is a trivial subject best approached from the early Twentieth Century. Let us keep to the elements.'

'The Twentieth Century' – Joseph's mind was still staggering but he managed to continue. 'Sir, that is what I most wish to know. Are the elements as Aristotle described?'

'Aristotle was a prick! Excuse me. My language and behaviour have deteriorated sharply since television was allowed into the Supreme Parliament. Let me phrase my sentiment another way. The great Ancient Greek philosopher's view of the nature of the elements is no longer considered to be relevant.'

By this time, Joseph had noticed that the professor was wearing odd socks. Surely this could not be correct even in the unfamiliar ethos of some future era? The observation emboldened him.

'Then what are the elemental substances? The Philosophical Mercury and Sulphur, I know about, but what is the status of Salt?'

'Ha!' said the professor contemptuously. 'You know about mercury and sulphur! Like Hell you do! Yes, they are elements. But not the Philosopher's Mercury and the Philosopher's Sulphur. Forget all about this Philosopher stuff – the Philosopher's Stone, the Philosopher's Air, the Philosopher's This and That, the Philosopher's Arse. And don't call them "Our" Mercury and "Our"

Sulphur either! They don't belong to you. They belong to us all – men and melons, buds and bedbugs. What you regard as the common sulphur and common mercury are the real elements.'

Joseph was in shock. 'Do you mean that the everything that exists is made of the common quicksilver and common brimstone?'

'Certainly not! Listen carefully. There are ninety-two elements in nature – and counting. I will name the more commonly found elements for you and describe their properties and relationships. You may suffer from information overload, but the subject can be systematised to a considerable extent through a framework known as the Periodic Table. You can tell the World about the Table too and they won't have to be bothered with that little Russian fellow, Mendeleyev. You can spike his guns all right, and some other guns too.' The thought obviously caused the professor a great deal of mirth and pleasure.

'Ninety two!?' said Joseph faintly, after the professor had calmed down.

'Yes. And increasing every year. I will name the metallic elements, at least the ones with which you are familiar – gold, silver, copper, lead, tin...' The professor listed the seven metals that Joseph was accustomed to acknowledge. 'And these, the non-metallic – sulphur, arsenic...' Another dozen or so names followed.

'Then if these are elementary and have nothing in common, it is not possible to change one into another? The transmutation of common metals into gold is not possible?' Joseph could feel the earth shaking beneath his feet. 'Then all our effort, our work of centuries...' He began to stumble for words.

The professor helped him out. 'Is wasted.' Another bout of merriment overtook him. This time it was short-lived, though. He broke off suddenly, perhaps in response to the dejected body language of the apothecary. 'Cheer up,' he said. 'I have come to make you the most powerful intellect on earth. Transmutation *is* possible, but it is very difficult and requires methods entirely different from those you envisage. Probably you could make gold with a cyclotron, but certainly not enough to buy the cyclotron, or even the fuel needed to operate it.'

'Cyclotron?' muttered Joseph, entirely bemused. 'But I have seen a gold ring which was made from a plain copper band.'

'You were not given the chance to examine it properly. But look – let us not talk in this fragmentary manner. Now I shall teach you all those elements of chemistry that you need to know at present. Later we shall have more sessions and get on to the advanced stuff.' And the professor proceeded to explain the electropositive series, the composition of the common acids, the way to prepare oxygen and its central role in the composition of many compounds, as well as its importance in combustion and respiration. He described the preparation of nitrous oxide, nitric oxide, sulphur dioxide, carbon dioxide, carbon monoxide and hydrogen. And he was told about the atomic composition of the mineral elements and compounds – the concepts of atomic weight, atomic number and valence. Next time, the professor assured him, he would be able to understand isotopes and radioactive decay.

'That's enough for the time being. Even a receptive listener like you won't be able to absorb more information in one session. But we have put Priestley out of business. He will be able to make his escape to North America much earlier. Dalton will be compelled to seek other employment. As for Lavoisier, poor fellow, he will be able to devote more time to keeping his head.' He began to chuckle uncontrollably again. When he stopped eventually it was only to say – 'I'll brighten up on my biology too and tell you about evolution by natural selection. Then Darwin can become a vicar or go for more luxury cruises or crawl into another wormhole.'

All these names of course meant nothing to Joseph, but he caught the drift of the argument. When his teacher had at last finished enjoying these thoughts, he said, 'I am full of gratitude that you have communicated these profound matters to me. You have given me an opportunity which no man before me has ever enjoyed. But if I understand correctly what you have been saying, my revelation of this information to the world will deprive these men – Priestley, Dalton and the others – of the discoveries that they would otherwise have made.'

'That is true. But they are all ingenious men. They will begin with knowledge and assumptions different from those that they would have had if you had not spoken. They will make further advances. And if they do not do so, then you will have saved them from the birth-pains of creativity, from the *hubris* that must accompany discovery, from the angry or violent reception of their work when it does not coincide with the prejudices and beliefs of their fellows. You may deliver them from the politics of their day, perhaps from excruciating conflicts between a perceived necessity of revealing what they know and their perception of personal moral duty.'

The previously jocular manner of the professor was replaced progressively as he spoke, by a deeply serious tone, heavy with sorrow and perhaps anger. Joseph noticed the change, but did not dare to question him.

'But,' said Joseph, 'this is nothing less than changing the course of history. I do not know whether you have made original discoveries yourself – I can readily tell from your wide erudition and ease of exposition of the complex knowledge which you imparted, that you are a man of high distinction – but if you have made such discoveries and if you decided, from whatever motive, to explain them to me, then your own life, which you have already lived, would be inexorably altered. I am fighting with a great paradox.'

'Apparently you have some brains after all. You are correct. And this issue has been discussed throughout history. It is popular with those authors in my age who write what we call science fiction and who like to build their stories around time travel, either into the past or the future. The dilemma becomes even more acute if the life of the story-teller himself is manipulated by these new events from the past. His capacity to tell stories or even his existence may be threatened.'

Joseph protested. 'But the future is already written into the world. Only

God knows what will happen. Certain particularly honoured prophets or adepts may, by God's grace, have limited perception of future events. But these cannot be altered. There are many instances where prophesies of impending disaster have been made and heeded, but where the very attempts to avoid the inevitable have merely accelerated the fulfilment of the prediction.'

'But you believe, do you not, that man has free will?' asked the professor.

'Absolutely. The Holy Book and the creeds tell me so.'

'Then some limitation must be placed upon the predictability of the World. Because what happens is to some extent influenced by human choice, and not only of kings and princes but by the choices made by each and every one of the common people.'

'But', said Joseph, 'here I see chaos and anarchy. If God is not in control then how can we believe that there are rules governing the behaviour of the material world. How can I go into my laboratory and be confident that the actions which I took yesterday will yield the same result when I repeat them today.'

'God does not play dice,' said the professor.

'I am pleased to know that. But tell me, sir' – Joseph indicated the sentence which was still written across the heavens – 'what is meant by a 'scientist'. It is not a word with which I am familiar.'

'Quite,' replied the professor. 'It is what you might call an Experimental Natural Philosopher.'

Joseph had no time to respond. Suddenly the chair on which his tutor was sitting separated into its constituent parts, which dissolved back into the characters of the unknown language. They wheeled and whirled away into the radiant background, some fading gradually, exactly reversing their mysterious coming, others assembling themselves into a script. The professor was left sitting on nothing in particular, looking astonished and rather put out. He slowly toppled over backwards, fading as he did so. Before he had time to hit the floor, he had become invisible. The glorious colours of the background remained, filling the whole horizon with an indescribable tremulous peace. Written across the sky in illuminated letters, as if on the page of an ancient manuscript, were the words

***He who wishes to explore Nature must tread her books with his feet.***

# CHAPTER 12

Joseph awoke long after noon. His exhaustion had been banished by the long sleep, although the cure had left him with a slight headache. This he hardly noticed. Hunger was now in charge, but was challenged by a suppressed excitement. He had been given the keys of the Kingdom of Learning. His fame among men was assured, providing that he was careful in the revelation and dissemination of the knowledge he now had. There was much thinking to be done. The information he had been given was of the greatest benefit for his fellow man. He was to be entrusted with a immense power. By whom? He had signed no contract, sworn no oaths, promised nothing, placed himself under no obligation of any sort. This was not the work of the Devil nor of any sinister power. Surely such a thing could happen only by God's will. It was a part of the Creator's great scheme in which he, an unworthy human being, had been chosen as an important instrument. He had been chosen and would not fail in the service of God, who had selected him. At this point, the slightly troubling phrase swam into his mind from the depths somewhere below. The professor had mentioned 'the Supreme Parliament.' Did God have to suffer an Executive? Surely the Heavenly Realm could not be open to disputes of the type that were causing so much dissension here in England? On the other hand, if the number of the Heavenly Host is 301,655,172, as the Kabbalistic tradition maintained, there must be a considerable potential for anarchy.

He ate his mid-afternoon breakfast and thought further. Probably the best approach was to write a book, but who would read it? For that matter who would publish it? There was all the business of obtaining a licence for publication. The material was revolutionary, in fact 'revolutionary' did not do it justice. It signalled the beginning of a new era. It was bound to be controversial. It might result in his imprisonment or even his burning. He shuddered as his imagination threatened to suffocate him with smoke while the fat burst out of his burning flesh and began to run down his legs, provoking little explosions of new flame as it dropped on the hot faggots. There was no question of a clash with the Scriptures – he did not face Galileo's problem. That was not a difficulty. But they would accuse him of diabolical assistance. Also the printing of a book had to be paid for. His finances were not good, especially now that much of his apparatus had been wrecked by an explosion. A foolish thought! Of course he would not now need a laboratory. But then again, yes, he might. He would need to demonstrate the correctness of the new concepts to a sceptical profession. Perhaps he could use facilities of other alchemists. He had many contacts, and they would be spellbound by what he had to tell. They would be lining up to help him. Or would they refuse out of envy, or simply try to steal his work and reputation?

A better way would be to find a patron. It would be best to begin at the top, if possible. This was dangerous too. He would need to find someone of intelligence and learning. The new chymical philosophy and its applications could bring great benefits to a nation but might easily be confused with alchemy. Monarchs had historically shown a wide variety of attitudes towards alchemists. Henry VIII and Elizabeth were presumably advised of the existence of the law against alchemy passed by Edward III, but politely ignored it in favour of John Dee and others, to whom they gave covert support in the interests of national solvency and even national security, arguing no doubt that, although they did not really approve of the transmutation of base metals into gold, it would be a terrible disaster if another nation learned the trick first. Zygmunt II and Zygmunt III Waza received alchemists enthusiastically in Poland while the eccentric Emperor Rudolph II included alchemy among his scientific interests and was a notable patron. Some monarchs showed an honest but brutal ambivalence towards the profession – they wined and dined alchemists in anticipation of impending riches and promptly hanged them when the demonstration failed. Alchemists were a source of special pleasure to Frederick of Würzburg, who reserved an exclusive gallows for their use, reputedly made of gold. Unfortunately, Rudolph II was long dead. Better perhaps to avoid sovereigns and find one of the new breed of men from outside the aristocracy who had acquired, through intelligence and ability, powerful positions and influence at Court and who would be able advise him and prepare his path.

Joseph meditated upon these difficulties while he ate, then hurried to his desk. The essential thing was to write down for his own use everything that he had learned from the first lesson, before the memory dimmed. He picked up his pen and began. The elements were the first thing. But what had the professor said? He had understood it perfectly at the time. Had mercury been mentioned? Or sulphur? How about salt? Gold? The list was there in his mind; he could feel it, almost touch it. He could see one corner of the page bearing the list sticking out, just beyond his reach. He leaned over, straining. Now he had grasped the corner. He pulled, but the paper resisted. It would not budge an inch. Joseph rested and thought. He worked out several strategies for recalling the vital list from the depths of his mind. He worked through each method in turn. Nothing happened. The treasure was there in his mind, tantalisingly close, but irretrievable. He sweated and struggled. Eventually he capitulated on elements and went on to try atoms instead. He retrieved the name Democritus, which was familiar anyway, but what was the name of the future discoverer of the atomic system? And what was it that had made the discovery so important? Again he strained and perspired, and again he failed. He tried in turn every item of the subjects which he was sure had been explained to him. Not one would yield its secrets.

He sat with his elbows on the table and his head clutched in his hands. The headache was now in the ascendancy. Of course, he thought, it is always so with dreams however real and powerful. In the morning you know that you have had a potent experience, which may have been so compelling that you were awoken by it, but the detail has gone. Possibly everything has gone, except for the fact of the experience, and the headache.

The flaxen-haired boy had entered the room and was looking anxious. He touched his father's arm and asked, 'Are you all right, Papa? What did the professor say? Have you written it down?'

'I have written nothing,' said Joseph bitterly. 'I can remember nothing but the trivial. The professor exclaimed 'Bacon!' very forcibly. I think that he was swearing.'

'But isn't Bacon a philosopher, Papa?'

'Well done, my son. You are right to remind me. I have read some of Roger Bacon's books. He made useful additions to Aristotle's logic and was a many-sided man. He was an alchemist among many other things.'

'Isn't there a more recent Bacon too?'

'Yes. Francis Bacon, a Lord Chancellor of England, no less. Such people rarely have anything original to say in philosophy. Perhaps I should look at his books, though. He might be an exception, you can never tell.'

'But,' said the lad,' did the professor say nothing else?'

'Yes. This I do remember very clearly. He said, "God does not play dice".'

'Pooh!' said the flaxen haired boy. 'That's nothing. Of course God doesn't play dice. Everybody knows that.'

# CHAPTER 13

*The Book of the Universe... is written in the language of mathematics and its characters are triangles, circles and other geometrical figures.*
   Galileo.

Joseph sat in the imposing library of Sir William Richards, maternal uncle of Penelope, Baroness of Mixford, in the same room in which the Baroness herself had gained such insight into natural philosophy. The thoughts of Bacon! were his new concern, not the familiar Roger, but the new and more worldly Francis. He had a book open in front of him – *Novum Organum* – and was making notes. After the debacle of the alchemists' convention, the baroness's house was out of bounds. His return there was too dangerous, for the baroness as well as for himself. He had however received a kind offer from her of an introduction to the house of her uncle, to allow him to further his studies there. An exchange of messages between the baroness, her uncle and the apothecary had opened his way to the authors he needed to study. His first reaction was guilt. Was it proper to accept such kindness from a lady whose expensive laboratory he had just burned down? As he pondered the matter, he felt the headache beginning that always afflicted him when considering ethical questions. He reacted in the way that he always did when so afflicted – by directing his thoughts into another channel. After that he wrote a letter of thanks and acceptance. Joseph was well read but he was not university-educated – otherwise he would most probably have become a physician and not had to suffer the snubs and sneers of members of that profession. His learning was characteristic of the self-educated – vigorous and perceptive in those parts where enthusiasm had led him, deficient in others, lacking system and order. He had read the classical Greek authors. He was of course familiar with the alchemical literature. He knew Roger Bacon, Grosseteste, Aquinas, and was aware of the Copernican view of the solar system, without any detailed understanding of the arguments, and he was aware also of the controversies provoked by it through its challenge to Aristotle and Ptolemy and, arguably, to the Scriptures.

   He began to read the Lord Chancellor, ready to pour spirits of vitriol on the good man's offerings. Knowledge is power. Well, here was a surprise! – the author telling us that knowledge is power. No alchemist needed to be reminded of that. Trivialities of this kind were not worth the expense of binding. A man seeking to make gold is not creating wealth only, but the power that follows it, as the tail follows the horse. That is why monarchs, pretenders and power-seekers of all kinds were so interested in the possibility of transmutation of base metals to gold. That is why alchemy is so attractive and so dangerous. And the Philosopher's Stone – altruistic, yes, but bringing power over disease, over life, bringing fame, prestige and power to the man who could discover it. Fame was itself a kind of immortality. To this might be added the literal immortality that the secrets of the Stone would perhaps confer.

Joseph read on, sceptical, impatient and somewhat irritated. But here was a new idea, strongly argued, that advance in Man's dominion over nature was only possible by collaboration between human beings with the necessary skills. This notion was not entirely novel for him, nor indeed for the better kind of alchemists, especially for those who had banded together to form secret societies whose professed aim was to pursue a common purpose, to share information and ideas; the novel part was that such collaboration might actually be made to work. He reminded himself of the difficulty – *"so that seeing they shall not see, and hearing they shall not understand"*. Francis Bacon had clearly not attended a meeting of alchemists and certainly no occasion like the recent meeting at the house of the baroness. Still, Joseph could see the force of the argument. Less secrecy was essential, more active collaboration in day-to-day work inside and outside the laboratory, and – another crucial point that the learned Lord Chancellor had not pursued – a common language in which to discuss the difficult subject matter. No more Babylonian Dragons or Diana's Doves, unless carefully defined. Here was a truly revolutionary thought – that they should work together, and to this Joseph added his own caveat – that they should understand what each other was talking about.

And here was Francis Bacon again, this time with a totally indigestible idea. A lightning flash and a great explosion of thunder filled the landscape, gradually dying away. Final causes must be excluded from enquiries into natural philosophy. Joseph read and reread the paragraph, fearing a lapse in his ability to read and understand. But surely Aristotle had settled this matter nearly twenty centuries ago. There were four levels of causation – formal, efficient, material and final. Final causes were if anything the most crucial. With final causes we approach the very core of existence, we face the reasons why things are so.

But why bother with Francis Bacon? He was a theoretician only. He had made no advances in knowledge himself. In what lay his authority? His experience? His work was in Council Chambers, not laboratories. He had, it was true, devised an interesting idea for establishing some facts about the nature of tides in the oceans. The experiment had not been done. Would it have worked? Most probably not. It was all very well for philosophers to sit in their comfortable studies and write down facile schedules for others to follow. Clearly this had not been the way of Galileo.

Another great thunderclap rolled and echoed about Joseph's head, so loud and threatening that he instinctively ducked his head. Suddenly he recalled the words that he thought he had heard from the professor – 'and trust the Galilean.' He remembered the strange look from the professor on hearing his response. He had of course misheard. The professor must have said 'and trust Galileo.'

Now various books of the great Italian lay before him. He began with the *Dialogue Concerning the Two Chief World Systems* – a riveting presentation of dangerous thoughts. The discussion between three courteous gentlemen was learned and friendly, but the identity of the author was not in doubt. The whole script crackled with controversies that went far beyond the academic questions under consideration. The charred ghost of Giordano Bruno hovered over the writing. The Catholic Church was not Galileo's target. His enemy was the world view of Aristotle, and it was clear that, while he held the ancient philosopher in genuine high regard, he was intent on kicking him whenever he was in range. The Italian master was a brilliant and formidable polemicist with hints of spare bile, the yellow variety. Joseph had no strong reactions for or against the Copernican view for which Galileo was the protagonist. He had some mathematical training but did not consider himself competent to decide complex matters that required – and had received from Copernicus and Galileo – life-long study. The system argued by Salviato was neater. The Ptolemaic system had become increasingly unwieldy as it had acquired more and more epicycles, and had begun to look like the design of an over-enthusiastic wheelwright who had become confused and crazed in his dotage rather than a work of the supreme intelligence of God. The Copernican system, although an improvement, did not seem wholly to resolve this problem.

Joseph's concern, however, was not with the conclusions to be drawn by the reader as juror in this dispute between Simplicio and Salviati, but rather in the nature of the arguments used and the foundations upon which they stood. The crucial – and indigestible – development was that final causes had been discarded. The prejudice natural to all mankind, that they themselves must necessarily inhabit the centre of the Cosmos had existed since the Greek civilisation and probably before and had been taken up by the Christian Church without question: it was provoked by the conceit which he observed in all men, himself not least. The belief had enjoyed the status of an axiom like those of Euclid. Now it was replaced by another axiom – no, not by an axiom but by another class of statement – an *axiom* was a self-evident truth and one could not have two contradictory axioms. But one could have more than one *premise*. Upon each premise in turn, a logical structure could be raised and the result tested against observations of the real world. This represented a great clarification of method, but there was little in the astronomical arguments suggestive of techniques that might be applied in alchemical studies. The Book of the Universe might well be written in mathematics, but what had this to say in the Chapter of the Substances?

Next he began to browse in another work of Galileo, which promised even less relevance to his own interests, concerning the falling of bodies from heights and the path followed by missiles. At first he was a little disappointed, even irritated, by this book. Here Galileo was playing what was suspiciously like a tavern game that Joseph had seen somewhere, rolling little balls down a sloping board. As he read on and pondered, however, he began to understand the method the Italian was using. He was asking a single question, so that he could study that and nothing else. In time he possessed reliable, logically sound and carefully demonstrated answers to a series of questions. A pattern then emerged, or a structure, which could be summarised, either as a mathematical equation or as a principle stated in common language. Final causes were omitted. Moving objects were not assumed to be pushed by anyone, least of all by the various categories of angels.

He felt that he was making progress. It must be time for the next interruption. He was deep in thought and entirely unaware of his surroundings when a soft, tactful cough close at hand broke into his thoughts, and raising his head with a start he found a servant, dressed in the smart livery of the household – far smarter than anything Joseph possessed in his own wardrobe – holding out a silver plate on which lay a letter.

'I beg your pardon for the disturbance,' said the servant, 'but I have a note here from Sir William's daughter, Miss Nancy Richards.'

Joseph read,

Dear Müller
Please forgive me for disturbing your important studies. I would not normally do so. I have however a small but pressing medical problem, about which I am sure you are competent to advise me. Would you be so kind as to find time to join me for tea in the small drawing room at four o'clock this afternoon? William, who brings this note to you, will return your reply.
Miss Nancy Richards

Joseph wrote a brief reply.

Dear Miss Richards
Probably your need is for a physician rather than a humble apothecary, but I will gladly provide you with advice of a preliminary nature, if it is within my capacity. I thank you for your kind invitation and will do as you suggest.
Michael Müller

At four o'clock, and following a short but humiliating brush with Kepler's *Epitome* which he saw almost at once was beyond his comprehension, Joseph was conducted to the room where a table was laid for afternoon tea in a style which he had heard about only from the more boastful of his friends. Miss Nancy was already there and greeted him with politeness, edged with a warmth that surprised him pleasantly. He was unfamiliar with the dress codes of the upper classes and assumed that his lack of knowledge was responsible for his fleeting thought, immediately dismissed, that she was too carefully dressed for the time of day and the occasion.

The young lady was already practised in the social skills and he soon felt at ease. She began by asking him some questions about the town in which he conducted his profession, enquiring after its prosperity and health, whether he was able to make a good living and how individual inhabitants fared. She knew a surprising amount about its more prominent citizens, some of it scandalous, and clearly considered the present occasion a useful opportunity for extending her knowledge. From pleasant gossip she passed on to recent events at her cousin's house. This lit Joseph's signal flares. Beacons were blazing on every hill. Perhaps this was the real purpose of his summons to the drawing room. The unexpected and unconventional invitation to tea and the early pleasantries were softeners. He proceeded with caution, only to find that the young woman was already familiar with most of the information he had to give. When in the course of his narrative he had to refer to the members of the conference, he used the term 'natural philosophers' or just 'philosophers. At the third reference of this kind, he was interrupted.

'Come, come,' said the young lady. 'There is no need for circumlocutions or disguises. We all know they were alchemists.'

Joseph excused himself. 'But they like to think of themselves as philosophers. Some of them actually are. About three of them, I estimate.'

'Are you one of the three?'

'I certainly thought of myself as a philosopher until a few days ago. Now I know that I was not. I am striving hard to become one. That is why I am here in your father's excellent library.'

He went on to explain, somewhat haltingly, his growing disillusionment in recent months, culminating in the revelation of the pottery shard. Too many new ideas and too much novel and challenging information were competing for digestion by his mental viscera for him to express himself with his customary clarity or fluency. He was also still a little cautious and steered away from controversial areas, especially those viewed as heretical in other countries. The young woman showed every sign of genuine interest and sympathetic understanding, so much so that the time passed quickly as they talked animatedly over a range of subjects, until Joseph noticed suddenly that the light streaming in from the casement window from the garden was beginning to weaken and that the purpose of his visit, as laid out in the young lady's note, had still not been addressed. This was awkward, but he felt that he could not reasonably leave without his duty being fulfilled.

'Your note,' he said, 'mentioned a medical matter on which you need advice. I may not be able to assist but I have acquaintance with several physicians who have expertise in various branches of medicine. I trust that your problem is not a serious one.'

'No, not serious,' she answered, and from the slight blush – slight, but to his practised eye, readily discernible – he anticipated that her problem was one of the specifically female type. 'No, I am for some reason having difficulty in sleeping at night.'

Joseph was a little relieved.

'Ah! There are various medicines, quite gentle and reliable with which such a condition can be treated. My pharmacy possesses several such. However, they treat only the symptoms. It is always best if a remedy can be found in some adjustment to the daily practice of living. Even a simple improvement in the daily timetable may be effective. Do you take much exercise?'

'I take those types of exercise which my father thinks appropriate to the dignity of a young woman from the aristocracy. In particular I spend many hours riding and hunting.'

'That is good exercise for the horse!'

'Come, come,' she said – this seemed to be a favourite admonition of hers – and proceeded to scold him, although, to Joseph's relief she was also laughing. 'Apothecaries should confine their wit to the proper concerns of their profession, advising those who consult them. You know yourself that the rider of a horse is well exercised. 'And,' she added, 'may even suffer pain.'

Joseph glanced at her suspiciously. She knew a lot about everybody else. How much did she know about him? But the young woman's face gave nothing away. She continued;

'Surely you must have some medicine, some 'sweet oblivious antidote', which will banish away my restlessness and subdue my bad visions, perhaps even ensure dreams have an element of tranquillity or excitement.'

Joseph's warning beacons, which had almost guttered out, leapt into lively flame again. He had not yet been able to rid himself entirely of the suspicion that Miss Nancy's invitation to him embodied a purpose that was not the one expressed in her note. Did she want to experiment with the hallucinatory properties of his medicine cabinet? Such explorations were not unknown amongst the young. And this was a youthful girl, spirited and eager to engage with life, but confined, perhaps over-confined, by too zealous parents. He had learned during the course of the conversation that she was able to talk to him alone in this manner because her parents were away and she had been left in the charge of her elder brother who had, however, taken the opportunity, as Nancy tactfully put it, 'to enlarge his experience of urban life'. She too was about to break out in some direction. This was clear. He answered carefully. He agreed that he would send her a small amount of a soporific, but urged her in the meantime to solve the problem by some other means. Any doubts he had about the advisability of arranging to supply her in this way were rendered irrelevant by the knowledge that he was no longer in a position to do so. A further embarrassment was raised by her next question;

'Thank you. By the way. While on medical topics, I must ask you – I am curious to know – what is the nature of the sickness called the Red Blot?'

'I have not heard of it.'

The people of Cottesthorpe have. They are in a considerable panic.'

'Oh my God!' thought Joseph, suddenly remembering his device for getting rid of Thomas Tatt. Clearly consequences had followed that he should have foreseen. He flinched but replied calmly.

'I am confident that there is no such disease. Otherwise I should certainly have been informed. No doubt the panic is the response of untutored villagers to an unconsidered statement by some foolish or malicious person.'

Nancy seemed satisfied with his response and changed the subject dramatically.

'This estate has great beauty. It is my home. I love to wander in the grounds. The trees date back, they say, to the time of the Conquest. The lake is one of the few natural ones to be found in the great estates in this area. Its depths are full of inexpressible colours. Sometimes I try to paint them but it is not possible to represent them on paper. They wriggle away and escape at the last moment. You can see one corner of the lake from this window. Come and look.'

She indicated one of the smaller windows in the room and, to his astonishment placed her hand on his arm and drew him towards it. Nimrod opened both eyes and rose to his feet. His ears flapped about as he shook the sleep from his head.

'Is that not beautiful?'

'Indeed, Miss, it is a lovely prospect.'

'I love it best when the moon rises above Thorner's Hill and is shimmered into a small rippled folds on the surface of the water. I would love you to see it then.'

Nimrod pricked both ears and began to wag his tail.

'I fear that I shall never have that privilege. Your father would not invite me, even if by some chance he learned of my existence.'

The young woman laughed. 'He is not here. Nor the rest of the family. I am my father's deputy. I know of your existence and am in command. Would you like to see our beautiful lake?'

Nimrod forgot that he was on a chain and almost strangled himself as he leapt from the kennel.

The arrangement was carefully made. Joseph would have to leave and be seen to leave. He would leave immediately before dark. He must ask the servant for his coat, making some leisurely talk about the state of the impending conflict. And similarly with the ostler, making his departure easy and natural but a little memorable. Outside the gate was a bean field with a hitching post used by the local farm workers. It would not be in use and no one would see either him or his tethered horse at that time of the night. He would walk back to the lake where his conducted tour would begin.

The young lady rang the bell and the servant who had ushered him into the drawing room reappeared. Joseph thought that he glanced disapprovingly at the girl. The proprieties were not being observed. The medical interview had been too long. As a servant, of course, he could not *prevent* but he might *report*. He was instructed to escort Joseph back to the library and to serve him with some sandwiches there when the dinner bell rang.

\* \* \* \* \*

The first pewter and brass of the dawn were in the eastern sky as Joseph, tired and with his head spinning from the delights, not of the lakeside only, left the Ragley estate and turned into the bean field. He expected to hear at any moment a whinny from his horse and perhaps the stamp of a hoof as the animal heard his approach. There was no sound. Nor, when he reached the hitching post was there any sign of the animal, and at first the Joseph thought that he had mistaken the field, or the point in the field, where he had tethered the horse. A minute or so of reflection and checking his bearings persuaded him of the worst. Blackstone had been stolen. There was nothing to be done. He might at other times have reported the theft, but it was too early in the day for reports, and in the circumstances a report was not an option at any time of day. There was only one thing to do – face the fifteen-mile walk back to the inn, and then somehow find the money for a new horse.

\* \* \* \* \*

Some days later the Baroness Mixford received a letter from her cousin.
My Dear Penelope,
I was alarmed to learn of the impertinent and insubordinate intrusion into your house by armed men. This is one of the many distressing events which have become our daily fare. The news from all over the region is alarming and who shall say when the present confusion will end or where we shall be led by the conflict between Crown and Parliament? Many of us here intend to stand aside from the conflict. Nothing good can come of warfare between these opposing sides, and we all pray to God for a peaceful resolution of the contentious issues. Perhaps the King and Parliament may be at last persuaded to compromise. May God guide Charles in all his words and decisions.
I trust you are well and happy and that you will soon have William back to comfort and cheer you. My father is also heavily engaged in negotiations and matters of public policy. I miss him sorely but I tell myself that the trials and obstacles which we meet in life are tests set for us, and that we may, if we react to them with courage and resource even discover in them benefits which we could not have predicted.
My health is much improved. Please send me another apothecary,

Your loving cousin,
Nancy Richards.

# CHAPTER 14

*Nor should it ever satisfy any man to look only at that which is placed before his eyes.*
Boethius. Consolations of Philosophy.

Anno Domini 1645 was difficult for the apothecary as for the whole nation. The military activity that had embarrassed the alchemists and terminated their meeting in spectacular fashion was in preparation for a great battle won and lost in June of that year. Joseph had not returned to his village dispensary. Instead, one day just preceding the date of his alleged return, according to the schedule he had given, the unfortunate Caroline, passing along the High Street had found the contents of the apothecary's shop being loaded into a wagon. The carter was under strict instructions not to divulge the destination of the cargo. The address he gave her, on investigation turned out to be a warehouse in London, where the goods and chattels were to be stored till further notice, and told nothing of Joseph's whereabouts. The carter, pocketing the money, went smiling to the tavern, and Caroline to her bed on which she wept bitterly. Joseph's urgent concern was to get lost again, preferably in some new region of England, where there would be minimal chance for his enemies to trace him. He used, or possibly misused, the hospitality of several adepti, friends, and friends of friends, in scattered parts of England during the summer months, moving on when he sensed a growing impatience on the part of his host, until finally he came in September to a village in the rural South West. The city of Bristol, not far away, aroused his interest as a suitable place in which to live and work. Big enough to provide employment; far enough from London to escape detection by pursuers; not so remote that contact with friends and colleagues was impossible; populous enough to absorb him with some degree of anonymity; it seemed a good choice. The city had been in Royalist hands for several years, but would almost certainly soon fall to the Parliamentary forces. Under new political management – and moreover a management with whose general aims he felt sympathy – and in the upheaval which would follow the capture of the city, he would set up his business as an apothecary. He might hope to prosper and perhaps enjoy a settled period of sufficient length to allow him to pursue his studies in whichever direction they might lead, perhaps undertaking even the long schedule required for preparation of the Stone.

Bridgwater had fallen to the Parliamentary forces on the twenty-third of July. The army under Fairfax moved to Bristol and for weeks was camped around the town, encircling it. The timing of the attack on the town was dictated in part by military logistics, but perhaps more influential still was the plague. It was one of the bad years for the disease in the town, rivalling 1603 and 1643. Already by May, three thousand had died. The Parliamentary troops finally entered on the eighth of September, after the worst of the summer epidemic, although there were many cases throughout the remaining part of the month. Joseph, who, like many other pharmacists and physicians, was a realist and knew that, even with his professional knowledge, he could provide little help to the victims of this terrible affliction, delayed his entry until the first of October.

He had made a tentative start with a new laboratory and a new approach to chymical philosophy. The philosophical approach was still largely unformulated. It was more a desire and intention than a method. Both Bristol and the approach were a long way away from their predecessors. In the case of the city, this was a major advantage – the benefits of moving, if he had to, of moving through large distances, was one with which he was familiar. It was wise not to leave forwarding addresses or else to select very carefully a very few trusted friends to hold them. He rented a shop that would serve his purposes quite close to the centre of the city. The site was spectacular. It was one of a line of buildings, mostly houses, built on a bridge over the River Avon. Outside the window was what a stranger would have taken for a wide street, if it had not been for the masts and rigging sprouting above it. At high tide large ocean-going ships began moving along it. These might be departing or returning from any part of the world, and often were completing journeys of many thousands of miles and many months, returning with exotic cargoes, sometimes with items which were entirely novel. It was an extraordinary harbour, six miles from an arm of the sea that was subject to some of the highest tides on the earth. When the tide retreated, Joseph was amazed to watch these great craft settle down into the thick mud deposited by the retreating water and by the rivers Avon and Frome to await restoration to their proper element by the next influx of the sea. The mud, the deposition by the inhabitants of a large town – one of England's largest – of their waste products into the harbour waters, and the general accumulation of urban rubbish brought a variety of odours as powerful and various, but of a different order of experience to those of the herbs and spices imported in the holds of the ships. Joseph, who was something of a specialist in bad smells, would, in hot weather, time his work for the high tide period when the acrid smell of hot sulphur stood some chance of competing with the external miasma and would bring a sense of purgation and cleansing to the room. The rats with whom he had sometimes to share the laboratory did not care for the odours either, and were noticeably reduced in number and enthusiasm. He became on quite familiar terms with some of these rats. He gave them names, often those of rival alchemists or other persons whom he disliked. The choice of the name Charles for the largest of the tribe was possibly treasonable, or would become so if the Royalists regained the ascendancy. The power and height of the tides saved the city, serving to flush out the worst of the harbour's accumulations, rendering life possible if not comfortable.

The town possessed one feature which was not seen anywhere else in England. Goods were drawn about the streets, especially in the harbour area, not by carts but on wheel-less sledges. The sight amazed new arrivals and often provoked sardonic comment. When Joseph questioned the practice, it was pointed out to him that the streets were relatively clean and this was in some part credited to another unusual feature of the town, namely the placing of the drains under the streets. These were at no great depth, and the distributed weight of the sledge was less likely than cart-wheels to disturb this fragile arrangement. He treated this explanation with some scepticism.

In the interests of avoiding unwanted attention, he assumed a new name. The surname Edwards attracted him. It called out echoes of an earlier apothecary of that name in Exeter who in 1603 had won in Star Chamber a libel case against a local physician, a feat that endeared him to all other apothecaries. The name also had an attractive English ring about it. Unfortunately the same could not be said about his voice and manner of speaking. In particular, the English use of the letter 'w' continued to elude him, and his introductions of himself to patients and business associates led to him becoming known in the town as Ed Vords, of more usually, Ed Fords, or just plain Ed.

The considerable distance of Norfolk from Bristol reassured him. By contrast, the gap between his new approach and the methods and assumptions of many years, was almost unbridgeable. He was engaged in a revolution in his thinking, radical but tentative and fumbling. He had to shift his way of thinking on to an entirely new plane. And he was overwhelmed, many times in the day, by the conviction that this was a lower plane. He began to alternate between depression and euphoria in a manner that he had not experienced since his juvenile years. Yet some ferment inside him kept working away, sometimes sending heady substances to his brain. The obsession of the adepts for hundreds of years with mercury, gold, sulphur, silver, cinnabar, copper and the colourful things that could be made from them, and with the remarkable shapes of the regulus of antimony, and with all the other fascinating phenomena which were the common concern of the alchemists, was somehow not the point. Their grand ideas were not producing anything. They knew the secret for making gold but mostly lived in dire poverty. Some were rich, but these seemed to have great skill in obtaining money credited against their reputations for skill in making gold, and to move on frequently and with suspicious haste.

On a shelf, gazing sternly across his tables and benches, was a crudely framed picture of Galileo. This he had furtively torn from a book in Sir William Richards's library – an act which he admitted to himself was reprehensible, particularly considering the kindness of the family in arranging the use of the library and other facilities of the house. He was haunted by the picture of Galileo rolling balls down a sloping table. There was something new, refreshing, even noble, about this superficially trivial activity. The great Italian was asking small questions, one at a time, and trying to find an answer to each with which he could feel certain before moving on to the next. But what was the equivalent in chymical investigation? Where to start? Like many before and after him, faced with the dilemma of initiating creative effort, and finding the possibilities too many in the richness of the surrounding world, or too few in the paucity of imagination, he fell back upon his own early experience.

His mentor, Michael Sendivogius, had been captivated by the properties of nitre. In one possible view this was a dirty white substance extracted from soil, the fouler the better, and from urine, the more the better, and when obtained its chief use was to blow men apart. In Michael's view it was a kind of Philosopher's Stone of the air. He had sensed a connection with the air we breathe. The thinking was obscure and leant heavily on intuition. It was a substance with power and it needed nurture. It was life-taking but also life-giving. It came from living creatures and from the soil. Its return to the soil was remarkable. The plants growing there responded as though infused with new life. They were granted a renewed vigour. Starved, weary, yellowed plants, fit only to add their widow's mite to a compost heap, became strong, healthy and green. To prepare nitre, the foul mixture of soil and human soil must be given air; it must breathe like a man or an animal. The nitre beds must be carefully prepared to allow in air, and carefully maintained by prodding and turning to allow air to seep into the unpromising heap of rubbish and excreta. Otherwise none of the prized crystals formed, and the nitre bed deteriorated into a stinking pile. Nitre was a substance of immense power. Locked in this unlikely powder was a great force, which could be used to destroy in an instant the walls of a fort that had taken months or years to build. It was not difficult to understand Michael's fascination with this stuff, why he had enlisted its help in the preparation of the Philosopher's Stone. At least three of Aristotle's elements were here. Nitre was formed in the Earth but not without the Air as an agent. Its influence on the sulphur, charcoal and other quietly burning materials was spiteful – malign even – Fire was bound somewhere within it, waiting impatiently for a chance to get out.

He had become uncomfortably aware of the strange behaviour of Galileo on the mantelpiece. The old man's impassive expression, which he seemed to remember when he first tore it from the book, now seemed to be in continual flux, like an Ionian philosopher's Universe. Sometimes he seemed to be vaguely encouraging. More frequently he frowned or looked contemptuous, the disapproval carrying with it an unbearable force generated by such a massive intellect. Sometimes Joseph felt almost sorry for the Roman Inquisition who had felt it necessary to deal with him.

His tutor, Michael, had evolved a standard method for preparing spirits of nitre in which he heated the nitre with calcined soil, taking up the orange fumes in a collecting vessel containing water. This was where Joseph, after much thought, decided to begin. But calcined soil possessed none of the virtues of a sloping table on which balls were rolled. Soil was not clean and simple; soil was a lottery – you used the one that you were given in the place where you were born and made the best of it. It came in all sorts of colours, textures and abilities for nurturing crops. He thought that soil was best left out. Both he and Michael had in the past heated nitre alone in a retort or crucible and had made careful notes about what they saw. This was as simple as anything that could be conceived and had the additional merit that he already knew what to expect. It was as close as he could get to rolling balls down a table or hanging a chain between two hooks. Start with the known – a difficult but secure port, like Bristol's harbour – and begin the exploration from there.

He began by heating nitre itself in a retort. The Spirit of the nitre began to separate from its Body. Or that is how he thought of it. He glanced furtively at Galileo, who had assumed the alarmed look of a professor who has just realised that he has taken on a hopeless student. Perhaps the old man would find "vapours" or "fumes" more acceptable than "spirit". He obtained the orange fumes from the bare nitre anyway, just as Michael had – so what was the calcined soil for? That was too difficult a question for the moment. The vapours were orange in colour and extremely acrid and, as he already knew, poisonous. He directed them into water. It was essential not to breathe them in. Michael must have been a particularly careful and skilful worker. He had lived to the age of seventy. Three score and ten might be the biblical estimate of the life of man, but the scriptures had not included alchemists in its calculations. If they escaped the malevolence of certain rulers, they were not infrequently poisoned by their own workshops or even by their own medicines. Joseph tried to exercise the care taught him by his old master. And, also following his instructor, he kept careful notes. He began his new approach by browsing through these. Much of what he read was not relevant to his new interest, some of it he remembered anyway without the benefit of notes. But one observation – or irritation rather – which he had recorded and forgotten, caught his attention. The orange fumes from the nitre were not all absorbed by the water. This was understandable as no operation in chymistry was ever totally efficient. The point of interest though, was that the fumes not taken up by the water were pallid compared with those rising from the nitre itself. He had seen many times when preparing spirits of nitre that too much of the vapour was escaping as bubbles. But it was pallid. He tried attaching a second vessel to take up the fugitive vapours, on the principle of a second pressing of the grapes, but had abandoned it promptly because the handling of larger amounts of weaker spirits brought extra effort and small benefits. So the potency of the nitre's effulgence must be lost through contact with water. In consequence it lost its colour. No surprise, really. Water was an element, a premier substance of great power. It was the principle of coolness and wetness. It would of course calm the fiery corrosive nature of the nitre fumes.

The months went by. The ocean obeyed the clock that the Creator had given it. Twice each day it sucked out the harbour's poisons and twice each day tried with partial success to replace them with clean water, while the populace continued to oppose its efforts. The masts rose up every twelve hours and every twelve hours fell again, usually slopping over slightly to one side or the other. Joseph was busy with his work as a provider of medicines and was in haste, sometimes in too much haste, to get back to his studies with nitre. These increasingly occupied the night hours, irrespective of the tides. He attached further wash-bottles, in sequence, so that the stream of nitre fumes had to pass through all of them. Once he used, fortuitously, salt water from the harbour and noticed an enhanced cooling of the hectic orange fumes. On better days, it appeared that the stream had been wholly calmed, entirely mollified. Its dangerous colour and corrosive nature were gone. It was tamed. It revealed its presence only as colourless bubbles in the final wash-bottle. Perhaps this was an aerial Stone. Joseph gave a nervous sidelong glance at Galileo and administered himself a sharp kick in the mental groin. This was the kind of thinking from which he was trying to escape. What he should be considering was why he saw it in some trials and not in others. It was bafflingly inconsistent. Sometimes the cooled nitre fumes could not be seen at all. The orange fumes were wholly taken up by their first or second bath to provide the familiar acid spirit. He pondered over the possible differences. He began to suspect that the occasions on which he had seen the cooled fumes had also been those when his furnace was not heating properly. Accordingly, he tried limiting the temperature. At first he thought that this was a failure. The nitre was reluctant to give up its orange fumes. But then he noticed that the wash bottles didn't care; they were bubbling enthusiastically. This was a major shock, which threw Joseph off balance. Pondering the matter later he realised that the fiery nature of the orange fumes must be a gift to them from the flames of the furnace. This made good sense. Fire and water were opposed. The fieriness was removed by the passage through water. He had a satisfactory explanation after all. He went to bed and slept well.

He was awoken next morning by the flaxen-haired boy.

'Papa. Why don't all things give up fiery fumes when you heat them?'

His first impulse was to give the boy a thick ear. He groaned aloud instead and grumbled 'Can't you think of a more suitable question for the time of morning!?'

'Sorry, I was only trying to help. I'll get breakfast.'

His next days were very busy, providing medicines that would probably not work for people who, all too often, were too ill to benefit from them and sometimes past caring. He did not get back to the studies of nitre for about a week. By the time he did, his mind, like the stream of orange fumes, had cooled and cleared. First he must be able to produce the cooled and colourless fumes to order. Like a good general he must secure his position. After that he might be able to study the fumes in some way, without the frustrations and disappointments of their sporadic non-attendance at his sessions. It was said that Galileo had invented a device for measuring the intensity of heat, but made of glass, and water-based, so that it was no use for work using a furnace. He had also heard that others were trying out various materials and liquids so as to extend the usefulness of the device. Joseph had no such tool and had to rely upon the traditional way of alchemists and those who were sometimes, rather dismissively called "vulgar chemists", of judging the heat of the furnace by the colour of an incandescent iron rod placed in it. This clumsy method was hardly sufficient for his purposes especially as he soon found that discouragement of the tendency of the cooled fumes to play truant required the furnace to be kept relatively cool. To get the best result he had to rely on experience and intuition.

Eventually he found that he could best secure production of the cooled nitre fumes by keeping the furnace just hot enough to melt lead.

So the fumes bubbled out fairly reliably into his room adding itself perhaps to the complexity of the town's odours. Joseph sniffed it cautiously. Taste and smell were important, if hazardous, methods of analysis. But it seemed not to smell of anything much – provided that the orange colour had been dismissed. He did not know whether to be disappointed or relieved. The flaxen-haired boy was not impressed.

'If you can't see it, Dad, and you can't smell it, how do you know it's there!?'

'Be quiet! It bubbles.'

'So can I. Watch!'

'Stop that at once!'

Joseph was uncertain as what to do next. One morning he was washing glass vessels – one of the necessary daily routines of his work. One of the bottles had some air trapped inside it and began to float upside down. The incident was of almost daily occurrence. He had seen it a hundred times before, but on this occasion it suddenly and uniquely made a connection with a totally unrelated matter. It was as sudden and surprising as the sensation he had sometimes experienced when touching a metal object on a dry winter's day. He saw in a moment how to proceed with his study of the cooled nitre fumes.

The next day he would be free enough of his duties to try it. He passed the day with impatience, and the next morning rose early, started his furnaces and set to work. When the wash-bottles began to bubble, he placed the outlet tube from the final wash-bottle under water in a flat vessel, filled a tube with water and inverted it above the tube from which the cooled nitre fumes were issuing. The tube slowly began to fill with the bubbles which would have liked to escape but could not, but instead had to join forces and become one large bubble at the top of the tube, looking exactly like the bottle in his sink. In fact for a moment he asked himself, almost in a panic, whether he was merely collecting air from the retort, but was able to reassure himself immediately, since he had long ago dismissed the possibility that the bubbling in his bottles was merely displaced air from the apparatus. If it was air, it must come from the nitre. This was a possibility and an exciting one. Nitre needed air for its coming into existence. Perhaps it was now, under the influence of gentle heating, yielding it up again. Soon his arm ached and impatience overwhelmed him. He replaced the small tube with a larger bottle and used a clamping device to hold it in position over the bubbling tube. Now he could watch and think. Things were going very well. Freedom from interruption made such a difference to working efficiency.

He ignored the first salvo of hammering at the door. A second followed, and this time one of his names was being shouted. He cursed vigorously. Perhaps some urgent medical problem demanded his immediate attention. It was not uncommon for a messenger to be sent to his shop by a physician or directly from a suffering patient. He strode to the door and threw it open. A scruffy youth stood at the door.

'Letters for Michael Muller. Is that you, sir?'

Joseph nodded distractedly. The interview would have ended there had not the courier unwittingly asked the question that always caused him extreme aggravation.

'Cor, What's that smell!?'

'It's you,' snapped Joseph, emerging suddenly from his reverie. 'It wasn't here a minute ago.'

'Have a heart,' said the boy. 'We 'aven't got no pump near us. But I had a wash all the same, last Tuesday.'

'In the harbour, I think.'

'Crikey, what have I done to you? I've no ideal,' said the lad, adding the strange final 'l' to 'idea,' as was the peculiar custom with the locals when they feared that a word ended too indefinitely to stop itself and might go rolling uncontrollably on for ever if it didn't get some additional help.

'No ideal.' Joseph mimicked the local accent. 'That's the trouble with young people nowadays. You ought to get an ideal somewhere. In this town, you'd probably have to buy it.'

'I wouldn't look for it here.' The boy was rousing to the fight and made a creditable attempt at the Polish accent. 'Are you a spy or something?'

'Yes. The Emperor has sent me looking for boys to capture. He cooks their bollocks with onions. He likes the English best.'

'Only ones with bollocks big enough to bother with.'

'They get that way from over-use.'

'We know how to do it. Where do you come from anyway? Somewhere with a lot of trees, I bet!'

'Better than being spawned fatherless from the mud.' Joseph nodded towards the deposit left by the fast-receding tide. 'What a dump' – with another nod, this time towards a passing sledge – 'look, they haven't even heard about the wheel yet!'

'Took you a long time to answer the door. What were you doing – shagging the cat?'

'I was thinking,' said Joseph. 'Ever heard of it?'

The contest, never elevated, was deteriorating. The depths that it might have explored were never to be determined. A sound, somewhere between a swoosh and a hiss, issued from the direction of the laboratory. It was followed by a loud crack and then by a confusion of noises resembling an explosion. A cloud of steam and smoke billowed out around Joseph's shoulders, momentarily and inappropriately haloing his head. He knew instantly what had happened and cursed himself as every kind of fool for standing at his door having an absurd and unnecessary exchange with another fool when he should have been attending his work and guarding against the familiar suck-back. He could picture it exactly. The vessel in which the nitre was being heated had cooled slightly and the water from the wash-bottles had been sucked back into it. The vessel was still at near red heat and the influx of water was instantaneous and catastrophic. It had burst, generating a spectacular belch of steam. The nitre had been cast into the coals where the fire gratefully accepted a further donation of fuel and proceeded with some whole-hearted and uncontrolled chymistry of its own. He anticipated the scene as he dashed from the outside door to the laboratory. There would be pieces of the pottery all over the floor together with glass from the wash-bottles, possibly with bits of burning fuel which he would have to extinguish hastily. There would be puddles of acid on the floor which he would have to circumvent. The scene was exactly as he imagined excepting a few details that he had omitted. For example, some splashes of liquid had reached the walls where they had apparently met old friends in the plaster. They were bubbling away happily together. A similar rejoicing was in progress in the puddles on the floor. And a hole was rapidly appearing in his notes. Scattered in the puddles was a profusion of sharp fragments with the glint of newly created surfaces – clearly recognisable as the shattered remains of the bust of Hermes Trismegistus.

Joseph put Law One into immediate operation. Deal with the pan of fat first – or in this case, with some scattered coals. A bucket of water added to the confusion on the floor. It was now safe, and the letters were more important than clearing up. Correspondence was rare and usually conveyed weighty matters. He ran to the door expecting to find the boy. The letters were there, still floating, fortunately, in the puddle into which they had fallen, but the boy had gone. He was a Law Four man. He was a hundred yards away already and still accelerating. Joseph returned to his room, and, in accordance with his rapidly improvised list of priorities, put the letters safely aside while he cleaned up. When that was done he would settle down to give them his calm attention.

# CHAPTER 15

Joseph opened the first letter.

From Reverend Alistair Douglas to his esteemed Brother Michael Müller.

Dear Brother
I was unable to find you after the unhappy ending to your talk. I am happy to learn that you escaped somehow the rapacious intentions of the agents of this appalling conflict, which has so damaged our once-happy kingdom. I was captured, released and captured again, then escaped again. During the pursuit I had the doubtful good fortune to walk into the estate's cesspool. I was lucky to have been able to extricate myself. When I had succeeded, I found myself surrounded by soldiers who seemed, however, uninterested in pursuing the matter further.
I am writing to recommend to you a gentleman named Paul Fourques. He has recently had some amazing experiences concerning discoveries, apparently of great antiquity, made recently in the Holy Land. You may be hearing from him in the near future, possibly with a proposition for your involvement. Consider carefully what he has to say.
I was appalled by the witless and unmerited devastation caused by the troops who interrupted our conference. For no comprehensible reason, they burned down the laboratory belonging to the Baroness. It was one of the best equipped in England and was utterly destroyed.
I have enclosed also the letter that I promised you when we last met. There is no doubt in my mind that you will find it of surpassing interest.
These are difficult times, which by the grace of God, we shall survive. I pray for you especially,
Yours
Alistair Douglas

Joseph wriggled uncomfortably. The Reverend Douglas had a knack of affecting him that way. He took up the next letter.

From Christ's Pilgrims of the Cross and the Rose to their beloved Brother Michael Müller.
Honoured Brother in Lord Jesus Christ. The whole World admires your travail and glories in a life selflessly directed towards the release of your fellow men and women from the bondage and affliction which has subjected them from the time of the first offence of Adam against God. In the search for that essence, which, by the purity of its substance, by its potent virtue and

incorruptible nature, will cleanse the human soul of the corruption and rust that has accumulated like a patina – no, not as a patina only, but as a vicious corrosion penetrating to the very core of the body and soul – you are known as one of a select and eminent group of leaders. Your incomparable skills and profound knowledge of matters that will, in the fullness of time and with God's guidance, redeem us from our past and enrich our future, are famed through all countries and across many seas. On the nineteenth day of January, our Brotherhood met with the sole purpose of discussing the ingenious and important analysis of the connection between the renewal of health in the body and the animation of Mercury, so lucidly set out in your essay 'On the spirit of man and the metals.' All present were astonished and grateful for the insights obtained from this marvellous work and unanimously agreed in a devout wish that you should become one of our Family. Then we might benefit from your erudition and in return pass to you whatever shards of knowledge the Brothers are granted by the favours of Almighty God. We fervently hope and pray for the success of your glorious enterprise.

But Sir, you are in danger! All who follow our calling, all who seek the Light that shines through the Ages, must face terrible hazards every day of their lives. To the routine but always imminent risks of loss of limb, loss of sight – and through these injuries, loss of the means of support for the Adept and his family – must be added the dangers inherent in the regrettable attitude of many in Authority in whose hands power has been invested – but not recognising Whence that power stems – who do not hesitate to inflict arbitrary and cruel punishments upon those working ultimately for the benefit of Mankind including, not least the Rulers themselves. Ah, my friend, you also have suffered. You will know all too well that we speak the truth. But there is hope. Unity begets strength. We invite you to join us. And the benefits to you lie not only in the opportunity to refresh yourself at the rich springs of shared knowledge. The Association takes care of its Brothers whenever they meet with misfortune, bringing succour and financial support to any member who, through his efforts in the Great Cause, has lost his livelihood through illness, accident or persecution. You are already elected for Membership. If, as we pray, you accept, we must ask – it is a regrettable necessity – but this is the means by which we support each other in vicissitude – for a fee of one hundred pounds for the first year, with subsequent annual donations of fifty pounds. Alternatively you may fulfil all obligations to the Association for life by means of one initial payment of five hundred pounds. If such sums are difficult to find – as they may be for even the most earnest and gifted of our members, we do attempt to make special reductions according to individual need.
Please join us. We wait, breathless, for your answer,
Yours in the Lord Jesus Christ
Sergio Fratinelli.

Joseph dropped the letter perfunctorily into a box on the floor in which he accumulated kindling. It would make a small but useful contribution to the lighting of his next furnace. The chosen name of the Brotherhood, if it actually existed, was a nauseating attempt to ride on the back of the

Rosicrucians, and the mention of 'shards' conveyed him instantly back to the recent explosion in his laboratory and his new purpose and resolve. If ever he had the good luck to acquire a hundred pounds, the least probable beneficiary would be Signor Fratinelli. He opened the final letter.

> From Paul Fourques to his friend and Brother Michael Müller
> Dear Brother
> I am writing to you as one who has expertise and has earned fame through many countries in a difficult endeavour that is our common purpose. I hope that you may by now have heard of my name through our friend Alistair Douglas who I believe we hold in mutual esteem. It is because you are a renowned leader in our discipline and a man who, through his idealism and high purpose can be relied upon to respond in a manner befitting to news of this magnitude, that I believe you should know of a strange and exciting event that recently occurred in the Holy Land. Because of the insecurities of conveying important information by letter, I suggest that we should meet. By this means I can inform you fully of what has happened and discuss with you its likely significance at length and without fear of the information falling into irresponsible or mischievous hands. I cannot hope of course to interest you and trespass upon your time without giving you some hint of what is involved. Suffice to say that a discovery has been made in a cave near the Sea of Galilee of important manuscripts of great antiquity together with a vial containing a red-gold liquid that we believe to possess extraordinary properties.
> I trust that you are in good health and spirits,
> Yours
> Paul Fourques

The letter hovered for a second or two above the box where Joseph accumulated tinder. Then he returned it to the table in front of him and re-read it. Both letters implied that he had an international reputation, a fact that had previously eluded him, unless having fled hastily from several countries was a suitable qualification. 'If you want a man to slip down, first cover him with butter,' thought Joseph. The letter from Fratinelli offered him the role of victim in a shameful fraud, a part that he did not fancy. But the third letter was more difficult to assess. The two letters shared a fulsome tone, Monsieur Fourques's more discreetly. The idea of the discovery of a possible elixir in a region loaded with such historic significance and momentous importance for the World inflamed the imagination. And the letter was sent, not by an unheard-of Signor Fratinelli who might or might not exist, but by a man recommended by a personal friend of known integrity. Deciding to think more carefully and at greater length, he put this letter aside with that of Alistair Douglas.

It had been an eventful day. He was tired and must defer consideration of this unexpected influx of correspondence until tomorrow.

\* \* \* \* \*

Joseph had decided not to replace the bust of Hermes. He had other pressing concerns. A week passed following the explosion in the furnace that had ended his studies of the Aerial Stone – in spite of glacial glares from Galileo on the mantelpiece, he could not quite free himself from thinking of it in those terms – generated from nitre. He was eager to learn more if he could. Gradually, during moments wrested from his other business, he reconstructed the apparatus and eventually, one morning, with the help of Signor Fratinelli's letter, was able to rekindle his furnaces. It was a blustery day – one of those days hated by the people of the town, when the sky seems almost at touching distance and gale-force gusts of wind blow in from the nearby Atlantic. He had some trouble getting the fire started because of the draughts of air which found their way all too easily into the leaky old house. Once kindled, he heated the nitre carefully, prayed that no one would call bringing post or pest, and began to collect the mysterious Air in an inverted jar, watching with excitement as the water was displaced. At last the jar was full. Before he sealed off its top, he applied the analytical tool with which God had provided him at birth. He sniffed the contents carefully. There was no sensation at all. He carried the sealed jar over to a window and examined it against the light. There was nothing to be seen. Whatever it was that he had with such difficulty succeeded in collecting, it was entirely transparent and invisible and had neither odour nor colour. He was increasingly convinced that he had released the air from the nitre by which it had been trapped during the growth of the nitre within the soil of the nitriary. But how would one know? He pondered. The familiar air around him had two characteristics that could reasonably be tested. It was absolutely necessary for combustion. And also for the continuance of life. The first was easy to test, but dangerous. It could be established immediately. The second would require more notice and the enforced co-operation of one of his neighbourhood rats.

He had heard many horrible tales from other adepts of the dangers of testing the combustibility of unknown airs. Sometimes they proved to be very, and instantaneously, combustible, with a price of blinded eyes and missing fingers. Accordingly he built a simple guard from pieces of wooden panelling, enough to protect his face and body, and it was from behind this that he advanced a lighted splint to the jar, at the same time slipping aside its cover. His expectation was – so convinced he was that he had released the common air from the nitre – that the splint would go on burning. If he were wrong then it would be extinguished. Neither thing happened. The erratic weather of the West of England intervened with another gust of wind that echoed through the room as a draught sufficiently strong to blow out the flame from the splint just as it approached the mouth of the jar. Joseph had barely time to curse, and not time enough to pull the splint away from the jar for another try, when to his utter astonishment he saw the splint's flame burst out again at the bottle mouth. He could hardly believe what he thought that he had seen, but since the air in the bottle seemed not to have ignited, he could try it again. This time he did not rely on the vagaries of the climate but blew out the flame himself before applying the glowing end of the splint to the jar. What he had seen before was genuine. The flame was rekindled. He repeated the trial a number of times, with the same result every time.

The following days Joseph spent in a state of febrile excitement. He could not quite believe that he had been able to prepare the Aerial Philosopher's Stone. He was ecstatic. His head was full of joyful words. Singing triumphantly in his head was a passage from Hermes Trismegistus, from the *Corpus Hermeticum*. It had expressed his credo as long as he could remember. Hermes is explaining to his son;

*You see that the world is always one, the sun, one, the moon, one, the divine activity, one. And since all is living, and life is also one: God too is One.*

*Is God then in matter, O Father?*

*Where could matter be placed if it existed apart from God? Would it not be a confused mass unless it were put to work? And if it is put to work, by whom is that done? The energies that operate in it are part of God. Whether you speak of matter or bodies or substance, know that these things are energies of God, of God who is the All. In the All there is nothing which is not God.*

Several times he had to reassure himself about his discovery by repeating the whole procedure, beginning with the lighting of the furnace and ending with the mysterious and exciting moment when the glowing splint burst into flame. Finally he was assured that he really could do what he thought he could do – indeed that he would be able, if required, to demonstrate the process to others – that he would be able to say – 'here you are, you can see for yourself: you can see that it works' and that he would not end with a red face, an army of limping excuses and a badly mauled reputation, as had been the case in many of the attempted demonstrations of transmutation and other phenomena which he had witnessed. But who would want to see such a thing? The gold-making community might say 'What has this to do with us?' The iatrochemists, because of their concern with medicine, might be interested. The danger with them was that they would rush away and use it to cure every existing disease. Galileo, he was sure, would have approved of his method and of what he had done so far. He would certainly have questioned the significance of his finding, and expressed his scorn for the lack of a theoretical framework. He would ask 'What next?'

'Yes indeed – what next?' Joseph felt stranded, washed up on some remote beach. Who could help him? Where was the Galileo of the substances? Van Helmont would have been intensely interested but was recently dead. Joseph's master, Michael, would have been pleased with him at last, would certainly have considered it as an enlightenment and confirmation of his own suspicions. Cornelius Drebbel was also dead. He was of the same generation as Sendivogius. Perhaps the story of the underwater journey from Westminster was true and the air from nitre was the same principle that had sustained the sailors. Did the super-air support life? The trial of the air from nitre as a support for breathing became a priority. The warehouse rats were in danger.

# CHAPTER 16

Plague was troubling the city again and medicines were delayed by the rigorous restrictions on entry at the city gates, especially if the travellers were from London. He had been identifying genuine merchants, arguing, sometimes pleading, with the city authorities to admit those bearing medical supplies. With relief he settled down in the evening to read. He had recently rescued a book from his store-room where it lay partially buried by the detritus of a busy and rather untidy man. He had forgotten this book, perhaps through shame. It had come from Sir William Richards's library and he had intended to return it. The flaxen-haired boy was looking shocked. This was not the behaviour that his father had taught him. Joseph tried to excuse himself:

'Honestly. I really meant to return it. Circumstances beyond my control. Fate intervened. Anyway, Sir William has too many books and never gets round to reading them. Probably does not even know what is there...'

This way a headache lay in wait. He brushed the thoughts aside and picked up the book. It was obviously a work of great learning and likely to demand all his attention. He had been attracted to it by its long discussions of Hermes the Thrice-Great, Hermes the Blessed. Perhaps the author had new insights into the greatest of all the great sages before Christ, a man older than Socrates, living and thinking even before Moses, the writer who had inspired generations of those wishing to understand the ultimate secrets of Nature...

He began to read. But this could not be right. Hermes's great books dated from the third century after Christ! Impossible. He threw the book aside in anger, and then, after several minutes, hesitantly picked it up again. The writer had no idea what he was talking about. And yet... there was evidence of exceptional erudition here. Monsieur Isaac Casaubon was a man with vast knowledge and an inexorable way of bearing in upon every point in his argument, so that there was no escape in any direction. He pulled out each brick from the fortification, examined it thoughtfully, while almost absent-mindedly avoiding an arrow or two from above, catalogued it carefully and finally dropped it casually into a waiting wagon. Eventually the whole edifice collapsed with a sickening crash. Sickening in the apothecary's stomach, that is. He felt bad – and progressively worse as he read on. Finally he threw the book aside and went in search of some air. If he could find any – the tide was out. It was not his lucky day.

The next morning he awoke with the sick feeling still there in his guts and an aching head. Well, it served him right for having stolen – no, I beg my pardon – having failed to return the book. There was no doubting it – another statue had fallen from its pedestal. Another piece of his early life had crumbled into the sea, never to be restored. He looked pleadingly at Galileo who merely offered a smug, could-have-told-you-so smile.

His ill mood continued for many days. Perhaps it was his punishment for illegal possession of goods. He was quite unable to think about the discovery that had so captivated him, his rescue of an imprisoned aerial Essence or Stone from nitre. He buried himself in his work as an apothecary, tried to concentrate his mind on the gloomy work of providing, for his threatened fellows, defences that did not defend, cures that did not cure. Two weeks passed. In desperation one evening he muttered half-aloud in the direction of Galileo, 'what am I to do?' To his astonishment, the old curmudgeon's lips seemed to move. No sound came, but Joseph read his lips.

'Rats!' he said.

'That's not very nice!' complained Joseph.

The next morning, in despair, he addressed the flaxen-haired boy: 'What *am* I going to do?' The lad replied, with ill-concealed scorn, that Galileo's remark might have been a reminder rather than an exclamation. Indeed, had not something of this sort happened before? He could not think where. With a new resolve, he resumed his studies of nitre. He had not expected rats to be interested in the advancement of knowledge and so was not disappointed. They moved with extraordinary speed and he was forced to devise a trap, consisting of a box with a hinged lid propped open by a bar that would be displaced when the rat tried to take the bait. The rats were sceptical and too well fed. It took some days for the trap to work and the victim was, unfortunately, not his old enemy, Charles. It was a small rat of half-starved appearance, which he named '*Espoir*', largely because it was such a poor specimen, and had obviously gained so little from the past that it might as well commit all of its aspirations to the future. He was not clear why he had chosen the French word in naming the unprepossessing creature, except that the English tended to use a French word for anything unpleasant – perhaps he was unwittingly absorbing English mental attitudes. He must watch this. More to the point – the hope was for himself and his next experiment – that it might be successful and that he might be approaching new revelations.

On the next day available for such work, he lit his fires and prepared a jar of the Vivified Air. The rat, although captive, still had to be removed from the trap and was no more inclined to be co-operative than before. It bit a considerable hole in his finger. He was obliged to apply one of his own remedies against blood poisoning. 'Well,' he muttered savagely as he finally succeeded in thrusting the unfortunate beast into the jar, 'have a taste of that. That will settle you down.' But it did nothing of the kind. The activity of the animal was redoubled. This was not difficult to understand since it did not approve of its situation. It was appalled by the unfamiliarity of its surroundings and by the confined space. It was indeed very cramped and Joseph noticed that the rat shared with wasps, flies, birds and other beasts an incomprehension of the nature of glass. If you can see something desirable – food or freedom – you ought to be able to crawl, fly or wriggle to it. This was the reasonable logic of the rat, which chose jumping. He watched with gathering excitement as the minutes went by and it not only refused to expire but seemed if anything to increase its struggles to free itself from its predicament.

He spent the next hours pondering the bizarre new facts that he had uncovered. The nitre, then, not only required air for its growth in the nitriary, but in some way was able to enhance it. And when it was forced to give it up again it was the enhanced air that was released. He felt very isolated. He needed other minds to look at what he had found, but from a cool distance. Unfortunately he knew few people here who would be useful for discussion. Oh for the benefits of a University position or even of residence in London where he had a few contacts with men, who, though not necessarily specialists in pharmacy or chymistry, had fine analytical minds. He would have been able to sit down at a tea table or in a tavern with someone with penetrating vision, someone who would inevitably look from a different perspective. He had found the Aerial Stone of his Master. In the absence of living confidants, he turned to the gallery of dead Masters. Michael Sendivogius smiled upon him radiantly but offered nothing. Francis Bacon said 'do more experiments: get more facts: write them down for us all to learn from.' Galileo scowled from his picture. Probably he approved Joseph's experiments but did not think much of his interpretation and deplored his terminology.

There was a banging at the door again. He should have expected it. He was making too much progress. Not the constables, for God's sake! – most probably a sufferer who hoped that he could cure the pox. Or scrofula. He would advise a visit to King Charles. The knock was too brief and too emphatic for a patient. It was followed by the sound of hastily departing footsteps. Throwing open the door, he was just in time to see the rapidly retreating back of the young man with whom he had enjoyed the previous altercation. Clearly the young man had not enjoyed it. Propped against the wall was a letter.

> From Paul Fourques to his friend and Brother Michael Müller
> Dear Brother
> I wrote to you recently in the hope that – beset, as I know you to be, with the daily labours of your profession and with your incomparable efforts in our great cause – that you might nevertheless find an opportunity to meet me in London to consider participation in an important project. I hoped by now to have received your letter in reply, but the chaotic state of England continues and no one can see an end to the unrest and confusion which affects especially our courier services and hinders free passage on our roads. Doubtless your answer has been delayed, destroyed or even impounded by the Authorities for God-knows-what reason. Or it may be that you have not found the time or the quietude required to consider the prospect of such a difficult journey. In that case, please accept my profound regrets for having troubled you.
> I would not be so inconsiderate as to add further to your burdens with a second unsolicited letter were it not for the news of crucial developments

reaching us from Germany and France – developments which lead us think that at last we stand at the Golden Door. I cannot be specific in a letter, which may be opened by those who would misinterpret or misuse the information, and at present we have no agreed code that might allow us freer communication (this also we might correct when we meet). Our studies of the phial from the Holy Land have granted us unique revelations. <u>Sufficient now to say that we have important new insights concerning the intimate connection between the Aerial Stone and the Elixir.</u> They are indeed devoted brothers, so devoted that, where the first goes, the second must of necessity follow.

I trust that you are in good health and spirits and hope to meet you before the summer is finished,
    Yours
    Paul Fourques

Monsieur Fourques's choice of targets was perceptive in the extreme and his aim unerring. His mention of the caves near Galilee in the first letter had saved his letter from the furnace. The opening paragraph of this second letter had merely irritated Joseph. He hated repetitive efforts to get him to do something which he was reluctant to do – but then he admitted to himself with a half-hearted self-reproof that he had not replied to Fourques's first letter, had not actually declined to meet him. But Fourques's hint about developments with the Aerial Stone set his own internal furnace raging. He had not known before that he could experience so many emotions simultaneously. First a consuming, passionate interest generated by his recent experiments and discoveries with the Vivified Air. Second a resentment that someone else might have anticipated his discovery.

He looked up to find Galileo glaring at him. Not staring or scowling, but glaring. In fact Joseph could have sworn that he was grimacing in fury. He seemed to be working through a series of facial demonstrations, all expressive of disbelief and anger and each more eloquent than the previous. Joseph began the descent from the heights. His intellect showed signs of taking control again. He sat down and tried to assess the Frenchman's letter more calmly. But first he turned the enraged Galileo towards the window, where he could pull faces without troubling his host. He muttered an apology, as he turned the old man round, that the prospect through the window was not that of Pisa or Florence. For that matter, although a ship happened to be passing along the water-filled street, the prospect did not allow him with any conviction to offer Venice instead. And why was Galileo so scornful?

The examination of this last question proved to be the most difficult but the most fruitful. To answer it he had first to think himself into the Master's mind as best he could via the few manuscripts that he had read.

He sat for some hours in deep thought not noticing the fall of night and finding eventually with surprise that he was sitting in darkness. He rose and lit a lamp. He knew that his concern must be with his recent discoveries. He did not know where his new thinking would lead him, but he had a deep sense of excitement and an inner conviction that with his studies of the Vivified Air he had turned in an important direction. He reread Fourques's letter and wrote a reply. He would not come. But he could not quite bring himself to refuse a meeting outright, but deferred a decision until he was less busy, until his health was better, until such and such obligations had been met, until, until...

Some days he almost forgot the temptations of Paul Fourques and his own defection from the cause beloved of adepts. At other times the voices of the past overwhelmed him. Particularly on those days – which were a heavy majority – when his work with nitre yielded nothing except boredom and frustration, he would testily ask himself why he was bothering with small questions when there were so many large ones that required answers. 'What is happening', he had asked himself, 'when a piece of chalk bubbles when placed in vinegar?' A stupid question, surely, with an unimportant answer that would benefit no one. He would return instead to the great subject of the incorruptibility of gold and the fallibility of flesh. Then he would curse himself for allowing his seduction by trivialities. His thought would turn like the lodestone towards the Pole Star, and the magnetism of London and his fellow alchemists would exert its pull upon him. But the trials with the heating of various substances began a counter-pull. Benefiting from his experience with nitre and its clear lesson in the importance of controlled heating, he repeated his distillations several times in any case where he suspected that an air was being generated. Paul Fourques could pursue his mysterious projects without him. He would not go to the capital...

* * * * *

Paul Fourques was a handsome man, large but of that kind of bulk which would in a few years run to fat. His manner was affable and his personality charming in the best Gallic manner. His features were unremarkable except for an extraordinary small patch of brown pigment in one of his eyes, which were otherwise blue. They met in a tavern in Blackfriars where they ordered ale and sat exchanging cautious pleasantries. These gradually became less cautious and Paul's idea of a pleasantry was not always to Joseph's taste.

'You are pale. I think you are working too hard and not getting enough sunlight. I trust you are not unwell. I hope your back is not troubling you still.'

This was accompanied by a hearty laugh, an attempted poke in the ribs, which Joseph managed to squirm away from, and a slap on the back, which he failed to avoid and which would certainly not have effected a cure if the problem had still existed. They exchanged views of the state of various countries, declining through the adjectives 'dire, direr, direst' for England, France, Germany. They also exchanged information – largely one way on account of Joseph's recent isolation – about acquaintances employed in their own dubious profession. Joseph learned that Francis Neil had abandoned chymistry entirely – unsurprising considering his increasingly corrosive relationship with the subject and its practitioners – and had become a chief in the Secretary's tax collection department. Joseph shuddered and hoped that he never met Francis in his professional capacity. He could imagine the man's polite but chilly reply to a peer's own estimate of the tax that he was required to pay, and the excited tremble of the point of his nose – 'How interesting! But puzzling. I must have made a mistake. My calculations suggest a small enhancement of your estimate, about five times that amount, actually. Perhaps we may work through the calculations together…' Eventually the small talk and the good offices of the beer brought sufficient relaxation and confidence to allow some serious discussion. Joseph made the first move. He was anxious to conceal the intensity of his interest in the supposed developments concerning the discoveries in Galilee, and so began with another topic.

'Are there any further revelations of the nature of the Aerial Stone?'

For a moment Monsieur Fourques appeared not to understand.

'Pardon? Ah – yes. Yes indeed, the Aerial Stone. No we have no further information. To tell you the truth, the whole subject of the Aerial Stone has been neglected recently, such has been the excitement generated by other events. Yes indeed, I have a further riposte from our source in Jerusalem. We were slightly malformed, but only concerning the location of the caves. They are not actually at the Sea of Galilee, but are about thirty miles south close to the Dead Sea. There is a ruined building close by, known as Qumran.'

Joseph's bewildered expression persuaded Paul Fourques to start again.

'But of course, I did not explain sufficiently in my letters. It is not known what the purpose of the building was. But many scrolls were found in the caves close by. And many must also be hidden still. There are clear signs that the Bedouin tribes have also been in the caves quite recently.'

'But they would not be interested in scrolls. What would they use them for?'

'Not to read, certainly. These are illiterate nomads who would not even be able to read their own language. They would have neither the means nor the desire to read ancient Hebrew or Greek. They might use them to keep out the wind from their tents, to saddle their camels or for less mentionable purposes.'

Paul laughed his jolly and very public laugh at this last thought.

'What do we know of the content and origin of these scrolls?' asked Joseph, who was too intensely preoccupied to be amused even if the remark had been to his taste.

'Nothing much. To tell you the truth, the lines of communication have gone very quiet. I do not know why. Maybe our informants have been captured or murdered. There are many who wish them dead and many more who would wish to arrest their secrets from them. And there is the always possibility that the informants themselves – although we try always to choose only the most trustworthy – may defect, may prove to be traitors from our great cause, intent only upon their personal gain.'

Joseph had noticed many times in the past that the phrase 'to tell you the truth' invariably indicated the opposite. He pursued the issue further.

'So these scripts may be a list of grocery stores from some community or fort in the desert – of no possible interest to anyone?'

'Ah, not so. Whoever placed them in the cave was intent on hiding them. And not only hiding them but preserving them through long ages.'

He leant forward conspiratorially.

'It is my belief that these manuscripts originated in Egypt. That they may concentrate in one place the incomparable wisdom of the Pharaohs. Here possibly are the final and ultimate thoughts of the Thrice-Great himself.'

'Surely,' said Joseph, 'Isaac Casaubon has shown that the so-called works of Hermes Trismegistus are Third Century inventions by a mischievous apologist for the Christian faith – a faith so evidently true that it does not need such support. Nor does the faith approve or promote such dishonesty.'

'Not everyone believes that Casaubon has proved his point. And as for dishonesty in the cause of religion, you should remind the leaders of the Church on this point.'

'I would welcome the opportunity to do so – particularly the Pope and the Holy Catholic Church, but only from a safe distance. I recall the burning of Giordano Bruno and the long imprisonment and threatened execution of Tomasso Campanella. I have not the stomach for martyrdom.'

'You are right,' conceded Paul Fourques. 'Martyrdom is strictly for specialists. But I have to tell you that one of our men who was involved in the discovery of the treasures in the Holy Land has been found dead. He was not a martyr but he died in pursuit of a cause, which amounts to much the same thing.'

'The end result is similar,' agreed Joseph. 'But how did he die?'

'We do not know. His name was Jan Bynkershoek. Officially he is believed to have died from a seizure, but he was in perfect health and had indeed survived a very difficult expedition to the desert, surmounting many hardships. We suspect that he was poisoned.'

'So Jan Bynkershoek is dead anyway. And that is the end of the business. But why would he have been murdered?'

Paul Fourques, who had been speaking more and more softly since the mention of Galilee, glanced carefully around the restaurant and dropped his voice further, almost to a whisper.

'He was one of us. He was our language expert. He assumed the task of translating the scrolls. In one of the caves, along with a number of scrolls, was a small vial. This contained some crystals of unknown substance and origin, of a red or gold colour. The label had long ago corrupted away, but the bottle and the glass of which it is made clearly identify it to be of great antiquity, probably from the time of Christ.'

'Was the bottle in his possession when he was killed?'

'No. The scrolls were. But we have the vial. It is in a secret location in the South of France. We believe it to be of the greatest impotence -

'Importance,' suggested Joseph.

– importance. One or more of the scrolls we believe may relate to its production and the way in which it is to be used.'

'What happened to the scrolls when he died?'

'They disappeared. Whoever killed him must have them. But we found documents that we believe to be his translations of the scrolls. They are coded. At first we presumed that they were the translations that he had made for us, ready for dispatch. But we found that the code was not the one we had prearranged. It was then that we realised that he must have been working for some other persons, swindling us, presumably thinking he could obtain higher rewards elsewhere.

'Joseph laughed. 'Perhaps the documents are not coded, but are simply in Dutch. Dutch is its own concealment.'

'We do not know what language is involved. Bynkershoek must have used keywords that were not the pre-arranged ones. Our frustration is extreme.' Paul pushed a document across the table to him. 'This is an example. It appears to be a letter with an attached document, apparently both in the same code used for the translations. Others beside ourselves were interested in the caves and what they may contain. They share our interest but may lack our altruistic motives.'

'Ye-e-s,' said Joseph dubiously, leaving Monsieur Fourques to decide which part of his last statements had provoked the doubt. 'You use the word 'we' a lot. Who are your collaborators?'

'I have a trusted friend, Richard Costeaux of Toulouse. He is an alchemist of great skill and knowledge, and has a laboratory of sophistication. He was excited by the news of the findings in the Holy Land, especially by the discovery of the vial.'

'And where is the vial now?'

'With Costeaux. You may see it for yourself if you wish. But you would need to come to France.'

Joseph did not answer but instead took up the papers – two sheets fastened together – that Fourques had offered him. At the bottom of the first were two words that might be a signature. The handwriting was clear and elegant but made no sense whatsoever. The words appeared at first glance to be arbitrary combinations of letters not possible in any language.

'What do you make of that?' asked M. Fourques.

Joseph studied it in silence for a few minutes before replying. 'It is certainly a code of some kind. There are no characters that would not be present in English, French or Latin. It is using a familiar language from Europe, but it is not possible to know which one. The most puzzling feature is that none of the short words is repeated. One usually expects repetition of some common words, such as 'the' in English for example. In such cases one can establish three letters of the code. Here it is not possible. The best hope would be to take it to an expert in codes. There are men in London or Oxford who might well be able to decipher it.'

'Indeed there are. They are mostly in the pay of the King or Parliament. They would be very interested – not only in the nature of the code but in what was being said and by whom to whom. Since we do not know for certain the nature of the message, we do not know who may be harmed nor what enterprises of excellence may be betrayed by allowing it to be interpreted by someone with links to authority.'

'I hope you are not offering it to me to translate! I have enough problems already'

'You are a man of outstanding intelligence. All your friends and fellows in the Great Search tell me so. I have asked many people independently who they think might help me. Many have suggested your name.'

Joseph laughed. 'Their opinion does little to recommend their own intelligence. Perhaps you should find some less stupid referees.'

'You do them and yourself an injustice. And perhaps I can divide you with a possible starting point although it has done little to solve the problem so far. I do know that it is common practice in communications of this sort to use a code in which a keyword known to both sender and receiver is used to construct a particular rearrangement of the alphabet.'

'How does that work?'

'Two rows of letters are assembled. The keyword, which must be shorter than twelve letters and contain letters that occur only once, is written down to begin the top row. The rest of the upper row, and the whole of the lower row, is filled with the remaining letters of the alphabet, either beginning with 'A' or carrying on from the last letter of the keyword, until the alphabet is complete. Letters that appear in the keyword must not be used again. Here are examples, showing the two variants.'

He pushed across a paper in his own hand-writing.

N I T R E a b c d f g h
j k l m o p q s u x y z
    or
N I T R E f g h j k l m o
p q s u v w x y z a b c d

'Each letter of the message is then substituted by the corresponding letter of the adjacent row.'

'Do you have any feeling for what keywords might possibly be used?'

'I have tried many. But there are so many to try. You may as well try and find a particular fish in the sea.'

'In my experience,' said Joseph, 'when anyone selects a keyword, he chooses one which is significant to him. If he is wise he avoids using his own name and the name of his correspondent, although I have known cases where such foolishness has been indulged. Generally people turn to the next layer of thought in their mind. Musicians use the names of musicians or technical terms in music; builders use the names of materials or of famous houses or palaces. Alchemists – who are the most obsessed of all workers – will certainly prefer to use words that are redolent with meaning for them. This – and the requirement that the word contains no repeated letters should narrow the possibilities sufficiently to give one a chance of interpreting the code.'

'Obviously you have a talent for this problem. May I leave these papers with you? Please disport immediately any success you have. If I can help in any way, you have only to ask. I suggest that we ourselves use a code for our letters. As you so rightly point out, those who correspond in code like to choose something from their profession. I suggest the word 'physick.'

# CHAPTER 17

Joseph admitted to himself that he did not know how to proceed with his exploration of the Aerial Stone – he hastily corrected himself with an anxious glance towards Galileo – that is to say, the Vivified Air. Since it encouraged burning better than air itself and was able to support breathing, at least of a rat, would it perhaps assist, or even cure a breathing disorder, like croup or consumption? Such a trial might be possible eventually – perhaps requiring co-operation from a physician.

His recent findings were exciting, spectacular even, but also baffling. But now he entered a period of slow progress, which lasted for many months. The meaning of the discoveries he had made eluded him, but he thrust this difficulty to one side and began to collect airs from any conceivable source. He was already aware of many reactions that he knew or suspected to be such sources. These he tested using the new method for collection over water. And when he had exhausted the list, he simply worked along his shelf of substances, bottle-by-bottle, studying each in turn. He would heat each one as carefully as he could, gradually increasing the intensity of the furnace and watching for the tell-tale bubbling into the collection vessel. He did not possess a portrait of Francis Bacon, but was sure that the one-time chancellor would have smiled upon his efforts. The thought helped him resist the equivocations of Galileo who seemed to be caught between nods of approval and sardonic laughter. Once Joseph thought he caught him grinning and holding his nose.

Joseph was at once elated and frustrated. He found that he needed to cultivate a new combination of internal qualities. He had to temper the exuberance, which he customarily brought to his alchemical work, but must be careful not to extinguish it. His enthusiasm must burn slowly, steadily but brightly, illuminating the boredom of repetitive work and consuming the frustrations that arose from mistakes, accidents or – most characteristically – from nothing happening at all during days or weeks of endeavour.

A letter arrived from Fourques, this time delivered by a new courier and without unscheduled incident, enquiring after his progress with the decoding.

The letter concluded:

…….Please continue your efforts in our great cause. We wish you good fortune with the manuscripts that you are so assiduously studying. I am sure that the rewards will be commensurate with your labours and that virtue will be many times multiplied.

Your friend and fellow-voyager,
Paul Fourques.

Joseph was vaguely uneasy without being able to determine why. He had better begin assiduously to study! But he lacked further ideas of how to proceed in deciphering the documents, and the engaging problems of the vivified air kept tugging at his arm.

He kept careful notes of everything he saw. And he had added a new item to his routines. He had been told of van Helmont's five-year experiment with a young tree and how he had proved beyond doubt that the substance of the plant came only from the water supplied not from the soil. Michael had been impressed by this experiment too but had sniffed at van Helmont's conclusion. He had muttered something about it proving that air was the basis of everything, not water, but when asked what he meant, had found something urgent needing immediate attention. Joseph had gained the impression that Michael meant something but was not himself sure what it was that he meant. The lesson to be gained, Joseph thought, was not the primacy of one element or another, but the importance of weighing, not for preparation merely, but for interpretation. He had several weighing devices and used them daily in the manufacture of medicines, measuring defined amounts as prescribed in time-hallowed recipes, unlike many of his calling who measured quantities by eye. He also used them in his alchemical ventures, the success of which was deemed to be dependent upon – among many other things including the proper state of spiritual grace of the alchemist – choosing the correct quantities. This was a part of his training about which Michael had been insistent. But now he began to be interested in weighing for entirely new reasons. When for instance nitre was heated and mysteriously generated vivified air, did it gain or lose in weight. Did the vivified air itself weigh anything?

The last question was a thought wasted, since it would clearly not be possible to weigh anything as imponderable as an air.

The weeks passed by and the journey along his shelves of substances was not paralleled by a journey into new realms of knowledge. A substance heated in his retort failed to yield anything, or merely yielded itself as it condensed unchanged on the cool parts of the apparatus or collected in droplets at the surface or bottom of the water of the collecting vessel. At other times it seemed to yield some new thing that simply disappeared into the water of the collection vessel.

On one occasion his exploration along the shelf brought him to a white powder of unremarkable appearance that decomposed on heating, as he already knew it would. The water trap began to bubble, but reluctantly. Whatever it was that was produced was mostly disappearing into the water. This was becoming an event of irritating frequency. He persisted however and after some minutes, the displacement of water from the collecting vessel began to run quite freely. Soon the vessel was full. This was one of those moments that made the whole of the patient, frustrating and sometimes dangerous work worthwhile. Now he could move on to the few simple but informative tests at his disposal. He began by applying his nose, but could detect no odour. He crouched behind his shield as he tested for combustibility. The flame of the burning sliver of wood was not extinguished. Blowing out the flame and reintroducing the glowing end into the jar, he was surprised to find that the flame re-ignited, though rather more reluctantly than with the vivified air generated by the heating of nitre. Was this the vivified air again? Or another kind of vivified air? He was confused. He also felt slightly light-headed and found himself giggling at nothing in particular.

'What do you think of that, Galileo Galilei?' he demanded cheekily of the portrait, which grinned sourly, perhaps, thought Joseph, with a touch of envy.

\* \* \* \* \*

'Milk with oats. Milk with apple. Milk with bread.' The flaxen-haired boy had been complaining about the daily routine and boring meals in particular. ('Lucky to have milk at all,' Joseph had retorted.) Now he had a sudden thought. A code could work like that. Suppose that one keyword was written out repetitively beneath a message and then each letter of the keyword used to modify the corresponding letter of the message? Any particular letter of the alphabet in the original message would be represented by a different letter of the alphabet in the encoded message each time it occurred. The result would be indecipherable by all normal methods of decoding. Moreover, there would be no observable repetition of short words, a circumstance that had puzzled him in the text he had been given. His leisurely stroll home turned into a brisk walk.

In his shop, he deferred supper and instead sat down with the documents, which Fourques had given him, together with a list of possible keywords chosen upon the hopeful premise that they would be alchemical terms. He took the first keyword in the list and copied it repeatedly under the text, aligning the characters of the keyword with those of the text. Next he replaced the letters in both keyword and text by numbers representing the position of each in the alphabet. Use of such repetition by the encoder would mean that any particular letter of the alphabet used in the message, for example the letter 'd', could be represented in the cipher by any one of the remaining letters of the alphabet, or in a few instances, by itself.

A neat idea, but the initial excitement soon evaporated as the use of the first keywords yielded only a nonsense which made no more sense than the original. He had to remind himself that he was merely testing yet another possibility among many ways in which the code might have been constructed. The mundane thought allowed him to hear at last the complaints of the flaxen-haired boy that he had not had supper and was starving! After eating he returned to the task, which was now an automatic and unexciting routine. Another hour of labour passed.

Beginning with the premise that the text would be in Latin – it was plain from Fourques's descriptions that any conspiracy that existed was of an international nature and the means of communication would probably be Latin, which in any case was the familiar language of academic exchange and certainly that favoured by most alchemists. He reached 'argentum' in the list of keywords, starting again at the first word of the message. He took the first letter 'a', worked out its position in the Latin alphabet, and then did the same for the first letter of the keyword. Then he subtracted the second of these numbers from the first, made the necessary adjustment for the length of the alphabet and reassigned a letter to the resulting number, obtaining the letter 'b'. Applying the same method to the second and third letters gave 'e' and 'n'. He found himself staring at the partial word 'ben,' which had stepped out dramatically from the nonsense. That was nothing, he thought, a mere coincidence. Three letters only. He had already had sequences forming longer words, which had proved to be the chance, inconsequential meetings of a few letters. It was a possible lead though and must be examined. He continued and obtained, unmistakably, a familiar man's name.

```
a l f e l q m a f z v z z
a r g e n t u m a r g e n
b e n j a m i n g r e e n
```

He hurried on with the task in mounting excitement. Benjamin Green was the man who had attempted to abduct him from the meeting at the Baroness's house! Another hour of work and the whole letter lay before him. The language was indeed Latin. Soon he had the whole letter deciphered and rendered into English.

Benjamin Green from Jan Bynkershoek March 15 1643
The news that you bring of your conversion is welcome to me, to all of us here and, I am sure, to the angels on high and to the great God himself. I believe that, although you may not yet discern the Throne before you, one more turn of the Pilgrim's Way will bring you to a place from where you will behold with joy the light spreading from under that door to which you, and you alone, now clutch the key.

Take care, though. The Dark One lurks always in the shadows. In the hope that I may be of assistance in this ultimate passage – as I hope and believe it to be – I include with this letter instructions that we have found to be of a crucial answer to the question that such an adversary may put. Use it well and bring to it that courage and ingenuity that you have demonstrated so gloriously at all previous times,
Your loving friend
Jan Bynkershoek

Bitter disappointment followed. Using the same keyword produced nonsense. There was nothing to do but work through the list of words again. He tried seven more without success. He was tired. He was about to give up for the day, promising himself one last effort before retiring. He chose the word "aurum", picked out one of the three lettered words in the middle of a sentence by placing the keyword beneath it and working systematically through the five possible positions. The fourth one began to make sense. With hardly containable excitement, he worked back to the beginning. He could barely believe what he was seeing as the words were revealed when decoded and translated:

*Some have called him the Green Lion; to others he is the Babylonian Dragon. We speak no more...*

He translated no further. Screwing the offending piece of paper into a tight ball he hurled it in his fury at a rat which had just poked its nose out from under a cupboard door. All his brilliance and tenacity had been expended on this worthless concoction of obscurity and banality. The flaxen-haired boy, mistaking for once his mood, thought there was a fun game beginning and hurled the missile back, further enraging him. He carried the sheaf of manuscripts to the grate and was about to conduct a study of calcination. The fire was low, though. It was late. He had not bothered to add more wood. The sheets crinkled at the edges like some unfortunate heretic, but did not ignite. For some reason that he could not explain, he pulled them out of the fire and threw them into a cupboard, and trudged off, muttering, to a disgruntled bed.

The next morning he was very busy with pharmacy. He found time, however, to write to Fourques explaining the basis of the code that had been used in Bynkershoek's documents. Later in the day, as the demand eased, he found to his surprise that he had a warm glow inside as though he had just enjoyed a glass of fine brandy. Apparently his Archeus was in good repair – or his soul – or some component essential to his well-being. This was something of a surprise, especially when he identified the previous evening's work as the source of the elevation of his spirits. On reflection he realised that the intellectual satisfaction of breaking the code far out-weighed the disappointing nature of the material that had been revealed. In short, he was pleased with himself. 'And I've every right to be!' he told the flaxen-haired boy, who merely put out his tongue.

# CHAPTER 18

The skies were terrifying, although Joseph was under the impression that he was sleeping a normal sleep, in an unremarkable night, at the close of a routine day. An unearthly light seemed to grow from the wrong part of the horizon, expanding gradually from where the sun had set. It was no ordinary sunlight but was tinged with strange colours that aspired to, or tried to escape from, the colour green. It was the skyscape of twisting storms. And there were strange objects, difficult to define, moving among the viridescent clouds, perhaps birds, perhaps those strange flying craft about which that eccentric Italian artist had liked to fantasise. After a time these began to assemble themselves gradually into patterns, perhaps characters, at first misty and jumbled but gradually sorting themselves out, becoming at last clear and distinct, forming a kind of banner with huge letters which seemed to fill the whole sky,

***Truth is the daughter of humility.***

Joseph wriggled uneasily. Of what did this remind him? He watched in disbelief as more of the whirling objects appeared. He expected another message but instead the mysterious fragments began to assemble themselves into wooden spars, and then into a chair. And on the chair a vague shape, no firmer at first than an hallucination or desert mirage, so tenuous that he was not sure it was really there, began almost imperceptibly to clarify, solidify, and acquire, as humans should, a shadow. This human was a man of distinguished appearance with an intellectual head – wide brow, coruscating eyes and a luxuriant bush of white hair. He was expensively dressed, but one of his shoelaces was undone and the bottom of one trouser leg was hitched up on the sock. Surely he knew this man, had met him before, but where?

'Good evening,' said the strange visitor, coolly but courteously. 'You will probably not remember me. I am Professor…'

He spoke no further, for he was interrupted by the collapse of the chair, which disintegrated in spectacular fashion leaving him sitting on the floor amid the wreckage with a surprised look on his handsome features. From all around the great ring of the heavens came an invisible chorus of laughter, male voices, female voices, old and young. The professor examined one of the fractured legs of the chair, which had quite clearly been sabotaged with a saw-cut, and then angrily shook his fist at the laughing voices. He was still shaking it, first in one direction, then in every other in turn, in a democracy of rage, when he slowly faded away. The first message also faded. The pieces of shattered chair suddenly whirled up into the sky and rearranged themselves into a sentence, transforming at the same time into characters whose beauty would have graced an illuminated manuscript.

***Vanity of vanities; all is vanity.***

# CHAPTER 19

Several letters bearing news from France arrived in the following months, passed on to him by Paul Fourques. They were coded by the relatively simple method agreed at their meeting and in each case a new keyword for decipherment was given in a separate and prior letter.

    To Paul Fourques from Richard Costeaux                     June 3, 1646.
    Dear Paul
    The Golden Way is open. The route through the grim landscape, so long frozen, is clear after the long night of winter. Before us lies the New Eden, a land indeed flowing with milk and honey. What a prospect for mankind!
    A brilliant Star has come out of the East. Nothing comes from nothing. As we were told by the Highest Authority, talents must be put to work. But we can take the small treasure which God has given us and multiply it not twice, but ten times, a hundred times and this not once or by chance, but according to recipe. <u>Jerusalem, in her bounty, gave us the key.</u>
    We congratulate and thank from our hearts our new friend and comrade Michael Müller for his breaking of the code and providing a means by which the manuscripts that we possess could be interpreted. The clues provided have already proved invaluable. Moreover we have yet to complete our study of the manuscripts and our understanding of their symbols and images. These, we do not doubt, conceal further information crucial to the completion of our work. We hope before the year has passed that we will be able to consolidate our friendship with Michael – which we feel already exists strongly, although we have not met – by personal acquaintance. We know of course that there are many demands upon his time and talents but hope nevertheless that he might be able to accompany you when you next visit us in Toulouse. You will both be received with the greatest warmth.
    When can you come to Toulouse – to glimpse the Millennium?
    Your loving friend
                Richard Costeaux

Joseph decoded the second letter and when he had obtained the letter in its entirety, he understood what had prompted the selection of the keyword 'pyrites' – often known as 'fools' gold' – for the key.

    To Paul Fourques from Richard Costeaux                   December 15 1646
    Dear Paul
    Our greetings and our love to you from this sad place. We hope that

fortune, after spending such lavish favour upon us through the past few years, and having now deserted us entirely, may be with you instead. Alas! Our enterprise upon which the sun shone so brightly is now consumed by the darkest of nights.

But I must not talk in riddles, and instead shall explain to you the dilemma with which we are confronted. The problem is one of *reversion.* Not of ourselves, for our will and purpose remain as steadfast as ever, but of those materials with which we work, and most especially with the final product of our many years of effort. Yes, transformation of base metals into those of noble quality is possible – this much we have shown beyond doubt – but we had not reckoned with the fluidity with which these substances may inter-convert. The crystals work their ancient skills upon the Widow's Mite of gold which we donate and lo! we have multiplication – so much so that the eyes can scarcely believe the evidence of the wealth growing before them. But the worm of corruption is with them; the seed of their own destruction is there at the time of birth. For in some few month's time – nine perhaps will suffice, we see a small change in the surface aspect of the new gold, an ineffable dullness, easier to recognise than to describe, and in the course of the next weeks this terrible infection spreads ever further into the core, until the whole of the proud, once-glowing metal is degraded into a dull and worthless mass.

You may imagine that we are in despair and indeed we have been locked for long hours in that terrible dungeon. But we have by the grace of God escaped, and our determination is renewed. Now our understanding must also be refreshed. We do not know in which direction next to proceed. Perhaps there is someone who can help us, someone who can contribute that final piece of understanding. We look around us and we find few who may possess that vital spark, and no one who may possess it and with whom we feel at the same time aligned with the nobility of our aims – we seek those who have some present understanding of, or potential insight into, the corruption with which our treasure is afflicted, the scourge of apostasy to which it is subject.

We are separated from the Promised Land by a small stream just too wide to leap. If you have any knowledge that will enable us to bridge it, or possess any knife which may serve to sever the bonds of Tantalus, please bring it to us, if you continue to love us and our enterprise. We wait with impatience to hear of your health and fortunes,

Richard Costeaux.

# CHAPTER 20

*If you do but consider the whole universe as one united body, and man an epitome of this body, it will seem strange to none but madmen and fools that the stars should have influence upon the body of man, considering he, being an epitome of the Creation, must needs have a celestial world within himself... Every inferior world is governed by its superior, and receives influence from it.*
     Nicholas Culpeper


The Heavens and the Earth were One. By day the radiance of the sun stirred the dead to life as certainly as Christ had raised Lazarus. Tonight Joseph looked up through the lower spheres and saw the macrocosm in its perfection. The immense black dome of the skies testified to the glories of the Creator. It was difficult to find the path, to see where to place his next step. But then the moon came, standing above the tree tops, huge, and for a few minutes the colour of an orange, before settling to its more familiar pale but welcome light, bringing illumination and help like a mother. And above it the stars, in their unchanging patterns, symbols of eternity, arranged into constellations, shapes which reiterated and spoke almost inaudibly, so quietly that only those could hear who devoted their lives to listening. And if he looked at the skies closely enough, often enough, he would become aware of the planets, wanderers like himself, obeying laws no doubt, but not those simple laws acknowledged by the stars, obeying other rules that could be appreciated only by patient observation, through the wisdom of many years of accumulated knowledge. Above the stars again was the sphere of the Angels, the Archangels. Beyond this, unknowable, was the sphere of the Prime Mover, the Creator, of God himself.

The words of the Emerald tablet came to him:
*That which is above is from that which is below, and that which is below is from that which is above, working the miracles of one.*

Because the Heavens and the Earth were One, the life of men reflected the movements of the Heavenly bodies. The microcosm echoed the macrocosm, the echoes ringing off many cliffs, each becoming fainter and more distorted than the last. In this way the stars and the planets determined human fate. This was his understanding from childhood onwards. The accumulated wisdom of philosophers and natural philosophers through the ages supported this view. Here in the open, with the great gorge, through which the River Avon passed at last to the sea, yawning before him in the darkness like the vast gap in human knowledge, and a hint of moonlight sparkling on the tidal river below, he meditated again on the immensity of the Cosmos and the place in it of Man; its tiny, tortured creature; its minute, flawed mirror...

'First, I must ask you for the money,' said the astrologer.

Joseph blinked. 'You mean you want to be paid in advance?'

Anthony Burbage replied in his deep, gloomy tones. 'Alas my good friend, yes, in part. I deeply regret such an unpleasant necessity. You are an honest man – not only honest but one committed to the healing and well-being of your fellow men, a veritable Samaritan. One glance tells me this is so. But not all of my clients are guided by the same high principles. In my youth I was trusting – ah! how trusting!' He sighed deeply and Joseph wondered whether he was about to weep. 'And I lost such a proportion of my just reward that sometimes I went to bed hungry at night. And so I made this rule. One half in advance, and one on completion of my services.'

'That is a fair policy,' agreed Joseph, adding cheekily, 'but it is a lot of money. I could look up the tables myself if only I had the time.'

'Ah, but my friend, you do not have the time, nor the access to the tables, nor the expertise to read them or the experience to interpret them.'

'That is true. I was being unfair. I would complain bitterly if one of my patients grumbled at my charge because he had once cured his aunt of a headache by brewing herbal tea. What do I need to provide for you?'

'Only the day and place of your birth. I suppose that you know them. And the time – that is important. Most people – even the most humble – know the day of their birth, but the hour – ah, my friend that is different – that is a time of doubtfully competent, usually illiterate midwives, of confusion, of anxiety, of celebration, a time of foolish, sometimes drunken gossips, of the whole village craning in at the doors, and no one – but no one in all the raucous, ignorant throng noting the time. And where is the priest who should be available to conduct an urgent baptism if the child seems unlikely to survive its first hours – an all too frequent eventuality – and to record the birth? Best not to ask – he will be punished eventually.' His tone became luxuriously mournful. 'And then they expect descriptions, predictions, advice and the Lord knows what else.'

That was Joseph's first meeting with Burbage. The next steps to be made in the study of the vivified air still eluded him. He lacked any real confidence that his new way of study, with its requirement for utter devotion to minuscule properties of the natural world was worth the frustration, the bewilderment, and the probable irrelevance to the World's practical concerns that accompanied it. Important decisions must be taken. Paul Fourques had answered his letter, and had congratulated him in effusive terms on his success in deciphering the letter. He was not short of suggestions. Fourques wanted him to travel with him to Toulouse to decode the manuscripts and – more excitingly – study the red-gold liquid with its mysterious crystals. The enterprise was attractive but smelt dangerous, and it was to try to explore its likely success and to discuss the most favourable times for departure that he had come to consult Anthony Burbage. Two weeks after his first visit he returned to the astrologer's residence to benefit from his research and deliberations. Burbage greeted him in his customary style, speaking as though to the most remote audience in the gallery of the theatre.

'Ah! Mr Edwards! I am glad to see you again. I trust you are well. For you I must be clear, brief and exact. You will not tolerate anything less, for you were born when the sun was in Virgo and as such you are a devoted life-long self-improver, intent upon acquiring further skills. You need precise information, not vague assertions or opinions based on emotional judgements.'

Burbage's conversion to brevity struck Joseph as one of the less probable events of the week, but he was suitably impressed by the sketch of his character, which was both accurate and relevant.

'That is correct, and I am confident that you will provide it.'

'The Ruler of Virgo is Mercury, the winged messenger, fleet of foot, who passes to the farthest corners of the Cosmos before we can blink or think, and who appears anywhere and everywhere. Remarkably, on the Fifteenth day of September, in the Year of Our Lord 1614 – on the day of your birth, Mercury was placed in the constellation of Virgo, reinforcing its influence upon your life. One cannot tell definitely – one must always take into account the disposition of the other heavenly influences present at birth, but we can say that the people of Virgo may be destined to travel often and far. Their journeys may well be for the purposes of communication, usually of those matters which are the subject of their inner intensity. You, I believe, are particularly talented, particularly successful in the exchange of knowledge with your fellow men.'

Joseph replied, 'I have travelled a lot. But your assessment of the purpose of these wanderings does me too much credit. Sometimes they are made for the purposes of acquiring knowledge or imparting it, but mostly to escape from some difficult situation, sometimes from physical danger. As for communication, my desire to communicate is very much greater than my achievement. Sometimes I think that I am a total failure in this respect. For some reason which I find difficult to analyse, my intentions and indeed my plans to share my knowledge, apparently well-conceived, seem frequently to be turned aside by unforeseen, sometimes by unseen, obstacles.'

Burbage was not at all put out by this unexpected reverse. He frowned purposefully and ostentatiously over his notes for a minute or so. The silence was so concentrated that Joseph felt that the faint susurration of his own breathing was an improper intrusion. Suddenly Anthony Burbage's face was illuminated by a revelation and inspiration worthy of an Old Testament prophet.

'Tell me,' he said. 'The problem is that, much as you wish to, you finally turn aside from imparting your message?'

'It is not that exactly. I enjoy speaking with those whom I meet. I enjoy discussion and argument. I feel there to be no obstacle on my side.'

The astrologer leaned forward portentously. 'Ah, but do those, with whom you attempt to discuss and argue, understand what you are trying to share with them?'

'Frequently not. Sometimes they do not even understand my questions. Sometimes I do not understand my questions myself. And this began early. I recall that one evening, when still a very small boy, I was walking home with my parents, several miles through the meadows. I noticed that, while everything else in the landscape moved in position as we walked – a tree, for instance, was in front of us, then above us, then behind – the moon stayed always in the same direction, apparently in the same place. 'Mummy,' I asked, 'why haven't we walked past the moon?' 'Don't be silly, dear,' said my mother who had clearly not comprehended my difficulty and had probably suffered long hours of infant babble. I was sufficiently aggrieved at this response to have remembered the incident to this day.'

'And this, said Anthony, 'I think became a pattern for your life? Most especially in regard to those closest to you. Do you have a wife?'

'Yes. In Poland. She does not understand me.'

'You are lucky. Mine understands me too well!' Burbage allowed himself a sonorous chuckle, then added sentimentally, 'Bless her!' He tapped his notes dramatically.

'It is all here. I should have understood your difficulty immediately. But I am under such pressure. So much work. So many clients. Ah! my friend, these are bad times...'

'When were they not bad?'

Burbage ignored the interjection.

'...Civil war, Royalists and Parliamentarians, a treasonable House of Commons, divided families, unrest, strife in every community. And illness – you must yourself be in the centre of that affliction – the pest, the ague. And the King – our blessed King! – in danger, imprisoned, his life threatened maybe, by the very subjects he has fought long and hard to protect. I am glad to tell you that the signs of the heavens favour a long and prosperous life for him and triumph over his enemies. So many difficulties and dangers. So many come to me – I cannot describe to you in what state of anxiety – fearful for the future, asking my help. I do my best for them. But I am overborne, almost, with work. I overlooked an important feature of the day of your birth. Of course, all is clear now. Mercury, the Ruler of Virgo, was on the day of your birth, in Virgo but moving with retrograde motion, as it had been for several days and would be for some further time.'

Joseph was not overjoyed at the news of King Charles's longevity, but on account of the need to plan his future moves as best he could, and remembering the shillings he had committed to the purpose, he chose not to admit his doubts. Instead he asked for a clarification of the significance of a planet heading in the wrong direction, against the general stream as it were, like the Sectaries. Burbage continued:

'The planets vary in the frequency and length of their retrograde passage, but for one or another to be in that state is common. It is not necessarily a bad sign, but it is a signal to exercise caution. It is good at that time to pause and reflect upon those parts of our lives that are affected by that particular star. And when we are born under a retrograde, especially the Ruler of our birth sign, we may expect a life-long difficulty, or at least equivocation, in those areas of our activity. In your case, communication particularly may present problems of unusual difficulty which you may, with reward, address with great care. Your past experience, especially the experience with your mother and the moon – which in another sense is mother to us all – supports my conclusion, and was certainly a Heaven-sent warning to you of a problem which might attend you throughout your life.'

'I thank you for drawing my attention to this point.'

'I have not yet spoken of the Moon. This is a sign almost as important as the Sun, or more so. On the day when you assumed our mortal cloth – it was rising from the half to the full. This circumstance invariably influences creativity in a most positive manner. And, on the day of your birth, not only was Mercury in Virgo – as I have said – but Jupiter also, with the happy result that you will have been the fortunate recipient of two great powers – the force and expansiveness of the greatest of the gods with the delicacy of insight and precision in performance that lies in the gift of the shining maiden. The stars speak with one voice – your destiny is that of the pioneer, though it may be your lot to fight grimly for the recognition and understanding of your fellow men – to fight grimly even to be heard.

'Were any other planets adverse in the manner of Mercury?'

'Saturn was the only other planet in retrogression. But this is a minor influence for you and, in any case, this planet is so frequently retrogressive – four months or so in every eighteen months – that these periods of reversion are of less effect. It weakens an already weak case, so to speak, by going on too long and too often – like Ireton and Cromwell and the rest of the Parliamentary rabble.'

'And have you considered also the matter of when I should set out on a journey which embodies also a hazardous enterprise.'

'Mercury – to whom, as I have said, you should pay particular attention – is retrograde quite frequently, but for short times only. The next occasion is on the tenth of May and lasts until the twenty-fourth. Avoid that period for your departure. The present time might also not be propitious. Jupiter and Mars are both retrograde, Jupiter until March the twenty-second, Mars until the fifth of the same month. Jupiter who attended your birth must be especially considered.

'Thank you for work on my behalf.'

Joseph had been extraordinarily impressed by the accuracy of the astrologer's description of his personality, allegedly read from the stars. But he was reminded of something from his own past? Of course! – Bob Nob Job!

He had watched that virtuoso performer in metoposcopy assess young Isaac's character and potential from a few scraps of conversation, then solemnly deliver his conclusions as though he had read them in the child's cranium. Was this not the same trick, but worked by the talented Anthony Burbage and attributed to the stars? Then against this was the fact that he had himself noted long ago, and wondered over, the accord between his own temperament and the characteristics traditionally considered typical of one born under the sign of Virgo. He had not even needed Burbage to draw his attention to this strange coupling.

'Sir,' he said, 'I have the greatest respect for your learning, but can I really be certain that our temperament and our fate are written in the starry skies? How can it be that these beautiful but remote lights can affect the constitution of our minds and influence our lives? There are those who entirely deny this as a possibility and I believe that your English poet had said "it is not in our stars, but in ourselves, that we are underlings".'

'He was correct to a point,' said Burbage gravely. 'We are indeed underlings but we are underlings to whom God has granted free choice. The problems of our temperament to which the stars are infallible pointers are not inexorable determinants leaving us no choice. They draw attention to our virtues, that we may empower them, and to our difficulties, that we may assuage them. And the great art of astronomy draws upon the experience of many centuries, marrying the intellectual penetration of the Greek philosophers, fifteen hundred years ago, to the accrued understanding of the Magi of Persia, extending back many more centuries still.'

'Then there is nothing more to learn of the relationship of man's destiny to the stars and planets?'

'The essentials were determined by the Ancients, by the accretion of wisdom of the East, of Ancient Egypt and the great Hellenic civilisation. Men lived nearer to God in those days, who are now foolish and corrupt.'

'Then the art is not only surely founded, but no further additions of real substance are necessary or possible. It is not only true, it is exhaustive?'

'That is so.'

'But I have a difficulty here. We know that Galileo turned a glass on the skies and found that Jupiter has moons. Could it not be that soon – perhaps even this very night – with the aid of an improved instrument – another planet will be discovered. And this planet must surely, as Jupiter, Saturn and the other planets do, have been exerting its influence upon our birth and our subsequent destinies?'

Anthony Burbage answered confidently.

'That is impossible. There is no other planet. Of this you can be sure. There is no room for it.'

'There is a whole sky waiting for it!'

'That is an answer, if I may say so, at the most trivial level. There is no room for another planet. There are ten spheres. The most lowly is the sphere of the earth and the four elements. Above them we have the seven planetary spheres of Lunar, Mercury, Venus, Sun, Mars, Jupiter and Saturn. Above again is the ninth sphere of the fixed stars. Above all things again is the Primum Mobile. There is no room for another planet.'

'But why ten? What is so special about ten?'

'Ten is agreed by all the wise. The Greeks knew that ten, being the sum of one, two, three and four – one, the minimum required to define a point, two for a line, three for a plane, and four for a solid – is of the greatest importance. Ten therefore encompasses all things. The Egyptians divided the year into decans, intervals of ten days each signalled by the passage of a new star over the horizon at dawn. God through Moses issued ten Commandments. The Sephiroth of the Cabala has ten names or spheres as does the Universe of Aristotle. Ten is the number on which all calculation is based. The mundane, physical expression of this great number is seen in our possession of ten fingers.'

'Perhaps there are ten elements, not three or four,' muttered Joseph, half to himself.

'I beg your pardon.'

'Merely a foolish thought, relating to my own discipline. Does not the displacement of the earth from the centre of the macrocosmos create difficult problems for astrological philosophy?'

The answer was contemptuous.

'If you are referring to the theories of that foolish Pole' – here Burbage paused in slight confusion and added hastily, 'an unworthy representative of a great people!' before resuming as forcefully as ever – 'then my advice to you is to reject such theories. Have nothing to do with them.'

'You sound like the Roman Inquisition!'

'Not at all. The structure of the earth and the heavens was settled for once and all by the great observer, Tycho Brahe. He established beyond doubt that the planets, excepting the earth, move in circles around the sun, which, in its turn, revolves about the earth. The earth is at the centre of all things!'

## CHAPTER 21

The apothecary walked home from the astrologer's house through a night of unsurpassed beauty. A frosty clarity abnormal in the moist atmosphere of the west showed the constellations at their best. His own protectress, Virgo, was not visible. She was cautiously approaching from below the eastern horizon. Ahead of her were a Lion and a Crab of similar size but of uncertain scale and temper, so that it was best to move with care, especially as a Scorpion – in tradition her particular enemy – moved with a steady purpose not far behind. Further to the west was the magnificent Orion. He had acquired a shining dagger and, like any man or army possessing a fine new weapon, was certainly seeking an opportunity to use it. He would soon stick it into something, without a doubt. Behind him ran his terrible dogs, one small but fierce and cunning, the other stupid but large and strong. Almost beneath Orion's feet was Lepus, the hare, who surely stood little chance. He was destined for the pot. Ahead the seven sisters of the Pleiades, and the rest, glanced anxiously over their shoulders at the hunter. They were all too aware of the reputation of Greek gods and demi-gods who made hectic love, which was fine, but tended to forget to ask permission first, which was not. And the ravishers' fertility was legendary. They never failed. Pregnancy was a mixed blessing, and who fancied a man made out of urine anyway?

The skies to the east showed few stars. Joseph was familiar with the comparative paucity of stars in the groups that followed Leo across the heavens. God had not been even-handed in distributing stars. Come to think of it, God had not been even-handed in distributing anything. The comparative dearth of stars eastwards was accentuated by a glow in the sky that seemed to emanate from the ground, a glow that Joseph had seen elsewhere but, being deep in thought, did not immediately recognise.

Joseph took himself to task for his undisciplined imagination. It was a recurrent problem. He had given up trying to suppress it. He hoped that it might prove to be an important, if uncomfortable, component of his talents. He directed his mind back from the celestial drama to the interview with Anthony Burbage. He had won an intellectual battle or two in their closing discussion but probably could be said to have lost the campaign. He was annoyed that he not thought quickly enough to point out that Tycho Brahe's and Copernicus's systems were geometrically almost identical. Ah! The arguments and witticisms, the rejoinders, wise words and jokes that one thinks of when walking down the street afterwards! But his main purpose had been accomplished. He had the astrologer's opinion concerning the proper time to start his new venture.

But his mood was radiant. The magnificence and mystery of the night sky reminded him of the convictions he had held from childhood on. The harmony of the world, recognised by Pythagoras and Plato, supported and sustained the mundane world and the heavens above. Kepler had tried to relate the musical intervals to the motion of the planets. Surely the great astronomer must have been correct, at least in principle. The conviction – that all things are interlinked and joined together in one great anthem – had begun to penetrate Joseph's work. Beneath the apparent chaos of facts that had emerged from studies of his predecessors across the centuries, and the new but confusing discoveries he himself was making, must lie an order that could be ascertained by patient endeavour. One day, the harmony would be heard, understood and written down, perhaps even sung.

He was nearer home now, and suddenly emerged from his deliberations with alarm. The mysterious red glow had intensified, and was no longer a steady stain on the sky. It flickered dangerously and it smelled and crackled. Something was seriously on fire – and in the district where he lived and worked. Inadvertently he began to walk faster. The closer he drew to the blaze, the more it centred upon his own neighbourhood. Rounding a final corner, he found himself among a great throng. It was not a house on fire; it was a whole street. People in various stages of agitation or panic, were running, standing, swearing, pulling possessions out of their houses, carrying pathetic buckets of water, desperately searching for children, parents or friends or just standing about like statues paralysed by the scale of the disaster. It was not just the remainder of the street that was threatened – the whole town was at risk. The fire had spread rapidly along the houses on the bridge and was heading thirstily for the main town with its narrow streets and closely packed houses. Warehouses loaded with riches, some of them inflammable, and innumerable churches lay in its path. It was obvious to Joseph where the fire might eventually stop – at the far end of the city when it ran out of buildings to use as fuel. Fortunately others had anticipated this danger too. Because the city possessed a wealth of optimism, a renowned reluctance to spend money and in consequence no fire-carts, a gang of men had begun to take the only action possible to confine the fire. They were busy dismantling houses at both ends of the street to create a space the flames might not cross. They had fetched the grappling hooks, fixed on poles or ropes, which were kept especially for the purpose of making fire-breaks. They pushed aside the protests of the owners and, when necessary, the owners themselves. There was no need to dismantle the apothecary's shop. All that remained of it was a smoking pile of ashes and rubble among which occasional flames still licked from the larger beams of wood frustratedly seeking something else to consume. Joseph fought his way through the crowds as best he could. The protective walls and rails at the sides of the bridge had been burned away and he nearly suffered the same fate as an unfortunate woman who had been apparently inadvertently pushed from the unprotected sides into the river below. Hindered by the press of people and the heat from the burning buildings, Joseph could not get close to his shop, but he came near enough to see that nothing was retrievable. His only possessions now were the things that he had with him in the street.

When later in his life he looked back on the few hours following the discovery of the wreckage of his home and livelihood, he found it very difficult to recover the state of his mind or to account for his actions. Certainly he was stunned and for a few minutes wandered distractedly about the street. Eventually he found himself staring vacantly at the squad of men who were dismantling one of the houses towards which the inferno was steadily and purposefully working. Suddenly he was pushed roughly in the back and a voice said, 'Don't just stand there like a turd in a tuft!'

With this he returned suddenly to the world where people lived and where they died, often prematurely, and joined the gang, mostly volunteers, who were stripping wood and slate from the top of the house that was to be the first line of defence in the fire gap. Joseph noticed several of the elite from the City administration, bustling about being useful or not, getting in the way or not, attempting to comfort those who had lost homes with the promise that they would receive help and – more imaginatively still – reassuring those whose houses were threatened that further help was at hand. The real hero was a man whom few people knew. He was obviously a builder with a thorough knowledge of the construction of the houses and therefore of their dismantling. His usual unassuming manner dropped away and was replaced by a calm authority, which probably he had not known himself capable of, as he welded the random collection of individuals into an efficient team. He had ordered tools to be fetched from his own and other workshops. Hammers, axes and crowbars were arriving and being handed around. Joseph found himself carrying tiles, beams and panels and other materials from the summit of the fast-diminishing structure to waiting carts and sledges which had been hastily fetched from the nearby warehouses, or, when transport was not available, simply dragging them along the street to a safe distance. The scene was apocalyptic. The noise of the fire and the shouts of the crowd were deafening; the gusts of smoke and heat blew in waves along the street.

Now it was far into the night. The dismantling was not finished, but Joseph was. He was close to exhaustion but now there was a sufficiency of helpers engaged on the task of confining the fire. It looked as though the race would be won. The fire-gap would be completed in time and the rest of the city would be safe. He sat down in a doorway for some minutes and then, slightly recovered, got up and began to wander again with no clear purpose and nowhere to go. He found himself at the end of the line of burning houses. The fire had by no means abandoned its enthusiasm for masonry and wood, especially wood. Bucket lines had been organised to bring water up from the river below. These were at first poured on to the fire, into which they disappeared with no perceptible effect – discounting a spectacular hiss. Later they were emptied more realistically on to the threatened but still unkindled houses – preventative medicine, thought Joseph. He watched in horrified fascination as the fire spread to an adjacent house. A few flames licked speculatively at the next prospective meal for some minutes, apparently without any real appetite. So little happened for some minutes that he almost began to wonder whether the fire would peter out. Then quite suddenly a panel of wood burst into flames and in a few moments the whole room became an inferno. Nothing the inhabitants of the street could do was successful. The mood was close to hysteria.

As he turned away from the house, which was now thoroughly ablaze, he collided with a young man who was standing with a group of men and women who had collected behind him. Some of them had empty buckets in their hands. Saving the house was no longer an option. A woman was weeping bitterly and several others, men included, were in a state of distress. He was trying to thread his way through the group when the youth with whom he had collided suddenly shouted out, 'it's him! It's the man from the house where the fire started!'

Joseph stared in disbelief at the youth. The young man's face seemed familiar although he could not tell why. It was bad enough that his house had been burned and with it his livelihood. The news, if it were true, that the destruction of the whole street had begun in his shop was truly terrible. His mind flashed back to his departure this morning. Had he been negligent in any way? He was relieved to find his conscience to be clear. No furnaces had been lit, nor any fires for warmth. All candles had been extinguished. He was meticulous about such matters. The small crowd found a new focus and began to crowd around him.

'It's him! He started the fire. I've seen him try to do it before.'

Joseph remembered – this was the young courier with whom he had an altercation interrupted by an explosion. He replied with an exasperation born of anxiety, and in his unfortunate mid-European accent,

'Don't be ridiculous. It has nothing to do with me. I've been out all day. I got back here only this evening.'

This fuelled another fire, and not of houses this time.

'Hark at the way he talks! He's not English!'

'Yes. Spanish. I know their way of speaking anywhere.'

'Spanish, that's right. He's from Holland.'

'From France, you fool.'

'Huguenot scum.'

'Huguenots are all right. They're against the Pope, like us.'

'They take our work!'

'He's a spy.'

'A Jesuit snake.'

'A stinking Royalist!'

The last accusation was more controversial and left several of the crowd glaring at each other. Joseph liked to consider himself both cosmopolitan and eclectic, but the crowd's attributions of his nationalities and religions were excessive. The mood was nasty and dangerous like dry-distilling nitre. It needed only one more aggressive individual to take action and his limbs or even his life might be in danger. One such person was indeed available. A red-faced man, with arms like a butcher's, took a step forward.

Fortunately for Joseph, if not for the residents of the next house in line, whatever it was that the crowd was thinking of doing to him was forestalled by a massive roar as the roof and upper storeys of the fire's latest victim, the property nearest to them, blew up in a massive fireball and then collapsed. A blast of heat scattered the crowd, and everyone, including Joseph, was showered with a drifting storm of red-hot flecks and black smuts. Joseph spent half a minute brushing pieces of burning material from his clothing before he was able to take advantage of the diversion of attention away from him. Luckily his accusers were occupied with the same task. This was his cue for exit. He stole away through the gust of smoke that followed the fire-storm, walking with large steps and on tip-toe, as if he was stealing out of the bedroom of a troublesome child who had at last fallen asleep, although an army with iron boots would not have been heard in the din of fire and fire-fighters. He did think however that he heard someone shout 'after him!' and at this point broke into a run, pushing through the mix of helpers, dispossessed and voyeurs as fast as he could.

He was away from the area of the fire and paused, gasping for breath, to listen. There was no doubt. He was being pursued and by someone who knew how to run. Fast running footsteps were approaching, fetching echoes off the walls of the buildings in the narrow street. He set off again and tried to accelerate, but succeeded only in slowing down. From the sound of the steps there appeared to be only one pursuer. The man was obviously more athletic, or had not spent the last few hours wrestling with pieces of building. The footsteps were now close behind him and catching up fast. It would be only a matter of seconds before he was caught. There was no other choice but to turn and confront the enemy. He stopped suddenly, swung round with crouched body, clenched fists, raised arms and an ugly snarl, generally trying to look as formidable as possible. He had assumed this attitude on a few occasions before – he called it the Trapped Bear. The prognosis was bad – the man was tall and powerfully built. Joseph's pugnacious attitude counted for little. The man grasped his right arm in a strong grip that immobilised it. Joseph was about to punch him with his free fist when he realised that the hold on his arm was not unfriendly. In fact his hand was being shaken in an enthusiastic and comradely fashion. The man spoke in a rough but amiable voice with a heavy local accent.

'Congratulations. That was a wonderful piece of work. But you should have burned down the whole God-forsaken town!'

'I did not start the fire,' protested Joseph angrily.

The strange man glanced along the street in the direction of the conflagration. A sound of pounding feet – not of one person only, but of many – was growing louder every moment.

'There is no time for modesty. They are after you. Down here. Follow me.'

They burrowed into a darkness of alleyways and packed houses, following a route that led first back towards the river, downstream from the fire. It divided and subdivided among warehouses and dockside offices. No one was going to follow them through this maze and they were soon, to Joseph's relief, able to adopt a leisurely walking pace. He was thoroughly lost but his companion was obviously familiar with the area. They snaked away from the river again to the oldest part of the city, a district of narrow streets and dense housing punctuated liberally by churches. At the door of one of the houses, the stranger paused and with a nod gestured Joseph to enter. There seemed nowhere else to go. They climbed two flights of stairs to a floor consisting mostly of small rooms. One door however opened into an unexpectedly large space. Three of the smaller rooms had been converted to one larger chamber. This was empty except for a lectern at one end that looked as if it might have begun its days in a small church, and this, together with the size of the room and absence of other furniture, suggested use for meetings or religious services of some kind. The lectern was much too large and grand for the modest room. It announced in beautifully carved words, but without conviction, "Church of the Holy Trinity".

Joseph could now see his companion clearly. The hat was an exceptionally large affair clearly intended to make a loud, if ill-defined statement of some kind. Its size and shape reminded him of a vessel from his laboratory.

He made two mercy missions on Joseph's behalf. The first was to bring him water to drink. The other was in the form of a straw palliasse, which he threw on the floor. Joseph acknowledged their delivery eagerly and in the most practical manner, drinking thirstily and then sinking with relief on to the bedding.

His rescuer, who was a man of few words, spoke for the first time since their brief struggle in the street.

'Tell me' he said, 'did you use gunpowder or lamp oil or just knock a candle over? But I believe that you have a special formula.'

There was no answer. Joseph was already asleep.

# CHAPTER 22

The strong light of mid-morning and the sound of deep voices, insufficient alone, together woke Joseph from his sleep in the corner of the strange house. Two men had entered the room along with the man who had befriended him during the night. A question was put to the latter by one of the strangers.

'Sid, this must be the man who lost his house in the fire?'

'Yes,' said Sid. 'It began in his house. He started it.'

'Nonsense, you useless toad. I know this man. This is Ed Fords, the apothecary. He is a good fellow. He treated my cousin and aunt for no fee and putting himself at risk too.'

Joseph arose unsteadily to his feet. His head felt like a baked chicken, which had been stuffed by a taxidermist rather than a chef.

'Arthur Goodrich,' the speaker announced, shaking Joseph's hand warmly.

'How are your cousin and aunt now?' enquired Joseph.

'Dead.'

Joseph muttered his regrets.

'You did what you could. The Lord had spoken. And plague has no respect for victims, nor for apothecaries or for their medicines.'

Sid was not defeated yet.

'Well, he may be an apothecary, but the fire started in his shop, didn't it?'

'You unreformed twit! Would a man start a fire by burning down his own house?'

'He might,' said Sid, sullenly.

'Well, *you* might I suppose, you gormless poltroon.'

Arthur turned to Joseph. 'Don't mind him. He's harmless really. He's never set a fire in his life except in his own hearth. It's just his diseased imagination. His ancestors must have been incendiaries of the top class and it's left some sort of stain in his mind. They set fire to Troy, Carthage, Rome and Alexandria, I shouldn't wonder, and would have burned down the Holy Christian city of Constantinople if the Roman Catholic Church hadn't done it first.'

A dark doubt crossed Arthur's mind. 'You're not a papist, are you?'

'No. I am an Antediluvianarian.'

'Sir, every day I lament my wretched ignorance and the discriminatory education system which has deprived me of the learning which should be mine by right. I regret that I have no knowledge of Antediluvianarians or of their beliefs. I am hearing of them for the first time.'

This was not surprising. Joseph also was hearing of them for the first time. He replied, 'please do not address me as 'sir'. It pays me too much respect. I too regret the paucity of my own knowledge. In fact the more knowledge I acquire, the more I realise the depths of my ignorance – or perhaps I should say, the depths of *our* ignorance. But I think that you greatly exaggerate your lack of erudition. I have already noticed that you are acquainted with the history of the Ancient World and with the Crusades, the Fourth in particular, and of their disgracefully mixed motives.'

This little preamble was a genuine compliment to Arthur Goodrich towards whom Joseph intuitively warmed. It also gave him a little time to think what an Antediluvianarian might be, in anticipation of the next question which followed immediately.

'What in general does an Antidiluvianarian believe?'

Joseph cursed the little demon that provoked him to these fantasies, trapping him in tight corners.

'You will be familiar,' he said, 'with the words which God spoke to Noah as the flood-waters receded.'

'Of course,' said Arthur, 'Genesis chapter eight. While the Earth remaineth, seed time and harvest, and cold and heat, and summer and winter, and day and night, shall not cease.'

'Exactly,' said Joseph. 'We do not dispute of course that these words were spoken. We do not question their good faith. We believe indeed that the seasons will continue with their potentiality for fruitfulness. But we think that the words have been misinterpreted in the sense that men have since underestimated the extent to which the Creator requires them to apply their hands and minds to the Earth's continuing fecundity. And most particularly their minds.' (Francis Bacon was riding to Joseph's rescue.) 'The name of the movement is perhaps unfortunate in that it may suggest a movement backward in time and man's attitude to knowledge.'

Before Arthur Goodrich had time to reply, another voice broke in to the conversation. 'There is no point, no purpose at all in trying to improve our lot.'

Joseph had not noticed that the room was beginning to fill up with people. All were dressed in the normal Puritan style of the day, especially the large hat, which they all removed on entering the unprepossessing room.

'Why is there no point nor purpose?' asked Joseph after Arthur Goodrich had introduced him to the newcomer whose name was Robert Forsythe. 'Do you not believe it possible to advance our understanding of God's world and for example to find ways of avoiding the bad harvests which are causing us so much hunger, misery and even death?'

'It may be possible but it is not desirable. Or rather it is not relevant. It would be desirable if we had time. But there is no time left. Time itself is coming to Harvest. And there will be misery and death for many. It is the event that we should hunger for. It is all written here.' He held up with a flourish a worn Bible, which flew open obligingly at a page where it had been opened many times before. 'One thousand, two hundred and sixty days is the rule of Antichrist. The days are years. And the identity of Antichrist needs no explanation. We need name no names concerning Antichrist.'

'The Roman Catholic Church?' suggested Joseph unnecessarily.

'Exactly. Of course.'

'I understand you,' said Joseph. 'I have written in my youth on this subject myself. I still have the manuscript.' The enormity of what had happened to him had not yet registered in his mind. He corrected himself. 'Or I did until last night. The difficulty I found was not in the attribution of characters, especially not of Antichrist, nor were the interpretations of time and the calculations of lapsed time difficult. The problem lay in decision as to which was the appropriate year to calculate from.'

'That also is written here with clarity'

Joseph was less than assured by the speaker's notion of clarity. He was not sure that he wanted to know. But he was going to hear about it anyway.

'The true beginnings of the Catholic Church, so called, can be traced back to the year 387. Not to the year of Nicea, 325, although the disgraceful manœuvrings of the elders of the Church at that infamous meeting generated the false doctrine of the Trinity, a wholly unbiblical but characteristic Catholic invention.'

'I admire your thinking.' Arthur Goodrich had rejoined the conversation. 'Christ will certainly return to hold the World to account. But I am not so sure about your mathematics. Did you not collect us all together on that mountain in Cambria seven years ago, praying and awaiting the great event? And what happened? A serene spring day of great beauty, with the birds in their most triumphant voice. It was a memorable few days in the Welsh wilderness celebrating the beauty of the World that our Lord has given us. I learned a new appreciation of God's munificence towards us, of the wonders of the forests and mountains. But what happened? Nothing!'

'I was young then and lacked experience. Now I understand things which have gradually been revealed to me. Christ's return requires preparation. It will not happen suddenly, all at once and unheralded. In the same wise as Babylon gained her power so shall she lose it. By inches. By the barleycorn. And the rood. Then the furlong and mile. And the process has started. It is there for all to see who will. Just as it is difficult to determine when Rome gained its foul influence over the true Church, so it is hard to determine when its powers will end. But I have done so. You say that nothing happened. But that is not correct. It did happen. But not in the Welsh mountains. In Parliament in London.'

'You are referring to the reconvening of Parliament after eleven years? That hardly earns the picturesque imagery of the Book of Revelations.'

'Symmetry,' said the young man mysteriously. 'Apocalyptic symmetry. The pattern can be traced through history if we study it. The stone rises, reaches its zenith, then must fall. What is the date when the true church was reborn?'

'No doubt of it,' replied Arthur Goodrich. '1517. When Martin Luther manufactured the Catholic coffin by banging nails into the church door at Wittenberg.'

'Of course. And in the year 257, one thousand two hundred and sixty years before, Stephen, who already dared to call himself 'Pope,' declared that he, as the Bishop of Rome, held authority in doctrinal matters over the universal church. It was the first grasp at the throat of the Christian Fathers. It was the foundation stone of Babylon. And as it was made, so must it crumble.'

'I think I take your meaning. There was timed plan for its building and another, which mirrors it, for its destruction. But what event provoked our journey to Wales to await the great return?'

'In the Year of our Lord three hundred and eighty-two, Damasius, another infamous Bishop of Rome, at a synod held in that city, made the hegemony of that accursed city an official act. Twelve hundred and sixty years later, in the year 1642, the time when you say that nothing happened, the walls of Babylon were breached. The Lord took up arms against the King and, through him, the Pope. Those who would revert to the ways Antichrist and restore his powers were confronted by the armies of God.'

'And the next development, what will that be. What is the next reflection in your mirror?'

'The synods of Chalcedon and Ephesus, where the Catholic heresy of the nature of Christ were finally established, bring us to 1691 and 1711. I feel that Babylon cannot survive longer than that.'

Joseph noticed that more and more people were coming into the room. They looked purposeful, sometimes conspiratorial.

'Is there to be a meeting here?'

'Yes. Actually an act of worship might perhaps be a better description.'

The wretched imp of mischief once more went to work on Joseph's left ear. He said, with a gesture towards the lectern.

'Oh, I see. A Divine Service. This must be the Church of the Holy Trinity!'

Arthur looked deeply embarrassed. 'Not exactly. The lectern was donated by the Church of the Holy Trinity.'

A new voice spoke up from behind Joseph.

'Yes. In the middle of the night. They found out the following morning about the donation they had made.'

The accusation was made by a newcomer who had approached the group unnoticed.

'But that is theft of consecrated property,' protested Joseph.

'Consecrated property, my arse,' replied the young man. 'It was desecrated property. It was the property of the Whore of Babylon. It was a prisoner of the Antichrist. We have rescued it.'

Another young man, who was introduced as David Jack, was nodding enthusiastically and Joseph guessed that both men had participated in the mission to release the prisoner. He expressed a reasonable doubt.

'Surely though, the Church of the Holy Trinity is a member of the Reformed Church of England which dissociated itself a century ago from the Church of Rome, risking invasion, bloodshed and oppression as it did so?'

'Reformed!' David Jack answered with a sneer. 'As reformed as my cock. Which never gives up trying. Always plotting and planning. Rome will be back in its full hideousness, if Charles has his way – back by the back door – or the front.'

'It has never truly gone away,' said the Revelations expert.

'No – by Christ!' The lectern rescuer spat enthusiastically and copiously on the floor, to the evident discomfort of Arthur Goodrich. 'They have substituted one load of idols for another.'

'We believe that The Church of England has only gone half way in its reforms.'

'Half way.' The young man spat again. 'It's hardly begun.'

Joseph became aware that the source of Arthur Goodrich's disapprobation was not only the manners and language of the young men. He whispered to Joseph. 'This happened only last night. When everyone was distracted by the fire.'

'Tell them to take it away again,' suggested Joseph simplistically. 'Or change the inscription.'

'I have no authority to do so.'

'Well, talk to the person who *has*.'

'There is no such person. All actions here are taken by vote or at least by an evident consensus.'

Joseph tried to visualise how this might work but his imagination failed him. The Athenians had tried it, and look what happened to them. A small crowd had gathered around the lectern, some admiring it.

'Are we now called the Church of the Holy Trinity?'

'Over my dead body.'

'Lovely carving, innit?'

'Three Gods is Catholic heresy.'

'The Fathers said nothing about three.'

'Nor the Bible either. I've read it.'

'A chair's good enough to stand on, or a box.'

A slight diminution in the noise in the room, which had been growing steadily for some minutes, and a perturbation in the doorway, signalled an event of some sort. Arthur Goodrich muttered an apology to Joseph. 'Our speaker,' he said, 'You shall meet him.'

He hurried to the door. Many of those present also wished to meet the speaker and crowded around the doorway. They were eager to offer opinions, to give advice or ask for it, to question, to harangue, and it was some time before Joseph was able to get a clear sight of – preacher, priest, minister, incendiary? – of the man who was to address them. His attention was suddenly arrested by a new voice at his elbow.

'By Christ, we shall have some fun today.'

'How is that?' asked Joseph. 'I thought this was a serious meeting, for worship even.'

'Some may think so. But you keep an eye on Frank Peet – Frank Prank, we call him. It's not everyone who can belch the words "Archbishop of Canterbury". And there's no doubt. You can really hear them.'

'Is that so?' answered Joseph politely. 'It's proper that everyone should have some accomplishment. He must practise regularly.'

'Every day. At least he does it every time I see him.'

'Perhaps he thinks you are a candidate for the position.'

The man, who was small and unkempt, spoke with a thick local accent and had an unfortunate twitch in one cheek. He offered Joseph some further advice and copious bad breath.

'But that's nothing to Tom Tum. He can fart tunes. He can fart "Gathering Peascods". There's no doubt about it. You can really hear that too.'

He indicated a bald middle-aged man, conspicuously over-weight. Certainly, thought Joseph, contemplating the vast abdomen, he has a capacious wind-chest, like a bagpipe or organ, adequate for a tune or two, although "chest" was anatomically confusing in this connection. His informant provided some further illumination.

'Tom Tum's not his real name, you know. He's really Alf Rumbelow.'

'Is that so! Is he performing today?'

'Don't know. Depends on what 'e've ate!'

And the little fellow laughed uproariously at his joke, with another blast of foetid breath in Joseph's direction.

Any further revelation of the anticipated programme was interrupted by the arrival of Arthur Goodrich with the speaker. Joseph's informant disappeared mysteriously without actually having been seen to go, a talent which, Joseph suspected, he had cultivated through years of practice, inspired especially by the arrival of the Law. Arthur had noticed however and was worried.

'Was that Tim Little I saw talking to you?'

'He didn't tell me his name. He seems to be expecting a party of some kind.'

Arthur turned to his companion apologetically. 'I fear there may be disturbances.'

The speaker showed not the smallest sign of anxiety. He had the air of one who had already seen everything.

'No matter. All God's children must play. Some just go on longer into life than others.'

He spoke with a strange speech defect, which Joseph could not identify, although he had met many cases of people afflicted with tumours of the mouth or tongue, by hereditary defects or by accidents. An odd clicking sound decorated the harder consonants and an occasional hiss accompanied some of the vowels. Arthur introduced them.

'This is Ed Fords, an apothecary who has done us all great service. Ed, this is John Freeman our speaker today.'

There was nothing remarkable in appearance about John Freeman, excepting the eyes. He was of average height. His ruddy complexion and rough hands suggested hard work in the open air. His hair was sandy and slightly receding but was grown very long at the sides, concealing his ears. His nose was not inclined to apologise for itself. His eyes, or gaze rather, reminded Joseph immediately of Reverend Alistair Douglas. He should have felt uncomfortable. The Recording Angel was at work again. His sins were on display. Strangely he did not feel threatened by this man. After a few polite enquiries as to Joseph's present problems and past history – which Joseph answered with the usual mixture of candour and half-truth – John Freeman went on with Arthur to open the meeting. As they left him, Joseph could have sworn that he heard Freeman ask, 'But, Arthur, what is his *real* name?'

The opening of the meeting was delayed for a few more minutes. Attention turned once more to the lectern. Freeman stared at the lectern uncomprehendingly. The great man's puzzlement was obvious. He smiled faintly.

'Is there a prize if I guess right?'

The embarrassed Arthur Goodrich explained, emphasising that the lectern's sudden appearance had not had his blessing. 'We were discussing what we should carve in its place, what name we should give ourselves.'

'No name,' said John firmly, adding with a click or two. 'A name is a sentry set at the gate to exclude those we would wish to be here. Labels are for those who prefer not to think. And this lectern is too big for the room. Also – I give a personal opinion, which may not be shared by those who do not have my loud voice – I do not need or wish to speak from a height. Every man here is capable of preaching God's word. We are all on the same level and should speak from the same level. We are all puny in the sight of the Almighty. I shall speak from the floor, which is my proper station. I am certain that the Church of Holy Trinity would be glad to have helped warm the poor.'

Arthur's relief was evident and he could not hurry enough to gather a lectern-disposal party. The offending piece of furniture left the room accompanied by the scowls of the young men who had acquired it, on its way to provide a little short-lived warmth for the needy.

Joseph was given what he recognised as a seat of honour next to Arthur Goodrich, although the Church or Society or whatever it might, in spite of Freeman's wise words, eventually be called, was trying to be non-hierarchical. Arthur whispered an answer to the question in Joseph's mind without him needing to ask it.

'He was tortured. Tongue boring. And he hides what is left of his ears.'

Joseph winced, but had no time for further questions. The meeting had started with a brief prayer from Arthur who simply stood up from his seat. 'O Lord enter into every one of us that we may be of the right mind to worship as we should worship and to decide as we should decide.' Anybody who wished to pray then did so in the same manner. The laconic remained laconic in their prayers and the windbags remained windbags.

The meeting then proceeded to a discussion in which matters of any kind were aired, mostly social and theological. Joseph kept his reactions strictly to himself – he was a fortuitous guest who had been rescued from a difficult situation. He was amused by the naivety of some of the points raised and amazed by the sophistication, profundity even, of others issuing sometimes from quite plain people.

*'Is there a natural law as distinct from the law of the land or from God's law as given in the Bible?'*

*'Who first lit the fires of Hell – God or Satan. And how was it done?* (This was from Sid, Joseph's rescuer.)

*'Who took Joseph from the pit? Was it the Ishmaelites or the Midianites? Genesis, chapter 37, v.27 to 36. How can God's word be so ambiguous on such a simple matter of fact?'*

*'How is it possible for the Book of Deuteronomy to set out rules for the treatment of slaves, thereby implicitly accepting slavery as a proper practice?'*

*'Is not predestination just another device for denying ordinary people comfort in the next world by those who deny it to us in this?'*

John Freeman, in spite of the democratic nature of the meeting, was expected to take the lead in the discussion. He was being given a hard time. A Catholic Priest might have sneered and said, 'Told you so! Look what happens when you let anybody and everybody read the Bible.'

At one point a figure, draped but obviously female, rose to her feet. Joseph was confused and not a little shocked.

'A woman?' he whispered half to himself.

David Jack, who was sitting next to him on the other side from Arthur, answered, 'Well spotted, Apothecary. You're growing up! She's a woman. You should try one out some time.'

Arthur Goodrich was more helpful. He whispered: 'with us, women are allowed to speak. We are all God's children.'

Joseph sat back, trying to digest this idea. As far as he knew, women never spoke in public. They just made up for it at home. The woman had a controversial point to make.

'We all know that John Lilburne is in the Tower, suffering for speaking the truth. His wife and child are without support. Should we not make a contribution to his family?'

There were murmurs of approval, and of dissension, and a voice, perhaps

Tim Little's, was heard to say something indistinct, apparently addressed to a neighbour. It sounded suspiciously like, 'You could send them a fart!'

John Freeman, Arthur and various others glared at the corner of the room from which the offer had been made, before Freeman answered that the woman's idea was laudable but that he was reliably informed that Lilburne's friends and supporters in London were already providing for the family.

*'Has not Christ's redemptive death freed us from guilt?'* The question was asked by a man with thick black hair, a broad back and a neck that hardly existed so that his head seemed to sink into his shoulders. His face wore an expression that should have been fleeting but which had become permanent like a mask; it suggested mischief and a sneer at the same time. He was sitting with the army of Tim Little's associates but had placed himself at a safe distance from Tom Tum's one-man entertainment show. Joseph immediately gained the impression that he was the intellectual leader of the group. He was surly-looking until he broke into a brief, sarcastic smile at something that had been whispered to him while the speaker was replying. For the only time during the meeting, Freeman showed some sign of departure from his usual measured tones. His voice acquired a slight edge and although his eyes looked directly at the questioner as he answered, his face was turned slightly aside like a man expecting a blow. His reply took several minutes and included one or two allusions, obscure to Joseph, but clearly relating to incidents that many of those present would recognise. Christ's sacrifice, he pointed out, alleviated our guilt, but our personal responsibility was increased, not diminished.

An exchange of glances between Arthur and Freeman was sufficient to signal the end of the discussion. Another, with Freeman's sermon as its subject, would follow after he had spoken. There was no formal introduction of the speaker, and a hum of voices still sounded around the room as he made his only concession to special status by walking to the front of the room. Nothing worse than a titter and one half-suppressed belch came from the corner of the room where Tim Little and friends sat. John Freeman began:

*Be strong and of good courage; be not afraid, nor be thou dismayed: for the Lord thy God is with thee wherever thou goest.*

His first words rang around the room. He paused dramatically. A total silence descended upon the congregation. There followed one of those rare moments when every one present seems to have stopped breathing for a few moments. Freeman continued:

'I do not usually speak from a text. Today I shall compensate by speaking from two. For the second I shall quote three verses from the Acts of the Apostles.

*And the multitude of them that believed were of one heart and one soul: neither said any of them that ought of the things which he possessed was his own; but they had all things common.*

*Neither was there any among them that lacked: for as many as were possessors of lands or houses sold them, and brought the prices of the things that were sold.*

*And laid them down at the apostles' feet: and distribution was made unto every man according as he had need.*

Freeman had mastered the dramatic pause and made no apologies to himself or to God for using it. His gaze moved round the room, seeming to catch every eye in turn. Eventually he continued in a quiet voice:

'I do not wonder at your astonishment. My first text you may have heard before. One hundred years ago or so, when God was only with the Pope – with the Grand Merchant of Rome or with his shop assistants in the Churches of England – you would not have heard it. It was not in the Church's interest for you to hear it. And you have never until this day, I swear, heard my second text.'

Freeman put away the viols and brought out the trumpets. 'And why have you not heard it? he asked. 'Why is it never heard?'

No one doubted that he would answer his own questions.

'Because, my friends, the priest at the Church of the Holy Trinity shudders at the idea of planing a yoke or fitting a door. The lectern, which you have so wisely donated to the poor, was made by a man who could barely afford to feed his family. The priest will *break* bread but does not wish to *make* bread. He is pleased to hold a carpenter in reverence, but is reluctant to pay him. Listen again to the words of the Acts of the Apostles... *Neither was there any among them that lacked* ... and listen again... *they had all things common*...

So this passage from the Acts of the Apostles is not the stuff for pulpits. The Reverend Father Holdfast does not want you to know how the Fathers of the Early Church lived. He does not intend that you should know that those who were our Fathers in Christ were also, to each other, Brothers.

Who then should we look to? Who will encourage us to ponder this text – the Bishop of Bristol perhaps, or the great Earl of Somerset?'

Here he paused and waited expectantly. A few laughs from the quicker-witted gradually spread like an infection through the room, until Joseph's ears were hurting with the cacophony of guffaws shaking the small room.

The speaker continued in the same vein – not for long, because he knew the value of brevity, particularly for an audience of this type. The slight speech defect added a strange exotic edge to his natural eloquence. His theme was simple and clear. Christ had been reclaimed by the individual after long imprisonment by the Churches. Christ was in everyone. All were potentially saints. Now the time had come to reclaim England for the saints. The time had come for a new brotherhood in Christ, for a recreation of the Early Church.'

John Freeman concluded; 'a great gale has blown through our nation. England has suffered a mighty earthquake, shaking its foundations and bringing down many structures. Last night your town experienced its own actual and devastating fire, still smouldering this morning as I speak. But England has suffered a greater fire. It will never be the same again. A great flame is raging through the whole country, burning away the old structures, baring a space in which we can build the New Jerusalem.' He finished with another text.

*'Go forth and stand upon the mount before the Lord. And behold the Lord passed by, and a great and strong wind rent the mountains and brake in pieces the rocks before the Lord; but the Lord was not in the wind; and after the wind an earthquake: but the Lord was not in the earthquake: And after the earthquake a fire: but the Lord was not in the fire: and after the fire a still small voice.*

From somewhere in the room, an unfortunately timed sneeze, which the originator had been desperately trying to imprison for some minutes, finally burst like an over-inflated balloon. The silent spell that might well have followed Freeman's inspirational talk was broken. An extraordinary noise broke out, like distant thunder perhaps, or the muffled under-the-Earth roaring of some mythical monster, perhaps the preliminary grumbles of an imminent volcanic eruption. It was followed almost immediately by what were quite unequivocally words, which all could recognise in spite of their unusual dress – Ar-r-hchBichchcshochp ochf ChChanter-r-rchbchury! ArchchBichchcshochp ochf ChChanterchbchury! ArchchBichchcshochp ochf ChChanterchbchury!' Frank Prank was addressing the meeting. Joseph began to interpret the rumbling noise too. It had a definite rhythm. It was presumably 'Gathering Peascods', although he would certainly have not recognised it but for the earlier conversation with Tim Little. It was very good on rhythm. This excellence was not matched by its control of pitch, which was frankly abysmal. The tunedid not come through at all. But in case the audience had not recognised the melody, all doubt was dispelled by Tim and several others who began to sing along – unfortunately not with the familiar words of a popular song, but with those of an anonymous local poet, the theme having more to do with Gathering Codpieces.

Several bottles had been opened by the group at the back, and it soon became clear that they did not contain Holy Water. One of the bottles was being passed from hand to hand, with copious swigs being taken at each stop. The reactions of the congregation were divided between outrage and a curiosity to see what would happen next. Of the former, many were shouting 'Sit down,' 'Shut up,' 'This is God's house' and similar discouragement. A more muscular bunch were assessing the possibility of physical ejection, but, after estimating the size of the opposing forces, changed their minds. Others were staring stiffly ahead of them, as though it were possible to ignore the unignorable.

The *coup de grâce* to the meeting was delivered by a young, but not very young, woman at the back, who – helped on by whoops of encouragement from the drinkers (edged by disbelief, because even they did not really believe that she would dare to do what they hoped she would do) began to pull off her skirt. Joseph was not among those staring straight ahead, but curiously he was not moved in the way he would have expected. Nimrod stared in puzzlement, then slunk back into his kennel. The woman began to whirl the garment round her head in time to the singing, until she had a better idea. Immediately in front of her was a bald gentleman who was one of those dealing with the situation by staring fixedly ahead. Blindfolding him from behind with the skirt, she shouted, 'guess who! Guess right and you can have one free!'

Nothing appeared to surprise John Freeman. He could not perhaps have reformed the devils in Hell, but he would have given them a good ticking off. He did not spoil his response with anger, but spoke with measured authority. 'It is you who will bring our movement into ruin.'

Turning away from the frivolities, he waved the outraged remainder to one side of the room where they could confer. Or rather where he could tell them what was to be done next.

'We shall take our ministry to the people. I shall complete my address in the open air, in public, in a place where all who care to, may hear. We can hold our discussion there. We may have trouble with the Authorities of this town. I urge you to have courage and join me. The pigs we shall leave to feed on their excrement until they are sated or sick, or turn back into humans.'

The congregation divided, but unlike the Godhead, into three. The revellers remained. Frank Prank was pouring spirits over Tim's private part – 'to harden it up,' he explained. Freeman and Arthur Goodrich and a small band of followers proceeded to the market place to face whatever would come. The fainter spirits, or those less dedicated, or those who weighed the integrity of their cause against that of their family and found for the latter, dispersed quietly to their homes. Joseph did not fancy risking imprisonment in support of a cause which was not his and which he had not even succeeded in defining clearly. It seemed to contain whatever was available, like a labourer's stew. He was at a loss what to do next, not seeming to fit with any of the three groups.

As he stood wavering, he felt a hand on his arm. It belonged to Sid the Fireraiser. 'Come with me,' he said mysteriously. A few minutes' walking and they reached Sid's mean residence. Here Joseph stayed for the rest of his time in Bristol, sleeping as best he could, curled up in a cramped corner of the kitchen. The arsonist proved to be the very soul of kindness and – within the limits of his family's meagre abilities – of hospitality. Even so, Joseph looked around nervously each night for kindling or inflammable materials before he slept.

\* \* \* \* \*

Joseph boarded the coach that would take him to London, where he would stay with, and be helped by, James Fisher. Then he would find Paul Fourques and discover what the Frenchman might propose. Not only had he been housed and fed by Sid, but also he had received clothing and a small amount of money from a collection organised by Arthur Goodrich – enough to get him to the capital and his friends. There was plenty of thinking time ahead of him, although he was unsure whether the buffeting and shaking he was to receive for the next thirty-six hours would stimulate or suppress contemplation. He did not have to look for material. Thoughts, sensations, reactions and ideas surrounded him completely, laying siege to him. He steadied himself and attempted to address his attention to the most heavily threatened rampart. He had been caught with the drawbridge down. He had lost everything in the fire. There seemed little left to lose. His life, which had been settling down, allowing him time and creativity, had suddenly been tipped upside down on the floor. The World turned upside down. His among many others.

His delicate negotiations with the stars and planets via Anthony Burbage were in a thousand fragments on the floor. He had to leave now, ahead of the most auspicious astrological time, on the next stage of his life, whatever the opinion expressed by Mars and Jupiter.

He had been treated with wonderful kindness in his misfortune. He had witnessed extraordinary scenes of sense and nonsense. Some of his companions of the last few days were as barmy as spring peewits. And, he feared, less skilled at pulling out of crash-dives. There was every sign that they would end with broken necks, some of them possibly with assistance from the hangman. The first impulse on meeting them was to laugh at the crudity of their untutored opinions and the impracticability of the course – or rather multiplicity of courses – to which those opinions had committed them. His second reaction was to admire their sincerity and humanity. Inevitably he had become aware as he went about his daily work of the trends in thought among the people of the town, but he had never previously visited intellectual headquarters. England was awash with new ideas, bad, good, sublime, ridiculous… but bold. He must bring the same panache to his own work. The disquiet of Parliament over the last years and the victories won by the New Model Army had broken into some previously untouched layer of the ground beneath them. What gushed out might be clear water, or a deadly potation. It was certainly powerful and had been flowing there unknown and under great pressure for a long time. Their thinking was weakened to the point of failure by chaotic indiscipline, and he was alarmed by the way in which their forces were fanning out in many directions, into a vast plain, into unknown and certainly hostile territory, their units becoming ever smaller and more vulnerable, inviting disaster. But they were vitally concerned with matters that were central to human life – to liberty, to just treatment, to the great questions of good and evil, and some part of him wished he could join them. What had his laboratory and its bubbling water-traps, its inverted containers, to do with the central problems of existence, of life and death? Nothing probably. But he knew that, however much he might approve and support these people, his destiny was not with them. His purpose, confused and inadequately formulated though it was, lay somewhere else.

# CHAPTER 23

*If you don't know where you are going, any road will get you there.*
    Lewis Carroll.


The journey to Toulouse with Paul Fourques was as difficult and uncomfortable as expected. The spring was a particularly wet one and they suffered both diversion and delay on account of roads flooded or rendered impassable by mud and debris. The frustrations of the journey were to some extent alleviated by Joseph's companion who possessed a deep knowledge of the regions of France through which they passed and was at times an engaging companion. At other times he was silent for long periods, which was to be expected during the forced association of such a long journey, but silent in a way which was peculiarly discomforting, perhaps because of its contrast with his usual bonhomie or more probably because Joseph had been unable to develop an intuitive feel for the core of the man's personality or the nature of his motivating energies. His local knowledge seemed to include an exhaustive knowledge of French criminology and he was able to point out every prison, gibbet and stake between Paris and the south-west and to relate who was hanged or burned there, and why. Gibbets seemed to be a particular speciality.

After days of travelling, the walls and towers of the city came into view. They stayed two nights there. Their real business was not to be conducted in the city itself, but in a village about twelve miles away. On the third morning they set out on horseback to find Richard Costeaux. Joseph was too familiar with the difficulties and dangers of his profession, and with the ambivalent attitude of the authorities towards it, to require any explanation for Costeaux's reason for conducting his activities in a remote location – but one not too far removed from an urban centre where he could obtain equipment and other supplies without too much difficulty.

It was not difficult to find his residence, although it was some distance from the village and from any other habitation. It was a typical Sixteenth Century farmhouse with numerous out-buildings one or more of which, Joseph guessed, would be workshops and laboratories not devoted to agricultural matters. Some people had all the luck. Joseph assumed a rich, probably noble patron somewhere in the background. They were met at the gate by a servant who was apparently employed full-time as a gate-keeper, since he was provided with a very neat and comfortable sentry's hutch.

'Monsieur Costeaux is concerned about security too,' muttered Joseph to the flaxen-haired boy, 'and well he might be if the documents we have seen give a true indication of the nature of his studies.'

Further speculation was interrupted by a greeting from a very small, very neat man, who recalled to the mind of Joseph something decorative he had seen in the past, perhaps a figure from an ornamental clock. Clearly the formality of announcement and escort by liveried servants was not a priority of the establishment although several more figures, presumably attendants, could be seen hovering in doorways or peering with failed discretion from windows – for the diminutive man was indeed Monsieur Costeaux who was quite happy to introduce himself standing before the house on the forecourt, which stretched about them like a muddy carpet on which he and several others had apparently been playing boules while awaiting the visitors arrival. The Frenchman's greeting was at once effusive and courteous. Joseph was conducted into the house and provided with refreshment. Fourques also welcomed him, just as though he were the joint-proprietor – 'You are most welcome here. We rarely have the pleasure of such distinguished company. Please, while you are with us consider all the comforts and faculties of the house and laboratories as your own. We shall enjoy a very profitable exchange of inspirations, of that I am precedent.'

The quaintly worded offer relieved to some extent the tension that Joseph still felt. His first impression of something sinister in the house and its accoutrements persisted. The farm was definitely unsettling. Perhaps it was the lurking, unexplained figures or just the presence in his mind of too many unanswered questions concerning the purpose of this place.

Costeaux welcomed him. 'It is late in the day – too late to show you around our workshops. Tomorrow I shall introduce you to our laboratories and you will see for yourself what passes there. In the meantime, please rest, and I will be pleasured if you join us for dinner – you will meet also Professor Charolet, who is staying with us.'

Joseph had never heard of Professor Charolet, but then, there was no reason why he should have. A servant conducted the two men to very comfortable rooms. Still he could not dispel his unease. The rooms were too comfortable, not at all what one expected from a farmhouse. Someone had spent a lot of money. Considering his own troubled background and especially that of his master, he should not have come here – perhaps would not have done so but for the disaster of the fire and the difficulty of his circumstances. Nevertheless he was tired and slept until it was time for what he hoped would be an evening repast superior to the improvised meals of their travels.

A servant, also in uniform, escorted Joseph to dinner. On the way a strange incident occurred which did nothing to reassure him. He had a sudden feeling that he was being watched. Looking round he momentarily caught sight of the face of a young woman. The face should have been pretty, beautiful even, since it possessed those mysterious ingredients which usually assemble to a whole of exceptional loveliness, but the summation process had failed somewhere, and there was a hardness, a suggestion perhaps of cruelty, which drew its shadows around the mouth and eyes. Moreover the woman was watching him closely, with more intensity even than one would expect from an inhabitant of a remote dwelling inspecting a new arrival. It seemed to him as though he was being subjected to a physical scrutiny. Such appraisal would not normally be unwelcome to him, and certainly not to Nimrod – who, to Joseph's surprise, flapped an ear and began to haul himself on to his hind legs – but the woman's gaze seemed to imply a different kind of inspection from those with which he was familiar. It reminded him more of a farmer's examination of a heifer at a market. He shuddered slightly and walked on.

They had passed through several rooms and hallways, keeping roughly to the same direction, and had almost arrived at the room where they were to dine with their host when Joseph suddenly noticed the same face, the face of a young woman, with the same sequestered beauty and the same animal look of appraisal, this time peering at him through a partly open door which was still some way ahead of him. There was no time, surely, for the woman to have passed between the two parts of the house, and no easy way to do so in such an elaborate place with its awkward corners and heavy doors. He was temporarily unnerved, even to the point where his manner faltered slightly as he was greeted affably by their host.

'Are you comfortable? There is nothing wrong I hope? This is Professor Charolet.'

Joseph shook hands with a young man who was as tall and powerful as Costeaux was tiny and dainty. A fine table had been put out for the visitors. Obviously he must be considered a distinguished guest.

The conversation was amiable, sometimes animated. The young man with the muscles was curiously quiet. 'A trait not familiar in academics,' Joseph thought. In fact he began to suspect that Professor Charolet was under instructions from Costeaux to remain quiet. At one point Joseph could have sworn that Costeaux had trodden on the hefty young man's foot as he was about to speak – a liberty which he would not have dared to take himself.

When the conversation had been sufficiently warmed by the fine food and the exceptional wines, Joseph ventured a question – with especial care as he was unsure of the status of Professor Charolet.

'Clearly, your excellent establishment here is not solely devoted to agriculture. I do not doubt that your efforts are directed towards some even greater end. May I ask what is the nature of your work in which you are so busily engaged?'

Richard Costeaux paused a little before replying. He also was going to choose his words with care.

'Our inspiration,' he said at last, 'is from sources two thousand years old. Heraclitus regarded all things as composed of fire and saw around him a world in perpetual flux. Tomorrow we will conduct you around our estate and you will see for yourself how we attempt to realise his philosophy. I believe that, from the superiority of your intellects (here he used the plural, but his eyes particularised Joseph) and on account of the vast experience you have in the study of medicine, you will be able to contribute much of value and perhaps even to resolve certain dilemmas that we have encountered.'

Joseph nodded, then replied, 'Many of the wise consider Fire to be an element present in all things. And one may argue with some force, as did Heraclitus, that it has a place, special even among the elements. Certainly Fire is an agent of magical, almost divine, powers. But it has been in use by the Magi through the ages, and for myself I cannot claim to have found any new way in which to use it.'

Joseph was being excessively modest. But caution was the priority. From both sides, information was to be proffered one penny at a time. His caution was mirrored by Costeaux's.

'We have no special skills with Fire, either. But other aspects of Heraclitus's thinking are our inspiration. We believe that all things are subject to endless change, and most especially that opposites define and balance each other. We may assume too that the dream of many of the cognoscenti over the years that disease may be transformed to health, that poverty may be changed to riches, that the sick and poor of the earth may no longer suffer, that the rocky places may yield food, that noble metals may be released from the base metals which imprison them, that lead or iron may be transformed to gold.'

'The latter is impossible,' said Joseph in a manner that was absurdly confident, peremptory even. 'Lead, iron and gold are elements.'

An astonished silence followed this unforeseen breach of Joseph's caution. Joseph was as astonished as the others. He became aware suddenly of the absence of man-generated noises in this country place. The only sound was of a distant owl. The stare which the three men turned upon him was composed of three parts bewilderment and two parts disbelief. Possibly with a trace of fear.

Fourques recovered first. 'Why did you say that?'

Joseph's reply was entirely honest. 'I have no idea.' His sudden outburst had amazed himself. The notion had entered his head unaccountably from nowhere, like a disease.

Now Costeaux recovered too. 'I think I take your meaning. If lead and gold are elements, it follows that they are present in all things, even in the sea and the wind. This is hard to register, but indeed it may be said that these natural forces partake in some sense of the properties of the base and noble metals. If you are right then it is even more reasonable for the alchemists to suppose that one may be converted into the other, since each must be present in each.'

'That is so.'

Joseph's agreement was both polite and tactical. He recognised that Costeaux had been thinking aloud and in bewilderment engendered by shock. The thinking was muddled and illogical. Joseph realised also that the unconsidered remark he had made was a defining moment in the development of his own thought. Something extraordinary had happened. He must go away alone and work through its implications.

\* \* \* \* \*

The next day dawned as one of those peerless mornings of Southern France. As Joseph dressed he had the good fortune to glance from the window just as the first glowing segment of the sun lifted above a distant hill. In a few moments the room was filled with red gold. There was no colour like this gold. To see it one must be in the right place at the right moment. It could not be imitated by any process, natural or unnatural. It was all the gold that we should need, he thought, as rare and more beautiful even than the metal dug from the ground. Such priceless moments cast the mundane concerns of humanity in cheap alloy.

*What here is made plainly visible, presents the invisible reality whose splendour permeates the world.* He could not think where he had read these words.

Even his intellectual adventures – and certainly the present rash excursion into an unfamiliar land and circumstance – seemed irrelevant, dissociated from the true core of the spirit. In a few minutes the red gold was replaced by the always welcome, but commonplace, yellows and blues of daylight. The morning was crisp, clear, and flooded with light. The day was waiting to be used; a page waiting to be written on.

His mind was refreshed by sleep and elevated by the beauty of the morning. Ideas were crowding in on him, nudging him, treading on each other's toes, falling over each other, provoking him, even as he urinated. He recalled suddenly his unconsidered statement of the previous evening concerning the status of the three metals. For some time his mind must have been working through logic and fantasy, making connections, without his conscious participation. He had plenty of time to ponder as he prepared himself for the day. One thing that surprised him in this house – on which in most respects no expense had been spared – was the absence of flushing toilets. Perhaps the excellent work of Sir John Harington had not penetrated to provincial France. If he had the chance he would contribute to the house in return for its hospitality a copy of the great man's book *The Metamorphosis of Ajax*, in which the invention was described and from which the "jakes" had derived its name. Perhaps Harington had contributed more to mankind than Galileo or Harvey. In the meantime he must use the chamber pots provided.

Breakfast was satisfying. He and Fourques ate together without other company. Shortly after the meal, Costeaux appeared, courteous, effusive, enthusiastic, eager to introduce them to his domain. Heraclitus was in evidence once more, as his host dispensed his personal philosophy in generous amounts. Joseph was less happy with an igneous World. It seemed to him that fire was becoming an unfortunate and probably repetitious theme in his personal Universe. He suspected too that Costeaux commonly used the Greek philosopher's fiery metaphysics as a screen to hide his real interests.

Envy was not a prominent member of Joseph's cabinet of sins. One thing that could certainly and instantly promote it was a laboratory like the one through which he was now conducted. Here were flasks, beakers, stills, retorts, alembics, furnaces of every size, shape and purpose. The laboratory of the Baroness (he squirmed uncomfortably as the thought came to him) was a street-side pauper compared with this one. It could only have been built by a rich noble or merchant or by someone with access to wealth generated by some mysterious, perhaps illegal, means. The laboratory comprised several rooms, or more accurately there were several laboratories that looked to have divided functions. Two of them were clearly designed for larger volume work, almost industrial scale. Costeaux talked only in the most general terms, giving little indication of the aims of his work here. Joseph pocketed his impatience. His host could not continue the tour indefinitely without revealing his interests and purposes. Joseph tried to encourage him with little scraps of information about his own work, and by asking occasional questions.

'What is the purpose of that building?'

The building in question was an unusual octagonal structure in ugly contrast to the traditional French rural architecture of the farm. A peculiar and rather revolting smell was hanging in the air and seemed to originate from the structure. Joseph, who considered himself an expert on disagreeable smells, was surprised to find that he could not identify it.

Costeaux answered politely but coldly. 'You would not be interested. We are studying a new approach to sanitation and the disposal of human waste matter.'

'To the contrary. I would be interested to see the processes and equipment used.'

'I regret to say that is not possible. Not today. It is in the process of redevelopment.'

Costeaux talked increasingly of social obligations. Heraclitus returned, this time with his public programme.

Joseph proffered Sir Francis Bacon in return.

Costeaux said, 'I have not read him. I must do so. But was he not imprisoned for fraud? How can such a one recommend a policy directed to public benefit?'

Joseph laughed. 'Call it creative hypocrisy. A man's ability to see how the world should be organised, does not mean that he is able to exercise the same high moral principles in his own life, however sincerely he recommends them.'

Monsieur Costeaux looked dubious. 'How are we to distinguish creative hypocrisy from the more familiar sort?'

'I don't know. It is a problem for all visionaries. Ask the poets. They are the worst – or the best. It depends which way you look at it.'

He was glad that Costeaux had changed the subject. The ethical subject matter was already provoking the first throbbings of a headache. It was dispersed instantly by a massive shock. At a corner of a passage connecting two of the laboratories, they met a man coming from the opposite direction. Joseph almost collided with him, so that he was confronted without warning by this grotesque creature. Momentarily he shrank away in fear. He had seen many frightful sights in his work and had for the most part become inured to physical degradation and decay. But this confronted him with the memory of a deadly disease, considered so infectious that its sufferers were isolated for life in communities denied all connection with normal life.

'Leprosy,' he thought.

In a moment he recovered his self-control and his more normal response returned. He began to reach back into his memory for a diagnosis. He had seen collapse of the nose many times before in cases of pox and indeed of leprosy. But here the nose and upper jaw were intact. It was the lower jaw which had been affected, and in a manner which did not suggest any disease that he had ever met. The man glanced at them furtively, mumbled some kind of apology and hurried on. He became aware that Costeaux also was apologising.

'It is no good,' he said. 'I must dismiss him. He has skills that I shall miss. Otherwise I would have done so before. But he frightens my visitors. He is no risk to us. He is suffering from the indiscretions of his youth, which are only passed by misconduct.'

As the day went on, it became clear that Costeaux had indeed a hidden purpose. He began by casually asking Joseph's advice on particular questions in chymistry, and then questioning Joseph on what could best be done with facilities like those available here. The hints became less subtle and more explicit and Joseph was not surprised when Costeaux suddenly said, 'we are honoured to have a man of your talents and background here. Why don't you stay and work with us. We could make progress which would startle the world.' Joseph's answer was cautious, neither dismissing nor welcoming the offer. He was greatly appreciative of such a generous offer and would give it his most careful consideration.

Costeaux bowed in assent. 'There is no hurry. Perhaps I can show you something which may influence your decision.'

First, via a servant, he summoned Professor Charolet. Together the three men passed along a passageway and turned into a room that he had not yet seen. Costeaux removed a formidable bunch of keys from a pocket and unlocked the door. The room was entirely bare and windowless, but let into one of the side walls was a heavy iron door with two locks, clearly a safe of some kind. Costeaux lit a lamp, dismissed the guard and closed the door to the room. The lamp was a poor thing after the brilliance of day but Joseph was just able to see Costeaux again produce keys from his pocket. The door of the safe swung open and at first Joseph could see nothing in the darkness of its interior. Gradually his eyes adjusted. First he saw a pile of some two dozen rectangular bars apparently of iron. There was nothing else in the safe. His vision adjusted further. Costeaux's lamp swung slightly. From the bars there came a momentary wink of reflected light. The lustre was unmistakable. This was gold. More gold – much more – than he had ever seen or was likely to see again. He became aware that Costeaux was examining his reactions closely.

'Yes,' said Costeaux after a few moments' silence, 'you are amazed naturally. But you may touch it. Here.' And he reached in and handed one of the bars to Joseph.

Recovering from his initial wonderment, Joseph began to inspect the bar, turning it over and over in his hand, trying to estimate its weight, assessing as best he could its quality. It certainly seemed to be genuine. A small irregularity – a faint discolouration in the smooth surface attracted his attention. He caressed it with his finger thoughtfully trying to imagine what fault in the separation of the gold from its ore or in the manufacture of the ingot had caused the imperfection. Costeaux, who was still watching him closely, spoke again. 'You have divined our problem. This is the reversion of which I spoke in a letter to Paul. The contamination, this disease of the metal will gradually spread through the whole bar until it is utterly spoiled, until it is hideous in appearance and of no value, entirely worthless.'

'You mean that this gold bar – all these bars which I see – have been made by transmutation from a base metal. But that in itself is an outstanding achievement, a unique achievement. Surely you cannot now be far from total success. Surely it must be but a small step to identifying the cause of the reversion, and thus devising a way in which to stabilise the converted metal?'

'That is what we hope. That is what we dare to believe. And that is why we want you to stay here, to work with us, to help us solve this problem and, of course, to share in the rewards.'

# CHAPTER 24

Night-time was for Joseph a time of problem-solving. The night seemed to be able to accept into its black cauldron the multiple sensations, difficulties and thoughts of the day, and then by some mysterious process of which he had no understanding, sometimes – rarely, it was true, but on important occasions – he would the next morning find in its dark depths a residue of true metal. After the offer of co-operation with Costeaux, the previous evening he was euphoric. The restoration of his fortunes was imminent. He would work in these beautiful surroundings with every facility which anyone could wish for, on a project which might perhaps bring great benefits to his fellow men and fame or fortune – or both even – to himself. His knowledge and abilities were at last being recognised. He had cause for self-congratulation. This present vein of good fortune had begun with the breaking of the code, which had clearly made a considerable impression on Fourques and Costeaux and whoever else was involved.

When he awoke in the morning he was almost startled to find that he had reached an unequivocal and opposite conclusion. He would not stay in this place. He would not accept Costeaux's offer. The reasons for this had to be dragged out of their hiding places. In the first he had never taken to Fourques and simply did not trust Costeaux. He did not like Costeaux, Costeaux's Heraclitean pretensions or Costeaux's associates. The establishment was too good to be true – or perhaps to good to be good – with its unaccountable wealth, as testified by its rich facilities, and by the contents of the armoured cupboard that he had been shown. And its atmosphere was eerie and unsettling, with its magically reappearing female apparitions, its disfigured attendants and thinly disguised bodyguards. He was aware suddenly of a craving for his humble shop on the bridge in Bristol. But that was gone. Heraclitus had spoken!

Costeaux joined the apothecary at breakfast. Joseph had decided to make his decision known without delay and, after coffee had been delivered to the table, came straight to the point. He thanked Costeaux for his warm hospitality, for the fascinating insight he had been given into his host's work and philosophy and most especially for the unprecedented opportunity that he had been given. With deepest regret he had concluded after prolonged thought that he could not accept. Costeaux was distressed, but courteous as always. He must respect the decision, of course, but would not Joseph please come to the laboratory once more before he finally rejected the offer that had been made, as he had one remaining thing to show him, which might yet persuade him to change his mind?

Accordingly Joseph, matching courtesy with courtesy, met Costeaux and Fourques in the laboratory. Professor Charolet was there too, looking heftier than ever. He expected to see another demonstration of the wealth available to the laboratories or perhaps to be introduced to a new process for the preparation of the Stone. Would he now be shown the red-gold crystals from the Holy Land? Instead, Costeaux merely began to reiterate the arguments that he had put at the breakfast table as to why Joseph should remain and work there. In conclusion he pointed out that Joseph was virtually destitute as a result of the fire and might welcome a refuge and a period of remunerative involvement with the subject in which he possessed a life-long interest and expert knowledge.

'Nevertheless,' replied Joseph, 'I have commitments in England of a personal nature which must be honoured.'

'If your commitment is to a woman, then I suggest that what we have proposed is of more immediate importance than any such. And in the long run she can only benefit from the delay.'

'I admit the force of your arguments and acknowledge your kindness, but I must leave.' Joseph's tone was firm and final.

'I am afraid, Monsieur Skledowski, that you are not free to leave.'

The use of his birth name was unnerving. But a few people knew his origin and it was not entirely surprising that Costeaux had discovered it. The idea that he was not free to leave was presumably a joke. He smiled at Costeaux as though the statement was indeed a jest. There was no answering smile, only a cold, impassive stare. Joseph's smile slowly guttered out. His head turned involuntarily towards the door from the hallway. One of the armed guards stood there. He turned to the door which opened into the courtyard. There was a guard there too. And, for good measure, the formidable Professor Charolet was blocking his path.

'You cannot keep me here against my will. This is a breach of hospitality and an offence against the law.'

'Yes. Both. But it is necessary. We need your skills and your knowledge. And we shall acquire them whether you wish it or not.'

'I have no knowledge which you do not have yourself or which is not freely available in the multitude of books that have been written on those subjects familiar to me.'

'You know yourself the obscurity of alchemical texts. You have complained of this obscurity yourself in public lectures. Many successes are claimed and it is not possible to reproduce them because the authors do not care to share the knowledge of their methods.'

'You are well informed about my opinions,' said Joseph dryly. Costeaux nodded and smiled ironically.

'We have made it our business to know. And we have much information too about your late master, Sendivogius.'

'That is common knowledge. His reputation embraced several countries.'

'Yes, but we have uncommon knowledge too. And we believe that he made more progress in our Great Task than anyone else has at any time. And we believe that these secrets did not die with him but were passed on to you, his protégé and heir.'

'No such secrets were imparted. All that he knew on the subject has been printed and is readily available to you.'

'We do not believe so. And, as you will know better than anyone, to follow processes from a written description is no substitute for personal tuition. Written descriptions fail to include that multitude of tiny but crucial details on which success depends.'

'That may be true. But you have no need of help, written or otherwise. You have already solved the problem – and in spectacular fashion. You showed me the very beautiful results yesterday.'

Costeaux laughed, heartily this time. 'That was a reprehensible deception. But it would be hypocritical of me to apologise. The bars of gold that you saw were born in the dust and dirt of the earth in the conventional manner. Boring, I know, compared with yesterday's account of their origin. But true, I regret to say.'

'Or may be particularly good examples of substitution?'

Costeaux shrugged. The extent of the plot against him began to flood into Joseph's mind.

'And reversion?'

'A picturesque detail to capture your interest. Reversion is no more a problem than transmutation was a success. No transmutation, no reversion.'

'And the coded letters?'

'Forgeries. We invented the code ourselves to engage your interest and talents. We congratulate you again on the ingenuity that you displayed. We felt that you would succeed and that your success would make you feel an important part of our enterprise.'

'That will never be so,' said Joseph firmly. 'Now let me go please.'

For answer, Costeaux nodded to the guards, and not many seconds later Joseph found himself in chains.

An old cellar of the farm had been converted into a dungeon. It was extremely dark with a feeble light filtering in reluctantly from some unidentifiable source. For a long time Joseph could see nothing. He was in a state of shock. His thoughts plunged about like soldiers in the later stages of battle. He was every kind of fool for having exposed himself to the possibility of such a development. After all the care he had expended through so many years of hidden identity and change of address, he had been tricked by a charade. His very anonymity and concealment would now work against him, a conclusion that Costeaux had doubtless also reached. Few people knew that he was in France and no one would remark or worry about his absence for a very long time. He was not the first of his profession to be abducted. It had been a common enough occurrence. Anyone credited with the ability to create wealth from dross was at risk. His own mentor had suffered the same devastating experience, not once but several times. He had been imprisoned at the court of Frederick of Wittenberg where an attempt was made to force him to release his supposed transmuting powder and on two other occasions he had been abducted while travelling, once by a rival alchemist and once by a hard-up Moravian nobleman. The only ray of hope – as uncertain as the ray of light entering the dungeon – was that his mentor had survived and lived to enjoy old age. Sendivogius had been too valuable a property to harm. But it was not likely that the same would apply to Joseph in his present situation.

His eyes gradually adapted to the near-darkness. There was little enough to see in the room. He was not about to be made comfortable. He eventually discerned what appeared to be a bundle in the corner. Dragging his chains he crossed the room to investigate. The bundle was a sleeping man, apparently in wretched condition. The stranger was middle-aged, unshaven. His clothes were torn; his face was unmarked but he seemed to be in considerable pain, since he kept shifting his position uncomfortably. Occasionally he would groan in a way that overwhelmed Joseph with compassion for the sufferer's situation but also with a growing apprehension for his own fate. There was nothing that he could do for his cell-mate except let him sleep on while he was able. In the meantime Joseph sat at the stranger's side, the bond of shared circumstance growing rapidly. The man's groans gave way occasionally to a muttering, not quite understandable but clearly recognisable as a German dialect of some kind. Suddenly he shrieked out words that were all too plain, punctuated with screams.

'No, no. Not again you bitches! No, not there! A-a-a-a-gh! I didn't call you bitches. You misheard. No! A-a-a-gh!'

The stranger was sweating. So was Joseph in spite of the cold clamour of the basement. He could only sit through more of the same for what seemed to be hours, while the victim groaned and babbled. The man's distress rendered consistent thought impossible. It was clear only that Costeaux had the power and methods to reduce a presumably normal individual to a pulsating mess. Joseph was trying desperately to bring his thoughts to order like an unruly meeting, when he noticed his companion's eyes open. The eyes stared unseeingly for a moment and then focused gradually on Joseph's face.

'Not again,' he screamed. 'Leave me alone. Don't touch me.'

'It is all right. You have nothing to fear,' said Joseph softly, and, his natural sympathies aroused, he reached out a soothing hand to touch the man's arm, merely eliciting another yell. He withdrew the hand hastily and instead put on his best manner for distressed patients, which although he was supposed to be merely a provider of medicines, he had practised considerably over the years. Eventually the sufferer became calmer and at last recovered sufficiently to talk rationally.

'You must be a prisoner too. Costeaux must have got you too. What have you done?'

'It's not what I have done, but what he wants me to do.'

'Ah! It is the same for me. It was information he wanted. And he knows how to get it.'

Joseph drew a wrong conclusion. 'You are trying to make gold for him too?'

'No, said his companion contemptuously. 'I doubt whether such a thing is possible. My view is that of Avicenna – that it is possible in principle but not in practice. No, I was a chemist in Dresden, a follower of Paracelsus, trying to prepare useful things like medicines. Uwe Schliessmann is my name. We were looking for a life-supporting principle in urine. It was based on the idea that an important essence of life and health leaks gradually away from the body and might be recoverable in a concentrated form. Paracelsus himself prepared something from urine, which he described as "icicles, which are the elements of fire". It's impossible to tell exactly what he did or what he obtained, but we followed a similar logic. We collected buckets and buckets full of piss – anybody's piss – got it from any one we could persuade. Then we left it to rot for days. Pwaah! O Christ, I can smell it now! Then we boiled it down. That was even worse. When it had turned into a paste we distilled it. And that was the remarkable thing.'

For a moment the prisoner's misery evaporated and his eyes sparkled. He spoke almost dreamily. 'At the second distillation, the contents of the retort began to shine in the dark and a glowing liquid dripped from the end of the retort. An elixir. No doubt. The life-bearing principle that runs continuously away from us, eventually taking our health and strength with it. If anything deserves the name of elixir it is this. It is an extraordinary substance, the most remarkable I have seen, fascinating and terrifying. It seems to be a distillation not of urine or of water, but of fire. It has fire in its very essence. Perhaps we may be able to explain these things better one day. It is some kind of brother or first cousin to fire. It is so fiery that it must be kept under water. You must never allow it to dry for, if you do, it bursts into flame without the need for any fire or spark to arouse it.'

'Fire from water.' Joseph muttered involuntarily. 'Just as Aristotle said.' He looked behind him in alarm, in case Galileo was listening, forgetting for a moment that a house fire had done for the sage what the Inquisition had failed to do.

'Some day it will be our greatest benefactor. Or our most implacable enemy. We began work to incorporate it in medicines, to restore to the human body that which is lost, perhaps even to restore the immortality lost by Adam's action. Now I fear that the knowledge of its preparation will be lost forever.'

'Does anyone else know how to prepare it?'

'No. Apart from my assistant in Dresden who has only partial knowledge. And those here, who extracted my knowledge from me, but no longer need me. I know also that a young man named Brandt in Hamburg has become interested in the possibility of preparing an elixir from urine, but any success he may have lies in the future.'

'How then did you come to be here in this terrible condition?'

'I was betrayed by the assistant I mentioned. Betrayed to those for whom the life-preserving essence of the elixir is of no interest. To people for whom its importance resides only in its incendiary qualities.'

'As a weapon?'

'Exactly,' said Uwe. 'What is certain is that the military would love it. And that's why it is of deep concern to Costeaux and his gang.'

'So that is why chamber pots are used here,' said Joseph thoughtfully. 'A flushing toilet would introduce unwanted dilution. Does Costeaux have army connections?'

'To the Hapsburgs. And before that to Catholicism. And Emperor Ferdinand is in a corner. And with him the Catholic Church in the Hapsburg territories, and – who knows? – perhaps in Italy and other countries too. The Swedes and the others have won a series of victories in Germany. Soon they will be at the gates of Vienna and Prague. Perhaps they already are. I don't know. I am not in a position to be informed about that or anything else.'

Joseph broke in. 'The last I heard was in mid-March. The Bavarians had made a separate peace at Ulm, gravely weakening the Hapsburg cause.'

'Exactly as I expected. And the Emperor is desperate for a new weapon. The old ones will not save them. A fire spreading devastation and panic among the troops is just the kind of invention that they pray for. A bitter war may become more bitter yet. That is why Costeaux is trying to build a stock of white fire, as they call it. Eventually it will be shipped to Germany, as ready-to-use weapons, so he hopes, that will bring terror, disfigurement and death on common soldiers who know only how to thrust and hack.'

'And you have been compelled to join this search for destruction?'

'Yes. By the most brutal means.'

'Hmm,' said Joseph ruminatively. 'The military are always the first to show interest in any new discovery.'

'And they have no scruples as to how they will get their hands on it,' said Schliessmann grimly. 'Unfortunately we do not know, when we begin study, where we shall be led by Nature or what use may be made of anything that we may find.'

'Then our trade is evil, you think. Or too dangerous. So dangerous that we should not meddle with things that are best left unknown or known only to God himself. It is a variant on a common argument.'

'Dangerous it is. But not evil. And the point at which we begin to apply our new knowledge and our skills to the deliberate purpose of producing a weapon is usually quite clear. And the choice is ours. To prostitute a great ideal to the pain and destruction of our fellows or not.'

'Then we must refuse?'

'Yes. If it possible. But they will muster powerful arguments. They will plead defence against evil enemies. They will say that if we do not do this, others will. They will pay. They will seduce. They will, if necessary, enforce.'

'And the sinister man with the deformed jaw – he is your torturer, I presume?'

Uwe stared in surprise. 'No. He is another unfortunate, a local man. He was of normal appearance when I first came. The awful disfigurement is I fear – I can't be sure – a result of daily contact with the white fire, which they pay him to manufacture. That is done in the building of peculiar shape, behind the laboratory. Inside is a large vat, which by now must contain enough of the white fire to threaten the existence of the farm. No, the fiends who have reduced me to the state which you see are two sisters, two sisters so like each other that no one can tell them apart.'

'Women!' said Joseph in astonishment. 'Women as torturers. Surely it is not possible!'

'Ah, but it is!' Uwe spoke in grim tones, which occasionally wavered in mid-sentence. 'Who better to punish men? Consider. Or – for all I know – look into your own conscience. We have been mistreating them for hundreds of years. Regarding them as a lesser kind. Denying them a voice in all the affairs which directly affect them, denying them opportunity and satisfaction, persecuting them, burning them as witches even, using them for our own physical satisfaction and then oppressing or deserting them, viewing them as breeding machines, domestic servants or receptacles of lust – or for all of those things at once. Some of them can't wait to avenge themselves. Christ! You should just hear Douce and Aigre on the subject – between jabs and blows.'

'Douce and Aigre,' muttered Joseph faintly, having wriggled uncomfortably several times during this list of indictments. This was worse than Alistair Douglas. 'Are those their real names?'

'It is what they like to call themselves. I don't know what names they were given by their parents, if they had human parents. But I *can* tell you that they like to play a game where one of them strikes me and I am supposed to tell her name. If I get it wrong, God help me.'

'Ah, "tell who it was who struck Thee".'

'I am not Jesus Christ but I might end on a cross. I would not put it beyond them. At least in the guessing game they give me an even chance. Which is unusual.'

'Apart from blows, what tortures do they use?' The subject was assuming a pressing importance.

'They, they take, take…' Uwe's voice trailed away. He had fainted. Best to leave Uwe to recover in his own time, thought Joseph. He would have to start thinking hard and soon. Costeaux and Fourques – or worse, Douce and Aigre – might return at any moment and begin making demands of one sort or another which would have to be met or endured by some means. There was renewed movement from the unfortunate man. His eyes re-opened and he spoke again in a barely discernible whisper.

'Listen carefully. The secret preparation of the elixir I will try to describe to you – otherwise it may be lost forever. But first, let me tell you this. It may be of the greatest importance for you. I brought with me from Germany another substance. It is a virulent poison, the most deadly known to Man. It was distilled from the seeds of a plant brought back from the Indies. The seeds also provide an innocuous and useful oil, but this deadly spirit must be removed first. When I first arrived and was still a guest I was demonstrating a method to Costeaux and Charolet in the laboratory. That morning I began to suspect that they had no intention of allowing me to leave. I could not let them find it on my person, so I hid it in the simplest way possible. I made out a harmless label for it and placed it openly on a shelf along with one or two other common substances that I had brought with me. It is a hundred times more deadly than any other known poison. There is sufficient in the bottle to kill most of the inhabitants of Toulouse.'

'And the label…?' asked Joseph.

'It claims to be Oil of Almonds. Use it to kill yourself if you can no longer endure imprisonment here. Or better, use it to kill the fiend Costeaux if you have the chance. But I do not know how you might achieve that. He is very careful and you will have little chance to use it.'

His eyelids began to flutter. This time Schliessmann relapsed into a longer sleep, disturbed again by the terrible experiences of the recent past. Nor did he wake again that night. No one came. The daylight – or what little reached him – waned and the night passed, the longest night he had ever known. It was cold, he was hungry, and there was nothing but a thin pile of straw on which to sleep. He was being given thinking time, or simply being broken in like a young horse.

Shortly after first light he heard movements and two of the guards entered. They roughly shook Uwe awake and gave him a plate with some food that looked as though it might have been something the farm animals had refused. Joseph received nothing but was taken from the cellar and seated in a small room. To his surprise, he was brought a plain but palatable breakfast, which in the circumstances tasted like a royal banquet. He ate it with the guards standing above him watching every mouthful. When he was finished, the plate was removed and Fourques and Costeaux appeared in the doorway. With the unfailing courtesy of well-bred Frenchmen they stood aside to allow two women to enter first. Joseph had seen them before, but separately. It was not possible to tell them apart. No doubt they had made use of this in their childhood to hoodwink adults and indulge in all kinds of the self-serving mischief uniquely possible to identical twins. Now they were just sinister. And sinister in spite of their present appearance, dressed in simple elegance, in garments indistinguishable from those of a simple French country girl, except for the superior quality of the materials. They affected the unsophisticated and demure. Costeaux introduced them.

'I would like you to meet two of our helpers, the Mesdemoiselles Paulet. They are keen students of chymistry.'

'I am pleased to meet you, sir,' said Douce – or was it Aigre? – with a well-oiled curtsey. 'Is there anything that we can do for you today?'

'No thank you. I hope not. I mean that I would not wish to trouble you.'

'No trouble at all,' said Aigre – or was it Douce? 'We shall be happy to oblige you in any way that we can devise.'

Their air of rustic simplicity would have won a more complete success if it were not for the hungry manner in which they were studying Joseph, as if they were measuring him for some apparatus or the other.

'You may go now, ladies,' said Costeaux. 'No doubt you will be meeting again later.' And the two ladies curtseyed daintily and left the room. The slightly exaggerated depth of curtsey and the inappropriate chivalry shown to a man in chains carried with it a sarcasm not lost on Joseph. His confinement for a night in the cell with Schliessmann had clearly been intended to demonstrate the consequences of non-cooperation and to frighten him into submission. And frightened he was.

Costeaux turned to him with a new grimness of tone. 'Now, to business. I profoundly hope that you will cooperate with us. There is much to do.'

'Certainly. I see it as in my best interests.'

'That is sensible. But then you are an exceedingly intelligent man. First some questions.'

'Your mentor, Michael Sendivogius is said to have received a red transmuting powder from Alexander Seton. Where is that powder now?'

'The powder was stolen before Michael had any chance to study it. I must point out once more that he died a relatively poor man, encumbered by the debts which were kindly left to him in a legacy.'

'We believe that it was you who stole it.'

'I am even poorer than he was. A penurious apothecary. And if I had ever had the powder, it would have been lost with all my other possessions in the fire which destroyed my house in Bristol.'

The answer had an extraordinary effect. Costeaux was infuriated, not with Joseph fortunately but with Fourques, to whom he turned in anger.

'I have told you many times that it was an act of extreme stupidity to set fire to his house. Never exceed your instructions again or you will regret it for the rest of your life.'

'But it got him here, didn't it?' said Fourques defensively. 'He would not have come to France if he had not been desperate after the loss of everything he had.'

The argument was terminated abruptly by an exclamation from Joseph. He had speculated endlessly on the causes of the fire but had never suspected arson. His future, possibly his life, was at stake. This was a time for swift and effective thought. He was in no position to show anger. The words that came into his mind were censored at source. After a long pause he said, 'if Seton's elixir was made once, it can be made again.'

'You mean that Seton passed on the secret of its production to Sendivogius?'

'No, not to my knowledge.'

'I do not believe you', said Costeaux. 'We have information to the contrary. And your master himself has written of the preparation of the Stone. You must have yourself considered attempting its manufacture.'

Joseph answered defensively. 'I have been too busy with many other concerns. And I have had reason to think – now confirmed – that I was being pursued, and so have had many addresses, not staying long in any one place for fear of capture or injury of some kind. All authorities agree that the process which produces the Stone is a long one. In Sendivogius's account, at least one hundred and seventy days are required to produce a tiny amount of the Stone. Then further time for its multiplication or amplification. And more yet again for projection upon a base material to produce gold…

'But that is months!' exclaimed Costeaux, 'we do not have months. Or may not.'

Joseph shrugged. 'It may be possible to accelerate the reactions. I do not know and certainly do not know how.'

'Then you are going to attempt both the manufacture and the acceleration for us?'

Joseph had already decided that it was best to agree.

\* \* \* \* \*

On the evening of the day of his enchainment Joseph was returned to the dark pit where he had spent the previous night. His fellow prisoner was no longer there. The day had been spent in discussion – frosty it was true – but both parties had of necessity to assume some semblance of courtesy as the manifold requirements of a complex project were discussed. Much of the apparatus required was already available, and many of the materials also. Some were not, and would have to be acquired; the acquisition would take some time. In spite of all the arguments Joseph could muster, Costeaux was adamant that he would have to remain in chains. An assistant would be provided as necessary to bustle for him and follow his instructions. A special living-room would be prepared to make him as comfortable as the circumstances would allow. Regrettably he would have to spend one more night in the cellar.

Joseph had plenty of thinking time. No shortage. At first he blamed himself for cowardice. Then he remembered the pitiful state of Uwe Schliessmann, the isolation of his own position, and the pointlessness, as well as the pain, of being handed over to become a plaything for the sisters Paulet. He must use every internal resource that he possessed and most particularly his intellect. It was best to cooperate and to await his chance. Costeaux and Fourques would have to grant him some measure of freedom, even if it was only the freedom of a canary in a cage. They would also need to put some powerful tools in his hands. His situation demanded patience and ingenuity.

The next day started badly. He put the wrong foot forward by asking after Uwe Schliessmann. Costeaux stared coldly and answered in tones as bleak as a new tombstone.

'He was surplus to requirements.'

Joseph clamped his mouth firmly shut on the anger that was trying to get out. His brief encounter with Schliessmann had generated great respect for the man. In the next months he became familiar with the taste of anger. It accumulated inside him instead, threatening dyspepsia. In a voice that had a strangled quality from the words trying to force their way out against the counter-current of his disgust, he compelled himself to begin the necessary discussion of the strategies to be followed in the pursuit of gold. He would follow the Cosmopolite's instructions, which, contrary to the lies he had told Costeaux, he knew by heart. First he would prepare the Universal Solvent. This must be made from the Volatile Salt, the Fixed Salt and Spirits of Nitre. The process was one that he had conducted before, with Sendivogius and alone. It bore some resemblance to the preparation of the Vivified Air. It would not take long. A day or so would suffice once he had assembled the apparatus and materials. The next stage was to place gold, mercury and the Universal Solvent in carefully measured amounts in a tube, which must be heated for forty-five days at moderate heat and then for another forty-five days at greater heat. At the end of this time, he would find a small crystal, the colour of ruby. Mixing again with the Universal Solvent and heating for further ninety days would give a red powder, the long-sought Stone.

For Joseph there were two problems. First, there was much to be done initially, for a few days, then nothing to do but wait. What would he do, or be allowed to do, in the these long periods of time – periods which would seem long in any circumstance but which would be interminable and unendurable during his imprisonment? And when at the end of the interminable, if he had failed – as he now believed he must fail – how would he survive his captors' wrath? He had to find a convincing means to keep himself busy at the stills and furnaces, partly to retain his sanity but also in the hope that he might invent some means of engineering his escape.

'How are you going to get us out of this one, Papa?'

The flaxen-haired boy spoke with a touching confidence in his father's abilities. Joseph glanced in pity at the boy, who was also chained.

'We shall think of something, with God's help. First we must be alchemists and nothing else.'

'Aren't we alchemists already?'

'We were. Now I am not sure. Men, in good time, become what they suppose themselves to be, and I had begun to imagine myself a Natural Philosopher,' replied Joseph. 'Now we are alchemists. We do not have much time, though. In another sense we have too much. But whatever we were once, or intend to be in the future when we have escaped this place, now we must be alchemists. We must begin by concentrating on the Philosophic essences.'

Joseph was made comfortable – as comfortable, that is, as chains would allow. He was not returned to the dungeon but given a room with a beautiful view from which the heavy barring at the windows considerably detracted. Every morning he was escorted down to the laboratory where he began work on the production of the Universal Solvent and the Philosopher's Stone. He could move about with difficulty only and was provided with assistants who could work according to his orders. At least one guard, well provided with some uncomfortable-looking weaponry, was always in attendance. He was well fed and considerately treated. Costeaux was clearly concerned to maintain him in first-class working order. But God help me when I am no longer of use, thought Joseph. That day must be postponed by every possible means. His largest problem was how to occupy the huge stretches of waiting time after the athanor had been set up in which the Stone would grow gradually, month by month, like a mysterious plant. Here his ability to fantasise, which he had many times regarded as a curse leading him into difficult or embarrassing self-inflicted situations, came to his rescue. He would seek to break new ground by attempting – or appearing to attempt – to find ways of accelerating the reactions leading to the transmutation. Costeaux kept a close interest in the processes and Joseph was forced to expend much ingenuity in satisfying him. Fortunately Joseph's knowledge was much the greater of the two and Costeaux seemed happy enough at Joseph's approach to the problems, although he was continually urging upon Joseph the urgency of finding a solution quickly. The relationship between them was cool but courteous. Their interdependence and the intricacies of the studies involved forced upon them some semblance of civilised intercourse, although Costeaux was not above occasionally and for no apparent reason breaking into a sudden homily on the beauty, virtue and good health of the Paulet sisters. Indeed these two charming siblings would frequently come into the workshop and Joseph would be required to satisfy their enthusiasm for chymistry with an explanation of the progress of the project. The visits were clearly hints, not especially subtle.

The preparation of the Universal Solvent was achieved within a few days. It was only necessary to assemble the apparatus from readily available components and begin distillation of some common substances. But the next ninety days were the longest five years of Joseph's life. For forty-five days he subjected small slivers of gold and shining globules of mercury to moderate heat together with the Solvent. Then, following the Cosmopolite's instructions, he intensified the heat and tried to face out the horror of another forty-five days' wait while the mixture did little except omit an occasional belch or hiccup. He set up a series of such experiments with slightly varying conditions or slightly differing ingredients, this in an attempt to retain his sanity by engaging in some kind of continuing activity, and in the hope of diverting Costeaux's attention when the first project failed – as he feared that it would fail – to others still allegedly burgeoning with promise. Each day he must exercise his ingenuity in explaining his actions to his to his dangerous and suspicious captor – a particularly testing exercise because Costeaux was by no means ignorant of chymical knowledge. The mental effort of producing credible fantasies helped him in his fight against the fear and boredom of his situation, which might otherwise have overwhelmed him.

His explanations brought with them also an unexpected and valuable by-product. In attempting to explain to Costeaux the rationale of what he was doing, he came to realise with a new clarity how little rationale there was available in the processes which he had set up, and how little was to be found in the prescriptions of the alchemical books with which the laboratory was of course well-supplied or even in Sendivogius's writings, where the practical instructions were of impeccable clarity, but the reasoning behind them sometimes of impenetrable obscurity. He was reminded of his talk on the last eventful afternoon at the Baroness's house, and the realisation confirmed his disillusionment with the old ways of thinking and constituted another step in the sweeping clean of his mental cupboard. The weakness of the rationale was of course on his side in deceiving Costeaux who was entirely of the Old School.

The mental problems of imprisonment were occasionally relieved by conversations with the guards, most of whom were objectionable and sometimes sadistic. Any potentate or criminal who wants to do evil, thought Joseph, has no difficulty in recruiting menial assistance. There is a small but perpetual reservoir of thugs available anywhere, awaiting hire. Arnaud was the worst. Beneath prominent cheek-bones that gave his face the friendly look of a rock-face, his animal nose was turned up at the end revealing nostrils that seemed to point at Joseph like the double-barrelled pistol that he carried. He delighted in taking aim at Joseph with the pistol. He was clearly practising speed of response, of firing and reloading. He was improving all the time. He would also take out a sword and pass away the boring hours of duty by rehearsing sword-play against an imaginary opponent. Sometimes he would vary this with dagger work. In one exercise of which he seemed particularly fond, he was unmistakably immobilising a victim from behind by gripping his hair and then cutting his throat. With one of the guards he felt a certain sympathy. This was a large shambling fellow called Bernard with halting speech who should have been cleaning out the cattle stalls in some neighbouring farm. Presumably he had been lured by better pay. He had a certain charm of the mentally slightly insufficient, a kind of attractive naivety belonging to a man too simple to be blame-worthy.

One day Bernard was on duty, but behaving eccentrically. He was shuffling from one foot to the other and muttering incoherently. Joseph had difficulty in deciding whether the words were addressed to him or not. Eventually it became clear the guard was trying to ask him a question. Why this exhibition of embarrassment from an armed man who could shoot him down in a moment? At last Bernard managed a recognisable question, recognisably addressed to him.

'Don't mind me asking, do you? But you're a doctor, aren't you?'

'I am not a physician. I am an apothecary.'

'Oh, it's no good then. I want somebody who knows about medicines and things.'

'That's all right,' said Joseph patiently. 'It's an apothecary that you need. Perhaps I can help you.'

'Well,' said Bernard, haltingly between shuffles. 'It's like this. I like children. Sometimes anyway. Bloody nuisance most of the time. But it's my wife particularly. She's very keen. But none come. We don't have any.'

This was familiar territory. There was a set of standard questions to work through.

'I see. But tell me, do you have regular intercourse?'

'Don't think so. But we fuck a lot. Or we try.'

'Ah. You try. But you don't succeed?'

'No, it's not good,' said Bernard shamefacedly.

'Is the trouble with you or with her?'

'I'm all right. There's no problem with me. It's my baby-maker, my Dick. It don't seem ready.'

'Ah! You cannot rise to the occasion?'

'That's it.' Bernard was obviously relieved to have delivered his message.

'Stop worrying about it. Worrying makes it more difficult still. I will give you a remedy which I am sure will help you.'

The conversation provided a welcome diversion to help fill the long hours of imprisonment. In the lavishly equipped laboratory he had no difficulty in preparing one of the traditional remedies for the man's problem.

The first crisis came after the second period of forty-five days. A scarlet crystal, according to the wisdom of the books, should have formed in the container. Examination revealed a rather dingy sediment of a rusty colour which might, to a man of imagination, be a collection of very small crystals but was definitely not scarlet. As a scarlet crystal it needed a little help. Luckily help was available, since Joseph had foreseen this eventuality, and had ready one that he had prepared earlier. Constant surveillance of his activities was easy for Costeaux to arrange, but constant surveillance by someone who understood everything that he was doing was not possible – even Costeaux could not comprehend entirely all that his prisoner was doing and Joseph made sure that it was as complex and confusing as he could make it – and in this lay his hope. Luck was with him, and a few minutes, when only the guard was present, sufficed for an instant enhancement of the unpromising residue. The next morning Costeaux was excited by the transformation that was beginning before his very eyes. Later in the day his excitement was tinged with suspicion. From that day forward, Joseph's activities were watched even more closely than previously.

The next and ultimate crisis was approaching. It was now sixty days into the ninety-day period that was supposed to end with the El Dorado of the multiplication of the gold. Costeaux and Fourques became increasingly restive. No changes were apparent in the stills. Visits from those eager students of chymistry, Douce and Aigre, became increasingly frequent as well as more prolonged and threatening. They attended rapturously to his explanations and hovered close to him in a way that should have been enticing but was actually infinitely terrifying. Joseph was running out of time and ideas. The situation was becoming critical. One day he was working with a liquid which had begun its life as spirits of nitre, but in which the several metals had disappeared with the familiar turmoil. Was the reaction complete? Had the spirit of the acid been killed by the additions he had made? He applied the age-old tests familiar to generations of alchemists. First he cautiously applied his nose to the flask. Then he touched the surface of the liquid with his finger and tasted the finger with his tongue. He had been explaining his latest idea to Costeaux and Fourques who were still standing by. He turned to them and asked their opinion. As on previous occasions when he had been discussing the work with them, each in turn did exactly as he had done, and as they had done themselves countless times in previous laboratories. They smelled cautiously. They tasted cautiously. At that moment a travelling huckster whispered in Joseph's ear.

'Psst!' he said. 'Wanna buy an elixir? Cure anything. Solve all your ailments and problems. Called Oil of Almonds.'

'Got some already,' replied Joseph.

That night he returned to the idea. Not a good one. He possessed a powerful poison, true. Or was it true? – he had only the word of the poor crumbling Schliessmann for that. In any case he could not administer it to his captors. The traditional tasting test had provided him with the original idea, but there was no way that Costeaux and Fourques could be persuaded to taste anything that they had not seen him taste first. He dismissed the idea and went to bed. But he could not sleep. The symptoms were familiar. Something was working there in his personal compost heap. Towards dawn, a possible solution occurred to him, desperate certainly, but so was his situation.

In the next few days he experimented tirelessly and was particularly agreeable and co-operative, taking especial care to consult Costeaux or Fourques, or preferably both together, for their opinions. The *sniff it, taste it* routine was used on several occasions. In fact he positively encouraged it. He had to await his chance. In the meantime, at night, he practised. The weather was hot and his request for a glass of water at his bedside was granted without question. What he now had to learn was a trick which he had seen performed somewhere by an itinerant conjurer making a few florins perhaps, or possibly someone showing off at a party, he could not remember exactly the occasion. At night he practised what he came to call the Wrong Finger Trick. Dip one finger and suck another, creating the illusion that the dipped finger was also the one that was sucked. The forefinger and middle finger were the obvious candidates. He practised, not dozens but hundreds, of times until he thought that he had perfected his act. His performance had to be faultless. His life depended upon it. If the ruse were recognised, he would be thrown to the wolves, or more precisely handed over to Douce and Aigre. If he contaminated the sucked finger with a trace of poison from the dipped finger, he would die along with his captors. The chains attached to his wrists were an extra hindrance. In the room was a mirror. With some difficulty he moved it from the wall where it hung, balancing it on a table where it was at hand level. Now he practised many more hundred times until he had convinced himself that his conjuring trick was not only totally convincing to the onlooker but also repeatable without flaw. After each session he replaced the mirror to avert suspicion.

## CHAPTER 25

Joseph's life was approaching crisis, perhaps its final crisis. He needed a moment when only one guard was on duty and both Costeaux and Fourques must be present and in the mood to talk about his accessory experiments in preparing the Elixir. Through long weeks the circumstances refused to conspire. There were only twelve days to go before the elixir was supposed to come to fruition, when Joseph's chance came at last, one day towards the end of summer. It was the Sabbath and there were very few of the staff in the building. About noon, his two captors came to talk to him. He kept a distillation apparatus running for this very purpose. He shuffled across to the still where an amber-red liquid was collecting.

'I need your opinion, he said. 'First I need to add some drops of acid and then some tincture of Almonds.' He transferred the amber-red liquid to an open vessel and added some drops from a bottle, which in reality contained water, not acid. Then he added one half of the contents of the bottle posing as Oil of Almonds. This was no occasion for economy or timidity. Only a minute quantity of liquid would be carried from finger to tongue but if the bottle really contained enough to kill the population of Toulouse, it should be sufficient. The other half of the bottle's contents was for himself if he failed. He swirled the mixture ruminatively, holding it up to the light. For some minutes he continued alternately examining the liquid and talking, explaining learnedly, pattering like the conjurers he had sometimes seen in market squares. At last he was satisfied.

'Ah. I think that is it.'

He was ready for the smell and taste routine. He placed his nose carefully over the beaker, smelled cautiously, and then went through the critical finger-changing routine. He sucked his finger thoughtfully.

'I taste only a slight almond flavour.'

He offered the beaker to Costeaux who followed what he thought was the same procedure. Joseph prayed to God not only that he would receive a fatal dose and that, on the other hand, the poison would not act immediately. If Costeaux was ill but recovered, Joseph was a dead man. If Costeaux fell dead on the instant or showed any signs of distress, Fourques would certainly not taste, and the consequences were unpredictable, probably catastrophic. To his relief both men tasted and then continued talking calmly. After a few minutes they departed with no more than some familiar veiled (and unnecessary) hints from Costeaux about what would ensue if his work for them failed.

That afternoon he grew increasingly depressed. Schliessman had been wrong about the Oil of Almonds. It was not a poison. Or he had been wrong about the dosage. His captors had absorbed far too little. Then again, perhaps Schliessman had been correct, but the poison had a limited storage life and had simply deteriorated, as many substances do, and the intervening months had rendered it useless. He tried to get on with the tasks in which he had no faith or which were creatures of his own fantasies, invented to fool his captors and provide himself with some occupation. Some hours passed in dejection and apprehension.

About mid-afternoon Bernard came on duty, replacing Arnaud. He was behaving even more strangely than usual. He wanted to tell Joseph something. The symptoms were unmistakable. He was flushed and shifting uneasily from one foot to the other like a flamingo with verrucas. Joseph thought it kind to lend assistance.

'How are you getting on, Bernard?' he asked pleasantly. 'Did the medicine work?'

'Oh yes,' mumbled the guard. 'Oh yes! Yes, my God it worked!'

'That's wonderful.' Joseph replied enthusiastically, but sensing that something was still troubling the man.

'It was. Fantastic. But she didn't think so.'

'Ah!' Joseph began to comprehend. 'Perhaps you were too enthusiastic. How long did it last?'

'Dunno. Haven't got one of them clocks. Two hours maybe.'

'Two hours!' Joseph's voice was half astonishment, half envy.

'Yes. Perhaps I was too keen. But it had been such a long time since the last.'

Joseph assumed the bright manner suitable for a patient troubled by a minor difficulty. 'Well, don't worry about it. Next time just show a little more care. Try and think of it from her side. If she needs encouragement, I can provide another formula which will help her feel more welcoming towards you.'

'You don't understand. She's left.'

'Left?'

'Yes. She's gone to her mother at St Genis.'

'Then you must fetch her back. Speak nicely and humbly to her. Just explain how you felt and apologise. Tell her that you love her. I am sure she will respond. St Genis is only a few miles away.'

'You don't understand that either. It's St Genis in Alsace.'

The man's difficulties were assuming a new scale. Joseph's reassurance routine, perfected at many bedsides, began without him having to think about it. The rule is – improvise soothing words which one hopes will comfort the patient while allowing time for some serious reflection on his problem. Joseph's words and further deliberations on this delicate matter ceased abruptly, however. He became aware suddenly that Bernard was no longer listening, but was staring over his shoulder as though he had seen some strange spirit or jinn. Glancing behind him he saw the odd phenomenon which was the cause of Bernard's preoccupation. The door from the corridor was opening. There was nothing unusual in that – Costeaux often visited at this time in the afternoon. But on this occasion, the door appeared to be opening without human assistance or any visible agency. Bernard had turned white and was crossing himself. Joseph was momentarily startled and bewildered. After a second or two he recovered his equanimity. There was a rational explanation and only one. Someone or something must be pressing against the lower part of the door that was concealed from them by the bench. He shuffled as best he could to a point in the room where his view of the door was unobstructed. It was indeed a visit from Costeaux, but he was no longer able to stand or walk. He was crawling painfully into the room across the floor. Joseph watched in awe as the Frenchman made slow progress towards him, stopping at times to clutch his abdomen. He was trying to say something to Joseph but his voice was weak and the sense of his speech was interrupted by groans. By a great effort he managed to reach where the two men were standing but then his arms gave way and he collapsed at Joseph's feet.

Joseph looked down at Costeaux and a spreading pool of vomit. The Frenchman was beginning to convulse. A boiling mud-pool of hatred and rage, repressed for months, came gushing up from subterranean depths. A severe headache would have been added to Costeaux's rapidly lengthening list of symptoms, but Joseph's foot was restrained by a sudden awareness that Bernard was no longer at the door but standing instead three feet away from him. A pistol, for which – as with all the other items of Costeaux's establishment – no expense had been spared, was pointing at him. He could see the beautifully fashioned and polished iron tubes reflecting the afternoon light. The picture lived on in his mind for many years. A calmness that he did not feel, conceived in desperation and nurtured by repeated rehearsal in his imagination, now served him well. He thanked God that Bernard was on duty, not Arnaud. He smiled disarmingly at the guard and addressed him in casual tones.

'Perhaps you would like to see where the gold is kept?'

The guard looked at him with extreme suspicion.

'What gold?' he said.

'The gold in Costeaux's store room.'

The implication of Joseph's suggestion spread slowly through the guard's mind like the reluctant beginning of a summer day. Dawn began somewhere in the eastern region of his eyes and spread slowly to the west and south, brightening as it went. By the time it had reached his mouth, it had become a radiant sunrise illuminating his whole face. After a second or two a cloud came over the sun.

'We don't have the key. And we don't know where the store is.'

'I know where to find both. But you must release me first. Costeaux carries the keys to my chains.'

Still suspicious but with an eagerness he could not suppress, the guard fumbled for the bunch of keys attached to Costeaux's belt. As the chains fell away from Joseph's feet and then his wrists, he felt an unprecedented sensation as though he was flying. His arms particularly, weighed down for some months, were literally rising involuntarily as though they had developed an ambition to become wings. He had no time in which to enjoy the sensation. Was the key to the gold store among the keys? If not, Bernard, who was still suspicious, would certainly become very unhappy, with consequences that could not be predicted. The point was underlined by the manner in which he walked a step or two behind Joseph with the pistol directed towards Joseph's back.

There were twenty keys at least in Costeaux's bunch and two doors to unlock, the first door being the entry to the store-room. The guard fidgeted impatiently while Joseph tried each key in turn, but avarice had now outvoted the other candidate emotions. Key number fifteen proved successful and in a few seconds more they stood before the armoured door to the gold store. Joseph prayed even more fervently than before. Please God let the both keys be here in the bunch! He was aware of the guard fiddling with his pistol. If he failed after raising the guard's expectations to such a height, he might soon have one orifice more than the body needs or can cope with. His prayer was answered. The eighth key clicked encouragingly in the first lock; the second yielded to key number three; after a little trial and error and some pushing and pulling, the door swung open. More prayers! Would the gold bars still be there? And still shining and unreverted? He stopped breathing as the door swung open. There they were – in fact rather more of them than when he had first been shown around the store. The guard gave an exclamation, eloquently expressing disbelief, excitement and anticipation in one syllable. A new life was in prospect. His pistol was forgotten, thrust back into its holster. Joseph no longer existed as far as he was concerned. He was too busy experimenting with all the ways in which heavy bars of metal can be secreted about the person. Joseph had long ago made his own estimate of the worth of the bars and of the problems of transporting them and had decided that two would secure his future very nicely without constituting an impossible encumbrance. He took three bars – perhaps the third would be needed as a bribe somewhere. Now he positioned himself behind Bernard and raised one of the bars ready to pursue the next part of the plan. The guard's newly risen sun was about to set prematurely. He hesitated with raised arm, then lowered it again. He was not violent by nature. Such actions were best left to those born under Leo. He had no quarrel with the guard who had clearly forgotten his existence. A Virgo would simply slip quietly away leaving the guard to his rewards, just or otherwise.

Outside in the corridor he turned in the direction that he reckoned would provide the least chance of meeting trouble. He cursed suddenly to himself. His luck was at an end. Turning a corner he was confronted by another of the guards. The man stared at him in surprise and then his right hand began to travel towards his sword. Before it could reach its destination, Joseph grabbed his left hand and placed one of the bars in it, smiling charmingly as he did so. Its weight necessitated the rapid return of the other hand. The guard was left staring in astonishment at a fortune that seemed almost to have dropped into his lap from out of the sky. By the time he recovered his thoughts and looked up, Joseph was gone. The keys would be an inestimable benefit: he planned to spirit himself away in some remote part of the establishment, locking as many doors as possible behind him, and stay there until after dark. One of the adjacent buildings might offer the best hope. Keeping in the shadow of the buildings and choosing the route that offered the best cover, he tried to assess which was the most secure hiding place. Eventually he decided upon the octagonal building of whose purpose he had received rather different accounts from Costeaux and Schliessman. Choosing a door on the side remote from the main buildings, he began to work through the keys again. He started suddenly at the sound of a sharp report, clearly a pistol shot, coming as far as he could determine from the direction of the front courtyard. It was followed by some shouting, the sound of clashing swords and then another pistol shot. Presumably the unusual appearance of Bernard, listing like a badly loaded ship, and his sudden change of shape and gait since he came on duty in the morning had attracted attention. Joseph guessed that a debate was now in progress among the guards as to who would finally own the bullion. More shots and clashing ensued, and further confused shouting in which he recognised the voices of several of the guards, a final shout of pain, and then silence.

   The interior of the building bore an almost unbearable stench so that he wondered briefly whether he could tolerate it for long, but he had generated many worse smells himself by choice and could doubtless live through it. Eventually his nose partially adjusted to the smell so that it became less overwhelming – a characteristic response of noses in general. Noses educated by his own trade seemed to have particularly effective escape routes. In any case, his professional interest was soon engaged by the contents of the laboratory. He had seen nothing to compare with this for sheer scale. It represented a giant magnification of the equipment with which he was familiar. He walked systematically around the building working out the functions of each item. Most of the pieces of equipment were for distillation, that was clear, but they were many times larger than anything that he had ever met before. Presumably – if Schliessmann had been correct – they distilled urine and its products. Hence this stifling atmosphere which he was, fortunately, no longer noticing. Everything was of immense size so that he had to fetch ladders and step-ladders to examine some of the apparatus. The building he realised was a factory rather than a workshop or laboratory. Largest of all was a huge vat in the centre mounted on a platform with four stout legs. Using the steps he climbed up to investigate the contents – or rather to confirm his conclusions and Schliessmann's account. At the bottom of the vat was a thick layer of some yellowish substance, which he judged to be about several inches thick. He could not see it clearly because it was covered by a water, some feet deep and occupying the rest of the vessel. This was presumably the storage arrangement for the final product, the incendiary material that had been described to him.

It was getting dark. His exploration had taken several hours, which had passed very quickly because of his study of the mechanics and chymistry of this remarkable building. He would wait for another few hours before he attempted to leave, in the hope that any remaining personnel would have departed, assuming they had not already completed the process of killing each other. He would not be bored in the meantime for he had one final task to accomplish. The Emperor was not going to receive his gift from Lucifer. It would be simple to set the building on fire, but that would merely bring attention to it and to him. He needed some delayed action. The factory contained everything he could possibly need. There was a whole store-room full of pipes and tubes of many sizes, presumably used for the construction and maintenance of the equipment. Choosing the widest bore he could find, he assembled an assortment of connectors and tubes of various lengths to make a flexible hose about thirty feet long. When complete he filled this with water and plugged the ends with corks. Climbing to the top of the vat he leaned over and dipped one end of the hose beneath the surface of the water and removed its cork. Then he pushed the hose down to a level just above the surface of the yellowish substance in the bottom of the vat. He secured the hose to a support on the outside of the vat and left it dangling with the free end coiled on the floor. The water would siphon freely from the vat when he removed the second cork. A satisfactory spurt of water came out when he tested it. He replaced the cork and looked around thoughtfully. Armageddon might require some further encouragement. The building was copiously supplied with fuel that was obviously needed to fire the furnaces for the stills. Beneath the vat he built a considerable pyre of logs and charcoal. It was now late evening and dark. The time had passed quickly as it always did when he was gainfully employed. Now he must leave. He lit the fire under the vat and watched it flare and crackle in a quite homely fashion. It should warm up the contents of the vat very pleasantly and assist with the removal of the water. The plugged end of the hose he carried out of the building with him. At its furthest extension he removed the cork and to his satisfaction water began to gush out liberally on to the ground.

The moonlight was bright but he moved cautiously in the shadows of buildings, navigating towards the front courtyard. He had almost reached it, moving along a path between two buildings, when he tripped over something soft and almost fell. It was the body of Bernard, dead, with one side of his face shot away. Feeling slightly sick he muttered a few words of prayer for the man's soul. Joseph had come to regard Bernard as opponent rather than an enemy. His marital problems were now redundant. Joseph concealed himself in some shrubbery to one side of the open space where he had a view of the sentry's cabin. Lying openly in the courtyard was the body of another guard. He waited and watched for some minutes until he was sure from the lack of movement that the cabin was no longer manned. One last careful, circuitous glide in the shadow of the perimeter wall and he reached the gate, passing through into the freedom of the French countryside.

It was a long night's walk to reach the town, and at first he moved blithely with the joy of release. The morning would bring further demands upon his ingenuity. He was entirely destitute except for two gold bars that would hardly be regarded as negotiable currency, and would not be easily turned into a breakfast. Luckily one of his past contacts, a magus, held a good position in Toulouse and would probably help him. He was suddenly overwhelmed by fatigue. He was extremely weak after months of confinement. He would face these difficult problems after a sleep. He slept for two hours in a wood and then moved slowly on. The dawn was just offering a tentative glow in the eastern sky when he heard a muffled explosion from somewhere in the direction from which he had come. The sky began to offer a rival glow to that in the east. The light from a large fire was reflecting off the clouds. So Schliessmann was correct in his description of the mysterious substance's distaste for being exposed to the air. Joseph chuckled and then sighed. Now he had destroyed *two* expensive laboratories – first, that of the Baroness and now this one – facilities so splendid that he would never possess anything remotely resembling them. Fire was becoming a motif in his life. He seemed fated to be the perpetrator, the victim or the innocent bystander of gross acts of incendiary. He really must try and break the habit. In future he swore he would have no dealings with Lucifer or Vesper, steal no fires from Zeus, reject the philosophy of Heraclitus. He would even resist the temptation to study the White Fire whose preparation had been so well described by Schliessman. In future all flames that he lit or caused to be lit would be strictly confined to the limits of his own hearth or furnaces.

# CHAPTER 26

*On a huge hill*
*Cragged, and steep, Truth stands, and he that will*
*Reach her, about must, and about must go;*
*And what the hill's suddenness resists, win so;*
    John Donne

Joseph polished his retorts and placed an order for saltpetre. His studies of Vivified Air were about to be renewed. His optimism was renewed also. He ordered many other substances and the latest apparatus, which closely resembled the equipment in use for centuries. It gleamed invitingly in the morning light but would soon lose its pristine quality and acquire that used-and-abused look, like gardening tools. He was in the remotest part of the country that he could find and was now Thomas Backhaus. He longed to be Joseph Skledowski but the longer he lived the less likely it seemed that he would ever achieve this humble ambition, the use of his names given at birth, an ambition which most people fulfilled without taking thought. He had passed over his chance to finish off Costeaux. He and Fourques were perhaps dead, perhaps alive, perhaps very much alive and in pursuit of him still, this time with vengeance as an extra motive. He had therefore chosen this remote northern part of England, and yet another alias.

One important change had come to bless him. He was partially relieved from the daily struggle to finance his next meal. He was not rich. He still needed some income from working as an apothecary, but he needed only occasional money from this occupation and was largely free to follow his studies wherever they would lead. For this he could thank the acquisition of the gold bars. Changing them into useful money had been a difficult and hazardous operation, of doubtful legality and possibly inviting the death penalty, providing another reason for the remoteness of his address and his assumption of anonymity. The legality might be doubtful, but the ethics were unimpeachable. Of course they were. Weren't they? This morning he had found himself thinking about the gold bars, provoked by a passage from Bartholomaeus Anglicus that he had read a few days before.

*From a mixture of bronze and tin and orpiment and some other medicines in the fire it is brought to the colour of gold, as says Isidorus. It has the colour and likeness of gold but not the value. Vessels and works of art of various kinds, beautiful when new and presenting the appearance of gold, gradually lose their first brilliancy and become red and thus show by their coppery colour and odour the material of their origin. In such vessels food and wines when long preserved acquire a horrible taste from the corruption and odour of the brass. Yet salves for the eyes are medicines which are profitably kept in them and are improved by the strength of the bronze, as says Platearius.*

Of course the bars that he had taken from Costeaux's safe were genuine gold! There was no deception on his part when he exchanged them for real gold and silver coins. How was he so confident that they were genuine? Costeaux had told him! He had been assured on the matter by that most honourable gentleman! And Joseph had examined the bars himself and concluded that they were real mined gold, probably from Mexico. Had he not been uneasy about them? Certainly not! Anyway, if they were obtained by some other means, by transmutation for example, all the better. That was real and valuable gold – maybe even more valuable because of its exotic origin.

But Reversion – that troublesome little voice kept nagging at him – how about Reversion then? Perhaps even now the worm was growing within the beautiful metal, rendering it grey and worthless! Oh come on, Reversion doesn't exist – that was Costeaux's nonsense, designed to lure him. As for Bartholomaeus Anglicus, well – he had come to distrust Authority. Besides the people who exchanged the gold with him are nauseatingly rich, almost certainly by robbing everyone else. They can afford the occasional little accident and deserve it. Well, maybe, but how about those they owe money to – poor people some of them, with families who might be now deprived through his actions, starving even – who cannot now be paid? Very improbable – just scaremongering. Not much doubt about that gold. A little doubt then? Perhaps a little – not much – a grain only. Well, if there were any doubts at all, why were the bars not examined and valued independently before exchanging them for money? Clearly unnecessary and a waste of valuable time! Oh dear! Perhaps he should have followed Bartholomaeus and made them into eye baths! The Adam and Eve of all headaches was overtaking him. It was time to abandon moral philosophy and think about something else. Distillation and heat control of substances subjected to a furnace would serve.

He had shown that the Vivified Air – he was no longer tempted to call it the Aerial Stone and could safely have readmitted the portrait of Galileo to his shelf if he had possessed one – supported combustion, apparently better even than ordinary air. It permitted respiration too. What else would burn in it? Would metals or salts do so? This was a starting point. He began with copper. The beautiful metal charred in the Vivified Air, just as it did in the external air, turning gradually to a dingy black mass that crumbled away to an unbeautiful unstructured powder. He weighed the metal before he began and was startled to find that, after the combustion, the weight had increased, not lessened as he had anticipated. He had grown up with the idea that something was lost during burning. The evidence of the eyes required it. Burn a piece of wood or coal and the flame and smoke leapt from it, as eager as prisoners to make their escape. Ash and cinders were all that remained, sometimes barely anything at all. The gain in weight must be wrong. He tried again and found again an increase in weight. The same was true when he heated iron or tin. Other materials gave more puzzling results. He returned to the metals, repeating the combustion many times. Each time he found the same things happening. He tried burning the same quantity of copper and each time obtained the black powder and each time in the same amount – the increase in weight was always the same, within quite narrow limits. The much easier trial of combustion in the external air gave similar results and the same gain in weight. Apparently the copper gained substance from the Vivified Air and from the external air. But the two airs were not the same; they came from quite different sources. And the Vivified Air was obtained from nitre, a white powder, an improbable origin for an air of any sort, let alone one with such remarkable characteristics.

'How about quicksilver, Papa? I like that stuff. You haven't done anything with that for ages.'

'I was trying to avoid mercury – mercury is a temptress and she-devil.' Mercury was too much a harlot from the old streets, the ambassador of a world with which he was trying not to communicate.

The flaxen-haired boy had another suggestion.

'About elements, Father. You said that lead, iron and gold were elements. Is that right?'

'How do you know that I said so? You were not there. I was a guest at dinner. You were in bed.'

'I was listening at the keyhole.'

'You are an incorrigible rogue. You will most likely provide employment for the hangman. I am ashamed to admit that I had no reason for making a statement of that kind.'

'I had no reason for listening at the keyhole. So that's evens!'

What lay behind that gratuitous, unsolicited statement he had made at the dinner table that evening about the nature of gold, lead and iron? How do we decide that something is an element? No problem for the Ancients – they solved the problem by argument and making assumptions about the means by which proof can be reached. By taking thought, by the quality of logic. What would Sir Francis Bacon's approach be? Rush into the workshop and study something. Collect some facts. Build up a huge picture. Eventually everything will become clear. But life is dangerous and short, thought Joseph. Somebody else will see the whole picture, maybe – perhaps after centuries of time, but certainly not me. An alternative would be to study one tiny fragment of the picture and bring that to perfection. What would Galileo recommend? A sudden and vivid vision assailed him, of the old curmudgeon scowling from his mantelpiece. Scowling – and growling as well, in the gravelly voice that Joseph imagined the old man to have when he was not trying to sweet-talk Cardinals. 'Don't go anywhere near your workshop. Sit down. Decide what question you want to ask. Try and imagine a way of answering it in practical terms. Then – and only then – take up your tools and walk.'

Joseph sat down as instructed. In the first place, what do we mean by an element? Aristotle and the whole team of Greek philosophers may draw up different lists of the elements and argue as to which is more elemental than the others – have them jostling for supremacy and precedence like politicians or duchesses. Here another voice interrupted him. 'You can't think about elements without defining what an element is, you oaf! Begin by defining an element according to Aristotle or the Ionian philosophers.'

'Well,' said Joseph in surprise, 'they would define an element as that substance or essence which cannot be described in terms of anything more fundamental than itself and which resides in all objects and substances in the world, although in differing proportions.'

'But that is two definitions,' said the voice.

With this second voice came a flash of illumination like the miraculous cure of a blind man. It – and the illumination – were immediately replaced by a rougher voice, this time all too unmistakably external and real. 'Backarse, 'Backarse. Where are you, Backarse? When are you going to let me in?'

Joseph sighed. Would he ever get this business of choosing a name right? He thought that he had chosen well at last, but obviously he was mistaken.

'Give me a chance, Charley,' he grumbled. 'What's the hurry anyway? Are the constables after you again?'

He let the old cattle farmer, Charles Botham, in.

'Glad to see you this morning, Apothecary. How is your head?'

Joseph was slightly puzzled by the question. He was unaware that something might be wrong with his head. 'No worse that usual. It never works as well as I would wish. It works better than yours though.'

'Ay, and better than the King of England's, for sure.'

'For sure. His did never function. Or it functions only when he is being devious or stubborn. Which, now I come to think of it is most of the time. How is your foot now?'

Joseph had treated the farmer for an abscess on his foot.

'Much better since I left off the medicine you gave me. And better than the King of England's head.'

'What is all this about heads? What's wrong with King Charles's head now?'

'Nothing. It's perfect. But when he eats his oysters in champagne, they won't go far before they come out again.'

Joseph's professional interests were aroused.

'He's vomiting then. Is it bad?'

'Vomiting, nothing. Nah. His stomach's all right. His body's perfect. And his head is perfect too. It's just they're no longer connected.'

'Christ!' Joseph inadvertently crossed himself. 'You're not serious are you?'

'Ay. I'm serious. So is he. He may not recover! It's feared he might die. The priests are gathered round both of him praying he'll mend.'

'But who has done this? Hell! Why do I ask? The English Parliament of course.'

'Yeah. They had him for treason. Treason against the King of England, I suppose. Against himself. Was about to chop his own head off. Awkward thing to do. So they kindly did it for him instead. Fair trial lasting three weeks. All his worst enemies as truthful witnesses. Heads you're guilty. Tails you're even more guilty.'

'My God, there will be trouble now. The Royalists will be in arms again. More bloodshed.'

'Na, they won't. No bloody chance. Fairfax and that lot have got the Royalists by the balls. Not a chance, unless they can get the Scots in on their side.'

'Charles's son has to be reckoned with.'

'There'll be no help from that rake. Only from the Almighty. Charles was the Lord's appointed and anointed. The Old Man up there must be battle-mad. Some say we're in for a beating. Wars, storms, fire from the earth, snakes, quakes, the lot. All the plagues of Egypt and some more He's thought up since. Plagues and pox such as we've never seen the like of. Be all right for you, Buckarse – your cures will sell like water in the desert.'

'I doubt it. So, who is in charge now? Fairfax, Cromwell?'

'Ay. And all the rest of the crew who'll be screwing us in the King's stead before long – that you can be sure.'

'Probably. But there are some good people among them. And zealous too. Over-zealous some of them. I wouldn't put water in your milk again if I were you.'

'That was only once! Well, twice. And it was an accident. Any road, it was the best water. Not like Bill Herbert. He piddles in his, I shouldn't wonder. At least it tastes like it.'

Joseph dropped everything that he had planned. Instead he assisted the villagers in their schedule for the day – standing about in groups discussing the awesome news. The community was in shock. Everyone had known that the execution might happen, but no one believed it would. The event was too enormous, too mind-swamping, too far outside experience. Kings were a part of destiny, arrangements made by God in his incomprehensible wisdom, an item to be adulated – saluted, almost with reverence, raising one's hat – or to be suffered like plague or poverty. Certainly not disposed of by a court of doubtful validity. There were laws of God and of Man. This was not some foreign country after all. A minority of the villagers, usually vocal, were supporters of the Parliamentarians and a few had even fought for their army, but today they had little to say, partly because the mood of their neighbours was unpredictable and possibly fragile and might become dangerous, partly because they shared in the sense of shock, of a nation careering, perhaps out of control, in some undetermined direction.

Joseph, recognised by his companions as an intelligent man of wide if enigmatic experience, was canvassed frequently for his reaction to this momentous event and his anticipation of what was likely to follow. He dispensed his opinions generously and for nothing. Internally he had no confidence in his pronouncements. Many times his thoughts flew back to the days he had spent with Goodrich and the Sectaries in Bristol. Perhaps their hour had come. But they, surely, were too divided. Would Parliament be able to rise to the occasion? Probably not. He suspected that they too were divided. The Army then. But armies know a lot about one thing and little about everything else. The situation demanded vigour, imagination and control. His illumination of the early morning, concerning elements, had disappeared into the lank undergrowth of his mind.

When he resumed normal life some days later, it was to grapple with a developing problem. His isolation. And how to share and publish his thoughts and his experiments on the gain in weight of calcined metals. He needed contacts in the world of natural philosophy. The most likely people to help him might be Baron Mixford and his wife. Hopefully they did not know the identity of the arsonist of their laboratory. He prepared a manuscript describing the work that he had done, together with a suitably fulsome letter. The courier bore both documents to London.

# CHAPTER 27

Costeaux raised himself on one elbow. He felt terrible. All the noises of a full-scale siege were going on inside his head. The enemy was trying to take it over. He felt as though the walls had already been breached, apparently by undermining and blowing up with gunpowder. He was lying in a pool of vomit some of which he had breathed in. He had no idea where he was. Presumably in his own room. The last thing that he could remember was going there feeling unwell.

It was utterly dark in the room although he could see the faint glow of moonlight at a window above his head. His one desire was to get into his bed and either recover there or die in comfort. Putting out a hand he expected to feel the rug on the floor of his bedroom. Instead his hand encountered a smooth metal object. He tried to lift it but it resisted weightily. Groping further he identified it. A chain. Further exploration discovered cupboards and the edge of a bench. He was in his laboratory. The chain was lying in a shapeless heap. Clearly the prisoner had escaped. He clutched at his belt for the keys. They were missing too. But how far had Skledowski gone? The question induced an immediate panic. He might not be alone. Skledowski might still be in the room. He was extremely anxious not to meet Skledowski in the present circumstances. He lay very still and listened. There was no sound, near or far. Presumably Joseph had got away as quickly as possible. But he would have had difficulty in leaving the heavily guarded farm though. Perhaps Fourques would know.

Fourques's room was on the same floor. Half crawling, half staggering, he arrived at the door of Fourques's room. It was unlocked. After much fumbling he managed to light a candle. Fourques was lying on his bed, seemingly dead. Further groping revealed that he was breathing but unconscious. There was no source of information here. The room faced the octagonal 'treatment house ' rather than the front courtyard, which would perhaps have been more informative. But he might be able to call to someone and get assistance. He opened the window and leaned cautiously out.

It was fortunate for him that he had already opened the window. Otherwise it would have blown in on top of him and certainly have killed him. The flash seemed to fill the whole sky. It was followed by an immense burst of flame and heat as though the Universe itself had exploded. He was hurled backwards into the room. The left side of his face seemed to be on fire and he had been sprayed with particles that glowed even in the intense flickering light that now filled the room, threatening to set his clothing on fire. Brushing them off as best he could, and burning his hands as he did so, he crawled and stumbled his way from the room, down the stairs, through another room where the cushions and chair covers were already bursting into flames, out into the courtyard. He collapsed a few feet outside the front door to the house.

A conflagration on the scale of the burning of Costeaux's farm was an event outside the experience of those who lived in the district, excepting a few who had served in the bitter fighting that was still continuing in the German states, and even for them it was hopelessly deprived of context in the quiet French countryside. A considerable crowd soon gathered together with some fire fighters who were entirely out of their depth. The first of the onlookers arrived in a few minutes, but by then the main buildings were thoroughly on fire. Costeaux was taken away and subjected to the best medical attention. The treatment for external burns was well known. Human history had generated plenty of opportunity for studying burns and the remedies were unpleasant but effective. Treatment for internal burning and the complications that followed was more difficult. Nevertheless, in time, and after periods of equivocation between life and death, Costeaux survived. But nothing could be done to repair the left side of his face. From that day onward, those who met him for the first time, flinched away from him as Joseph once had flinched from the man who manufactured Costeaux's white fire.

# CHAPTER 28

The business of the nation was conducted by Parliament – in the House of Commons and the House of Lords. And also, in spite of the passing of the era of Monarchy, at the Palace of Whitehall. At least these were the places where seals were wielded, writs issued, demands for taxation made, death sentences confirmed. It could be said, however, that the decisive work was done, not there, but at various sites not very far away, in a number of firmly established offices of less formal nature which indeed could be mistaken for eating places, taverns and coffee houses. In one of the latter, in January 1651, His Honour Judge Francis Neil sat in earnest conversation with a prominent but eccentric member of the aristocracy – that is to say that he was regarded as eccentric by his fellow peers and most of the gentry. His own view of his presence here was that he was trying to assess the mood of the people, or at least of the Middle Sort who frequented such places. If Francis and the peer appeared to talk as something like equals this was because of the persuasive way that Francis was believed to have – or rather to have had until recently – with the Secretary of State who was ultimately responsible for the taxation of estates, but also in acknowledgement of Neil's sharp mind and habit of speaking what was in it, albeit as offensively as possible. For these characteristics he was respected and hated by many in about equal proportions. The peer, William Richmond, Baron Mixford, was speaking, not without sympathy.

'Yes,' he said. 'It's hard, I know, but we all have these downturns in our lives. The wheel swings down. We get sick, our sons spend too much of our money, the house burns down. We seek preferment; it fails. We have to pick ourselves up again. Get on the wheel again. The wheel swings up.'

'This is not the failure of preferment. I have been sacked. Just plain sacked.'

'I am afraid that you should have chosen a different occupation. You can't expect Cromwell to take the blame. You have made too many enemies and finally had to be sacrificed.'

'I know. Enemies worth making, many of them.'

'There you are. Recalcitrant as ever. Count yourself lucky. Henry the Eighth's first act on becoming king was to execute his father's tax collectors. An easy way of gaining popularity. He still collected the money though. You have lost your job only, not your head. And have been granted another highly respected post and given a comfortable property.'

'Yes,' said Francis Neil bitterly. 'Circuit judge, drifting idly and endlessly in Limbo between towns in barbarous parts of the country distinguished only by their designation as sites for Assize Courts.'

'But not so far from London and with a nice estate and a title to go home to.'

'I suppose so. And I have to thank you for that, I acknowledge. It might have been worse without your intervention.'

'Not "might". It would have been. Well, I have a small favour to ask of you in return. Your past occupation and interests are your own concern and beyond reproach I am sure. I believe that you had some interest in matters of philosophy – as I have myself – in particular that you may have had some experience, which I have not, in alchemy… '

'That was a long time ago,' Francis Neil interrupted, rather over-hastily.

The Baron continued calmly apparently without noticing his companion's discomfiture. 'It is a subject which I find particularly difficult, obscure and somewhat distasteful. My wife has a much better grasp than I have. She assures me of its respectability, at least in its potential as a branch of natural philosophy. She is not in London, otherwise I would have consulted her opinion on this manuscript which I have just received. I would be grateful if you would read it and give me your opinion, which I shall greatly value, concerning its soundness.'

Francis Neil glanced briefly at the title page, welcoming it with a twitch of the nose.

'Thomas Backhaus. Hmm. A Goth! Or a Vandal. Another refugee from that squabble in the Palatinate, probably. I have never heard of him. One of many German tinkers who thinks he has manufactured the Horn of Plenty, I expect.'

'I think not. He has a different tone from most of such writers. Fewer animals. Less ferocious monsters. Hardly a Cave, Flower or Star to be seen. None of these things, actually. Except once, when he forgets himself and mentions something called the Aerial Stone.'

'He won't fly far on a stone, even on an aerial stone.'

Francis Neil began to read rather idly, with a supercilious expression on his nose. After a few paragraphs, he rested his chin in his cupped hand. Something had caught his attention. A paragraph or two more and his brows contracted into a frown of concentration. Soon he was utterly still, reading intensely. A deep silence ensued in which his Lordship was caught up also. He had not expected this. He screwed his neck round rather painfully and not very successfully trying to re-read the script. The sculptural group at this table in an otherwise lively venue attracted some whispered comment.

'It's from the Dutch Ambassador.'

'Nonsense. He is only a tax official. It's a new ruling on Estates.'

After some minutes Neil put the manuscript down. William Richmond looked at him enquiringly, but received no response. Francis was still deep in thought. At last he spoke, apparently to himself.

'Of course, he is wrong about elements. That can't be so.'

Suddenly remembering the august presence which he had been ignoring for so many minutes, he apologised to the Baron. 'I beg your pardon. This manuscript is either complete nonsense or of supreme importance. I am unsure which.'

'I sensed something of the same myself, although I could not be sure. It is essential that we decide what its true value is. Clearly we need to pass it to someone who has real expertise in the subject.'

'That might be difficult. Experimentation has made significant progress in several fields in London – in navigation, in magnetism for example – but in our understanding of the substances and their interaction we are still with Gerber and Avicenna.'

'Gresham College might help us,' suggested the Baron.

'They might,' Neil replied doubtfully.' Over there I spot an assistant to one of the professors. Not much hope from him. He's an old sailor whom they employ for some reason. But he has some inside knowledge. He may know who it would be most profitable to approach.'

Neil crossed the room and spoke briefly to the man in question and shortly returned with him in his wake. The sailor bore marks of his former occupation. His face was highly coloured as though still exposed to the ocean winds. His nose was similarly reddened, suggesting that he had been enjoying the solaces of shore life. His gait compensated for the pitch of unseen waves. He was astonished to be introduced to a baron but not at all daunted by the experience.

'Pleased to meet you Captain. What can I do for you, my Lord?'

'You can start by telling us what a sailor finds to do at Gresham College,' said the baron pleasantly.

'Same as he had to do at sea when he was master of a ship, sir. Reads the compass.'

'But you know where you are now. Somewhere between Thames Street and Cheapside.'

'Ay sir. We know where we are but we don't know where we're going.'

'That's not much use for a ship,' said Neil with a twitch.

'It was the greatest use for Cabot, Drake and even that rascal Columbus.'

'I take your point,' said William. 'You are concerned with exploration.'

'Ay sir. We try. We teach, but we try to extend the subject too. William Gilbert is our Admiral, dead though he is these thirty years.'

'But he was a scholar – a University-trained man,' said Francis Neil offensively.

'He was indeed,' agreed the sailor. 'And he had to forget it in order to do something useful.'

'A hit,' remarked the baron with a smile that he did not attempt to conceal. 'And you will be telling me next that you don't know any Latin.'

'Not a stitch, sir. Although it would often be useful.'

William Richmond came to the point.

'Does Gresham College know anything about chymistry?'

The sailor scratched his head. 'Stinks?' he said, 'and poisons! And making gold out of rusting guns? No sir.'

Neil was a mine of information as usual. Gresham College was endowed for seven professors. It had to be a mystical number, of course, to prefigure its mystical achievements. Divinity, law, rhetoric, music, physic, geometry and astronomy. 'Not navigation or compass studies,' he added nastily.

'They come under other subjects. That's what geometry and astronomy are for,' replied the sailor.

The baron intervened. 'Sir Thomas Gresham doubtless took the view which I confess I have shared and possibly still share. Alchemy, or chymical philosophy, if you wish to call it that, is a dubious occupation for a person of repute.'

'Ay sir. But it has its place. The people who know about it are the smelters of metals and the makers of inks. Ask them if you want to know about chymistry.'

Francis Neil's nose had an opinion on this too. 'Those are journeymen who use it but do not understand it. Mere cooks.'

The sailor agreed rather reluctantly without looking at Neil. 'There is something in that. They should ask more questions about what they are doing.'

The baron nodded. 'Listen. We need an informed opinion on a matter involving chymistry. It does not sound as though Gresham College can help us. Nor the manufacturers of metals and smelters of inks.'

The sailor was speaking slowly and thoughtfully as though trying to recall an item of conversation that he had heard but taken little account of.

'There is a group beginning to meet. Mostly of Greshamites. My friend Seb told me about it. He was a ship's physician. They are loaned a room in Gresham College for occasional meetings. I don't know much of what goes on there, but I believe that a clever young fellow from Scotland – McPherson – has been making quite a stir with some new ideas about alchemy or chymistry or whatever you want to call it.'

'Find his name please and ask him to contact Judge Francis Neil here who will pass a manuscript to him directly for his urgent attention.'

'Ay, ay sir,' said Thomas, taking his leave with a smart salute. 'And mind the iceberg on the starboard side, sir. It's always there.'

'I will see you in court, no doubt,' was Francis Neil's parting shot.

'An impudent fellow,' mused the baron, 'but likeable. What did he mean by that last remark, do you suppose?'

'I suspect he was making an observation concerning life in general, but I fear that he may be referring also to your possible role as regicide, and the certainty of extreme retribution if the Royal party ever returns.'

'I was not a regicide,' protested William Richmond. 'I was in favour of banishment.'

'It is all the same. You were too close to those who killed the King. To them it would be all the same.'

# CHAPTER 29

The six horses stood munching contentedly in the town square, solid and stolid. Some of them had been brushed and buffed for the occasion; the others had been led in directly from the fields with mud and burrs still visible on their sides. Sunlight flooded the streets with a radiance that should have brought peace and good humour to all. It was certainly a good morning for the horses. They had been released from their familiar heavy duties of carting and carrying and were standing at peace in the town square, yoked together and munching some handfuls of hay, and even a few tastier objects that had been fed to them by onlookers. Perhaps this was the glimpse of a Nirvana for horses, the foretaste of an equine Paradise. It was not to last. A sharp word of command and a thwack or two on their hindquarters and they were at work again, lunging suddenly forward. The four condemned women rose into the air. Their legs twitched briefly and their bodies contorted in protest for a few moments before the supply of blood to the head and breath to the lungs failed, and the cares and injustices of the world faded into a welcoming darkness.

Through long months of the impending trial the townspeople had assumed a shared identity and had behaved as though with a common will. They knew what they wanted – to be rid of the misfortunes which troubled the community and to purge the neighbourhood of evil. And to be rid of the cause – women, mostly, with an evil bent. From the proximity of neighbourhood these were women with malign natures and exceptional powers acquired by wicked means. From a greater distance it might have been perceived that the accused shared certain characteristics which were undesirable but not necessarily sinister. One would perhaps notice that such a woman might, for instance, have a peevish and interfering manner, a habit of forcing herself forward by means of some inadequate pretext into households where she was not welcome, of brushing against others in the market place or pushing into situations which the more discrete would have avoided. Her manner might be brusque and offensive and her smell not good. And her remarks, apparently jocular – for she laughed at them herself, sometimes immoderately – were often ill-judged or just incomprehensible. There were some dissenting voices, but not enough, and not loud enough. There were a dozen witnesses and several magistrates hearing preliminary evidence, and the trial was conducted at Assizes under the proper procedures of English Law with a judge and jury of twelve men of substance, but the whole town viewed itself the real arbiter. As far as the community was concerned, the issue was decided in advance of the trial. The town had assumed a single personality and had spoken. Often the Court disagreed with them and the defendant was released – to continue, if still capable of continuing anything at all, her evil machinations.

The unanimity faltered with the building of the gallows. Suddenly there were doubters. And for every doubter, several repentants. The initiative had not been theirs. It was sad that these things happened but it was in the nature of things and how could it be avoided? What else could one do? The reality of the terrible end of members of their own community was with them and the drift and drive of the long process of accusation, trial and conviction, during which time views had been expressed, theories postulated, evidence gathered, interminable discussions held, was now evident in the scene in the market-place. A great deal of hand washing was beginning. Pilate's bowl was being passed from hand to hand.

Mark Horbling was a man of honour, a man of courage. 'Everyone else,' he would say, 'the farmer, the builder, the architect, has to see the end product of his work. What sort of man would I be if I put these months or years of effort, of desperately painful work undertaken to bring justice upon these wicked offenders, if I could not follow the logic of my actions to their awful conclusion?' And so he made a point of attending the final act, 'unpleasant though it be.'

'See you're back again.' Mark turned to find a townsman whom he vaguely knew from a previous visit. 'Come to collect your fee, no doubt! Doing all right, I expect?'

Mark's neck began to post its warning signs. 'I don't do this for the remuneration. I get nothing more than expenses, and it's hard enough to collect those sometimes.'

'I heard that you get fifty pounds a neck.'

'Expenses only,' said Horbling in a dangerously raised voice. 'Are you calling me a liar?'

'Certainly not. I wouldn't dare. How much *did* you get, then?'

Mark eyed the man thoughtfully. He was of dauntingly muscular build. Mark recalled from his earlier interviews that the man was a blacksmith. One must not over-react in these situations.

'Expenses only,' he said firmly.

'Your expenses paid for an assistant too, I see.'

Mark looked round, expecting to find Richard behind him. He was not there.

'I would go and find him if I were you,' suggested the blacksmith. 'I saw him go behind Carder's shop a few moments ago. He didn't look too good.'

Mark set off in the direction indicated. Richard was indeed behind the shop. He was as pale as the shrouds being prepared for the remains of the wicked women. In front of him was a voluminous, green pool of vomit, in which several flies were already showing interest. He was still resolutely but ineffectively trying to add to the size of the pool. He looked up briefly at Mark and then continued his efforts.

'I know it's hard', said Mark, gruffly but not unkindly. 'These scenes take years off my life too. You have to get used to this work. You have to harden up.'

The two stood for several minutes, the older man's hand on the youth's shoulder. Mark talked calmly of the details of the day's journey in prospect and of any other indifferent things, which came to mind. The young man was showing signs of recovering his composure, but suddenly re-addressed his ineffectual attention to the green pool. It needed a further half hour of Mark's conversational efforts concerning the prospective weather, the bad roads, the possible accommodation, before the young man was in the minimal state of health needed for the continuation of their day's work.

'We've seen enough of the Market Square. We'll go round by the rear of the church', suggested Mark. 'The sooner we get our horses and go, the better.'

The path they took was slightly longer but offered the prospect of an unhindered return to their inn. At least, it would have done so on a normal day, but today was far from normal and today it was partially blocked, not by a crowd, but by a single individual, crouched on his knees in the middle of the path. His eyes were closed, he was dishevelled and in distress. He was in the attitude of prayer. He was not only clasping his hands, but wringing them. Mark recognised him as the rector of the parish church of All Saints, who had given evidence against one of the accused women. The vicar was addressing the Heavens in a loud voice.

'Have mercy on their souls, O Lord. Have mercy. Have mercy on us all. We know not what we do.'

It was not an occasion for socialising, and in any case the incident obviously threatened a return of Richard's digestive problem. Horbling took Richard by the arm and they side-stepped the vicar, allowing him to continue with his intercessions. They found their horses and began the journey to their next rendezvous with maleficence.

\* \* \* \* \*

The market square in which Joseph found himself, not long after, was an altogether more cheerful place. He was in a small town not far away from the one where the executions were carried out. The streets were crowded. It was the day of the cattle fair and horse market and the whole population of the surrounding district seemed already to have arrived. Auction, barter and exchange of cash were already in full noise. Also in progress was the greeting of friends and distant neighbours, rarely seen, and the obligatory courtesy of drinking plenty of beer with them. Joseph could have avoided the thickest of the throng, but was tempted instead to the area where most of the trading in horses was happening. He did not have money to spare on horses or on anything else that was on sale, but he did like to look around these markets and perhaps spend a few token pence on some small object that he found attractive but did not need.

The town was a few miles only from the house of Sir William Richards whose library he had found so useful, and on which he had committed several acts of reprehensible vandalism. He was on his way to Cambridge. Some years had passed since his return from France, during which time he had worked and pondered in his lonely village among the wolds. His discoveries seemed to him to be of a revolutionary nature. He had a growing sense of the importance of his studies. Perhaps, on the other hand, his grand ideas were nothing more then mirages bred by the moorland and isolation. The time had come to weigh them and, so to speak, test their density.

The market provided an opportunity for a break from travelling. He really would need another horse – eventually. He would not buy one now – that was for some time in the future but he would just get a feel for what was available at a price which he was able to afford. His present mount very effectively conveyed him on the few long journeys which his interests required him to make, but its spirit reminded him slightly of all the women whom he had known with any intimacy – distinctive and energetic, slightly unpredictable, a little uncomfortable, unlikely to bore him. Such qualities were equally but more directly dangerous in a horse. Joseph liked to maintain the fiction that he was in control of his life. In his more lucid moments he knew perfectly well that he lived on a metaphorical bolting horse. Also that when he purchased eventually, from whim or necessity, an actual, unmetaphorical horse, he would find that he had bought another with exactly the same qualities. The analogy with his attitude to the women was apparent. Only fools made the same mistake twice, but in this respect he was an incurable fool.

He saw by chance a splendid animal, a chestnut with burnished back, black mane and muscles that might have been painted by one of the great artists. It would carry its next owner many miles, and swiftly. It had a great problem just standing still. Just like his present horse – restless and temperamental. He would not buy it – he did not have the money with him even if he wanted to make a purchase. The horse trader was in the process of negotiating a price with the seller. The trader had a long jaw and a somewhat equine forehead, and indeed altogether slightly resembled a horse himself. This set Joseph wondering whether people, after many years of work at their trade, began to take on the characteristics of the materials with which they worked. He shuddered at the thought. Maybe his complexion was showing tinges of yellow like sulphur or the green colour of the vitriol of Mars. It would be no surprise, given the foetid atmosphere in which he frequently worked. He dismissed the thought as too uncomfortable and went back to admiring the horse. The sale had been arranged and the seller was just departing. Joseph could swear that he had seen the latter before, but could not remember where.

He dredged through memory, making repeated passes and seemed almost to have captured the elusive association, but each time it slipped away and was fugitive still.

'Lovely animal, isn't he sir?' said horse-face. 'And a bargain for you. It's my birthday and I'm celebrating. I want everybody else to be happy too.'

'How much?' asked Joseph suspiciously.

'For an animal of this quality I would usually ask at least five pounds. But you've got taste and judgement, sir, I can see. To a gentleman like you, who obviously admires him and knows a good horse when he sees it, I would let him go for three-and-a-half, hurt me though it will.'

'It's tempting but I have a decent horse already and no money to spare. I must pass, I'm afraid. But tell me, please – I'm sure that I know the man who sold the horse to you. I can't think why. I am sure I have seen him somewhere before.'

'His name is Dennis. He is a servant at a big house near here – with Sir William Richards.'

Horse-face lowered his voice. 'He quite often brings horses in for sale – lovely horses most of them. I can't think where he gets them – a man in his position, just a servant. I'm an honest man, sir. I don't take horses when I know that they've been stolen. I've nothing against him. I just wonder, that's all. He doesn't get paid much, I suppose. Probably he trades horses in his spare time to make ends meet.'

Dennis! The servant who had brought the note that summoned him to the young Nancy Richards. The night his previous horse had mysteriously disappeared. And Dennis sold horses regularly and mysteriously at the fair. Could it be? If he had revisited some years earlier, would he have been able to buy his own horse? Surely not!

'Of course, sir, we could arrange an exchange with your present horse. If I could just have a closer look at her.' The horse trader broke off, noticing that Joseph was transfixed and not listening. 'Anything wrong, sir?'

'Not here. Pardon me. I have seen too much in too many countries. I have become too mistrustful, God forgive me. And surely, Poseidon and Aphrodite can never work together.'

No further exchange of words – and certainly not of horses – was likely. He was just about to walk away and was idly wondering how many birthdays the horse trader enjoyed each year, when the focus of attention of both men shifted. Adjoining the market square was the courthouse, and Joseph looked up just in time to see an official disappearing through the main door. The sound that attracted him emanated from a small group of people as a wave of comment and conversation flowed through them. Something of interest or importance had been posted on the board outside the court. Never one to resist the tickling of his curiosity, he walked over to join the growing throng who were attempting to read, or provoking others to read for them.

> This day, February 11th. 1650, notice is hereby given by the undersigned, that Alice Selworthy of the Parish of Cottesthorpe is summoned to appear before court of Assizes on April 20, to answer charges of maleficence and witchcraft. The presiding judge will be His Honour Judge Lancelot Francis Neil.

Again Joseph's mind had to undertake a journey – back through intervening and very eventful years. Francis Neil was easily reclaimed. So old Nose-Twitch was a judge now. The mystery of his first name was also revealed. 'Very appropriate,' thought Joseph with a sour smile. The name Selworthy caused him more of a problem, evading him at first as had Dennis's face. Its significance was almost but not quite in his grasp. The name should mean something to him, but what? He groped unsuccessfully for some seconds before the image came to him of the old woman with the birds, Caroline Albright's grandmother. A peculiar old woman certainly, but a witch? She had that reputation locally. Perhaps she was being punished for her unusual intelligence. Joseph shrugged and was turning away when he encountered the horse-trader who had come over to read the text. Here was a chance to hear local opinion.

'Will they convict her?'

'Almost bound to,' replied the horse-trader. Little chance for her, I should say. And serves her right too. These hags deserve Hellfire and the sooner the better. And there will be more trials to come. Plenty of them. Mark Horbling and his lad are in the district.'

'Witch hunters?'

'Ay. Horbling is notorious. And his lad promises to be tougher and cleverer still. Not much chance for Alice. And a good thing too.'

Joseph shrugged again. After a few more diversions among the market traders, he continued his journey. As he rode, he tried to anticipate the difficulties and hazards of the conversations he would have at the university. The professors there were exceedingly learned and inclined to disbelieve the possibility that there was intellectual life outside their walls. Indeed, it was true that this was one of the best places in England in which to hear commentaries on Aristotle. This was the method of teaching and by some unquestioned process had become the method of investigation. The group to whom he would be speaking had become, so he had heard, devoted to Plato. To convince them that he had something important to say about the structure of the world was a double challenge – first to his own confidence that this was so, and second as a challenge to a centuries-old tradition, in its own formidably fortified citadel. It was a desperate move on his part to try and find sponsors and supporters and to prepare the way for publication. To his surprise, his mind refused to grapple effectively with the rehearsal of his impending test. Alice Selworthy kept interrupting his thoughts almost as if she were stepping out from the wayside woods and bushes of his journey trying to scare his horse. After this had happened a few times, and his mind had once again failed to grapple with its proper business, he pulled up in irritation. What was Alice Selworthy to him or he to Alice Selworthy? She was no relation, not a friend. She was not even the mother of a current girl friend, but several stages more remote. A previous lover, half-forgotten, and the lover's grandmother only, an old, rather egregious woman who would die soon anyway. And there were many other witches. Should he not be equally concerned about them? Were they worth anyone's concern?

He had grown up in a world of witches. Their existence was taken for granted by everyone around him including his mentor and protector, Michael. Witches and evil spirits were very real and moreover enjoyed classical and biblical authority. Their existence was already known to Homer. Medea must have been the Black Princess of all witches. Saul had to hear of his death and the death of his sons from a witch. That was enshrined in Old Testament law:

*You shall not permit a sorceress to live.*

*There shall not be found among you ... any one who practises divination, a soothsayer or an augur, or a sorcerer, or a charmer, or a medium, or a wizard, or a necromancer.*

Christ himself cast out evil spirits. They were necessary. "If no devils, no God", someone had said. Authority and tradition favoured the existence of witches. Authority could not be cast aside as some radical opinion would prefer. He had met some such opinions in the Bristol community. If this was done, where was the authority of the Bible? At some point the questioning of Authority had to stop. Authority, he now believed, was to be respected but not worshipped. In Cambridge he would have to present this attitude with the utmost care.

He had not thought about witches for years. He had been obsessed with the explanation of obscure events in the nature and interaction of substances, a subject neither understood nor rated as worthy of consideration except by a few. He had – with extreme difficulty and through a process not yet complete – freed himself of some of the magic and mystery of his predecessors. Simple events in his laboratory had simple causes, or if not *simple* causes, at least causes which could be rationally questioned. Was this not also applicable to events in the World in general? Perhaps witches were no longer necessary. The landscape visible from the top of the hill had not changed. His *perception* of the landscape had changed.

Even if witches were redundant – if they now existed only as an unnecessary and unjust prejudice, the strength of his reaction to the news of the threat to Alice Selworthy still demanded explanation. He could not understand it. Her fate was none of his business. Her predicament should no more concern him than the fate of any other of Horbling's customers. He winced at the jocularity of 'customers.' This problem could not be dismissed with a mind-saving joke, a means that he too often used to dispel uncomfortable subjects. At this moment, a distant glimpse of the towers of

Cambridge intervened and with it came a renewed flood of nervousness. His mind returned dramatically to the business in hand which was likely to be an embarrassing affront to his self-esteem. For the time being, Alice Selworthy was forgotten.

# CHAPTER 30

From Judge Francis Neil to Michael Müller (Thomas Backhaus, John Edwards, perhaps Joseph Skledowski)
    Frawley Manor
    June 7th. 1652.

  Dear Müller
  I thank you for your letter and for your offer of interference in the case of the Crown against Alice Selworthy on a charge of maleficium and witchcraft. Your concern for an elderly woman with whom, as you maintain, you are hardly acquainted, is most creditable. In the circumstances of most trials of this kind, a character reference from a person so remotely connected, with respect to both time and place, with the accused, would not be helpful, as indeed it may well not be in the present case. Nevertheless, if it will ease your conscience, I suggest that you do write to the Court in her support. There are so few in the district of Cottesthorpe prepared to speak for her that any crumb thrown to this wounded bird (more about birds in a moment) may be welcome, although unlikely to affect the outcome. I appreciate that it would be an excessive trouble to you to attend in person since you are doubtless still engaged in projects of the utmost urgency to mankind – projects whose importance I was well able to assess for myself in times past.
  There are no fewer than nineteen witnesses giving evidence against Alice Selworthy, some of whom will swear that her actions have been responsible for death, in several cases of farm animals and in one case of a human child. The feeling against her is intense, approaching hysterical even, and I fear there is little chance for her survival. If the jury were recruited solely from the people of her village there would be no chance, but the minimum requirements for property and income exercised in the selection of jurors ensure that recruitment of superstition is geographically wider, and that a superior class of ignoramus is chosen to decide the case.
  The trial promises to be an unnecessary waste of my time – and of yours if you do abandon your work for the period needed to write a letter. The event has its unusual aspects that give it a small hint of interest. Birds are central to the accusations. They are viewed by those who have brought the charges against Alice as her accomplices, whom she teaches and from whom she learns. They gather information, conduct missions for her of an unremittingly evil nature, carry sicknesses to the objects of her malice, and may actually have taught her to fly. Central to the case is the disappearance of several items that are referred to by their owners, rather imaginatively one suspects,

as jewellery, allegedly carried to her by the same enchanted avians. In accordance with practice, statements have been obtained from witnesses and written down in advance of the trial, and these will be read in Court, but any witness may also be called to give oral evidence. I include a list of the indictments and a brief summary of witnesses' statements.

I await your letter with curiosity but little hope. Principal among the items of my fascination is a desire to become acquainted with further developments regarding your present opinion of your identity,
Sincerely yours,
Francis Neil

Joseph's reading of the letter was heavily punctuated by snorts. 'Sarcastic swine,' he snapped. 'It's lucky that I don't have to like him.'

He turned to the list of witnesses' statements. The first fourteen were much as expected. Number fifteen was astonishing and stimulated him to immediate action. Now he would provide better evidence than a character reference – much better.

# CHAPTER 31

An old drama was about to be restaged with a new cast. The penultimate scene was set in the court-house in the city that administered justice to Cottesthorpe and many places of a similar size and nature. A chorus of estimable citizens, distinguished by their capacity to accumulate a little property or wealth and their possession of the wisdom that such activity brings, sat ready to pronounce on the innocence or otherwise of the accused. A newly appointed judge, Francis Lancelot Neil, not seen in the town before, sat on a beautifully carved seat raised on a low dais at the end of a once magnificent court room that was beginning to reflect the poverty brought to the area by years of stress. He was immediately recognisable, even without his robes, by a certain haughtiness in his bearing and a nose which was as eloquent as his blue eyes were inexpressive. The Justice of the Peace who had decided that Alice Selworthy's alleged felony must be tried at Assizes, was expected but not obliged to attend. He had voted for expectation rather than obligation. The second of the circuit judges, Julian Petrie, though, was of more conscientious nature and had taken the trouble to be present at a trial where he was not absolutely required. He was a large imposing man with thick black hair and a deep voice. The two judges were attempting to confer by shouting into each other's ear, a circumstance imposed by the clamour from the benches provided for those of the public who had been fortunate enough to get in, counterpointed by the uproar from the street outside from those who had not. The atmosphere was one of public holiday with an underlay of resentment and fear. A constable was trying to preserve one of the benches for members of the accused's family – and if necessary to protect them. Among the latter sat Celia and Caroline Albright.

His Honour Judge Francis Neil was in charge. It was he who had read the depositions of the witnesses and studied any possible legal complications of the case. Julian Petrie was there to assist him, to offer support in a situation that even the most experienced justices could find taxing, and to provide, if required, a second opinion. His immediate contribution was to signal with a nod to the court usher, who rose to his feet and called for silence. This was much like tossing a pebble into a waterfall. There was no discernible effect. Judge Petrie clearly considered that the time had come to assist. He addressed himself to the room in booming tones, which would have silenced the Bacchantes, and which succeeded in turning a few heads in his direction. Another minute or two of the hubbub and it was Francis Neil's turn. He said nothing. He rose to his feet and simply stood, his gaze slowly rotating around the room. He was exercising one of his premier talents – looking ominous and rather nasty. The noise slowly subsided. When it had reached a workable level he spoke. 'Expel those people on the bench left of the door. They have mistaken the place. This is the courtroom, not the prison.'

The constables ushered out some protesting citizens after a slight altercation in which one of the benches was overturned. Francis Neil now had the courtroom in the palm of his hand, although the noise from outside was still considerable. He nodded to the usher. The defendant was brought in.

Alice Selworthy entered between two constables, a classic case of overstaffing, as one fourteen year-old child would have been sufficient for the task. She had a crumpled look. She had become exceedingly frail. Old age, no doubt, had worked its wicked trick itself, but there were tell-tail signs about her eyes and a more-than-usual pinched look about her cheeks, which suggested that stress and sleeplessness had assisted.

Francis Neil had assigned the humane tasks to his fellow judge who addressed the accused in his deep but kindly tones: 'Your name?'

The reply came in a voice so firm that it took everyone by surprise, like a scarecrow breaking into human speech.

'Alice Selworthy,' she replied and, forestalling the next question, added, 'of 1 Hawthorn Cottages, Cottesthorpe.'

'Alice Selworthy,' Petrie continued. 'You are charged with maleficium and witchcraft, for offences committed against the Law of England between the Years of Our Lord 1641 and 1652, in contravention of the statute of 1604. Do you understand the charges?'

'Yes sir. As far as anyone can.'

Petrie gave her a dangerous look, but continued, 'Do you plead guilty or not guilty?'

'Not guilty. The charges are ridiculous.'

'You are required to answer the questions, not to comment on them,' said Petrie severely. 'Since you maintain that you are not guilty, how is it that you have made a confession. I have it here, in my hand.'

Alice had been – with considerable difficulty – persuaded by her daughter and granddaughter that she must address the judges politely and correctly. She replied: 'So would you, sir, if you had been kept awake for three days and nights, and threatened with all manner of unpleasant things.'

Julian Petrie frowned. 'We have a statement here from those who questioned you, Mark Horbling and Graham Drover. They say that they questioned you closely "ensuring adequate rest periods." And later in their report that you "yielded the information in response to continual but gentle examination".'

'Yes sir. The rest periods were when they changed places.'

Petrie's voice registered surprise. 'You mean that they alternated – that is to say, they questioned you separately – and that one took over when the other finished?'

'Yes sir. They alternated. And the rest period was between one leaving the room and the other entering. Immediately. And their report is wrong. I believe that they meant "continuous" not "continual".'

'You are treading on the edge of impertinence. What schooling did you have?'

'I was taught by Charles Treadle of Cottesthorpe along with the other village children until I was twelve, when not needed at the farm.'

'A suitable education and competently taught, I am sure, but sparse. What makes you think that you understand these subtleties of language?'

'I have met many people while working in coaching inns. I have talked to intelligent people whenever possible. Not many about,' she added nastily with a pointed glance at the public benches, which responded with some sullen mutterings.

At this point the two judges were seen to confer although, their words could not be heard. Francis Neil said:

'I am going to call Horbling and Drover.'

'You cannot. They are not here.'

'I know that. I am going to call them all the same.'

Neil turned towards the usher. Call Horbling to the witness stand and warn Drover to be ready to follow him. The usher looked flustered and puzzled but started towards the appropriate door. The clerk of the court rose and said: 'Excuse me your Honour. The witnesses you name are not present.'

'Not present! Why is that?'

'Sir. Mark Horbling was under the impression that he was not required by the Court. It is not a necessary practice for those who have exposed the suspected witch to attend the trial. And Graham Drover has written a letter to the Court.'

'I can hardly believe it.' He addressed the usher. 'Please check whether or not Mark Horbling is with us.'

The usher disappeared and in a few seconds re-entered. 'Not here my Lord.'

'Preposterous! How can we be expected to conduct a trial where a woman's life is at stake if key witnesses are absent?'

Petrie turned to Neil and said aloud. 'We do have their deposition in some detail.'

'Yes,' replied Neil, also aloud, 'but I am not satisfied with the conditions under which the examination was conducted and would have preferred to question them. We shall certainly hear what Drover has to say in his letter later in the proceedings.'

The members of the jury were engrossed by this piece of theatre. Their eyes turned in astonishment from the clerk to the usher, to Neil, to Petrie – exactly as Neil had intended.

Petrie, who took a more proper view of court procedure, and disapproved of what was happening, was clearly annoyed as well as bemused and looked profoundly uncomfortable. Some of the jury were puzzled, some outraged. Francis Neil merely twitched his nostrils and continued with the next item.

The Court considered the first evidence. This concerned a small brown mark, slightly raised and of a curious oval shape, discovered on Alice's left shoulder during examination by Beatrice Weir, a licensed midwife who had been summoned to examine her – a witch's teat according to Horbling and Drover's report.

Next came a long and damning list of the injuries suffered by people in the district of Cottesthorpe, or by their animals and crops, provoked by the evil talents of Alice Selworthy. Several threads ran through the otherwise diverse accounts. The victim had engaged in some altercation with Alice, or had been glared at by her in a menacing manner. Both of these things were more than credible, and no one, even her nearest and dearest, would have disputed the possibility. In some the sufferer had been touched, deliberately or with purpose disguised as an accident, by Alice. There followed loss of feeling in an arm, mysterious deaths in the chicken pen, blackening of the ears of rye and a catalogue of other minor and major disasters.

A particularly colourful thread was provided by the avian theme. Birds kept coming and coming out of the skies and into the narrative, hundreds of them, singly or in great flocks. They looked in at windows, dived at heads, wove above the houses amazing patterns, black in colour and very complicated – inexplicable signs that were clearly harmful spells conjured by black magic. (At this point, Alice Selworthy interjected scornfully 'starlings – they do that everywhere' and was told peremptorily by Francis Neil to be quiet.) The birds shat on washing, even tapped on windows or, in one case, simply flew past in a way that was loaded with suspicion.

For most of these statements, Francis Neil refrained from calling the originator for questioning but satisfied himself by commenting to the jury, usually drawing its attention to the lack of evidence connecting the allegedly magical events to the injuries sustained. He did not persist much with this point. The jury *just knew* that there was a connection between events of this kind, and were not about to change their view of the world for a judge, however eloquent or persuasive. No point in lecturing them on the lack of uniqueness of an event or quoting numbers from all over England to show how often sheep fell dead or udders dried up. The jury would simply conclude that there were even more witches about than it had realised.

One of the accusations of maleficium stood out from the others and demanded especial consideration. An increased tension and attention on the public benches signalled its arrival. The birth of a child still-born, if attributable to human malice, would have constituted a felony even under the more lenient Act of 1564, which required proof of death of a human person to merit capital punishment. Under the harsher Act of 1604, which was relevant to the present trial, personal injury of any kind was sufficient to send the perpetrator to the gallows. Brownlea's paralysed arm would have been sufficient. But the death of a child in the womb was damning and particularly emotive.

Lucy Pridy, a thin, worn-out woman of about forty, the unfortunate mother, was called for questioning. This was Petrie's métier. He spoke to her gently, whittling his big voice down almost to a whisper. He enquired first the date and place of the child's death, then – rather unnecessarily – the effect of the event upon her and her husband. Then he turned to the episode that had engendered the accusation against Alice Selworthy. The two women had been at a market stall, buying vegetables. The potatoes were particularly cheap, were fast disappearing, and there was something of a mêlée of women around the stall. Lucy Pridy, who was in the early months of bearing the dead child, had inadvertently pushed in front of Alice, stepping on her foot at the same time. Alice had reacted. ('I'll bet she did!' whispered Celia Albright to her daughter.) She had made some picturesque, if inaccurate, observations on Pridy's parentage and, catching hold of her arm, uttered some further words that Pridy did not understand. She was certain that they were a curse. How did she know that they were a curse? Petrie had asked. Because of the venomous tone of voice and the subsequent still birth of the child, was the answer.

To the surprise of the court, not least to the surprise and relief of Lucy Pridy, Judge Neil did not question her, but merely warned that he might require her later. Instead he called a clergyman, Reverend Holly, vicar of the parish of Cottesmere. Josiah Holly was the successor to Father James whose possible assistance in a matter of the heart had been so scornfully dismissed by Celia Albright. Father James had died, supposedly from complications following influenza, although some were heard to mutter that the disease had been of a less creditable nature. Holly was man of middle age, not fat, but rotund. His rounded face, small nose and large eyes gave him an owlish appearance. He arrived blinking slightly.

'Thank you for attending, Father. You know Alice Selworthy well, I believe?'

'Fairly well. And for six years or more. She is my parishioner and attends my church.'

'Regularly?'

'No sir. Her attendance is unpredictable. But she is often there.'

'How would you describe her in person?'

'She possesses many of the virtues of Christian charity –' he hesitated, ' – but her way of expressing herself is easily misconstrued. She is impatient with those less perceptive. I would estimate her to be of exceptional intelligence for one of her station – one might almost use the word 'genius,' though undeveloped. If she has a sin with which to battle it is excessive pride in her superior mental powers.'

'Would you expect that her neighbours would find her of an easy nature?'

'No. She is eccentric, sometimes cantankerous and easily misunderstood. But she is of good heart.'

Francis Neil, to whom the parson's owlish appearance had not been lost, then said 'Father, we need to benefit from your wisdom as a man of the Church. There are one or two theological issues that have relevance to this trial. But first. Do you believe in the existence of witches?'

'Oh certainly. The scriptures are clear on the subject. The Law is clearly stated. 'Thou shalt not suffer a sorceress to live.'

'Does that imply that witches are always women?' It was Petrie who asked the question.'

'I do not pretend to understand why women are especially mentioned. There are many instances of sorcery by men.'

'But most cases involve women?'

'Yes.'

'Perhaps,' said Neil,' that is because the law is entirely in the hands of men – judges, magistrates, law enforcers and – in most cases – jurists.'

'But women are the most frequent accusers,' observed Petrie. 'In any case that I have seen, they are in the front rank of hostile witnesses.'

Neil restored the discussion to its proper course. 'Well, matters of gender are of great interest but are not our concern here. What I am puzzled about – and what may puzzle the jury too – is how these come about. In most cases where people die or suffer those misfortunes that afflict us in abundance, they are assumed to be the will of God. When they happen we pray to God in humility accepting His will. "Take this cup from me, but Thy will be done." Why in the cases we have heard today is it to be assumed that other forces are at work.'

'Because,' said the clergyman, 'other forces *are* at work as the Bible makes clear.

'But is not God omnipotent – all powerful?' said Francis Neil, remembering the jury.

'God cannot take the blame for the World's wrongs.'

'Then the Devil is responsible for all evil acts?'

'The Devil is powerful but God is immensely more powerful. The evil powers are effective to the extent that the voice of the Devil is listened to.'

'Does the victim of such an evil attack have no defence?'

'The victim may or may not have an adequate defence. The true believer may perhaps possess such a defence by the strength of faith as a shield.'

The point was of intense interest to Francis Neil. He leaned forward.

'So it may be said that the victim is to some extent in complicity with the witch's action.'

'Come,' said Petrie, that is a surely a misinterpretation of the good Father's words.'

'I am not trying to impugn the character of Lucy Pridy who is clearly a woman of the highest virtue. I am merely trying to understand how witch enchantment works and whether it was present in this case.' He turned back to the clergyman. 'What we are saying is that the true believer may have some degree of defence against evil which others attempt to work upon her?'

'That is so.'

'And could that defence ever be absolute so that the evil powers had no chance of success.'

Josiah Holly shrugged. 'Perhaps. But it might demand perfection in the spiritual state such as was given only to Christ.'

'Do you believe Alice Selworthy to be a witch?'

'Certainly not.'

Now the curious subject of birds, normally a gastronomic topic, had to be examined more specifically. Elias Pitt was the first witness. He testified to having seen the bird heading into Alice Selworthy's garden bearing Tatt's amulet. He knew Tatt? Yes, he was a good friend, and Tatt had occasionally shown off the amulet to him. It was Tatt's amulet that the bird had in its beak. Was he certain? He was questioned repeatedly on this matter. He was certainly certain that he was certain. How could he be so sure? He had served a period as a lookout in His Majesty's Navy and had been rigorously trained as an observer. But not of magpies surely, flying with pieces of jewellery? No, but the skills he had acquired applied to land-lubberly situations too and he had clearly seen the gold and silver winking in the light and dark as the bird flew through the light and shade of the trees.

Next to witness was Thomas Tatt himself. A rather plump man, he stood proudly before the judges determined to enjoy his moment of eminence to the full.

'Mr Tatt, I thank you for attending to give evidence at this important trial.' Francis Neil was proffering the same courtesy to the meat curer as he granted the clergyman, which was certainly suspicious. 'Perhaps you would be so kind as to describe the piece of jewellery which you lost.'

'It was gold and silver, sir, about so big' – his fingers constructed something like an "O" – 'with a lamb and a flag. Given to me by my father, and by his father to him.'

'Ah. An heirloom.'

'No sir. But it had been passed down the family. Very old, which gave it partic'lar value.'

'Yes. It probably would.'

Thomas Tatt continued unprompted. Francis Neil made no move to interrupt him. He was quite happy to allow Thomas Tatt the freedom of the court.

'Yes sir. And a powerful defence it was against all sorts of afflictions. My grandma herself was saved by it in the great plague of '25. She was in the midst of it, serving the others like, as they died all around her. And my Dad carried it against the Dutch. Spattered all over he was with the blood of his mates, but not a scratch himself.' He lowered his voice conspiratorially. 'It's my belief that it was stolen from me to open me up for attack by evil powers.'

'I see. Given its extraordinary virtue, it is remarkable perhaps that it permitted itself to be stolen from you.'

'Eh?' Thomas Tatt had not quite grasped this point.

'I was merely wondering at its failure to protect you from theft. Perhaps you would be so good as to explain to us the circumstances in which it was lost.'

'Yes sir. It was a beautiful spring day, very warm, sir, and I took a tub into the garden, filled it with water and stripped down for a good wash.' He made an attempt at joviality. 'You may understand, sir, that sometimes my wife complains that I smell like smoked mutton.'

'The Court will take her word for it, Mr Tatt. Please go on.'

'I took off the amulet to wash – to wash myself I mean, sir, not the amulet – and laid it down on the grass. I was singing to myself and splashing about and so did not hear the flutter of wings. But I have this sixth sense sir, that has often served me well in difficult times, and something was troubling me. I looked round just in time to see a big bird flying away into the trees. And the amulet was gone.'

'I see. Thank you for your very lucid account, Mr Tatt.'

'Very glad to oblige, your Honour.'

'Well, Mr Tatt, I think we may be able to reward you for the trouble you have taken. We may have good news for you. The Clerk of the Court is holding an object that you might find of great interest. We would be glad if you would tell us whether you have seen it before.'

The Clerk beamed encouragingly at Tatt as he held out the exhibit for examination. The expressions that he received in return encompassed astonishment, pleasure, fear and a whole pageant of human emotions in swift succession – not including embarrassment however, which was beyond him. He might just as well been confronted with the a unicorn or proffered a griffin's egg.

'The court is waiting hopefully for possible news of the object's ownership,' prompted Francis Neil. The answer came in indecipherable splutters. The judge put the question more baldly.

'Does it belong to you?'

Tatt finally managed to indicate the affirmative.

'The Court is delighted to restore it to you. I have bad news however' – the bad news was celebrated with an appropriate twitch – 'I am assured by an expert that the trinket is constructed from brass and tin rather than gold and silver and that its value – if you were as unwise as to attempt to sell it – would be about five pence. I may have some further bad news at the end of the trial concerning punishments for false witness. In the meantime, however, the jury needs to know the recent history of this amulet.' He addressed the Clerk again. 'Please read out Michael Müller's deposition.'

At the name 'Müller' there was a stir on the bench where the Alice Selworthy's family sat. It could not be the Muller that they knew – the only one they had ever heard of – could it? Probably not. But the connection at first dismissed was soon reinstated when the clerk came to the words – 'previously an apothecary in the town of Cottesthorpe'. This provoked much nudging and a pantomime of meaningful looks between Celia Albright and her daughter. The court was now remarkably silent as the simple and not particularly eventful recent history of the amulet was disclosed.

\* \* \* \* \*

Joseph's involvement had realigned dramatically in a much more useful direction when he had read the fifteenth item in the accusations listed with Francis Neil's letter. He was startled to read that:

'Benjamin Tatt will give evidence that a valuable amulet was stolen from him by a crow which he saw flying away in the direction of the defendant's house. The same bird was seen flying with the object into the accused's garden, as will be attested by Elias Pitt.'

Joseph's astonishment was replaced by some hard thinking. He entered his memory like a diver plunging for sunken coins. He recalled easily and instantly the incident in his shop where he had relieved himself of the presence of Benjamin Tatt in such a dramatic, if reprehensible, manner. He could testify to the incident without difficulty, even at the cost of embarrassment in his admission of the scare he had once caused. He would be much more likely to convince the court if the amulet could be produced as evidence. Did he still have it? Improbable. A worthless item, of no monetary or aesthetic value, acquired inadvertently seven years ago. Why keep it? At first he feared that it might have been destroyed in the Bristol fire, but there was a chance of its survival with those of his possessions that had remained with James Fisher. And he was convinced that he had seen it somewhere not so long since. There was certainly a magpie (but definitely not a 'crow') in his own house – himself. He hated to discard anything ('This may be useful one day') and tended to throw small items into a junk box, which overflowed rapidly and generated another junk box. The boxes seemed to breed at the same rate as the mice that nested in them. He had seen the amulet he was sure on the last occasion of moving house. If he was right it was in his attic storeroom. He had to crawl into the cramped roof space before he could dive. He came up after several hours, not with a coin, but with an itchy nose from the dust he had raised and the wholly charmless charm, dirty but clearly disporting its lamb and flag and its quotation from the Lord's Prayer. After he had cleaned it and himself, he sat down to write a statement for the court and, for good measure included the amulet with it.

\* \* \* \* \*

'It is time,' said Francis Neil, 'to return to the matter of the confession.' He turned to the Clerk of the Court. 'I believe you have a letter from Graham Drover. Read it to the Court please.' To the jury he said, 'Drover is the younger of the two men whose work identified the defendant as a suspect and who examined her and persuaded her to confess. This letter is of the greatest importance. Please attend to it carefully.'

To the Justices of the Court, matter relevant to the trial of Alice Selworthy.
From Graham Drover.
Sirs – it is with great regret and shame that I present this statement to the Court. Eighteen months ago I agreed to enter the employment of Mark Horbling as an assistant to him in his work of identifying witches and bringing them to justice. I was – and remain – a young man, the son of a poor farmer, with few prospects of advancement. The position that I was offered seemed to provide an opportunity too good to refuse, both in terms of my advancement and as a means of providing an important service to the community. I entered the service of Mark Horbling in hope and sincerity of purpose.

It was a grave mistake and one that I fear I shall regret for the rest of my life. I have come gradually to realise during the period of our work that the evidence that we have collected in many cases is of little worth, and that the methods used by him are reprehensible.

In particular I must report that the means my employer adopted to extract confessions from those accused of crimes – crimes that are rightly regarded as abhorrent – have been no less abhorrent than the crimes themselves. I have become increasingly uneasy about the nature of the pressure put upon defendants to extract evidence or even confessions from them. It has become ever clearer to me that these methods often produce false evidence, with the accused condemning herself or himself. The case of Alice Selworthy confirmed me in this realisation. Alice Selworthy proved to be a woman of great ingenuity and spirit. Three nights and two days of questioning, during which she was given little respite and insufficient sustenance, were required before she made a confession. My belief is that the confession is of little value and I would humbly ask that the content should be ignored by the Court.

For the reasons given above, I have left the employment of Mark Horbling and returned home.
I am your most humble and repentant servant,
Graham Drover

The reading of the letter reduced even the public benches to a brief silence. It was broken shortly by a voice shouting, 'that's how they should be treated!' and a renewed uproar of voices shouting agreement. Francis Neil was forced to rise to his feet again to repeat his silent menace act. As the noise died down somewhat, he turned to the jury: 'The confession made by the defendant is to be discounted. You must treat the confession as though it never happened. You must forget that you ever heard about a confession.'

The time was approaching when the court's decision and the future of Alice Selworthy's neck must be reached. He did not call upon Alice for questioning. This was again an occasion for whispering between the two judges. Like everyone else Petrie had expected and clearly thought it only proper for such a standard procedure to be honoured. To these anxieties

Francis Neil replied, 'No – she would lose the Court's sympathies immediately and condemn herself irrevocably.'

'She should be allowed the chance,' said Petrie.

'She is not going to get it,' was the reply.

Before the matter was passed to the jury, the judge in charge would address them. He could not – or perhaps more accurately should not – tell them what they must decide, but a judge might be very eloquent and persuasive. He might direct them or even threaten them. None of these, nor rhetoric was in Francis Neil's repertoire. He spoke throughout in even tones with no dramatic climax and without any modulations of his voice except those required to express his icy contempt for juries, public gatherings, fellow judges and indeed for the world at large. His scorn clearly included the evidence presented against the accused. He spoke of witches' marks. These he seemed to view as evidence of childhood illness or the injuries received in particularly difficult births. He praised the virtue, application and industry of witch hunters, and of Horbling and Drover in particular, with complimentary words, but in tones that somehow suggested that such persons might be putative highway robbers. He noted the frequent occurrence of misfortunes such as those that the villagers had suffered but in places where there had been no suggestion of witch activities. He did not dwell on the point. It might merely be taken as an argument for the further employment of such men.

He did discuss, however, at some length the religious attitudes and practices of the accused, and of Lucy Pridy, her alleged victim. He noted that Alice Selworthy attended church with fair regularity, and was of a virtuous if unattractive disposition. Pridy was a woman of renowned piety who would probably rise from her death-bed to attend a church service and hear a sermon. Here Francis Neil made a new and surprising point. Lucy Pridy he suggested was not of the type of the victim. Her faith in the Lord God, in Jesus his Son and in the power of the Resurrection, and in the continuing work of the Holy Spirit here on Earth, was total and unswerving. Such sincere and potent belief, the judge suggested, rendered her almost impregnable to the dire machinations of evil powers.

The judge reserved for his final words the item that might score most heavily with the jury. When he came to the subject of unreliability of witnesses and the dubious nature of evidence, there were some significant mutterings among the jurors. Several of them cast meaningful glances in the direction of Thomas Tatt, who should have been mortified, but who was actually waving the amulet at them and silently mouthing further explanations and justifications.

The jury disappeared into that mysterious realm from which travellers *do* return, but from which they bring back with them no descriptions of the ship-encrusted archipelagos or venomous interiors they have visited. They may have had great adventures but are not telling. It is a blind spot in the eye of history. They emerge eventually with a single value judgement, disappointing in some respects, but upon which the fate of empires may hang. Well, not exactly empires – smaller and more important than that – individuals, and how they are viewed and treated. But on these, perhaps, the fate of empires rests.

A small tide of murmurings accompanied the jury back into the room, falling away to silence. Eleven sat down. One remained standing. Petrie spoke.

'Has the jury reached a decision?'

'No, sir. We were unable to agree.'

'How did the opinion divide among you?'

'Five were for a guilty decision, sir. Six for not guilty. And one could not make up his mind one way or the other.'

Francis Neil conferred briefly with Julian Petrie. The he turned to the Court.

'The case against Alice Selworthy is dismissed.'

The relative quiet of the courtroom during the trial came to sudden end. If the judges were in any danger of thinking that their decision was popular, the possibility was now dispelled. A whole Naseby of sound swelled out and quickly spread to the street outside where news of the outcome of the trial arrived instantaneously as though by thought transference or divination. Getting Alice Selworthy home without the sentence, which she might have received from the court if found guilty, being pronounced and executed by the crowd, would not be easy. The few constables marshalled for the task would have failed had it not been for the voluntary assistance from a sizeable group of citizens who welcomed the verdict and joined an unofficial defence league. It was some time before the hubbub died away in the distance. When he could hear his own words, Petrie turned to his fellow judge.

'You are certainly a man of great talent with an assured future.' He was attempting with all the courtesy inherent in one who could trace the nobility of his descent, to make a point: 'But you are, of course, inexperienced and perhaps a trace impetuous – comprehensible of course in one serving only a second year on the bench. The handling of a trial must be balanced and – judicious in fact. I cannot feel that – with all due respect – that the balance was entirely equable in this trial of one who may, when all is said and done, be operating for dark forces.'

'It is time that that particular balance was disturbed,' replied Francis Neil with a twitch of the nose.

# CHAPTER 32

'Why the Devil does he live in a place like this?'

Doctor Henry Lamb was trying to wipe a cloud of midges out of his eyes without much success. Next he would attempt to dissuade those that were colonising his ears.

'These moors are not without their charms,' replied his young companion, lengthening his Os and rolling his Rs in a charming manner that immediately disqualified him as an Englishman. 'I was born in Scotland,' he added unnecessarily. 'Further north even than this. In good weather the hills and valleys have an incomparable beauty, not easy to imagine for a town man like you.'

'When the Hell do they have good weather?'

'Several days each year,' admitted Angus McPherson.

'Well, I'm damned wet.'

'Stop grumbling. The rain's stopped now.'

'Yes. And as soon as it stopped, the midges started.' He stared aggrievedly at McPherson. 'They don't seem to be interested in you.'

'No. That is because you are such an effective decoy. They will eat you first. My hope is that when they have finished with you, they will be sated.'

Lamb answered with a snort, defending the back of his neck at the same time. 'Thanks. Are they always this bad?'

'No. Only on certain days. Their Holy days and religious festivals. Then they sacrifice a human. I think you have been chosen on this occasion. Try to think of it as an honour.'

Henry Lamb snorted again and reined in his horse. 'I think we are lost. We just needed that.'

McPherson agreed. 'I have been worrying about that for the last ten minutes. I think we should perhaps have taken the other road at the fork back there.'

'Road! You call these roads! The other was just as bad. We had better go back.'

They turned the horses around and began to retrace. They were on the last difficult stage of the uncomfortable journey from London, a distance of nearly three hundred miles. The coach had brought them as far as the Crown Inn. There they had hired horses to ride to the village that Joseph had chosen as his working place.

'Hello – look there's life here after all,' said Lamb. 'He looks like a local. No mistaking them. He will put us right.'

The bystander was informative but not encouraging. 'Holkirk? Littlehope Common we call it. Ay. Some people go there. Don't know why. Not often. A few come back. Ay, you're on the wrong road. Go back. Take the left fork this time. And when you've crossed the bridge over the stream, you'll find the road divides again. But this time take the right.'

The two natural philosophers rode on with renewed confidence. The bridge was unmistakable. The right-hand track was plausible if not particularly convincing. After another twenty minutes of riding, they again spotted a figure standing by the roadside. As they approached nearer, the figure began to acquire a degree of familiarity, although this time he was holding a horse.

'My God,' said McPherson, 'it's the one who gave us the directions.' To the man, he said, 'Have we travelled in a circle?'

'Faith, no.' The answer was delivered with a rusty croak that could have held the suspicion of a laugh. 'No. I sent you this way because I thought you'd like to meet my friends.'

He whistled and the austere peat banks, which lay on both sides of the track suddenly, burgeoned with men, rough-looking men with an array of weapons including ancient but well honed cutlasses and a variety of outdated but probably functional pistols. These, and sheer numbers – half a dozen or so men – discouraged argument. A weathered man with a brindled beard, who seemed to be their leader, addressed them.

'Nice horses. Where d'you get 'em?'

'They belong to the Crown at Prenford,' answered McPherson.

The man with the beard laughed. 'Belong to Robert do they? Well, he charges too much for his ale, so this'll make it quits.'

'Take the horses if you must,' said McPherson, who like Lamb had visibly turned white. This was not the kind of debate to which they were accustomed. 'But let us go, please.'

'You town people are always in such a hurry. Enjoy our hospitality a little longer. We haven't talked about your purses yet.'

'We haven't much and what we have we need for our journey.'

'Walking doesn't cost much. And the poor need the money. Think of it as charity.'

Another of the band, who was brandishing what appeared to be a genuine eastern scimitar, explained. 'Ay, we rob the rich to give to the poor.'

'That's us,' said the man who had directed them. 'We're the poor.'

There was laughter all around, except from the two travellers.

'And by the way,' said Brindled Beard to McPherson. 'I like the kilt. I've always wanted a kilt.'

Many miles and hours lay between them and the Inn, but there was no alternative. It was almost dark when they reached the Crown, footsore and exhausted, though not quite dark enough to hide Angus McPherson's embarrassment. The next morning much persuasion was needed to get Lamb to continue with their mission, and would certainly have failed if it had not been for their expenditure already of the three hundred miles from London to the inn. After much argument, and delicate negotiations concerning the credit necessary to allow them to go anywhere at all, they set out again for Joseph's village some thirty miles away, this time with a guide and an armed escort, both of which came at a price, doubtless inflated in recognition of their predicament. Thankfully they encountered no bandits or midges. It rained piteously.

They reached the village just at twilight and had little difficulty in finding Joseph's house following the description that he had sent them. The house showed only an unwelcoming darkness, and persistent knocking evoked no response except from the local dogs.

'I told you so,' said Lamb. 'I was a damned fool ever to allow myself to be talked into coming to this barbarous heath. I doubt Thomas Backhaus even exists.'

'I told him that we could not predict our time of arrival within a day or so. I expect that he has been called out on some urgent matter. He is an apothecary, after all. Someone will know. They always do in these villages.'

The travellers enquired at a neighbouring house where a light was discernible. The old man who came to the door peered at them for a long time, as though they were a new and suspect breed of sheep that he was expected to buy. At last he said: 'Ay. Tom Backus. He came four years ago this Michaelmas.'

McPherson spoke patiently. 'We are not especially concerned with the time he came. More with the time he went. And where.'

'Ah, that's a difficult one. He's been treating Don Taggart's wife at Whiteford for colic. Never had it before. Came on sudden after her last babe.'

'He's there today?'

'Oh no. Some months ago.'

'For God's sake, where is he today?' asked Lamb.

'Dunno. Marksby maybe. With Jane Randall's child. It has the croup. Wasting his time. They never live long in my opinion. Not with croup.'

'When will he back from Marksby?'

'Who said anything about Marksby? I don't think he's there. I think they've gone to Newcastle.'

'They?' queried McPherson.

'Ay. Now I come to think of it. He left suddenly with his wife and child this morning early.'

'He's married then? I didn't know that.'

'No. He's not married.'

'Excuse me, didn't you say that he left with his wife?'

The old man pondered awhile.

'Never see'd the lady before. Not till yesterday. Came suddenly.' A gleam of life came into the old man's eye as though some remote memory had been stirred. 'And she stayed all night – and the boy too!'

'Come on. I've had enough of this.' Lamb turned away. McPherson thanked the old man courteously.

'Going already?' the man replied. 'I had more to tell 'ee. Ah well. I'll tell 'im you dropped by.'

It was less difficult to extract news at the next houses they tried. They enquired at several, on the new Gresham principle that important information demands multiple corroboration. A consensus was soon established. Joseph had left at first light that same morning with an unknown woman and boy. It was quite dark now. Except for Lamb who was glowing. He resembled one of the experiments he had tried as a boy, which had included highly inflammable materials and little means of controlling them. In vain McPherson pleaded with him. Henry Lamb was going on to Edinburgh where he had additional business and the Devil could have Thomas Backhaus and do whatever he fancied to him. The more patient Angus McPherson remained in the village for several days awaiting the return of the mysterious author of the manuscript that had caused so much controversy. At last he too cut his losses and returned to London.

# CHAPTER 33

Joseph was preparing for a momentous event. His work had at long last attracted the attention of experts in the new subject of experimental natural philosophy. Not only that – the experts were travelling some three hundred uncomfortable miles to visit him and discuss his work. He had the Baron to thank for making the contacts that he could not himself have made. His manuscript must have made a powerful impression. It was true that forty years ago Professor Briggs had travelled from Gresham College in London to Scotland to talk with Napier about the logarithms that he had invented, but John Napier was the Laird of Merchiston, a land owner to whom great respect would have been due. Joseph, an unknown alien, had no such advantages. They must have been deeply impressed by his work. He must receive them warmly and ensure their comfort. He must be well organised domestically and mentally. For some days he had been correcting those small faults which had accumulated in the house over a period of several years and which he had been too preoccupied to put right – a broken shutter, a creaking door, a dangerous floorboard. He attended to a hundred and one small items. As he did so he planned the dispositions of his main facts and arguments. These were not men who would listen meekly while he lectured them. They were men of the finest intellect, who would be questioning, rigorous, inquisitorial even. The ideas and evidence that he had presented were so radical that they could hardly be anything other than sceptical. He anticipated a hard time. If he succeeded it would be a miraculous, wonderful meeting, which might transform his life. If he failed to convince them the experience would be miserable and draining. These great men, moreover, would not be pleased at the scant rewards from their long, certainly uncomfortable, possibly dangerous journey. They had written to inform him of their date of departure and the probable length of journey but with the warning that the exigencies of travel in these troubled times (but when are the times not troubled? thought Joseph) rendered it unwise for them to name an exact hour or even perhaps day for their arrival.

All morning, Joseph was nervous and could not work, but spent much of his time fiddling with small domestic matters requiring no adjustment.

'You've cleaned that twice already, Papa,' said the flaxen-haired boy.

About mid-afternoon, a knock came at the door, surprising him since he had heard no horses. With his heart beating faster than usual he opened the door expecting to see two strange gentlemen, probably attired in the finest riding garments. He found instead a woman in common clothing, and a boy with blond hair, aged about seven. The woman's face seemed familiar and for a moment he thought that she and the boy were local residents calling on some matter that required medicines. But echoes from the past intervened. He had known this face very well; now it had lost its girlish bloom and, although still handsome, had been overtaken by the hard-to-define changes of maturity. It needed several seconds as his mind raced back through the multiple images of the hectic last years of his fractured life. At last he exclaimed,

'Caroline.'

Caroline nodded in reply without speaking. For some time they stood there in silence, gazing at each other, neither knowing how to begin. The spell was broken by the boy who began to hop round in a circle in the apparently pointless manner of young children, disposing, presumably, of spare and frustrated energy. Placing one hand on the child's shoulder to still him, she nodded towards the interior in a silent request that they might go inside. Joseph opened the door and gestured his unexpected guests into his house.

He began by fetching refreshment that he had reserved for the men from London and by improvising toys for the young lad. Both adults were aware of the potential for a disastrous opening to the conversation. They proceeded with the greatest caution, speaking quietly without emphasis, almost casually, as though what was happening was an event of no note, an everyday occurrence. In the centre somewhere lay Caroline's resentment at Joseph's treachery and by its side Joseph's shock at being hunted down and cornered – two explosive charges. The dangerous topics must be confronted eventually, but in the meantime they trod with extreme care, moving gradually towards the difficult areas like scouts reconnoitring towards an enemy camp through dense woodland. Exchange of neutral information provided a long, well-illuminated and safe passage, easy to negotiate. From the difficulties and discomforts of Caroline's journey with the boy, they passed on to Joseph's situation and arrangements, enabling him to buy further time by showing her, with some pride, his modest house and its adjoining laboratory. They passed on to his journeys, adventures and misadventures in the intervening years. There was plenty for Joseph to tell. Eventually it was Caroline's turn. Joseph enquired after her mother, the estimable Celia Albright.

'Very well. Very busy. As always,' She explained that her mother had invested the results of her many years of hard work and thrift in a part share of a coaching inn. Business was good. Many were travelling in these days at Government expense – a disgrace – but proprietors of taverns did not complain.

The stakes were now raised.

'And your grandmother?'

'She is alive. Just.'

Caroline paused. 'She was tried as a witch, but found not guilty. The trial has ruined her. They may as well have hanged her. It would have been quicker,' she added bitterly.

She resumed her normal tone and said calmly, 'But I think I am telling you what you already know.'

'Ah.' Joseph had been expecting this. 'Yes. You are right. I did know already the result of the trial. I had the news by letter. So that is how you came to know my address. Someone has spoken of my small role in the trial. Someone who was asked not to speak of that and certainly not to divulge my address. Francis Neil, no doubt. He would. Typical of him.'

'What you call your small role was of crucial importance. We are profoundly grateful to you, the whole family. My mother especially. She has asked most particularly that I pass on her heartfelt thanks.'

'You speak of family. But you have told me nothing about yourself. Have you married?'

'No. I am not married.'

'But the boy?'

Caroline hesitated for a several seconds. When she answered, her voice trembled.

'The boy is yours.'

She hesitated again.

'Is ours.'

For some time Joseph gazed at her without speaking. Then, to her alarm, rose to his feet. She arose also. The moment that she feared had come, the moment of immediate dismissal of herself and the child. Instead Joseph walked slowly to the laboratory door where he could see the boy playing with the glass marbles that he had given him. The usual function of the marbles was to rest in the tops of tubes to restrict evaporation, but the boy was working gradually through all the other things that marbles can do. First the familiar game of *Who Can Get Nearest*, rolling them up to a distant target. Then an unsuccessful game of *Patterns*, arranging them in various geometric shapes: this required surfaces more nearly level than the room could provide so that the marbles were uncooperative and moved off in arbitrary directions. *Preparing For Battle* – lining them up like opposing ranks of infantry. For this, various other objects around the workshop were co-opted as forts, siege engines, cannons etc. Then he provided the appropriate noises as the conflict commenced. Next of course, clashing them together in a game of *Cavalry on Horseback* or *Knights at the Lists*. Joseph watched in fascination vaguely aware that Caroline had joined him. After some time the lad sensed that he was being watched and looked up, expecting the puzzling adult game of *Stop It At Once*. The two merely smiled at him in concert, so he grinned back and returned to his absorbing sports. 'Marcus,' whispered Caroline for Joseph's information, a formal introduction having been omitted in the intensity of her arrival with the boy. They carried on watching for some time, then returned to the living room. It was time for explanations.

'But why have you come?'

'I was passing this way for the first and only time in my life. And I have thought for a long time that you should be aware of the consequences of your actions. Because you should be aware of the existence of your son. Should be aware of the suffering that followed from your actions. From my folly too. It was my only opportunity. It arose as a result of the trial.'

'How has that happened?'

'My grandmother's trial did not end with the verdict. There were ugly scenes when she left the courtroom. The streets were packed with people shouting and throwing stones and anything else they could find. The jurors were assaulted and one badly hurt. Nan – my grandmother – had to be escorted back to her home by the constables who were themselves in danger from the crowd. I can't describe what it was like. It was terrible. She spent one night at home. Mother and I stayed with her. It was terrifying. In the morning we realised that there was no chance of her living alone there in her own cottage, so we took her back to the inn to live with us. She has been there ever since.'

'And she is still there?'

'No. The harassment did not stop even then. We have our windows smashed regularly. Constant personal abuse. The business is beginning to suffer. Travellers want proper rest from the demands of travelling, not disturbance or a stone through the window. And her health has suffered. We decided that it was no longer possible for her to stay at the inn. My mother has a sister in Newcastle who has agreed to take her.'

'That is very good of your aunt,' said Joseph.

'I do not think that she will be troubled for long. Nan is very frail now. I did not think that she would survive the journey.'

'My God,' exclaimed Joseph. 'Of course that is why you are here. You have travelled with her to your aunt. Then where is she now?' He answered his own question. 'With your aunt already, of course. You are on your return journey.'

'Not exactly. You are almost right. My intention was to call on you after I had taken her to Aunt Liza. But she became increasingly tired during the journey. Yesterday I decided that we could not travel on immediately, but that she must rest. Today she was no better. I decided that we could not move on and that the best thing for me was to see you if possible at this stage, rather than later.'

'Where is she now?'

'In the inn at Wadworth. I must return there as soon as possible. I should not have stayed as long as this.'

'It is too late now. We can leave at dawn.'

'We?'

'I will come with you – if you will allow it. I may be able to help.'

\* \* \* \* \*

The inn at Wadworth was the kind of hostelry that would be recommended as 'inexpensive'. Caroline had paid one of the maids there to tend to the old woman until her return. As they approached the door of her room, they could hear voices from inside, the voice of the maid and a male voice that Caroline could not recognise. Before she could reach for the latch, the door was opened from the inside by a man who was just about to depart.

'Ah,' he said. 'You must be the daughter. I need to speak to you privately for a moment. Walk with me to the street.'

The maid left also giving Joseph an opportunity for a brief inspection of the old lady. A brief inspection was enough.

It was only two minutes before Caroline returned. She was clearly upset.

'He is a physician. The maid and the innkeeper were so worried by Nan's condition during the night that they called him in to look at her. He says that there is little hope for her recovery.'

She wiped a tear from her eye. 'They're not always right. Perhaps you can look at her.'

Joseph replied quietly. 'I already have.'

His tone rendered further questions unnecessary.

After Caroline had recovered her composure, they spent some time discussing what to do. They could not move Alice. One of them must watch over her, while the other looked after Marcus, occupying him with whatever was possible in this threadbare village. Most of the sick room vigil would be have to be conducted by Caroline while Joseph was child minder, but roles would be reversed occasionally for the sake of Caroline and the child.

Towards the end of the conversation they were suddenly interrupted by a single low musical note, the whistle of a bullfinch, apparently in the room with them. They turned in astonishment to see that Alice Selworthy, who had been lying quietly, either asleep or unconscious, had opened her eyes. The bullfinch's call was followed by the cascading song of a skylark. Alice lay on her back with her eyes open staring sightlessly at the ceiling. Over the next hours and days she drifted between states of semi or total unconsciousness and periods of delirium, when she would mutter, usually incomprehensibly, but sometimes all too clearly. In these periods she would intermingle her words with bird calls that lacked the strength of her old performances but had lost none of their accuracy. These uncanny displays of virtuosity brought sad smiles to the faces of the two nurses.

For five difficult days they worked a punishing schedule, not physically demanding but emotionally exhausting. Luckily Marcus seemed quite happy with Joseph, almost as if they were father and son, an irony that was not lost on Joseph. Finding things for them to do all day for so many days was a major test of his imagination. Another duty that he assumed was finding medicines with which to ease the last illness of the old woman. The experience served as a sharp reminder of the state of his profession. The local apothecary was a moth-eaten specimen of a man, decrepit and smelling powerfully of his shop and its contents. He tried to sell Joseph some truly disgusting remedies that must have originated from the Thirteenth Century. For the second time in his life, Paracelsus's words associating apothecaries with 'foul sculleries' and 'foul brews' came to mind. He came away after combining patience and insistence – latterly a heavy preponderance of the latter – with a simple drug to ease breathing difficulties, and an anodyne.

The periods of consciousness of the old woman became gradually shorter and rarer. She was past recognising Caroline and muttered fitfully. Much of what she said was incomprehensible, but sometimes they caught a phrase that unmistakably belonged to Alice Selworthy and no one else.

'You shouldn't have taken that, you bad boy. Return it at once!'

'Don't fight my dears. Just take turns.'

'When you come back next year, you can have the whole house.'

By the fifth night Joseph and Caroline were both utterly weary. The boy, who had for some days been most patient and amenable, was becoming fractious. And the inn was costing money, which neither could really afford. They had spent some minutes going over other possible courses of action, or rather of inaction, and had finally concluded that there was no alternative but to stay at the inn and wait. It was now dark and they had reverted to silence again, when they a heard a deep-throated whistle from the bed. The thrilling sound was repeated a number of times, seeming to become more intense and alive with each repetition. Then a pause. Followed by a sudden star-burst of song. The nightingale without a doubt, thought Joseph. For some minutes the wayward song continued, though punctuated by silences even more dramatic than the song itself, rising sometimes in a tense crescendo, at other times falling away, speaking always of faraway places, of other lives and other things unknown to mere human beings. It ended as it had begun with the repeated deep single notes, but this time gradually fading away, leaving an utter silence except for woman's shallow breathing which had subtly changed in nature. About one o'clock in the morning, Alice moved her head slightly and muttered the last words they heard her speak.

'Not worth cursing them. They're too damned stupid. All of you!'

From then on her breaths became more irregular and intermittent. By the time the first light was feeling its way to the window, Joseph found himself counting the intervals between breaths and waiting for the next intake. The pauses lengthened . Finally no breath came. After a few minutes of silence, he pressed Caroline's hand briefly and quietly left the room. When she emerged later he asked,

'What will you do now?'

'Arrange for the burial. Then return to Cottesthorpe. There is no point in me travelling any further. My mother badly needs help in the inn. I will write to my aunt today with the news and explain.'

'You will not be able to travel for several days. Best to rest at my house in the meantime. And cheapest.'

For several days Caroline stayed as quietly as possible. On the evening of the day following the burial, they were sitting together after supper. The boy was already in bed. It occurred to Joseph to settle a point which had roused his curiosity.'

'Why Marcus? It is a very unusual name in England.'

Caroline pouted in a manner which reminded him sharply of her old manner when she had been little more than adolescent.

'I was devastated. I hated you with all my soul. I swore to find a name that you had never used. You had used up a lot of possibilities that I knew about – and probably some more that I didn't!'

Joseph averted his eyes. Out of the window seemed the best place to look, although by now it was dark and there was nothing to see.

'Can you ever forgive me?'

'What you did was unforgivable by God or man. No, I cannot forgive you. To leave so suddenly. With no warning, no explanation. Lying as to where you were going, what you were about to do. It was unforgivable.'

'I know. I can only assure you that I believed my life to be in danger. Later events proved that I was correct about this.'

'You could have trusted me.'

'I felt that I could trust no one.'

'Thanks,' interrupted Caroline sarcastically.

'Well, you I should have trusted. I know. No doubt. But I did not know you all that well. We had not met long before. You were very young.'

'You knew me intimately. All over! You didn't mind me being young either.'

'That was a different kind of knowledge.'

'It is not different. And because I was young you should have taken especial care.'

The bitter discussion continued for what seemed to Joseph to be many hours, and was indeed several. He was desperately uncomfortable. His behaviour had been unpardonable. Cowardly as much as anything. It was not the first time that he had loved and left. It was the first time that he had been found again.

After they had bid each other a cool goodnight, Joseph was confronted again, but this time by one of his phantoms. This one looked a little like Galileo but had altogether different interests.

'Why did allow yourself to be found?'

'What do you mean – allow myself to be found? She found me, searched me out like a criminal.'

'You conspired with her. You helped her find you.'

'Nonsense. I did nothing of the kind.'

'Why then did you ever involve yourself with the trial of an old woman that you hardly knew? What did you want to get out of it?'

'Nothing. It was that awkward swine, Neil, who doesn't miss an opportunity to stick forks in people. He'll find employment in Hell, turning a spit.'

'You knew what he was likely to do.'

'Pity for an old, innocent woman, falsely accused. Charity. Concern for my fellow men and women.'

'Bollocks. You love only ideas and laboratories. And tits and bums. And why did you not simply turn Caroline away when she arrived here? And why have you gone out of your way to help her through these last days of trial and discomfort? And been prepared to face out the inevitable torturous discussion with her which you knew must come?'

Joseph did not answer.

'I rest my case,' said the phantom.

The next day was to be the last of Caroline's and Marcus's stay. No residue of the volcanic outburst of the previous evening was evident. The morning was clear and calm with the lucid, restrained sunshine of a fine summer morning in Northern England, and the mood at breakfast was similarly light and airy. The talk was of inconsequential matters – the eccentricities which his rustic neighbours had introduced into their tedious and poverty-stricken lives to render them more bearable, or the manifold peculiarities of travellers in their brief residence at coaching inns. For some of the morning Joseph entertained Marcus with engaging items from his laboratory. He had accumulated an impressive repertoire of mysterious colour changes, spontaneous combustions, assorted flashes and minor but spectacular explosions, mostly well controlled. As the day passed he became aware of a growing emptiness, which he ignored until it became utterly insistent. Something was stalking him relentlessly. When he at last turned to confront it, its identity was immediately obvious, but shocking all the same. For the rest of the day he was preoccupied and rather silent, so that Caroline presumed that he had become anxious to return to his work and was looking forward to repossessing his house and his time. For once she was mistaken. The truth was entirely the opposite. He was approaching a momentous decision.

It was dusk. Marcus had gone into the workshop to renew his acquaintance with marbles. Caroline was packing into a bag the few possessions that she had brought with her on the journey. Joseph stood watching her. They spoke intermittently of indifferent matters. The last of her items having been carefully placed, Caroline fastened the bag and straightened. Joseph had reached his decision. He stepped forward, re-opened the bag, removed the uppermost piece and placed it on a chair. Caroline watched him in astonishment as he went on to the second item, placing this carefully on top of the first. He passed on to the next item, and the next. By the time the bag was empty Caroline's astonishment had been replaced by understanding. They stood as they had on Joseph's doorstep a few days before, gazing at each other, silent and motionless. At last, Joseph spoke.

'You can't forgive, I know, but can you accept?'

He had forgotten the comfort of holding and being held, and the sweetness of kisses. He had to wipe away her tears and then his own. At one point, glancing over her shoulder, he suddenly caught sight of the flaxen-haired boy, behaving in a reprehensible manner. The boy was making obscene gestures in the direction of Marcus who was still in the laboratory at his war games. Really, thought Joseph crossly, I was not even aware that he knew that sign. Where do children pick up these things? As though for answer the flaxen-haired boy turned in his direction, looked at him for a few moments, smiled wanly, then gave a sad little farewell flap of his hand. He moved reluctantly towards the outside door and had hardly reached it before he faded into invisibility.

From the laboratory there came a sudden crash and the expensive sound of shattering glass. Presumably the fort had fallen at last, suddenly and irreparably. Caroline pulled away from him in alarm, with raised eyebrows.

'It doesn't matter, whatever it was,' said Joseph and began kissing that compelling round of flesh immediately beneath her chin.

## CHAPTER 34

Several years had passed since the news of Charles's execution. Joseph's mind was loitering with intent in familiar manner. This time he was in pre-Christian Athens. Here was the Parthenon. Below it the Dionysian Theatre. On the opposite side the Agora, bustling with merchants. Now he saw it again on another occasion, quieter and more orderly. The ancient philosophers were voting for the New Constitution for the Governance of the Natural World, no less. They were voting, these wise old men, raising their hands in turn. Thales voted for water, Anaximander for water and fire, Anaximenes for air. Pythagoras and Philalaus voted for five geometrical figures with which the others were indifferently acquainted and which had them scratching their heads. Heraclitus chose fire; Anaxagoras voted for everybody including flesh, bone, bark and leaf, possibly vitiating his ballot paper. Empedocles spread his bets by raising his hand for earth, air, fire and water, provoking Aristotle and Plato to do the same. Leucippus and Democritus voted for something that didn't exist, or at least in whom the others refused to believe. An amazing and inspiring scene. The birth of democracy. But was the Natural World democratic? Perhaps it was an autocracy or oligarchy rather than a democracy or ochlocracy. How had we paid so much deference to these old men? As pioneers they deserved our respect, but how could we have believed them all so uncritically. They couldn't all be right.

These rather disgraceful fancies concerning a virtuous congregation of great men, who had mostly never met each other and some of whom may not have visited Athens, disappeared in a flash. It was suddenly replaced by his recollection of the interruption he had suffered several years before. An important proposition had been made, only to be roughly overruled by the voice of Charlie Botham. It took some little time for him to reconstruct what had been said.

*'But that is two definitions,'* the voice had said, *'those are two separate dishes, potatoes and cabbage, not bubble and squeak.'*

'You are right,' agreed Joseph. 'Perhaps an element may be something which is itself and nothing else, than which nothing is more fundamental, and yet without need to be present in every other thing. He hesitated in doubt. 'But that is a different definition of an element.'

'So what!' said the voice, 'Are you some kind of shrinking virgin? Get some balls into your thinking!'

To recognise indivisibility, then – that is the first step. Forget whether it is present in everything else or indeed in how many other things it might be present. Concern ourselves with indivisibility only. No easy route here, though. How do you recognise the state of indivisibility? The copper itself might be elemental. Or the black stuff that forms from it when heated. He made a list of all substances known to him, placing them in categories – the elements he called Converts, the complexes he named Diehards. Better have a third category too – Equivocators – no way of knowing. Joseph began writing down three lists. Equivocators grew with alarming speed. Very few Diehards. Very few Converts. Converts made a particularly short list. The list of Diehards was not much longer.

The exercise was depressing so far. There was no compass and no stars, and therefore no way of establishing the cardinal points so that a course could be plotted. Where was north? His only hope was that the task might become simpler as he determined the status of more substances. The growing framework of the identified would perhaps assist with further identifications, like deciphering a coded message. If mercury was an element then mercurius calcinus was not. The Vivified Air might or might not be an element. Mercury combined with sulphur to form cinnabar from which the mercury could be recovered, arguing mercury's status as an element. If the Vivified Air was an element then sulphur, by analogy, might also be. Or not. Probably they were Converts. He thankfully wrote them in under this heading, which was in dire need of candidates. So far it contained only copper, tin, iron and lead. How about gold and silver? Gold was reluctant to combine with anything. Perhaps it had combined to its full extent already. Perhaps it was fully committed, all used up. Intuition rebelled against this idea. One moment though – gold was able to react with mercury. Therefore it had not already spent all its combining power. The thought issued his permit for re-entry to the workshop. Gold and mercury met like old friends – this he knew already. For the first time he weighed them. The total of their weights remained unaffected. They were indeed like old friends, meeting after a long time and dropping effortlessly back into their former relationship, as old friends do.

The months passed. The list of Converts barely lengthened while the list of Equivocators remained depressingly long. Perhaps he was straying into arenas of fantasy. He was too isolated. He must make contact. He must get other opinions. He must publish.

Not everything gained in weight on heating. Far from it. Limestone was an example. This was well known, certainly since Vitruvius had written it down in the first century BC, claiming a weight loss of one third, and it had probably been common knowledge among builders and practical chemists for some hundred – or even several thousand – years before that. Joseph was becoming sceptical about ancient authorities though, and chose to check it for himself. 'What does an architect know about it anyway?' thought Joseph – a further reason for doubt. He used materials as pure as he could find and discovered that this time Authority was correct, or approximately so. He obtained a figure of a little over a third for the loss in weight.

But why should some substances gain and others lose in weight? For some days he could find no way to resolve the dilemma. He was following a path confined by high walls on both sides, walls created by his assumptions with which he had grown up, supplied, you might say, in his mother's milk. When you heated almost anything it smoked, sparked, flared, spat... It lost substance. The bad boys in the class were the metals gaining weight, not the limestone losing it. So ingrained in his mind was the idea that an ineffable essence escaped during the heating process that he was blinded for some time to his next move which in other circumstances might have been obvious.

Soon the rest of the World – or those who cared – would know about the Vivified Air. He had just written two accounts of his work as three papers – one, purely technical, on the Washing Up method for trapping gases; one on the preparation, collection and characteristics of Vivified Air; and one much more speculative paper on his latest thoughts concerning the nature and identity of the elements. He was forwarding the three as one package but in two versions – one in Latin to authorities in the University of Cambridge and another in the vernacular to Gresham College in the City of London. The manuscripts lay ready on the kitchen table, where Caroline was about to parcel and address them.

Caroline came into the room to consult him about some matter concerning the welfare of Marcus. It was the fourth time she had entered his workshop this morning. Twice she had presented problems generated by Marcus. Twice she had brought refreshments that Joseph did not need and did not want.

'Damn it woman!' Must you keep interrupting it me? That the sixth time this morning.'

Caroline flushed permanganic with anger.

'I've been in twice. And don't call me "Woman". I'm your wife and I have a name. Caroline actually. Perhaps I may be allowed to introduce myself!'

'It's not just this morning. You're always doing it!'

'I never see you otherwise!'

There ensued a sequence of accusation and counter-accusation involving 'always' and 'never' – two words which are implausible in politics and should be absolutely taboo in marriage – and was concluded only when Caroline stamped out tearfully in anger. Joseph turned back to his limestone studies but dropped the flask with a comprehensive anthology of oaths.

Such episodes were fortunately infrequent, and perhaps because of their rarity were particularly upsetting. Their relationship was like one of the characteristic streams of the moorland which surrounded the village – running clear, limpid and sparkling, shallow for the most part, deepening occasionally into peat-laden, black backwaters where the current hesitated uncertainly and sometimes reversed into impenetrable hollows in which lurked bizarre creatures with elastic mouths and distorted limbs. Caroline was aware of her husband's restless and nomadic temperament and the life it had generated in the past; aware too of the rather arbitrary nature of their coming together.

Once she had said to him that he ran through her fingers like water. He had gently apologised and replied it that it might be a comfort to her to know – but probably not – that he ran through his own fingers like water too. On whose behalf had the union come about, she thought – hers or the child's? She was conscious too of their disparity in mental ability. The brilliance of Alice Selworthy had been progressively weakened by two generations of child-bearing, like the progressive dilutions that Charlie Botham made to his milk. In so far as Caroline's grandmother and mother could be said to have enjoyed any choice of marriage partner, both had discovered a predilection for men with barrel chests and well-filled trousers. But Caroline was intelligent enough to realise that shared intellectual capacity was not of the essence in their life together and, looking around her, that careful choice of partner was a luxury rarer than one assumed. Her nightmare – that Joseph would rapidly tire of her and find some other woman, or simply move on without her – gradually eased with time as she realised that he was content – with her, with Marcus and with his work. The latter was two-edged, though. The intensity of Joseph's absorption in his daily – and often nightly – activities in the laboratory elevated chymistry, a subject, which was entirely impenetrable to her and of no discernible use, almost to the status of a mistress. It was a kind of jealousy perhaps that provoked her not-always-welcome incursions into the territory of his preoccupation.

Perhaps Joseph had discussed the four Laws of Crisis Management with her, in whatever serious or jocular fashion. Certainly arriving back in her kitchen still in a rage and with tears running down her cheeks, Caroline resumed after a few minutes – angrily, rather blindly – the tasks on which she had been previously engaged, the addressing and dispatch of the manuscripts. The occupation gradually calmed her mood.

Supper time proved to be conciliatory. Meal times are potent reminders of the real structures of life. Caroline was the first to apologise – the order of apology not necessarily representing the order of offence – and the olive branch was immediately accepted with relief by Joseph. Eventually the conversation normalised and reverted to immediate practical matters. He said,

'I fear we lost our chance of getting Alfred to deliver the manuscripts to the courier in Newcastle. He was leaving this afternoon.'

'I gave them to him. I parcelled and addressed them this morning – to calm myself down.'

'Your soul is studded with diamonds and emeralds,' said Joseph. 'I don't deserve you.'

'I know.'

'You are not supposed to agree so readily,' said Joseph with a laugh.

# CHAPTER 35

*Mid way this way of life we're bound upon,
I woke to find myself in a dark wood
Where the right road was wholly lost and gone.*
          Dante. The Divine Comedy. Trans. Dorothy Sayers.

The fire burned bright in the scholar's hearth.

Henry Lamb was glad to get home after an exhausting day. Chymistry was not the cause of his fatigue – that was usually exhilarating. The problem was the long hours spent trying to gather money extra to that so wisely provided by the estate of the good Sir Thomas Gresham, and the even longer hours trying to ensure that the legacy was well spent. The round of meetings – either begging-bowl encounters with possible rich patrons – or, worse still, committees dedicated to saving money and wasting time, threatened to grind down his enthusiasm. He ground his teeth at the thought of the frustrations and abrasions of the last few days with Knapman the soporof, Creasey the sycophant, Digwell the obstructionist, Nigman the obscurantist, Larkins, Sitwell and Szabó-Tóth – and several others whom he now preferred to dismiss from his mind. But one of them had given him a manuscript, and he had – perhaps unwisely – brought it home. Just for a leisurely first perusal. Serious study could wait until the morning, if the contents seemed to merit further attention.

The script had been given to him by Buckfast, who felt that the task its content presented lay more clearly in Lamb's area of expertise. Lamb always felt himself to be on sufferance with his colleagues. His subject was still regarded by some as being not quite worthy of a place in philosophy. This particular thesis had been passed around in puzzlement or disdain. It had finished in the correct place, but its protracted journey in reaching it had given it a slight aura of defeat; it looked faintly battered and uncared for. Nevertheless he would give it his attention. Bad-tempered he may be, but he was fair-minded.

His first glance showed why it had been passed from hand to hand. His spirits drooped on the instant. It was written in Latin. This posed no problem of comprehension – his Latin was excellent. But the choice of language immediately suggested the old world studies on the dimensions of angels. Or of homage to Aristotle. Well, Aristotle deserved homage. But not bowing and scraping. And certainly not unquestioned quotation or pages spent discussing minuscule adjustments to his logic.

Who was the author anyway? Did he know him already? His Latin pseudonym was here. An anagram if the author was performing true to type. He rustled through the leaves. On the final page he found the author's name in English – no, actually German.

Henry Lamb had risen to his feet. His body was stiff with anger. His limbs were shaking.

'My God!' he said. 'My God! Backhaus. Thomas Backhaus. Not him again!'

The fire burned brighter in the scholar's hearth.

\* \* \* \* \*

Professor Charles Melanie sighed. A purge of the Universities was in progress. His longing for the comforts of the Roman Mass were known, fortunately, only to a few friends, any one of whom might betray him. There was no way of withdrawing the article he had written as an enthusiastic young man in support of Arminianism and Archbishop Laud. For once he was pleased that the piece had attracted no more attention than his subsequent writings. Probably it would not be noticed. But one could never be sure.

He did not feel well. The air of the flat countryside around Cambridge did not suit him. The east wind, spawned in Russia, laden with cold, dry black bile in North Germany and tempered by cold, wet phlegm over the North Sea and the fens of East Anglia, had entered his bones. Or something had entered them. Perhaps it was something worse. The Pest perhaps?

*Kyrie eleison, Christe eleison.*

More probably his youthful indiscretions were overtaking him at last. He had learned much on that journey to France and Italy as a young man, not all of it scholarly. Perhaps some part of his education was coming to its awful maturity. *Mea culpa.* And there were also his less-than-youthful indiscretions. To be awarded a Fellowship and seated on a Chair at the University one had to take Holy Orders. It was an absolute requirement. Holy Orders conferred much advantage and consequently did not necessarily acknowledge, much less guarantee, a pious and moral life.

*Qui tollis peccata Mundi, miserere nobis suscipe deprecationem.*

There was a distressing itch in his groin and his hands had been shaking a lot recently. Mercury was good, they said. Yesterday had been his thirty-eighth birthday. After the euphoria and celebration, he was confronted with the spectre of the day-after and the year-older. A quotation had circled endlessly around his mind these last few weeks, like a tune that one cannot get out of one's head.

*Nel mezzo del cammin di nostra vita*
*Mi ritrovai per una selva ossura*

*Chè la diritta via era smarrita*

He sighed again, this time with exasperation. It was bad enough to be troubled by a miserable poem. Worse still it was written in a vernacular. The lowly Italian language as used by mere working people. Dante Aligheri, to whom a philistine friend of Charles Melanie had once tendentiously referred as 'that rancorous Italian paedophile', had abandoned the magnificent language of his dead mentor, Virgil, for the language of mere peasants, tanners and carpenters. 'Nothing wrong with carpenters,' he added hastily to himself and to whoever might be listening.

And – Oh yes. Another sigh, this time showing clear signs of ambition to become a groan. Talking of vernacular writings, a script in English, claiming to be a candidate for academic consideration, had just been passed to him, or passed off to him more exactly. Presumably no one else wanted to deal with it. By a Thomas Backhaus, attached to no University as far as he could see. Clearly a German. Well, small mercies! – at least his youthful follies had not included a visit to Germany. He glanced at the title again. *A New Definition of a Chymical Element.* But all that had been decided long ago. Another shake and a slight feeling of nausea reminded him that it was time for his medicine. Attila's script could wait until the morning – or the morning after that.

He uncorked the new bottle of a medicine that had been prescribed by one of the University's distinguished physicians – medical advisor to the Master, no less, and prepared by an expensive apothecary using the finest Spanish quicksilver. One spoonful, once a day. The taste was so vile that he customarily measured the spoonful into a large flagon, adding water, honey and molasses. 'One spoon only. Do not exceed the dosage. Danger of death!'

He was overwhelmed with a feeling of nausea, not only of the body, but of the whole being. He glanced again at the manuscript. It seemed to typify the world he no longer understood, where his beloved England had come under mob rule, where the common people had become priests, where kings could be judged by their subjects and disposed of at will. The old verities were as nothing. The earth was a mere attendant among other functionaries, the heart reduced to a mechanical contrivance pumping blood around the body. It was a world where upstart foreigners wrote heresies in vulgar language.

Perhaps after all the earth did move. He felt once more its terrible lurch into darkness and disintegration.

He picked up the manuscript and, opening a cupboard, thrust it far into the middle of a paper mountain, which responded with a volcanic belch of dust and dead earwigs. He turned back to the table on which the bottle and flagon stood.

*Pater mi, si possibile est, transeat a me calix iste...*

He was not quite finished with Thomas Backhaus though. A charitable impulse prompted him to turn to the cupboard again. He was a generous man at heart. He pulled out the manuscript, wrote on the front cover,

Please send to:
Dr Henry Lamb,
Tannery Lane
Southwark.

and threw it on the table from which his mail was regularly collected by a servant.

And then he poured the whole content of the medicine bottle into the flagon.

# CHAPTER 36

*Think you that there is any certainty in the affairs of mankind, when you know that often one swift hour can utterly destroy a man?*
 Boethius, Consolations of Philosophy
 Trans. W.V.Cooper, 1902


From William Richmond to his beloved wife, Penelope.
The Tower of London, March 31 1661.

Dearest
In the last terrible weeks I have written to you my thoughts at length, as to how you and our beautiful children may survive the hardships of the coming years. There is little more for me to add to those suggestions - already too many and perhaps too optimistic or even fanciful - that I have made in my previous letters, and there is no time left for you to respond.

There is no time left.

It is now clear that you will not be allowed to retain the family estates. The King and the restored regime are determined to inflict every last penalty upon our family, beginning with my life. A grave injustice has been visited upon us. I do not complain that I have earned punishment. I have opposed the Stuarts and worked towards the deposition of King Charles I. I did not, however, wish or work for the death of that sly and stubborn man. I opposed his execution and would have been well satisfied with his banishment from the country that he served so ill. Many of those who wanted to kill him have escaped with far lighter penalties than the one that will be exacted from me at first light tomorrow.

This day is my last on Earth. During the last weeks, I have explored, I think, all the labyrinthine passages of the mind of man. I have huddled in the darkest cupboards of despair. I have walked on horrifying edges of fear where I have seen my body broken apart piece by piece as it fell from rock to rock on the mountainside. I have trembled in the courts of justice where my life has been exposed, item by item, with all those things that I have done awry or failed to do transmuted into accusers who have stood in the witness box, pointing…

I have prayed to my God, cursed my God, feared my God, rejected or despaired of him. I have read his word, found solace, then despair, then comfort again, then disbelief. I have accused him. Why, I cried, do you visit such an end, premature and terrible, upon an innocent man? Or, if not upon an innocent man, upon one who bears no greater burden of wrong than that which is our common lot, the inheritance we carry from our first parents?

I turned then away from the Word of God. In desperation I took up a book written in despair, the gropings towards the light of another man who faced the same injustice and a similar end to his life, eleven centuries ago, while his false accusers were free to laugh and rejoice outside his prison. Eleven centuries since the condemnation of Boethius! Have we learned nothing in the long and blood-stained years between?

We have learned nothing.

The realisation merely added to my sense of oppression and to the futility of seeking any form of solace. The author's clever arguments, seeming to suggest that the strong are weak, and that the weak are the truly strong, appeared as appalling ironies, terrible sophistries, self-serving theses born of affliction and the imminence of the destruction of the body. I threw the book aside. Having done so, I began to ponder once more – not on the content of the Consolations of Philosophy – but on the courage and lucidity of thought of the writer in such dire circumstances. In shame, I picked up the book and read again. Some mysterious unseen hand guides us at these moments, for I opened at the words:

'Now,' said she,' I know the cause, or the chief cause, of your sickness. You have forgotten what you are.'

Indeed. In such a condition – under the burden of daily accusation and false witness, with the threat and the reality of torture and faced with the prospect of being put to death like some unregarded animal – easy to have forgotten what you are.

Now I have remembered. Though heavy-hearted still, I can face what has to happen with calm and courage.

Now I have remembered. I am a man, not a scorned creature of the wild, a man not perfect, but with the dignity of an intellect given only to the human, to add to the Spirit that informs all living creation. I am a man, moreover, who has striven to give back to my countrymen, in some form, a part of those riches that it has been my good fortune to inherit; who has striven to understand the basis of our unhappiness as a nation and to make what contribution I could, however small, to the elimination of our discomfort.

I am a man blessed also by baptism in Christ and life-long participation in the sacraments. With these thoughts, I returned again to the Bible and there found solace and read of God's love and of the donation of His Son to suffer among us.

The great hymn of St Paul to charity I have read again with fresh hope, though nothing expresses my thoughts better than the words of our great and courageous author from the Sixth century – a Christian himself but writing a book not overtly Christian, perhaps in the hope of reaching out to all men:

*Through Love the universe with constancy makes changes all without discord: earth's elements, though contrary, abide in treaty bound: Phoebus in his golden car leads up the glowing day; his sister rules the night that Hesperus brought: the greedy sea confines its waves in bounds, lest the earth's borders be changed by its beating on them: all these are firmly bound by Love, which rules both earth and sea, and has its empire in the heavens too.*

Such love is all-pervading, has manifold presences. It has its special cases too. In our marriage I have found love such that I had not known myself to be capable of giving, or worthy enough to receive. Now I thank and praise God for such blessing. The chapter must now end. But the book is not finished.

In my last hours I pray for you and our children – that you may find the courage that you need, the resourcefulness that a harsh world will demand of you and, eventually, the better fortune that God may grant,

Now and through Eternity, I remain your loving husband,
William Richmond

# CHAPTER 37

The Clematis was blooming again. The lovely flowers were overflowing the stone wall of Joseph's garden. The sight gave him great pleasure every year, or a double pleasure – the beautiful long petals with their delicately painted lines and the luxuriant yellow centre, like a superior bottle brush, were in themselves exquisite, and additionally they affirmed that the winter had been dismissed and sent on its way. On this occasion the flowers evoked another response also. He was aware of a tug at his heart, a melancholy, almost as if the flowering indicated not spring, but autumn. How could this be? In a contemplative moment he returned to the question. The feeling of sadness had not been solely a response to the beauty of renewal. The problem was his growing perception that the plant seemed always to be in flower – or if not in flower then in bud, or in fruit. It seemed always to be about to flower, to be flowering or to have recently flowered. The year was contracting. Time was beginning to pass with ever increasing swiftness. And he had achieved nothing…

In the hope of banishing this feeling of failure, he returned to his notebooks. He was relieved to find that the depressing conclusion was not true. He had in fact achieved a great deal, more perhaps than any alchemist – or should he say *chymist* or *chemist* (he did not even know what to call himself) – had ever achieved before. The pleasure at this reminder was short-lived. Why then was his work still unknown? Why was he himself unknown? He was no longer a young man. He might die at any time, his life's work unseen, like a beautiful but obscure rowan tree in the mountains. Would anyone arrange its publication if he were gone? Caroline had neither the perception nor mental stamina to see such a difficult enterprise to conclusion. He must take action himself, and soon.

The possibilities were few, so few that the analysis did not take long. Many years had passed since he first came to this remote place. England had changed, dissolving the Rump, dismissing Praise-God Barebones, rejecting the temptations to King Oliver, disposing of the Protectorate, and finally lining the streets to cheer the return of the discredited Stuarts. It had gone full circle but somehow not found itself in quite the same place. Joseph's only real channel of hope for fulfilment had been the Richmond family. The baroness with her ruined life was unlikely to find the renewed strength necessary to help him, and her influence, following the disgrace of her husband, would be diminished or non-existent. There was one solution only to his problem. It did not take long to identify it. To summon the resolution required for action needed much longer. He must move to one of the centres of intellectual activity. Of Cambridge he had only bitter experiences. He recalled his seminar there with discomfort and contempt.

One of his tormentors had asked, 'You will doubtless concur, as I must, with the opinion of the divine Plato, and believe absolutely his conclusion that the four elements are prefigured by four regular solids – fire by the tetrahedron, water by the cube, air by the octahedron and earth by the icosahedron. Also that the dodecahedron – the fifth and only remaining regular polyhedron – is the summation of all of these and configures the Universe. How then can your belief that there may be additional elements be anything but fallacious?'

More serious, because more unanimous, had been the reception of his contention that the nature of matter was particulate, a conviction that had been forced upon him gradually as he began to realise that certain substances combined in simple proportions, a phenomenon that could best be explained on the basis of a some kind of theory of atoms. The attack had been led by a kindly, good-natured middle-aged gentleman who had put aside his natural disposition to voice his displeasure, apparently shared by most of those present, concerning particulate theories. These implied an unacceptable mechanical view of the Universe, leaving no role for God; the atomic theory had been invented by the impious blasphemers, Democritus and Lucretius – the latter having written his book after being rendered insane by a love potion – and atoms, in short, were atheists' bullets. In response Joseph had denied that particulate structure excluded Spirit from matter or God from the Universe, but his reply met with a frosty silence.

Cambridge might or might not have changed over the intervening years, but the choice seemed to lie between Oxford and London. The latter was preferable for several reasons. He had heard that a group of talented people interested in Natural Philosophy were meeting there and possibly may have found royal interest. That they had engaged the attention of the dissolute and extravagant Charles the Second was a surprise, but that was what he had heard. There were risks of course – from the pest, for example, but he had faced out those before – and from those who had attempted to abduct him. For many years now he had lived in obscurity and surely had been forgotten by those who once believed that he had valuable secrets to disclose; and by others of the opinion that he might have interesting evidence to discuss concerning bars of counterfeit gold. As for Costeaux, even if he had survived the poison and the conflagration, surely he could not still be a danger. He would long ago have abandoned any interest in, or hope of finding, Joseph.

An additional attraction of the city was finding a career for Marcus. There was nothing for him to do here. The lad had quickly become one of the loves of Joseph's life. The young boy had won him at first with the captivating charm that seems to be a characteristic of the young of most animals. And the boy had his own personal charm in exceptional measure. Also a talent for chymistry. Together they spent long hours, that passed very quickly, in the workshop, at first fooling about with substances for Marcus's entertainment, later working more seriously on particular problems generated by Joseph's studies. The boy's interest gave Joseph great delight and made a significant contribution to one of the happier periods of his life.

His enjoyment was to some extent tempered by Marcus's tendency to carry what he had learned in the laboratory to the real world outside it. The ingenuity of the boy was unmistakable, especially if you were an unfortunate villager who had picked up a candle from the street, congratulating himself on having saved a little money. The candle would indeed burn quietly and usefully for some time before it exploded. Such incidents led to several pursuits – by the villagers of Marcus, or if they couldn't get him, of Joseph, and by Joseph of Marcus with a stick which, however, when he had caught up with him, he found himself too indulgent to use. 'Childish prank' was his usual apology to a complaint, and he was rather taken aback when a farmer, in response, grimly showed him a finger with the top joint missing. On this occasion the boy had presumably got his calculations wrong.

As Marcus entered adolescence, Joseph began to realise with mixed feelings that Marcus's preoccupation with explosions and war games was beginning to assume a professional dimension. On the one hand, he admired and was proud of the son's cleverness and absorption in a subject close to his father's heart. On the other hand he disproved of what he regarded as a prostitution of learning. True, he understood the satisfaction of making bigger and better bangs. Doubtless this would continue until a whole town could be blown to pieces with a single act. A fascination with these instruments of destruction was shared by most people, and chemists had the opportunity, widely envied in secret, to practise it, but he had, in early life, found the military interest vaguely repugnant. Since then his opinion had received confirmation and clarification, receiving special impetus from his conversation with the doomed Schliessmann. He had tried to dissuade Marcus, in order to divert him into what he considered more desirable directions for the use of his undoubted talents – to medicine or discovery. Having failed, he had sighed and applied himself to the paternal duty of doing the best that he could for his son.

\* \* \* \* \*

The move to London threatened disaster. The challenge announced itself first to the nose. Joseph himself had almost forgotten the atmosphere of the city. It had become considerably worse even than he remembered. Caroline had never visited a large town before. She was bred on country smells. To these she was so habituated that she had come to regard the rich pastoral odours of the midden and the cow shed as a species of fresh air. The odours of the town

– of human waste and rotting carrion, of the industrial miasma that filled every street, though with subtle variation according to which particular trades were conducted locally – filled her with disgust. Marcus wrinkled up his nose too in horror but the excitement and stimulation of the new situation overcame his revulsion. Within weeks they were all sick in varying degrees. Joseph himself suffered headaches and vomiting. Caroline and Marcus had severe breathing difficulties, so much so that Joseph became fearful for their lives. The night was orchestrated with coughing. In despair Joseph sent them to Cottesthorpe to recover. After some weeks both returned. So did the coughing. After several such periods of respite their lungs seem to have hardened their attitude to the thickness of the atmosphere, so that the permanent flight back to the country, which Joseph had seriously begun to consider, became unnecessary. Caroline's possibly life-threatening cough reduced to a troublesome but not particularly serious daily hack. It became a chronic rather than an acute condition, much like the English weather.

Joseph had come to London to make contacts. He began by writing to or seeking out the few people with whom he had some acquaintance. These gave him further introductions by letter or in person. Such chains mostly died out. But one or two rewarded him eventually for his patience. One in particular led to some interesting private discussions of his work. He was sufficiently encouraged by these to apply to give some lectures at Gresham College but was disappointed. A teacher was already booked. Joseph had crossed off that particular opening from his list and was exploring other possibilities when, one morning early, he was aroused by a knock at his door. A messenger from the College requested his immediate attendance if possible to replace the preferred teacher, who had fallen ill. He must give the first class that very morning at ten o'clock. The lecturer would no doubt return next week.

Here he was wrong. The unfortunate man, Dr Burns, had been prevented from taking his class by a fever that caused him to sweat while at the same time chilling him to the bone. The next day lesions began to develop on his body and his glands swelled into agonising buboes. A terrible fear engulfed him and all those of his family and household. They knew these symptoms all too well. On the third day he was in terrible agony. On the fourth he felt better and rose from his bed with the intention of renewing his normal routine. The house was cold in a searching east wind. Picking up an armful of kindling, he dropped dead at his wife's feet.

Joseph received a further message. He was to give the whole course of lectures. A second chance. The first class had not been a success. He realised that he had spoken far over the heads of the eager but ill-educated class, too quickly and in a funny accent that they found extremely difficult to understand – a fatal combination. Fearing the worst, and finding that his expectations were fulfilled, he came to the second of the series of lectures to discover that the attendance had dropped catastrophically. Now though, he was better prepared and spoke clearly and slowly and with content better tuned to his listeners' background. For the third class the attendance had partly recovered. In the end the course of lectures was at least a partial success. His approach was new and strange and had some heads shaking.

There was one peculiar episode. He was in the classroom preparing to give the third lecture. Most of the class was already assembled. Joseph was taking a last glance at his notes. He looked up, ready to begin, and was just in time to see the back of a man leaving through the door at the other end of the room. The man had apparently entered with the purpose of joining the class but suddenly changed his mind. The man's back reminded him, with a start, of Costeaux. He dismissed the possibility as foolish and in a few moments was preoccupied with communicating difficult concepts to an unlikely mixture of students in a language not his native tongue.

# CHAPTER 38

The elegant Richard Costeaux was no more. Elegance was not possible for a man with one side of his face burned away. Forget elegance – even the mundane inelegance of daily life was difficult. Others shrank away from him. His infirmity disqualified him from all but the most menial jobs, not because of incapacity but out of fear and prejudice engendered by his appearance, or from the thought of those who might have employed him that here was a man who had been punished for some terrible sin he had committed, or for the sins of his family.

His personal wealth and the patronage that he had attracted – the patronage that had enabled the construction of the laboratory, had disappeared in smoke and ashes, had vaporised, or was spread about the countryside in tiny embers. He was fortunate – or was he? – to survive. Some times he thought otherwise. In despair he worked his way, existing by the grace of miserable payments for the lowliest of tasks, through France and into Italy, coming finally after many months to Padua. His destination was not coincidental. Padua was famous the World over for its medical skills. He had entertained a vague idea that maybe the clever physicians there might be able to help him. Each one had shaken his head doubtfully and passed him on to another physician who *just possibly* might be able to help, extracting a fee before he left. The final physician shook his head sadly and suggested London. 'Leyden?' asked Costeaux with raised eyebrows presuming that he had misheard. 'No, London,' was the answer – remarkable developments in understanding of the human body had been made in London. Not regarding burns however. But it might be worth a try.

He did not go to London, at least not immediately. The great centre for the human body having failed, his next destination was the centre for the human soul. Rome. Here, under the walls of the Vatican he found some comfort and occasional employment, and here it was that after several years, his fortunes changed once more.

He was working with a gang of men who were building a chapel to adjoin the house of a Senator of Rome who was also an assistant to one of the Cardinals of the Congregation of the Inquisition. Among the workers was another Frenchman. One day Costeaux was translating the instructions of the foreman in charge for this man who had very little Italian, when he was overheard by the Senator. Recognising the presence of an educated man in an unlikely situation, the Senator became curious and sent a servant to investigate. Having received an intriguing report from the man, he sent for Costeaux and questioned him himself. What he learned was of the greatest interest. Here was a man of intelligence and intellect with many skills, some of them with direct bearing upon military developments, a man moreover with command of several languages, including English. *Including English.* This was of special interest.

Costeaux was offered work. The alchemist, munitions expert and erstwhile builders' labourer became an agent for the Vatican. His first post was in London where he was required to do what he could to promote trouble between Parliament and the Army, an enterprise in which the participants eagerly assisted. Subsequently he worked in several countries. In 1657, he left Italian employment and began the same kind of work for the French king, working mainly in Spain or the Netherlands. In 1664 he was still active. This was the year in which the English decided to pursue commerce by other means. The prizes were the discouragement of the Dutch from their domination of the trade routes to the East, and the mouth-watering possibility of the capture of fat Dutch merchant vessels. Early in 1666 the French decided to grasp their opportunity. They declared war on England, as did Denmark.

Costeaux was sent to London with several specific tasks; also to find out anything additional that he could, and to stand ready for further orders. He arrived there two years after Joseph Skledowski had emerged from his self-imposed exile in the moorlands of the North.

## CHAPTER 39

Joseph was frequently asked what he did for a living. This should not have been such a difficult question and most people would have answered promptly without thinking. The easy and convenient answer would have been "apothecary", but he no longer regarded this laudable profession as his primary concern. 'Alchemist' was not an answer that he would have chosen to give, even in his younger days when it was certainly true. Such persons were frequently held in disrepute, as Celia Albright's comments had so eloquently demonstrated. Or the word aroused an elbow-nudging, eye-winking interest and risked immediate suction into some vicious whirlpool of nonsense, avarice or deceit. In any case he no longer considered himself an alchemist. He fought for another word. The term "chemist" was coming into use, but generally was another name for apothecary. 'Chymical Philosopher' was the most accurate description of what he was attempting. It resonated quite beautifully and should have impressed mightily. He had found however that, with the learned, it provoked scorn from disbelief that the two words could be put together. With others it brought the conversation to a puzzled halt and was guaranteed to change the topic. Van Helmont, whose experimental methods Joseph had come to admire, had found his personal answer to this problem. He called himself a *Philosophus per ignem* and the subject that he studied was *pyrotechny*! There was an air of realism about this choice, and the manipulation of materials by heat in many conditions was indeed an important tool (though not, as some had maintained, the only tool necessary).

For Joseph, van Helmont's self-description raised unfortunate memories. He had sworn to avoid both incendiary accidents and arson in the future. For once he had been able to sustain one of his good resolutions and, amazingly, had done so for a considerable number of years. He had even resisted the temptation to make the white fire for which Schliessmann had given him instructions. If the fires were to remain under control and in their proper place in his furnaces, it might be better to eschew van Helmont's title for the benefit of his own internal climate, and to avoid possible misunderstandings with others. He settled on 'chymist' or 'Chymical Philosopher', according to what kind of person had asked, the questioner's likely purpose in asking, and how impressive Joseph wished his answer to sound.

He now had a list of thirty substances that he believed to be elements. Elements that is by his new definition. He had come to believe also that at least one of the components of the air – and in all probability the Vivified Air

– were on this list. When he exhausted the ordinary air in a closed vessel by burning a candle inside until it no longer supported combustion, he found that the volume remaining was about four-fifths of the original, and also that a rat could not live in it. Logic triumphed over imagination as he named this leftover 'Depleted Air'. The Vivified Air disappeared into combination with many of the other items on his list of elements, in reproducible quantity, and from just a few of the resulting products it could be recovered again. A substance of this kind, apparently made up of two elements, he called a couple – and the event that produced it a 'marriage', revealing inadvertently that his thinking still carried residues of his alchemical origins.

He had now prepared several gases. In this respect he had gladly adopted van Helmont's terminology. He now preferred the term 'gas' to 'air'. It made a proper distinction and acknowledged the existence of gases having quite disparate and individual properties.

He could recognise several of these and prepare them consistently to order:

Vivified Air, which supported combustion and breathing.

Depleted Air, left behind after burning.

A highly inflammable gas released from metals by acids (or from acids by metals?), which he called *ignis fatuus*.

A non-inflammable gas, that did not support combustion, made by the action of acids on chalk or a mild alkali such as soda, or by burning charcoal in air. This was more difficult to collect because it tended to dissolve in water.

A gas prepared by heating sal ammoniac. This relit a splint but less certainly than did the Vivified Air.

One, possibly two, gases released by the action of nitric acid on metals or the heating of nitre. These were difficult to interpret and required much further effort.

Joseph gave thanks to his Maker, reserving a little credit for himself. It would have taken anyone else one hundred and fifty years to do all this, he modestly told himself. But the discovery that pleased him most was the latest. He had seen already, many years before, that the ignition of the gas from acid and zinc – the *ignis fatuus* – produced a liquid that appeared to be water according to any test that he could devise. Since ordinary air – 'but what is ordinary air?' he pondered, as he cautiously sniffed once more the appalling, malodorous miasma of the City of London – since ordinary air and the Vivified Air had a number of things in common, and since ordinary air reacted with the *ignis fatuus* to produce water, perhaps the latter would also yield water when ignited in Vivified Air. He collected them together over water in one vessel. On ignition he obtained water. He was ecstatic. The most probable conclusion was that water was a complex of *ignis fatuus* and Vivified Air. This was an altogether revolutionary idea. Two elements combining? That they might be elemental was even more revolutionary. He would have to prepare a very thorough defence.

He had also tentatively formulated a new principle that he called the Law of Constant Proportions. He had come to believe that combination always occurred between the same relative proportions of reactants. He could not be certain. His methods of analysis were too limited to examine anything better than a small number of instances, but these few were utterly reproducible, and he had come to suspect that the rule was generally applicable. There was no way that he would ever be able to prove it, and could never present it as more than a tentative suggestion.

He had argued further with himself – if the Law was true what did it say about the structure of matter? He had been forced ultimately to think in terms of combination between particles. The world was usually regarded as a continuum or plenum. From time in history, atomic theories had mysteriously erupted, rather like those sudden and unaccountable outbursts of hot lava from a hillside that troubled some countries. He thought of Democritus and Lucretius, but in more recent times and more persuasively – because they were chemists and puzzling over the same phenomena as he – of Geber and van Helmont. Descartes had argued a particulate Cosmos with some force. It was true that such a law of nature would lead to troubling difficulties concerning what existed *between* particles. It would generate profound questions about the nature of space and dimension. Those must be left for others to worry about. His task was to limit himself to possible explanations of the facts as he became aware of them.

Defence against what or whom? He must by some means, at last, discuss and publicise his work. Already he had been in London for two years. Most of this period he had been occupied by extracting a presentable kernel from fifteen years or more of intensive experimentation, trying to fill gaps in his arguments that opponents would otherwise exploit, strengthening and polishing, writing a series of papers. Sometimes he would pause and look at the growing mound of paper and become uneasy. It was vulnerable. He swore he would make double copies of everything important and lodge one copy elsewhere, probably with his wife's family in Cottesthorpe, but it was a daunting task and somehow he never got round to it. There were always more pressing matters demanding attention. Making contacts for instance. The obvious target was the newly formed Royal Society of London. It was not that he aspired to become a member – that was too much to hope. Or not immediately. He was entirely unknown. But he was very optimistic that he might be able to present a paper to the Society or get someone else to do so on his behalf. Who knows what then might develop?

The Society had firm roots in Gresham College. It had crystallised from an informal group that used a room there for many years to discuss problems in Natural Philosophy, and the Society, formed in 1660, was now housed there. The spirit of man, like the cosmos in general, was full of contradictions and surprises. The apparently feckless Charles II – in whom the determined, devious nature of the father had been replaced by extravagance and licence – had shown sufficient interest, two years later, to grant the Society a Royal

Charter. Joseph was in the right place. Gresham College was a mere fifteen minutes walk away from his home. Moreover he had already given a course of lectures at the College and knew some of the staff, including one or two members of the Society.

He knew by reputation though not in person, Robert Boyle, from a wealthy Irish family. Boyle had generated around him a new excitement in chymical philosophy, which looked as though it might gain acceptance as a subject worthy of consideration. A formidable man evidently. And here to prove it was his book, *Sceptical Chymist*. Joseph had read it with a mixture of irritation and admiration. The author was critical of almost everyone, but particularly Paracelsians. Unfair thought Joseph, who still had a soft spot for the great Bombastus, the idol of his younger years. Boyle didn't think much of the writers of chymical text books either. 'Vulgar Chemists' he called them. It was difficult to say what Boyle thought about transmutation and the chrysopoetic practitioners. Some sympathy apparently. It was difficult to tell, largely on account of the author's style, like tangled string, and complicated by his use of dialogue (but Joseph's revered mentor, Michael Sendivogius, had also used this form) that effectively concealed which of four participants conveyed the author's view. It was true that Galileo had also used this time-honoured method for his major works, but his presentation had been remorselessly logical and systematic with no problems of identity. He and Descartes had set new standards of clarity in the writing of Natural Philosophy. Boyle seemed not to have noticed. But then again, did not the uncertainty of his style, with its perpetual qualifications and fusillade of relative clauses, simply mirror the tentative nature, the vulnerability of a new and generally despised subject?

Fine to be *against* things, Robert Boyle, but what are you *for*? That is the crucial test of a man, what is he *for*? There are those who are *for* everything. *Glass ... is among stones as is a fool among men for it takes on any colour.* But the opposite was no better. To repudiate everything, to demolish, to destroy ... Well, now I discern that you have most scorn for the grand architects who construct giant, imposing buildings, suspended on hooks from the clouds. And as much for those who write chymical cookery books, full of household receipts, unaware, or uninterested, in the country or origin of the ingredients.

He had found one answer to his question. Robert Boyle was in favour of particles. This was what Boyle was *for*. Joseph was excited. He prosecuted his purpose of an introduction to the Royal Society of London and to Robert Boyle with renewed vigour.

# CHAPTER 40

There are numerous ways of being an agent and in his eighteen years of duty Costeaux had tried many of them. Being an intelligent man with good language skills, including immaculate English, he might have operated via the diplomatic service, masquerading perhaps as a secretary to the Ambassador, while gathering covert intelligence of the intentions of the host nation, the state of preparation of the military, troop movements, advances in weaponry, political intrigues, factions, power struggles within the government or nobility – any strength to define or weakness to exploit. He was indeed tried by his employers in this role, but the social disadvantages of his appearance proved overwhelming. People avoided him, excused themselves in the middle of conversations, or, if they talked to him at length, he was aware that for much of the time they looked, not into his eyes in the natural way, but a little to the left of his vision, at the terrible scar tissue.

He was a little more successful making contacts with military personnel. Several times he gleaned useful information from high-ranking officers in Spain or Germany. But here also he was hampered, not so much by his disfigurement – this could be viewed as a kind of badge of courage, an honourable wound suffered in the service of his country, something to be accepted or expected in one who had survived, as he claimed, several sieges in the recent wars in the German states – but because of his exceedingly small stature, which did not immediately suggest the warrior.

As a consequence he was reduced to minor roles, and these he hated with all his being, and as his hatred grew with the years it transferred to the cause of his disfigurement, Joseph Skledowski. He could not have proved in a court of law, or in a University seminar, that Joseph was responsible. He had not been attacked by him with a flaming brand or had acid thrown in his face, but he knew beyond doubt that the destruction of his laboratories and the ruination of his face and career had been Joseph's doing. But what was that to him now – he asked himself? Joseph might be anywhere at all, in one of many countries, perhaps in a grave. It was even possible that Joseph himself had been burned to death along with Fourques. The latter's charred body had been found, however, while no sign of Joseph's remains had emerged.

His form over the years was Protean. He had become diplomat, interpreter (this had been particularly informative), engineer, artillery man, plumber, beggar... the last was the easiest and one of the most convincing. His ravaged face drew pity like the North Star drawing a magnet. His benefactor would glance, throw a coin and turn hastily away. This was, for a proud and talented man, a drink of bitter aloes, of vinegar laced with gall. The incidental coins that he gained, he threw away as Judas had; not in the Temple with remorse, but with utter disgust into the depths of the black flowing river. In the meantime he had noted from a point below London Bridge the movements of shipping in the Pool of London or, more importantly, from various vantage points further east, the arrivals and departures, and especially the requisitions, of Royal Naval vessels at Chatham.

Now he had received a new project, delivered to him from his masters via a French agent by word of mouth. His superiors had come to suspect – the reasoning was not disclosed to him – that the English were developing a new and more powerful propellant for use in guns, particularly in cannons. The war between England and France was likely to be fought primarily at sea. The prospect of English ships, already formidable enough, being armed with more destructive or longer-range guns filled the French with alarm. His instructions were to find out all he could, from wherever he could, and by whatever means.

It was difficult to know where to start. It was likely that such a development might be conducted at one of the Naval establishments, perhaps Chatham itself. He might have to try and penetrate there. Very difficult. Very dangerous. Much preliminary work was required. Where, he asked himself, would the expert knowledge for such an advance be obtained? The worst possibility was that the Navy – or the Army – had established some time ago study groups with chymical expertise to work on explosives and that these were well isolated and carefully guarded within the military establishment. There was some chance, however, that help had necessarily been recruited from the academic community. Here was a possible lead. The first thing to do was to make a list of those who might have been consulted for their knowledge of combustion or related topics. The list was not too long. There was one Institution that immediately suggested itself as worthy of enquiry, which had by now gathered many years of reputation for excellence in natural philosophy, had a strong leaning towards practical studies and, most persuasively, had taken great interest in marine subjects of several kinds. Moreover, it was immediately accessible – only a few minutes walk away from his residence. A further fact, irrelevant but intriguing, was that its founder had himself been a secret agent in his younger days.

It was by this logic that he was now walking towards Gresham College. It did not have a notable involvement in chymistry, but then, where *was* such an involvement? From time to time, however, chymical experiments had been made there by Kenelm Digby and others; more to the point, the current list of lectures and courses included a title 'Combustion and Related Topics'. It was raining slightly so he walked at the side of the street where he was sheltered by the overhanging jetties or storeys, a common strategy, often a competitive activity, known as 'jostling for the wall'. It carried with it a diminished chance of receiving the contents of a chamber pot emptied from one of the upper floors.

At the College he was pointed to the appropriate room by an attendant. It was the shortest session he had ever attended. As he turned in at the door of the lecture room he glanced curiously around, wondering what kind of person hoped to benefit from free lectures in English. The *hoi polloi*, no doubt. The lecturer was looking down at his notes, his face foreshortened. Nevertheless, Costeaux was convinced immediately of the man's identity. He was in shock, but long practice in reacting to the unexpected had sharpened his responses. He swung on his heel instantly, just as the lecturer began to raise his head. He thought that he had probably not been seen. The attendant at the door was gazing at him in surprise, edged with the all-too-familiar blend of compassion and distaste.

'Did you not find the lecture on combustion, sir?'

'It was not the class that I expected,' replied Costeaux. 'Tell me, the lecturer's name is Edmund Burns, I presume?'

'No, sir.' The attendant was of a lugubrious turn of mind. 'Mister Burns is indisposed.' He paused. 'Indisposed by death, actually. Mister Thomas Backus has taken his place. In the lecture room, that is.' He paused again, becoming even more sepulchral. 'So far.'

'Hmm,' thought Costeaux. 'You are right. *So far!*'

He stood for a moment pondering his next move. So 'Thomas Backus' was Skledowski's latest name. He had never thought much of Joseph's adopted names. This one suggested horse races. But first he must be certain of his identification of the lecturer. His view had been the briefest of glances. The years had passed and would have changed Joseph's appearance; Costeaux's memory, however, was both sharp and bitter.

Opposite was a coffee house where there was good view of the door of the College. He ordered refreshment and sat there practising again the blend of patience and impatience that he had developed over the years during long hours of waiting – usually in less comfortable circumstances – for something to happen. He expected that the lecture would end as scheduled, on the hour. The time came; the various clocks about the city delivered their slightly differing opinions, but Joseph did not appear. Students – if that was not too a dignified a name for this curious rabble, thought Costeaux – and lecturers emerged, but Joseph was not among them. Damn, he thought, perhaps there is another door. At last, many minutes late, a small group came slowly out, oblivious to their surroundings, immersed in animated conversation. In their midst was 'Thomas Backus', older but unmistakably Joseph Skledowski, the centre of the intense discussion. Clearly it had been a stimulating class. Damn again! They were coming into the coffee house. He had, however, anticipated this possibility. He rose quickly and walked out through the door leading into the kitchen, taking care not to inspect it too closely. There was a certain category of information that even agents did not want to know about. In answer to his query he was directed into the 'garden', a mean yard containing a flimsy wooden privy with two overfull buckets whose contents should have been donated to the night soil men – a double structure, so that the occupants could have a pleasant chat to each other while performing. Fortunately he had no intention of using it. There was little obstacle to the next property and he was able to enter the adjacent house through its back door. It proved to be a butchery. Inside he pushed his way hastily through a room where a butcher glared at him menacingly. The man plunged his already bloody hand into the interior of a sheep, apparently with the intention of hurling something uniquely unpleasant at the intruder. Costeaux accelerated, and, as a fistful of offal squelched against the doorpost behind him, pushed past a man who had been stationed in the doorway to discourage theft. He escaped into the street pursued by nothing worse than a few muttered curses.

Again he waited. It was one of the premier skills of his business. He chose a place a short distance along the street, where he was largely obscured from view by the throngs of people passing, in seemingly inexhaustible supply. This time, three quarters of an hour passed. At last Joseph appeared, paused in the doorway to bid a leisurely farewell to the group of students and then, turning away alone, began to walk away from Costeaux's observation point. Costeaux dropped in behind him at a tactful distance. Another routine skill – tracking. He had exercised it countless times. He followed for several hundred yards. Today though, his expertise deserted him. Perhaps he was over-stimulated, too eager. Whatever the reason, after a few minutes he lost his quarry momentarily in a crowd and could not trace him again. Bitterly disappointed and very angry with himself, he gave up. But, he consoled himself, there were more lectures to follow. He would get a second chance.

At the same time the following week, he monitored Joseph's arrival at the College, and his departure. This time he succeeded. He followed Joseph the length of Bishopsgate Street and through Grace Church Street, on past the turnings to Fen Church Street and Little Cheap, into Fish Street Hill. Now the crowds had thinned and he must be especially careful not to be seen. At St Margaret's Church, Joseph turned to the left and walked into Pudding Lane. Here, after buying a loaf of bread from the baker, he disappeared into the house next door.

Costeaux had most of the information that he needed. He had been sent to London to gather information about propellants and explosives. That was the *entrée*. But killing Joseph Skledowski would provide a satisfying *hors d'oeuvre* or a tasty *aperitif*.

# CHAPTER 41

Joseph liked to have, hanging on the wall of his rooms, mottoes, pictures of things or people important to him, or reminders of his current aims and principles. He missed Galileo, frightening though the old man had been at times. Long ago, before the foolish journey to France, he had remembered Francis Neil's recommendation – almost indistinguishable from a gibe – that he should read Descartes, and long ago had accepted the advice. Now he had decided that the wisdom of Descartes was suitable for display and had written out, in the best script he could manage, the Rules.

(1) Accept nothing as true that is not self-evident.
(2) Divide problems into their simplest parts.
(3) Solve problems by proceeding from simple to complex.
(4) Recheck your reasoning, omitting nothing.

Very good!
He had taken the last three of these to heart and had applied them to the study of the Vivified Air and to everything else that he had examined. Every part of his studies with the Vivified Air he checked and rechecked until he was utterly convinced that he was not mistaken. But was it 'self-evident'? No. In that respect, what else that he dealt with was 'self-evident' – anything? Not much. The axioms of Euclid were self-evident. It was obvious, for example, that parallel straight lines can be extended indefinitely without meeting. But what held in mathematics was not necessarily true for other branches of philosophy. Chymistry seemed to be the least self-evident of all. He crossed off Descartes's first item and moved the others up one place. Now the boat was absolutely watertight. The instructions were unarguable and profoundly important, but – alas! – Descartes had scored only three out of four. A limb was missing. Two legs or four was workable. With three you fell over or walked round in a circle. The result was not a good wall hanging. He was beginning to suspect philosophers. Some had gone so far as to question the validity of the concept of proof. He tore up the poster and returned to the laboratory to try to prove something.

Descartes worried him. The emphasis on logical inference from what one considered to be an unarguable principle, worried him. Too little attention to observation and confirmation was implied. And the idea that a living organism was merely a collection of clever mechanisms was clearly wrong.

Not only wrong, but objectionable. It led immediately into an unacceptable world containing nothing but machines and mechanism. Unlike Galileo's work, Descartes's writing did not suggest a practical method for problem solving through experimentation. Galileo was a better model. He must look for another copy of Galileo's portrait.

He was very excited. In the following week he was to travel to Oxford to meet Robert Boyle and to discuss his findings and ideas. The long years of hard work were approaching consummation. The move to London had been crucial. His estimate that his enemies – and the Law – would have long ago lost track or interest in him was well founded. No sign of danger had presented itself in four years.

No danger of the human kind that is. But something else had been on the prowl with terrifying effect. The previous year, 1665, had been filled with the utmost horror. London, although suffering grievously in the years 1603 and 1625, had not seen the like since the Black Death in 1349. The usual cases of plague had been noted early in the year, not meriting exceptional attention or concern. The rise in the spring months was familiar and not especially worrying, though unusually steep. By high summer the sickness had reached proportions unprecedented in living memory and by August was becoming catastrophic.

In the early months the main effect upon Joseph was to fill his pockets, a welcome gift since London was expensive and he was beginning to run short of money. He ordered in bulk traditional and new remedies for the Pest and had no difficulty in selling them. Finding sufficient supplies was his main problem. In June he sent Caroline away to her mother's home for her own safety. Two weeks later he followed the example of the Court and most of the town's physicians, and left for the countryside also, joining Caroline in Cottesthorpe. He was not made of heroic materials, unlike Margaret Blague, the Matron of St Thomas's Hospital, staying at her post after the doctors had quit, or Dr George Thomson who remained to conduct the first autopsy of a plague victim and survived a consequent attack of the disease by applying a dried toad to his chest. And Joseph was a realist – there was little that he could do against God's will. And he had another kind of gift to make to the world.

When he returned in the autumn, the plague had subsided but its devastation was everywhere apparent. The beneficiaries were the pigs, crows and other carrion eaters, who were still feeding on the bodies of cats and dogs that had been slaughtered in their thousands – by order of the government, for fear that they carried the infection from house to house – and still stank at the roadsides; feeding also on human remains inadequately buried in the plague pits, as the normal methods of disposal had disintegrated under the weight of corpses. The town was alive with rats, which had plenty to eat and few of their hereditary enemies left to trouble them. Many of his acquaintances and some of his nearest neighbours had perished. Closest of all, his next-door neighbour Elizabeth Farriner, a pleasant lady with whom he had sometimes chatted, wife of the baker, was among the dead.

In the following spring, the survivors waited for the renewed onslaught, but none came, or nothing came that resembled the ferocious invasion of the previous year. God, it seemed, had exacted the measure of retribution that He demanded and was, for the time being, satisfied.

Now it was almost September. The terrible sickness had not recurred in the abundant measure of the previous year. He was at his home, with his wife. It was very hot and had been for many days, but his excitement carried him through the heat without difficulty. He was carving the final details of his work for presentation next week. His life was approaching consummation.

\* \* \* \* \*

Costeaux was very hot too. He dreamed of the French countryside where he would soon retire. The woods and hills might be as hot or even hotter than London but they were saturated with a relaxed charm as old and deep as the bird song that filled them, and they lacked the charnel house stink and the acrid reeking fumes of this damnable city. To cool off he walked at night, and recently his wanderings had gained a new and deadly purpose. London was too dangerous a place in which to go alone in the dark, and unarmed, so he was accompanied by a pair of pistols and a suave gentleman who was also in the pay of the French king. Together they made an exhaustive study of the geography of that part of the city just to the north of London Bridge, with special reference to Pudding Lane. The street was typical of the City, its houses several storeys high, with overhanging jetties, and bound together like an advancing Roman cohort. They established that Joseph slept in a room on the second floor, that he went to bed usually at a quarter to midnight and that entry to the house was from an exceedingly narrow passage, barely wide enough to walk down without scraping shoulders on its walls. The attack would be made as he slept.

Costeaux fetched out from a cupboard a smart leather case. Inside were six balls, beautifully made, apparently of wood and leather. He weighed fondly in his hand one of the mysterious objects – mysterious that is to an Englishman. A Frenchman might well have recognised it as an essential part of a set for playing Jeu Provençal, which Joseph Skledowski had so unkindly dismissed as aerial marbles played with cannon balls. Well, Skledowski was about to find out what could be achieved with aerial marbles. Costeaux pulled a second case from the cupboard. Inside were another six balls, apparently of similar construction and purpose, although perhaps a trifle larger. Whereas Costeaux had handled the first set with a certain reverence, now his actions suggested rather a nervous caution. He took one of the second set and turned it over in his hand, which it entirely filled. A small patch of dark powder was visible on one side of the ball. Brushing this away revealed a small hole in the casing through which the powder had escaped.

The first set had been presented to him at the French Court as a reward for services rendered. It was a gift set, something of a work of art, for display rather than play. The second was the result of several years of study by himself and others. After many trials of prototypes the balls for the second set had been made as close as possible in replica of the presentation set. The purpose of this was to facilitate the passage of the second set through border checks or examination by police or enemy agents, where both sets would pass notice as a harmless game or French foible. The idea had first come during some leisure reading of the Roman author, Livy, who had described how the Bacchantes ignited their torches by dipping them in water. Costeaux had paused at this point and asked himself if there was any means known by which this could be done. Further reading had taken him and his colleagues to a work called the *Liber Igneum ad Comburendos Hostes,* which in translation lost its academic ring to become *The Book of Fires for Burning Enemies,* attributed to Marcus Graecus writing, Costeaux believed, in the 8th Century. The innocent-sounding *Little Key to Painting,* from probably the same era, surprised the reader with some further recipes for arson.

Costeaux next took from the closet a small box of nails. He gingerly placed one of the nails in the small hole in the ball that he was holding and gently worked it in and out, checking that it ran freely. One of the great problems of daily living was the lighting of fires. Considering the frequency with which houses burned down in the big cities, it was hard to believe that the routine lighting of fires and candles was such an inefficient business. But the methods were indeed slow and clumsy, and the morning fumble with steel, flint and tinder was a recognisable near descendant of the primitive method of rubbing sticks together. Nowhere was it more inept than on the battlefield or at a siege, he thought. But no – correction – there was one place where the wrestle with flint and steel was even more undesirable, and that was in acts of sabotage. The last thing that was needed when attempting to destroy a ship in its yard or dock, in the silence of the night, was to stand immobile, clashing hard objects together and raising a miniature firework display of sparks.

He checked each of the six balls in turn in the same way, thinking about the long research that had been spent on the development of this weapon. The hole in the ball ran along a radius of the sphere, reaching almost to the centre. The point of a nail, pushed into it, abutted against a small central glass sphere containing water with the head of the nail just projecting from the surface of the sphere. Surrounding the glass sphere was another spherical compartment containing a mixture, the formulation of which had occupied most of the development time. Quicklime and naphtha he knew were two of the ingredients; other additives had been found necessary. The outermost compartment was packed with gunpowder and more naphtha.

Detonation was simple. One way was to push the nail in to its limit without applying pressure, and then to throw the ball into the target, leaving the impact to drive the nail into the glass sphere. This was almost certain to work, but there was just a small possibility that the ball might land or roll in such a way that the nail was not depressed. A better way was to tap the head of the nail against a wall or the ground first to break the glass, before throwing the missile. There was an interlude of a few seconds before the device exploded, presumably while the water penetrated the incendiary mixture and sufficient heat was generated to ignite it. This was the standard method but it required strong nerves.

He replaced the last of the spheres in its case, breathing heavily. Actually they were quite safe without the nail in place. They could even, he had been assured, be dropped, since the glass was sufficiently stout to resist minor challenges, although dropping was not recommended as a routine test. One trial had been made during their manufacture, when the two cases had been misidentified and a game had begun using the wrong balls. Luckily the first throw had been made by a strong-armed gentleman who had achieved considerable distance. No one was hurt but the little wooden target ball, the *cochinet,* stood no chance and was not seen again, nor was a shed that had stood nearby. After the contestants had picked themselves up, the game was declared a tie, and they moved immediately to the tavern to repair their nerves.

Now all was ready. It remained only to wait for a suitable moment. Flaming naphtha was about to be distributed over the bottom floor of Joseph Skledowski's house, probably as the flimsy floors above collapsed with the force of the explosion. Costeaux was well aware that he was disobeying instructions. The fireballs were difficult and dangerous to manufacture, and therefore in short supply and expensive. His instructions were to use them only against primary targets – ships or dockyard installations. He was going to make an exception in this case. He could always plead that he had destroyed a dangerous enemy agent who possessed expert knowledge.

# CHAPTER 42

Happy the man who had invested money in the beer companies. The sale of ale and small beers was beating all records. The weather was still hot. It was true that a stiff wind had been blowing from the east for several days; at other seasons of the year this would have brought chill winds or even snow, but at this time – the first day of September – continental Europe was roasting under fierce heat and could offer only dragon's breath. The great city was parched and the thirst of its inhabitants reached heights remarkable even for London.

Costeaux and his companion, Roland, set out to walk eastwards along Cheapside. It was a relief to be walking in the cool night air. In one of the mean streets just before they reached the main thoroughfare, Roland lost his hat in the surging wind, and the two had a merry chase before they rescued it, by which time the filth of the street had polluted it beyond wearing. Costeaux dispatched it into a philanthropic future with a well-aimed kick towards a group of shabbily dressed men and women, who were sitting in a doorway seeking some relief from the heat, and had found the unexpected free entertainment uproariously amusing. There was no doubt that someone would be glad to make use of the hat.

'That was *my* hat you gave away!' said Roland ruefully.

'Never mind,' Costeaux answered, 'it didn't suit you, anyway.'

'All right for you. You don't have to pay for a new one.'

'Cheer up. This wind is just what we need. The place will burn like tarred rags.'

'Yes.' A lingering doubt seemed to be troubling Roland. They had worked through this conversation before. 'A lot of people live in that house. Many are going to die just for the one man that we wish to kill.'

'They are English,' explained Costeaux patiently.

'Yes, damn them,' muttered Roland, but did not seem entirely convinced.

The two walked on, Roland lanky and spare, Costeaux tiny and doll-like, suggesting a stage comedy act. The chase had heightened the effect, especially as both had seemed strangely awkward and encumbered during the pursuit of the hat, whose progress had been decidedly frisky by comparison. Encumbered they certainly were – Costeaux by one of the balls of the non-sporting variety in his left pocket and a pistol in the right, Roland by two pistols also hidden away in his clothing. Fun was not the purpose of the night. The time was right, Costeaux had decided. He had thoroughly satisfied himself about the habitation and habits of Joseph Skledowski; there was a good wind blowing and the time had come to even the score.

They turned south towards the river. In Fish Street, Costeaux halted, sending Roland ahead into Pudding Lane to consult with another accomplice. This man, Gascon, had been given the onerous task of sitting outside the Star Inn all evening, drinking ale and keeping an eye on Joseph's house. In a few minutes, Roland returned.

'Skledowski is still awake. There is a light in the room and someone moving about.'

'Damn him. Well, we will come back later.'

There was nothing to do but walk. It was better than standing about, possibly arousing suspicion. They chose the easterly direction, along the river. They were close to the Tower and walking aimlessly about among the quays, when a strange incident occurred. A young man with a dangling arm and a peculiar stagger in his gait, which was clearly caused by lameness rather than inebriation, almost collided with them. As he brushed against Costeaux, he uttered an oath, unmistakably in French. Costeaux caught him by the arm.

'Where are you from?' he asked, also in French.

The young man glared at him suspiciously. 'Stockholm,' he said.

Costeaux smiled indulgently. He guessed that the young man had no English and continued in French. 'Stockholm! If you had asked me to guess, I would have suggested Normandy.'

'That's what I said. Normandy. Rouen. I'm going home to my parents.'

'That will be nice,' said Costeaux with a friendly smile.

'Bastards!' was the young man's response, accompanied by another glare.

'You don't get on with your father and mother?'

'Bastards!' reiterated the young man.

'A pity,' said Costeaux sympathetically. 'But then, why are you going back?'

'He made me,' answered the youth with a toss of his head in the direction of the river. 'The bastard!'

'You came off a ship?'

'Yes. The *Skipper*.' He pointed to a ship close by, clearly announcing itself to be the *Maid of Stockholm*.'

Costeaux was puzzled. 'Who is compelling you to go home?'

'The Captain. Master Skipper. The bastard! He didn't want us to come ashore.' The young man became even more rancorous. 'He said we were going to Rouen. And here I am in fucking London! Fuck him! Did he bring you here too?'

'No. We were here on business and have been trapped by the war.'

A new light came into the young man's eyes. 'Are you going to burn the place down?'

Costeaux was almost unnerved by this piece of prescience.

'Which place?' he asked, rather hesitantly.

'Fucking London.'

'No,' replied Costeaux. That far exceeds our ambitions. By the way. We did not introduce ourselves. I am Pierre Tailleur and this is Gaston Meunier. What is your name?'

'Hubert.'

'Hubert Who?'

'Robert Hubert. I'm a watchmaker.'

'This is the first time that I have had the privilege of meeting a one-armed watchmaker.'

'Fuck off!'

'I doubt whether I shall have so much luck – not tonight at least.'

They turned away from Robert Hubert and the unpromising conversation.

Hubert stood glaring after them, his arm dangling.

'Bastards! Fucking bastards! Fuck you!'

It was time to return to Pudding Lane. This time Costeaux accompanied Roland to the proximity of Joseph's residence. To his extreme irritation, the light still burned in Joseph's window.

'Damn him! Why does he have to behave differently – tonight of all nights?' He sniffed the air.

'Sulphur,' he said. Even through the assortment of appalling smells of the city, the pungent odour of sulphur was recognisable to one of the *cognoscenti*. 'He is working in his laboratory.'

'A shed in the yard, behind the house,' he said, in response to Roland's puzzled look. His left hand played frustratedly with the ball in his pocket. His right hand toyed with a nail. 'It looks as though we will have to postpone our operation until tomorrow.'

'Why not just go and get him? What are pistols for?'

'Too dangerous.'

'At this time of night?' Roland's question sounded more like a contemptuous sneer. 'We could do it and be streets away in a few minutes.'

Costeaux was aware of a deep reluctance. Perhaps shooting offended some higher artistic impulse. Or lodged somewhere in the human was a powerful impulse to match the punishment to the crime.

'There are many people living in the lower floor. They could make it very difficult to get out.'

'I'm sick of this street. I've spent too much time here recently, watching this damned house. I don't know that I can come back again.'

'You will do what I tell you,' said Costeaux curtly. But he still hesitated.

'I'll go and shoot him for you, if you like,' offered Roland.

To Roland's obvious approval, Costeaux pulled out a pistol. But he still had not convinced himself.

Further debate was interrupted. From somewhere behind the house came the sound of a muffled explosion. It was not very loud but the echo was repeated several times off buildings near and far.

'My God,' said Costeaux slowly. 'I believe he's done our work for us.'

'Can we go home now?' asked Gaston, who had just joined them and had obviously enjoyed his evening's vigil rather too well.

'No. We need to wait and watch. If Skledowski comes out, shoot him.'

They positioned themselves at the end of the alley, trying to look as casual as men can who are simultaneously trying to conceal, and hold ready, loaded pistols. For a few seconds nothing happened. Then suddenly there was a shout of 'fire!' followed by a confusion of noises. A few people emerged from the house looking apprehensive, while the sounds from the back of the house suggested that the rest of those living on the lower floor had launched a crude fire-fighting operation. From the street there was no evidence of fire for several minutes – nothing to hear except the babble of voices shouting contradictory instructions to each other – and nothing to see. Then suddenly there was flash from the sky, apparently due to the illumination of smoke that had been accumulating unseen above the house. The would-be fire-fighters came tumbling out of the entry in a great hurry, one of them with his clothes alight.

'It's gone!' someone cried.

'And the bakehouse too,' shouted another.

A woman began hammering at the door of the baker's shop. There was no response from inside. Men and women were rushing to the end of the street where fire-fighting equipment was kept. Others were bringing out tools from the neighbouring houses and were beginning to dig into the ground to reach the water conduit that ran the length of Pudding Lane. Through the windows of the baker's shop the fire was now visible, spreading from the back of the building to the front. A man joined the woman who was hammering at the baker's front door. For a minute or two, they set up a thunderous noise – still without sign of arousal of the occupants, until they were driven away by the heat of the fast-spreading blaze.

The conduit had been tapped and a miserable piddle of water, like an old man urinating, was issuing from the abused mud and cobble of the street. From these thin rations those who had returned with equipment were filling buckets with painful slowness, then donating their contents to the fire, more as a gesture of disapproval of its intentions than an act of containment. The lower floor of the baker's house was now thoroughly on fire.

A sudden shout of hope and fear from the street attracted Costeaux's attention. All heads turned to the roof of the baker's house where two figures could be seen – in shadow and smoke one moment, weirdly illuminated by the fire the next. They were making the precarious passage along the guttering towards the next house. They were treading the narrow way between fire and fall. Once it looked as though the latter might be the likely outcome, but the woman was steadied by the man's hand, reaching back. For a moment both tottered on the edge of destruction, before steadying themselves and edging on again towards the safety of the next house, which was still not seriously alight. To the relief of those watching below, they disappeared through a window and shortly emerged to the street.

They had made their passage to the next house only just in time, for the fire was now spreading to the adjoining houses through the garrets, which offered an efficient conduit. The woman, the baker's daughter, had serious burns. The baker was unhurt, but could only stand aghast as the upper floors of his house burst into flames. The wind was blowing as hard as it had all day. The appetite of the fire was whetted by its initial taste of tinder-dry wood and plaster. The roof of the baker's house suddenly collapsed with a roar and a glowing blizzard descended upon the street and upon the houses across the cramped space where the upper storeys were separated by little more than a handshake.

Costeaux put away his pistol and called off his dogs. His accomplices could be discharged for the night. There was no sign of Joseph who had most probably perished in a furnace of his own making, a fitting end for a *Philosophus per ignem*. Gaston lurched uncertainly away with evident relief. Roland had seen enough too and also left. Costeaux though was fascinated by the spectacle. The fire had already travelled through several houses and the Star Inn itself was under threat. At last, weariness overruled his curiosity. He turned to go. He had been standing outside the fourth house away from the baker's, which was already burning. He had not progressed many yards when the ground where he had been standing a few moments before, suddenly heaved. The street erupted like a pot boiling over. A huge fountain of soil, cobbles and red-hot stones, along with vast quantities of what appeared to be liquid fire, engulfed the houses to left and right and across the street. Some of the blazing black material fell at Costeaux's feet and he recalled that his exhaustive study of the area had identified a ship's chandler in business at the house. Presumably the cellar extended beneath the street and had served as a store for inflammable goods, probably barrels of pitch. Both sides of the street were becoming an inferno. It was time to go.

Towards the end of Pudding Lane, he stopped in surprise. The wind seemed to have changed direction. Because it had been blowing from the east and the street ran approximately north-south, he had been largely sheltered from it by the buildings. Now he felt the strong draught on his face as he began to walk northwards. The fire was beginning to supply its own larder. The massive upward current of hot air from the conflagration was renewing its needs by the easiest route, sucking air along the street, between the two lines of unburned houses that stood like prisoners awaiting the executioner.

\* \* \* \* \*

The time was short now before Joseph made his impact on the Royal Society. His discoveries were so revolutionary and, he believed, so profound, that he must anticipate a struggle in gaining acceptance or even perhaps a patient hearing. He was acutely aware of gaps in his arguments. He felt rather like a knight of earlier times whose preparation for battle had been interrupted by the battle itself, leaving him only partially sheathed in life-saving metal. There had not been time to pull on all of his armour. But that was nonsense. There had been many years of time. Where had they all gone, those hurtling years? He had not wasted them – at least he had not frittered them away – for he had pursued his chosen course unswervingly, working by night and day to achieve understanding, hoping that one day the accretion of the small pieces of the puzzle would bring him finally to a view, however hazy and indistinct, of nature's throne, that the shallow waters would slope gradually into profound deeps of comprehension. He was overtaken suddenly by nostalgia for his young days when it seemed as though the single act of forging the Golden Key could transform the whole world.

Nervous anticipation drove him back to the workshop. He could at least check one of the final points in one argument. He *must* do something. He was getting tired of the taste of his nails. Most of his time at this address had been taken up with thinking, reading and writing, interpreting his earlier experimental work, inventing and rejecting hypotheses, assembling arguments. He had a laboratory, it was true, not particularly well set up but serviceable. One of its disadvantages was its proximity to a large number of people living in crowded conditions, against none of whom he bore a grudge. Nevertheless, on Saturday morning he lit his furnace and began a study of iron pyrites. The time slipped – or perhaps skated – away, as it always did when he was engaged in such work, passing with extraordinary speed so that he was surprised when he found the light failing as the September evening, already over-hasty after the leisurely light of June and July, surrounded the house and the dusk began to spill through the window. At intervals during the day Caroline brought him food and drink along with sensible, sometimes sardonic, always unavailing suggestions that he give up and just relax.

He was still there at some time after midnight, almost ready to finish and go to bed, when the door flew open with a crash that startled him. A middle-aged man stood there, not a particularly large man but one whose bulky shoulders and arms instantly betrayed the presence of muscles well-trained by some form of manual activity. Joseph knew him slightly. His name was Sam and he lived on the ground floor of the same house and at times helped out in the bakery next door. Joseph had seen him loading wares into a cart ready for transport.

'Oh!' said Joseph, clutching at the region of his heart in theatrical style, 'I didn't hear you knock!'

Sam ignored this potentially important medical event. 'What's that terrible smell?' he said.

Joseph sniffed the air in histrionic fashion.

'I can't smell anything unusual.'

'It smells like prostitute's shit.'

'I'll take your word for it,' said Joseph. 'I don't move in those circles.'

Sam did something peculiarly aggressive with his eyebrows and moved up menacingly close. Joseph stood his ground.

'Don't be funny with me. I don't allow it. Summat smells terrible. What is it?'

'Really,' said Joseph, 'I don't know how you can recognise any unusual smell in this stinking town. The whole place smells like an explosion in Hell's cesspit.'

'Bin there have you?' suggested Sam with a grim attempt at humour. 'Look. I'm tellin' you straight – you're gonna stop this. People are complainin'.' 'Specially the baker. You are poisoning his bread with your dirty smells.'

'His bread's poisonous already. It doesn't need help from me.'

'He's a very good baker – one o' the best. He supplies the Navy with biscuit, by the King's anointment.'

'I've seen his biscuit,' lied Joseph. 'It's the only kind known where the weevils are already there when it comes out of the oven. If you tap it on the table and wait for the weevils to come out, they just put out their tongues and crawl back in. The sailors were reduced to using it as ammunition. As for the king, he never sees the sea. Lady Castlemaine's arse is in the way.'

'I could 'ave you for seduction. Where do you come from anyway? You're not English are you. Some kind of bleedin' savage.'

'I hope that you meant "sedition". I prefer to keep the race pure.'

Sam now had hold of him by two handfuls of shirt.

'Listen to me!' he said. 'I'm not gettin' nowhere, am I?'

'No. You're not. And the sooner you do, the better. I'm busy.'

And Joseph began an attempt to steer his unwelcome visitor towards the door. This was a gross mistake. When it came to steering, there was no contest. The muscular Sam gave Joseph a push in return that sent him staggering across the room. Joseph's personal history, the development of chymistry and the geography of London might have taken a radically different course if he had not collided with the portable furnace, which overturned and burst open, scattering red-hot coals all over the floor. This time the coals were not received by stone flags, but by wooden planking. Joseph grabbed a bucket of water and threw it over the developing blaze, but the volume of water was inadequate to quench all of the spread-eagled fuel. The wooden wall nearby, dried out by many days of drought and intensely hot weather, burst eagerly into flames. Everything else in the room seemed, almost in an instant, to take the infection. A wave of intense heat drove the two men out into the yard.

'Christ!' said a suddenly repentant Sam, 'sorry mate!'

'My fault, you oaf! Pumps! Quick!.' Joseph was equally distraught.

They turned to get help and equipment, only to find themselves immediately in a cram of people who had streamed out of the house to see what was happening. There followed some moments of confusion, a great deal of milling about and colliding – much as Joseph imagined that Boyle's particles might behave – before one of the newcomers took over and began to issue orders. Joseph was about to follow instructions and the throng, and to take up his not entirely unfamiliar role of fire fighter, when he was overwhelmed by a new and appalling thought. He stopped as though fixed by a sudden onset of a paralytic disease.

Inside the burning hut was his work of many years. The papers he had written for presentation were there. So was the book in which he wrote his ideas and conclusions. Neither of these mattered too much. He could rewrite the papers in a few days or, if necessary, present them to an audience orally with no more than a hastily scribbled note or two. The book of ideas and conclusions he used merely as a stimulus – he would thumb through it occasionally, hoping to beat more pheasants out of the bushes. He did not need that book either. It could be readily recreated. But his laboratory note books... They were there too. Not the original scraps of paper on which he had scribbled down observations and weighings, but fair copy books which held all the significant experimental descriptions and results of the last ten years. These contained the basic information, the evidence to place before the court, the detailed descriptions of key experiments – the record of conditions and temperatures, the volumes and weights of reactants and of products, the balance sheets of chymical reactions – an accumulation and summary of many years of practical labour on which the whole of his conclusions and hypotheses depended, a collection absolutely unique. The original scraps of paper were long gone. Many times he had thought how important it was to make a copy of this book, and many times he had failed to do so. The book was irreplaceable and inside the burning hut. He must retrieve it.

The blast of heat when he opened the door of the hut almost cancelled his rescue mission before it had properly begun. The intake of fresh air also encouraged the flames mightily; they gulped it in gratefully and suddenly roared up with a new appetite that clearly included the ceiling on its menu. Joseph dropped to his knees and began an arachnid crawl with his arms wide on either side, as flat as possible, but before long was forced to substitute the snake for the spider, worming painfully forward instead on his belly. The book he required was on a table halfway along the right-hand side of the room. Smoke was swirling everywhere about him, making location difficult, but he felt gratefully a leg of the table and began to haul himself upwards, straightening his legs ready to make a snatch at the book. Once in his hand he would drop down again and crawl or worm his way to the door. At the critical moment, when he had reached the half erect position and his fingers were almost touching the book, a flaming piece of the ceiling dropped on his back, setting his shirt on fire. With a scream, he dropped to the floor and began rolling back and forth on his back, denying the blazing garment air, until the flames were extinguished. Gasping with pain he hauled himself upwards again. But only to despair, only to witness the demise of his records. The book had also been the victim of burning plasterwork falling from above and was already beyond recovery or use. What ever it had contained of importance was gone for ever. Even in the middle of his sufferings from the terrible pain in his back and with his life in imminent danger, he had a sudden, absurd vision of the numbers, calculations, descriptions and technical terms spiralling upwards from the pages of his book towards the heavens, in some kind of Cartesian vortex or fiery ascension.

The only thing that could be saved now was himself. He began the interminable journey back towards the door, worming along the floor and gasping for breath as smoke denied his lungs their proper diet. The last thing he remembered from that day was the terrible pain that shot through his throat and into his chest as he breathed in hot air. He collapsed in the doorway with his head in the life-giving air but much of his body still inside the building with the flames beginning to flower above him like a wreath.

# CHAPTER 43

At first Costeaux was uncertain what had woken him. It felt very early. Because of the abortive hunt for Skledowski, he had not reached his bed until past three o'clock and had been confidently expecting to sleep until mid-morning. Something unusual was happening. There was a strange sound, a distant roar, like that of the sea. But the sea was many miles away. He lay there still, drowsily pondering what the sound might be. To the distant noise, suddenly, was added another sensation, a smell, a familiar and unmistakable bite in the nostrils. Smoke! He leapt out of bed. The great fear of the age grasped his guts. The harrowing, ever-present worry, especially of town dwellers – the horrifying possibility of waking at night to find the house burning underneath one, the stairs perhaps alight – was augmented by his own terrible experience at the farm. He was awake in an instant. Cautiously he opened the door of the bedroom, giving himself a view of the staircase and the hall below. No problem there. The way of escape was open. With relief he returned to his room and went to the window, which faced west. There was nothing to see there except the sunlit beginnings of another day, promising heat again, but with a strong leavening wind blowing, sometimes gusting. He crossed the house and entered a room with an east-facing window. The sound of the mysterious sea doubled as he opened the window. Among all the experiences of a tumultuous life, he had seen nothing to compete with this. Less than a mile away an immense wall of smoke rose hundreds of feet into the air, not vertically, but shaped off at the top by wind on its easterly side, so that it bent down towards him and towards the centre and west of the city like a giant, black, grasping hand. Beneath it, nourishing it, was a leaping, cavorting Hellish dancing-troupe of flames. Black smuts were whisking past his head and settling on the sill. The sound advanced and retreated with the wind like the noise of a battle and was spiked intermittently by brief rumblings that he guessed must be the sound of collapsing masonry. Coughing, he banged the window shut and dressed rapidly.

The distance to the Pudding Lane area was short, a mere fifteen minutes of walking, but Costeaux's passage on that morning took a full hour. He was battling against a current of panic-stricken men, women and children. Many of them were staggering under the burden of the few pieces of value – not usually of monetary value – but items for living. Sometimes the piece of value was a baby. Some had managed to load carts with their possessions. The streets were already partially blocked. He gave up the more direct route and turned southwards towards the river. His intention was to take Thames Street along the Embankment but the torrent of refugees was even thicker here than in the roads further north. Few seemed to be attempting the counter-current journey in his direction, although he did see some men with fire-fighting equipment and a number of soldiers moving, without much sign of organisation or purpose, towards the fire. He had to zigzag, his route mapping by inverse the density of distress encountered, sometimes using the riverside road, sometimes taking a course a few streets away from the water. This became increasingly frustrating as many of the smaller streets were orientated northwards. At last he abandoned any thought of making further progress towards the fire and decided instead to find some vantage point where he might better assess what was happening. He saw in front of him the church of Allhallows. He pushed his way inside and located the steps to the tower. Even here he was hindered, as many others had shared his idea, but after much pushing, and having received a brief but intensive training course in English oaths, he reached the top of the tower.

He understood immediately why progress had been so difficult in Thames Street. Access to it from the London Bridge end was completely barred by an immense arm of the fire that had spread through the buildings lining the river in the Fish Street area, barring it as an escape road from the flames. The crazed network of narrow alleyways and slum houses that lay between Thames Street and the water were under imminent threat from the fire and those who dwelt in misery there were spilling out from the woefully over-crowded tenements. Most of the buildings on Thames Street itself were warehouses, many of which were packed with combustibles ready for shipping out or carting away – pitch, flour, wood, wool, spirits, animal fats, oils, even gunpowder, and the fire was devouring these with grateful voracity and at terrifying speed. He had been watching for no more than a minute when one of the warehouses explored the heavens with a mighty roar, sending flaming brands into the houses in the next street inland and setting light to the premises next in line for destruction along the waterway.

Beyond the chaos of Thames Street he could see London Bridge. To his astonishment, this also was on fire. The flames had spread about a third of its length from the north bank of the river, writhing its way along the buildings that lined the bridge. As he watched, great pieces of masonry dropped hissing into the water. From the intensity of the fire and the lack of movement of people across the bridge, it was obvious that access from the northern side had been completely blocked by burning debris. Via that route there was neither escape from the fire, nor assistance to fight it. The river was crammed with debris and floating, sometimes blazing, furniture. Hundreds of boats were ferrying people to safety, at a price, he guessed. It was likely to be a profitable day for the ferries and the watermen.

As he watched, a flaming piece of wood was carried by the still raging wind a full two hundred yards across the water, where it landed like a seed upon one of the houses on the south bank. The house was soon in flower, its dry roof burning briskly, generating sparks and embers that sought to colonise the whole area.

Out in the street the confusion was even greater than before. No need to hold up a damp finger to the wind. It was from the east, blowing hard towards the body of the city and, within the constraints of weather prediction in England, likely to continue to do so. Any chance of arresting the fire had been missed in the early hours of the morning, and how much of London would be destroyed, Costeaux concluded, depended solely on the weather. An act of the Almighty was needed. If the wind dropped or heavy rain came, the city might be rescued. Otherwise nothing short of the arrival of the Army, highly organised and clearing huge fire-breaks using gunpowder, was likely to suffice, and this method carried its own dire risks.

He had work to do. Any temptation to linger further – and indeed the spectacle was enchanting, awe-inspiring even, a once-in-lifetime experience – was dispelled in the next few minutes. A scuffle was taking place on the corner of the street. A rough-looking man, immediately recognisable as a foreign sailor, was being beaten with fists and sticks by a group of half-a-dozen honest London citizens, apparently servants from a nearby large house. He was left bleeding and semi-conscious in the roadway. As he tried to crawl away, he disappeared from sight under the hooves of a horse that was pulling a cart. Costeaux had hardly turned away when a passer-by grabbed his sleeve.

'The Dutch have done this,' he said.

'Ay,' said another, 'the Dutch and the French. And the French army is a few miles away, at Gravesend.'

Costeaux nodded his thanks for this information. Long experience had taught him to react quickly and, in particular, when to speak and when to remain silent. His English was immaculate but his accent was not perfect. He could easily suffer the fate of the sailor.

His first task was to get the news of the fire and his assessment of its likely outcome to France. For this there were two lines of communication already in place and smoothly operating. One was conventional and involved fast horses and boats. The other was an express service, unreliable but swift, using pigeons. By this means the news of the disaster in London would be in France within a few hours, provided the birds evaded the activities of falcons and English sporting Lords. Costeaux had no part in the mechanics of either service. All he had to do was deliver the messages to couriers in London. Making contact with them occupied the rest of the morning. A little after noon he arrived back at his home.

It was now time to consider his own problems. If there was no change in the weather, the fire might well spread as far as St Paul's and the area around it, threatening his house. It was impossible to know how soon this could happen. He decided to remain for the time being, but began preparations that would enable his departure at short notice. First he must ensure that he had transport away from the fire. It would be in great demand and in very short supply. He must also find alternative accommodation. He spent the afternoon making the necessary arrangements via the French network. In the evening he packed his bags and boxes and by the end of the day was ready to leave at an hour's notice. During the evening's packing he almost injured himself by an uncharacteristic piece of carelessness. He picked up the case of balls – the presentation balls with which it was safe to begin a game. All the contents dropped on to the floor with a quite thunderous noise narrowly missing his feet. He must have omitted to latch the case properly when he had last looked at the balls. He recovered five of the balls and returned them to the case. The sixth had disappeared, probably rolling under one of the heavy pieces of furniture. Fortunately he had made no such mistake with the imitation set.

To say that the next day dawned would be a serious exaggeration. In Essex or Kent this may have been an appropriate description of the beginning of another hot day of late summer. In the City of London, and for many miles to the west, the daylight failed, or at least faltered. In Costeaux's house, the light barely penetrated at all. It had been almost impossible to sleep that night. He had fastened the windows securely shut, in spite of the oppressively hot weather. Even so, although the house was of superior quality to most of those around it, smoke still discovered ways in which to enter through previously unrealised pores, mostly places where the woodwork had warped, in some instances very recently in the exceptional weather. Its state of repair was being usefully tested – usefully, that is, provided it survived.

He had decided that, in any case, it was too dangerous to attempt a serious night's sleep. It was not possible to tell how fast the fire would spread through the city, and so he put himself into *night watch* state, a skill among many others that he had developed over the years as an agent. Every hour he woke himself up to take another brief look at the streets around his house. The fire was making spectacular progress but was still a long way off. Tomorrow was going to be another difficult day. He took gratefully what little sleep he could procure.

It was the most terrible Monday in London's difficult history. Even the glacial Costeaux was affected by what he saw as he tried to monitor the progress of the fire in preparation for another report. His difficulties in moving about the city were extreme, and worsened as the day went on. At mid-morning he arrived at Queenhithe docks, a large corn and fruit market at the side of the Thames, at the same time as a Royal party, among whom he could clearly discern King Charles. The market offered a large space that could be pressed into service as a fire-break and orders were given to clear the stalls away and pull down houses surrounding it. The King left for some other scene of destruction and was no longer present when the turret of a building on the west side took fire from burning debris flying on the wind. Within minutes the whole building and its neighbours were in flames; the fire-break – and the king's instructions – were briskly disregarded by the fire.

In the afternoon as one limb of the fire moved along Thames Street and the region by the river, a second arm flung out to the north throwing a consuming embrace towards the wealthiest districts. Encouraged by the rising ground and the still raging wind, the fire devoured the rich houses of Lombard Street and made a brief meal of the Cornhill, where the fashionable shops and merchants' houses offered little resistance. This left the Royal Exchange, the hub of London's trade, defenceless. The heat was now so overpowering and the risks of becoming trapped so great that Costeaux did not see the flames burst through the double galleries that ran around the massive central quadrangle of the Exchange. The appetite of the fire, trained on readily assimilable baby foods of deal and plaster, had adapted enthusiastically to an adult diet. Oak, marble and stone presented no problem to its digestion, nor for that matter did lead. It fed on all four in the Exchange. The sovereigns of England, all of whom were depicted there in marble, were deposed, some of them for a second time, within a few hours. Watching from a distance, Costeaux saw the final act of desecration in the great building as the gilded grasshopper emblem of Sir Thomas Gresham crashed from the tower into the furnace beneath it.

Several times during the day, he encountered a royal party, not the king this time but his younger brother, James, Duke of York, busily but ineffectively organising fire fighting and fire breaks. 'London,' Costeaux exulted in his next message, 'is finished. If the weather remains steady, the Palace of Whitehall and all of Westminster will be destroyed. The King and the Duke of York are men hunted by terror and the wrath of the God whom they have offended.'

Costeaux had seen enough during the day to make up his mind about his own affairs. That evening, after he had arranged the sending of information, he called for the cart that had been held ready for him, and the removal of his personal goods began at dawn the next morning. This was not too heavy a task since most of the furnishings belonged to the house and its landlord. His papers and few pieces of jewellery and furniture of his own were loaded along with a few miscellaneous items of value, actual or sentimental. Among these were the two cases of balls, one belonging to the former category, one to the latter. Now he had to face another appalling day of reconnoitre and reporting, a day of filth and danger, lightened only by the thought that the burning city belonged to the enemy. As he turned to leave, he noticed suddenly that the upheaval of removal had displaced one of the heavy pieces of furniture in the living room, revealing the lost ball of the presentation set. He picked it up, put it in a pocket and left the house for the last time.

The scenes in the streets were now Apocalyptic. The streets were jammed with a barely moving throng of people and carts and horses. Wagons were travelling – or attempting to – in both directions, some already loaded and seeking exit from the holocaust, some called in to evacuate goods from the great houses – the two being brought up stationary, head to head. Even progress on foot was extremely difficult, so much so that Costeaux decided upon his expedient of the first morning of the fire and found a viewing point – the church of St Michael le Querne. This time he was obstructed not by sightseers but by the homeless who had spent the night sleeping in the church. From the tower, he saw that an immense wall of flame extending along the Thames had already, in its westward passage, passed St Paul's to the south. To the east and north the fire was almost touching the City walls. The smoke obscured detail but he could see that the great ceremonial thoroughfare of Cheapside was becoming a flaming arrow directed at the heart of the city. If he wanted to know more he would have to map the conflagration the hard way – on foot.

He made his way to the river where the destruction had extended as far as Blackfriars and Bridewell, then northwards to the City wall to west of Drapers' Hall, which was at the end of its long history. He could not approach – nor did he wish to – nearer than about a hundred yards, the heat proscribed it. The heart of the fire was at white heat, and even looking at the fire so close was difficult. And the fire had made its own wind. True, the gale from the east was unabated, but the uprush of air from the intensity of the conflagration had created a fire storm, sucking in air from every direction, sucking in anything light enough or weak enough, threatening to pull in human bodies even – the poor, the greedy, the desperate hoping to save their possessions at the last moment – taking the lives of the honest and the thieves who had arrived at the scene like wasps at a beer glass.

Costeaux had not believed the accounts he had heard, from those who had been forced to flee from forest fires, how trees at a great distance, as much as a hundred yards from the visible conflagration, had burst into flames without a tongue of fire touching them. This Tuesday morning his scepticism was dramatically dispersed, not by one instance but by many. Indeed he nearly lost his own life, as many had already lost theirs. He was walking, or rather trying to push his way along. The next street away to the east was burning fiercely but there was no sign yet of trouble nearby. The heat was tremendous and rising every moment, so much so that there was a general nervous acceleration of movement. Suddenly the house next to where he was standing took fire and within two minutes was a blazing torch scattering shards of fire among the crowd around him. In the panic he almost lost his footing, which would probably have been fatal.

The atmosphere in the streets of London was approaching the hysterical. Someone must be chosen for blame. The traditional enemy, France was a likely candidate at any such informal ballot. The fact that there was war between the two countries was decisive. The French were unanimously elected to the Seat of Wickedness. They had fired the city – there was no doubt. Their agents had initiated it during the small hours of Sunday night. If any further proof was necessary – and really it was not – the evidence was provided by the spontaneous outbursts of fire in the city, sometimes at considerable distance from the massive wall of fire that was consuming street after street. Bands of French saboteurs were roaming the city, setting new fires everywhere. Some had already been caught with fire-bombs and had been handed over to the Trained Bands or had been summarily, but justly, dealt with on the spot.

All day he gathered information, walking many miles. By circumventing the fire to the north, he mapped the spread of the fire eastwards from its origin. For some part of the way he travelled through the fields outside the City walls, where thousands of the dispossessed had congregated and, if they could, slept. In this direction its progress, opposed by the wind, had been quite slow, but it was creeping up on the Tower. A feverish operation had begun to defend it and to remove its combustibles. A huge army of sailors was carrying barrels of gunpowder on to ships. Costeaux's information was that The White Tower held some five hundred thousand pounds of gunpowder, enough to destroy that part of London and all the shipping on the river downstream from the bridge. To set it alight had been one of his favourite and recurrent dreams. In practice it was far too difficult an enterprise. Perhaps Fate was about to arrange it for him.

Returning, later in the day, to the area west of the fire, he encountered once again the Duke of York's party. They were organising the blowing up of houses with gunpowder, in an effort to create a fire-break, wide enough to be effective, along the Fleet ditch. The natural light was beginning to fail, but an unearthly light rendered the sky luminous and flickered and fluttered everywhere on the surviving buildings. Costeaux was exhausted and half-suffocated. He was about to conclude the day's work and retire to his new lodgings, which were at a safe distance, when he became captivated by the situation of St Paul's. The great cathedral was being attacked from three sides by flames rising as high as the nave, yet it seemed to resist. Its walls were massive and not likely to give in easily, but as he watched he saw a fire begin in the roof, apparently in a portion where repair work had been about to begin. From this weak spot the flames ate their way rapidly along the whole length of internal timbers of the roof. Soon the great windows began to glow with strange colours. Blazing debris from above must have breached the building from inside like spies or saboteurs. Soon the windows began to fall out and flames took the place of the glass and the lead-work, licking out from the interior, tasting the walls from both sides. Suddenly he saw a glistening stream running from the burning ruin. 'Water?' was his momentary thought. It was not possible. Water did not glow with this eerie silvery sheen, nor spit out globules. As he watched he saw that everything it touched as it ran also burst into flame. It swept down the street in an incendiary fury. Lead, he concluded – molten lead from the roof. There must have been tons of it. Presumably it would run until it cooled and solidified on the ground or streamed into the Thames, boiling the water.

Now he really was going to end his day. He turned away, to begin the walk to his new refuge. Two hundred yards from the burning Cathedral a gang of men were trying to prepare a fire-break. Perhaps it was exhaustion that caused Costeaux to stagger against the man who was trying to secure a rope to a hook in the wall of the house. The man cursed as the rope fell to the street again.

'Watch where you're going, you ugly little runt,' he said.

Exhaustion, over-excitement from the extraordinary scenes at the Cathedral, anger at the insult – which he would in more usual circumstances have ignored as part of the day's work – induced a grave mistake. He had made errors in his life as an agent, rather few considering the complexity of the tasks allotted to him. None had been particularly serious in the long run. This one proved to be his last.

'No use making a fire-break here, you ape,' he said. 'It's too close to the fire.'

He knew immediately that he should not have broken the rule of silence that he had imposed upon himself all day. Why, in any case, was he offering good advice to the enemy?

'Where are you from?' asked the man in tones compounded of suspicion and aggression in equal parts.

Costeaux decided to repair the damage in the shortest way possible. He said nothing more. He swung round to go, only to collide with another large member of the fire-break gang whose interest had been aroused. Costeaux turned to the gap between the two men, only to find that it had been filled by a third man.

'Wait a moment,' said the first man. 'I asked you where you are from?'

'Ireland,' replied Costeaux.

'Oireland,' said the second of the men, whose name was Patrick. 'Niver in all the world is he from Oireland!' He turned to Costeaux. 'Whereabouts in Oireland?'

'Dublin,' said Costeaux.

'I'm from Dublin. I've never seen you.'

'I am sorry that we never met there. It's a big town.'

'Faith', said Paddy, 'nobody from Oireland speaks like you do.'

'That's because my mother was from Russia.'

'Let him go', said the third man impatiently. 'We've work to do.'

'We will', said the first man who was clearly the boss. 'But we'll search him first.'

Costeaux was now surrounded by all the members of the fire-break gang, five in number. He was clearly going nowhere.

A handful of gold coins was the first thing to emerge.

'My!' said the leader admiringly, but with a pinch of sarcasm. 'Where did you get these?'

'Cloth sales. I am a trader in woollen goods. I was paid just in time. If the fire goes on like this, the goods will all go up in smoke. Now let me go please.'

'Then what is this?' The boss man held up the ball for the Jeu Provençal.

'I don't know. I believe it is for a game of some kind. It was given to me as a courteous extra in the cloth transaction because the negotiations had gone well.'

Another man, who had not yet spoken, gave an opinion.

'This man speaks like the Frenchies do. I've worked with them on board ship.'

'Look,' said man number three, 'there's writing on it.'

The boss squinted at the mysterious sphere in the flirting light.

'Doesn't mean anything to me.' He peered painfully at the script again. 'Christ!' he said suddenly. 'Louis the Fourteenth! It says Louis the Fourteenth!' He placed the dangerous object gingerly but in haste on the ground and stepped back. So did his mates. 'A bomb', said somebody. The ring suddenly enlarged, but not enough for Costeaux to make a run for it.

The boss looked around it desperation. Water was his first thought. 'Here he said to Patrick. 'Dunk it the stool over there. That should settle it.'

'Jaisus! Whoi me?! Do it yourself.'

'Get on with it.'

Patrick picked the sphere up in his hat as though it might be hot or that the cloth would protect him if the device exploded. He walked the longest fifty yards of his life to the close stool and lowered the ball into the murky depths of the bucket, inadvertently donating his hat too.

'That should work,' said the boss.

'I hope I shan't be around here if it doesn't, said Patrick.

'What do we do with this snake?' asked number three.

'It's a frog. And a little one. Stamp on it,' said someone else.

'Wait a minute,' said the Boss with a glance down the street, where the fire was racing through the houses with the terrifying momentum that three days' practice seemed to have given it. 'Remember that he gave us some good advice. He was right about us making the fire-break too close to the fire.'

A small hope leapt somewhere in Costeaux's breast. He brightened visibly. 'Yes,' he said, 'you need to work a good quarter of a mile from the fire.'

The Boss continued. 'You are so right. We'll call it off here. We're too late. And I've thought of a better use for this rope.' And he began to make slip-knot in the end of the rope.

'Great,' said number three and the chorus of approval was taken up all around the group. Number two produced a piece of twine and in a few moments Costeaux's hands were tied behind his back.

'Look,' said Costeaux, 'I know that you don't want to do this to an innocent man. I have nothing to do with this terrible fire. I am a simple merchant.'

The point seemed not to register. He tried again.

'Let me go and you can have the sovereigns yourself. For your own use. Share them out.'

It was his last throw.

The Boss laughed.

'We were going to keep those anyway.'

The noose was already round his neck. This time there was little difficulty in throwing the other end over the hook in the wall. A concerted heave by all members of the gang – two would have sufficed – and Costeaux rose into the air. The sailor was singing what appeared to be the snatches from a sea shanty, perhaps the one for hoisting the mainsail.

Costeaux's body was dangling against the side of the building. His feet sought desperately for a foothold, for a crevice or coign in the wall. After a minute or two the legs became still. The men turned away to the site of their next hopeless venture.

Not more than half-an-hour later a lick of flame severed the rope, sending Costeaux's body crashing down into the flaming remnants of the house, where any strictures that the Popes and Cardinals of the Ages may have made against cremation were brutally ignored by the Great Fire. His remains, like those of hundreds, perhaps thousands of its victims, disappeared without trace.

# CHAPTER 44

Joseph turned his body into a new position. It was no use. A different pain shot through him. On the whole he preferred the first one and shifted back again. The sheets felt raw against his skin even though a considerable portion of his body was swathed in dressings. His chest hurt rather less than it had a day or so before, but his difficulty in breathing had not lessened. He had no recollection of how he had come to this place. His latest memory of that day was his collapse in the doorway of the blazing laboratory.

Now at least he had some minimal information. He knew where he was, if still ignorant of how he came to be there. The line of beds and the shoddy room had immediately announced 'hospital,' and a blue-smocked woman, clearly a nursing Sister, had paused long enough in her pressing and depressing duties to inform him that he was in St Bartholomew's Hospital. When he asked how he came to be there, she had shrugged and passed on.

St Bartholomew's was one of the better thoughts of King Henry the Eighth. Previously a monastery, it had been saved from the fate of most similar institutions and allowed to supply the City's needs as a refuge for those unfortunate enough to be both poor and sick. Joseph, having a family to support him would not normally qualify for its services. The expectation was that he would be tended at home, with the family engaging medical and nursing help as required. Part of the answer to his bewilderment was provided by another Sister, a remarkable woman whose efficiency permitted and promoted her communicativeness, rather than obstructing it. Her brisk manner was put aside and she sat down and talked to him briefly but informatively, in gentle tones – tones sisterly in all senses of the word.

Yes, she confirmed, he had been brought in from the street, unidentified, by whom she did not know. There had been hours – days in fact – of unprecedented confusion and unparalleled injuries. A massive fire had swept through the City of London, destroying nearly all of it. Many had suffered terrible burns; many of those brought in were unidentified. He was one of them, and they had thought that he would not survive until daybreak. Now he had recovered sufficiently to talk, they would be able to contact his relatives, who would be expected to take him away as soon as he was sufficiently well.

'Your name?' she asked.

There was moment of hesitation on his part before answering, during which she gazed at him searchingly and with a faint air of surprise, in a way that reminded him of Alistair Douglas.

'Thomas Backhaus,' he said at last, and gave her the address of his wife's family. An appalling thought now occurred to him.

'Is it known where the fire started?' he asked.

'In Pudding Lane. In a baker's shop, so they say.'

As the excellent woman's back receded, Joseph lay in shock. He seemed to be a thousand miles deep with great mountains piled upon his chest, stifling him. His breathing difficulty intensified. Thought was beyond him. He lay, overwhelmed, in a great darkness, lost in a blank, directionless wilderness. Occasional images presented themselves in random order, images of burning buildings, of fleeing people, of people losing their possessions or their lives, of the wrath of God, of the fate of Sodom and Gomorrah, of the Apocalypse, of Hellfire and Damnation. When at last a coherent thought occurred to him, he shuddered for another reason. 'At least,' he heard his own voice saying, 'they will not blame me. They believe that it began in the bakery – a likely place for a fire to start.' The ignobility of the thought, its sheer plumbing of the despicable, shocked him into a more rational state. For some reason that he did not understand, he had always been more resolute in facing physical dangers than in confronting moral problems. It's no good, he thought, 'I shall have to inform the authorities of what really happened. That decent man, Farriner, cannot be allowed to take the blame.'

Night came, like a sack lowered over his head. He felt himself to be suffocating. He lay for many hours under a terrible weight, unable to summon the sleep that his tortured body needed and longed for. He lay under a weight of guilt, of shame, of despair. So this is where his burst of bad temper had brought him – and not only himself, but countless other people also – to a black, smoking desert of ruins. His response to what was, after all, an acceptable question from Sam, who had come to him with a reasonable complaint, had been irrational to the point of absurdity, a self-indulgent display of invective and insult. It was true that Sam's manner had been aggressive and provocative, but these were problems that he had met and learned to negotiate in his dealings as an apothecary – in confrontations with supercilious physicians, dissatisfied patients, avaricious or swindling suppliers.

Sheer exhaustion brought him sleep, but not until the small hours of the morning. When he awoke, it was light. After a few seconds of intermission, during the first re-orientation after sleep, of reconnecting with his situation, the burden descended upon him again. But there was a new thought hovering behind it somewhere. He called it out, pulled at it until it was close enough for identification, and gradually it began to take shape; sleep had once again worked its transforming alchemy. He began to recall the many incidents that he had personally witnessed of potentially serious fires, where candles had been knocked over, embers scattered, or burning oil spread about. In most of these cases, swift action or sheer luck had averted disaster – or even major damage. He had seen a house burn, and in the case of the great fire in Bristol, which had so dramatically diverted his own life, he had seen a row of houses destroyed and a city threatened. But never a whole town consumed. To burn a whole town something special was required – a whole set of unique circumstances.

He thought of the situation of London and its citizens on the first day of September 1666 – a city constructed of vast acres of wood and plaster, tightly packed together, but not so tightly as to deny air to a developing fire, honeycombed with tunnels made by the overhanging jetties that presented channels through which a conflagration could rush. He remembered the prolonged spell of hot weather that had made life so unbearable in the days before the disaster. The wind, hot and dry as though from an African desert, had blown with unrelenting, malevolent force from the place of origin of the fire towards the heart of the great city. He recalled the inadequacy of the fire-fighting arrangements, both in equipment and organisation, inadequacies that he noticed many times and even complained about in his period of residence in the area.

The burden of guilt that he had first taken upon himself solely, should reasonably be shared. By whom, though? By the governors of the city who had failed to make preparations for a large scale conflagration. Certainly. By the designers of the city? But who were they? Had the city *been* designed? No. Or it had been designed only by indefinable mass movements of human folly, by tacit agreement between the needy and the greedy. How about the wind and the drought though? This, surely, was God's area of expertise. What part had God played in this? He sets the seasons. He determines the winds in their courses. And the floods and heat waves presumably.

He was inclined to give up at this point. His head was aching as it always did in response to ethical debate. Normally he would have given up and turned his mind to something else, but his head ached almost intolerably already, and every other part of him seemed to hurt. At least he had placed his guilt in a more realistic context. He was responsible certainly for setting fire to a hut by a reprehensible act of folly, but the blame for the catastrophic conflagration which had followed was not his, or his only in some miniscule part which he shared with many thousands of others, past and present. For that others must examine themselves. God should examine himself too.

*If God is, whence come evil things? If He is not, whence come good?*

One more step in search of a final cause and Joseph might have confronted Almighty God himself and been fried to a crisp like Semele, or torn to pieces by hounds. He was rescued from this fate by the appearance at his bedside of a beautifully dressed gentleman. The bag, and the expression on his nose, clearly identified him as a physician. At least, thought Joseph, I am not about to be consumed by lightning. A further glance, however, revealed another figure hovering deferentially in the background and immediately suggested to him that perhaps a quick thunderbolt might be his preferred choice. He knew this second man. He was a member of the Company of Barber-Surgeons and was active in the same area of the City in which Joseph worked. His name was James Hakluyt member of an immigrant family. Not the nicest of names, thought Joseph, but at least he does not have to bear the burden carried by a barber-surgeon he had known in Bristol, whose name was Thomas Carver.

James Hakluyt, who was known locally as Jim Trim, recognised Joseph too and smiled pleasantly – but a little too enthusiastically, thought Joseph. The rivalry, sometimes savage, between physicians, barber-surgeons and apothecaries had a long history. Generally apothecaries had won third prize in the contest. The barber-surgeons were able – and did not hesitate – to point to their incorporation in 1540, some seventy years before the apothecaries. They never tired of reminding Joseph that apothecaries had for a period been included with the Society of Grocers. 'What condiments do you have for the patient today?' they would ask him. 'Will you be applying a cheese, perhaps?' Physicians looked down from a great height on those of both professions – or tradesmen as they preferred to call them – men who had never seen the inside of a university and would not be able to conjugate a Latin verb, even if that indispensable ability replaced the reading of the neck verse – the test for Benefit of Clergy – as the requirement for avoiding execution. Joseph would reply that the prior recognition of barber-surgeons merely reflected the fact that everyone understood carpentry and plumbing – and carpenters and plumbers were two a penny – but only a chosen few understood chymistry. (After the revelation brought to him by the pottery shard, he realised that chemists did not understand chymistry either, but that did not inhibit him from making this rejoinder.)

The presence of these two practitioners immediately stimulated his talent for the Gothic elaboration of invective. A variety of complex insults swarmed into Joseph's mind together with the prospective pleasure of using them. But then, on the other hand... He looked nervously at James Hakluyt who, tactfully, was not carrying a bag. Joseph guessed, however, that his collection of saws, knives, scissors, chisels, adzes and hammers was not far away. He decided to postpone the pleasure until another day.

The physician examined Joseph's wounds, paying especial attention to his damaged leg. At last, after much hmmming and tutting, he said – somewhat reluctantly Joseph thought – 'you'll keep that I think.' Instead he turned his skills to Joseph's respiratory problems, placing a disdainful ear against his chest. Joseph rather expected him to wash his ear afterwards. Whatever it was that he heard there provoked some further mutterings. Next he required a sample of sputum, which Joseph was able to provide all too readily. Joseph recollected suddenly that Dr Menge was a great sputum doctor, in fact *the* great sputum doctor, the national expert. He could recognise all diseases of the lung from the patient's sputum, and not only of the lung but of all other parts of the body as well, including the brain. The colour, texture, consistency, density and patterning comprised an infallible guide to the nature of illness, as beautifully set out, with illustrations in the good doctor's book, where he had shared his discovery with the world. He was not about to share information with Joseph, however, and simply muttered something in Latin that defeated even Joseph's command of the language. Joseph's sputum was green and lumpy and told Joseph what he already knew, and did not need to learn from Dr Menge or any other physician – that his lungs were suffering congestion as a complication following damage to them by inhaled hot air and smoke.

The two medical experts departed. At least he was still in one piece. And had acquired – Oh, the great mercies of God! – a medicine the taste of which he immediately recognised. The physician in his wisdom had prescribed antimony. It would do him a power of good – mainly by exercising his mind in finding a way of disposing of it. The contact with other humans, however brief and unsatisfactory, had lifted his spirits. He felt more cheerful and a little better. It did not last. A fit of coughing, worse than any that he had so far experienced, left him feeling weak and helpless. The clouds of misery descended upon him again.

This time it was daylight misery. Where was Caroline? Had she survived the fire? He needed help, sympathy, understanding… His Aristotelian analysis of the fire had lessened his terrible burden of guilt. One might analyse perhaps the intricate anastomosis of cause and effect in an event such as London's fire, but neither the Greeks nor the Bible explained how the burden of guilt was to be distributed among the various levels of causation. As for *final* causes, these were just too difficult, too remote. Or were they too imminent and too dangerous? Or unreal? Perhaps even God had to answer to some higher authority. God must look to His own conscience. The blasphemy of the thought shocked him into other channels of reflection.

If he recovered, all would be well. There would be a delay while he found another place to work, acquired a suitable laboratory and restocked with the necessary apparatus and substances. His relationship with his wife's family, after the unfortunate beginning, had long ago normalised. They would greet him warmly, with evident and genuine relief at his survival and would help him to re-assemble the shattered pieces of his life. His books were destroyed but his mind was clear and his exceptional memory in excellent repair. His discoveries were the fruits of many years of exploration, of hard and lonely work, frequent disappointment, progress that seemed slow or even non-existent, navigation through a maze in which he took many wrong turnings, explored many blind alleys. Now he looked back and saw his years of struggle in perspective, saw the richness of what he had achieved. With hindsight, he would know exactly what he needed to do to recreate the information lost in the notebooks. The key experiments could be readily repeated. He knew what these were and exactly how to conduct them. In a few months he could collect persuasive evidence that could be presented confidently in front of the best expertise that England could assemble.

Another fit of coughing dispelled his optimism. He was very ill, would perhaps die within a few days. If he did so, all was lost, his life's work destroyed. A double blow – not only his life lost, but its purpose also. The prospect of the loss of the special knowledge that he now possessed added to his determination to survive. Probably most people would be content to allow their labours to slip quietly away from them. Why should he feel differently? Was his knowledge really so special? It had never been tested by critical examination, although that had been imminent. He would never know its real status until it had been judged by the best minds among his fellow men.

Supposing, as he fervently believed, that his discoveries *were* of fundamental importance – what made him think that they were unique or indispensable? He had come to realise during his reading how difficult it is to trace the true origin of any particular idea. There always seemed to be a precedent. Always someone had conceived the idea, or some closely related idea, at an earlier time. Sometimes discoveries had been made simultaneously but independently, presumably because the intellectual climate was such that it tended to generate similar notions. Somewhere, someone would have been wrestling with the same thoughts and finding the same solutions. If they were not doing so now, they would do so in the near future. His life's labours, seen in context, were of little importance.

Perhaps the cocoon of his secret knowledge did not need to take upon itself bright wings and show itself to the brutal world of pin-happy collectors and sniping swallows. And the splendid imago would, at best, last only a season before the chill winter brought its glories to an end. *Tempus, edax rerum.* And yet… and yet… He could find no ease. His labours and their fruits possessed a life of their own somewhere, were in some way wholly self-sufficient, existed and would continue to exist, admired by the Heavenly Host, by a chorus of the Ancients, by the Demiurge, or they would simply live in some rarefied space beyond the desire or need for use or admiration.

However ephemeral his discoveries, whatever the credentials of his ideas as representatives for the ultimate secrets of Nature, and regardless of their reception in the human community, they carried with them, in some sense, his immortality. And this was the crux of his difficulties. They represented that part of him which would live on. They were his children. This is why men had engaged in such bitter struggles to establish precedence for their ideas and discoveries.

True, he had real children. A girl many hundreds of miles away whom he had deserted twenty-five years ago and who may by now have children of her own. And a beloved son – where was Marcus at the moment? Doing what sons do – living his own absorbing life and turning up at home occasionally when he ran out of money, affectionate, grateful enough, but preoccupied.

Immortality was not in his hands. It had been given, albeit with important provisos, by a supreme act of sacrifice some sixteen hundred years ago. 'He that believeth in me shall have everlasting life'. 'In my father's house there are many mansions'.

The words provided little comfort. Eventually he slept. Several days passed. The daylight hours were filled with anguish, with coughing, with the struggle for breath; the night with feverish and hectic dreams, bordering on delirium.

\* \* \* \* \*

He awoke at dawn in a room not distinguished by any unusual feature. He became aware, however, that something very extraordinary was happening. The sounds were coming from outside and were not the familiar ones of the town or of the country. There was a clanking, a tinkling, a rustling – metallic noises of all kinds – gradually growing louder and apparently coming from all directions. Opening a shutter, he found that the familiar morning light had been replaced by deep crimson. Bathed in this light and reflecting it in a myriad of glowing points and patches were thousands of metal objects, moving under their own power and control, quite clearly alive. Some of them seemed to be animals, tiny or large, and of many different kinds, but all of metal. Equally numerous were what appeared to be flowers made of tin and other metals. Larger than most, and obviously in command of this singular creation were upright creatures made from metal cylinders and having legs and arms constructed from levers, giving them a strange air of parodying human beings. One of this latter kind was looking straight at him and gesturing to the others to follow him. They began to stream towards Joseph, who tried hastily to slam the window shut. He was too late and the current of metal creatures poured into the room. Momentarily he was terrified, but quickly realising that they were not hostile, but merely curious, he calmed down and allowed them to examine him. The one who had first pointed was certainly their leader and his cylinder bore a shining, yellow band, faintly reminiscent of a kingly crown. He was the first to speak, addressing himself to a lieutenant at his side on whom he trusted for expertise. He spoke in strange metallic tinkling voice:

'Is it from the next aeon, do you suppose?'

'No,' replied the expert, 'it's a primitive life form.'

'Careful what you say!' exclaimed Joseph indignantly, but no one took any notice. The mass of creatures had by now all seen Joseph and were reduced to what seemed an awed silence. The quiet was suddenly broken from somewhere at the back of the throng by a symphony of clashing, scraping, clattering noises resembling a serious collapse in a blacksmith's shop, except that the sound was sustained, on and on, although it came in waves, alternately falling away to a mere tinkle, then rising again in a mighty crescendo of bangings and bongings. Looking in the direction of the disturbance, Joseph could see that two of the human parodies were attempting to copulate.

The leader gave out a kind of scraping sound that was clearly a sigh. Turning to a lieutenant he said: 'Please go and remind them that we don't do it like that any more, and extract them two rivets.'

'Won't that kill them?' asked Joseph.

'No,' replied the leader. 'It's a first offence. But habitual criminals eventually fall to pieces.'

They continued their puzzled, but gentle and thorough examination of him, collecting flakes of skin and dabbing at the inside of his cheek with a swab. He became increasingly impatient at their treatment of him as a fascinating object and, as they were trying to extract a drop of blood from his finger, attempted to recover his captured hand. He blinked awake, half expecting to see some mythical animal, perhaps shaped like a kettle. A hand was resting on his arm and he found himself gazing up at the face of Celia Albright. The good woman had anticipated his next thought.

'Don't worry,' she said gently, 'Caroline is well. Everything is all right. She was unable to come herself, but she is well, or will be in a few days' time.'

'I am glad.' Breathing was difficult and his voice was weak, partly from days of disuse. 'And glad to see you. Tell me what is happening.'

'You have Caroline to thank for your life. She found you lying in the doorway of that shack – (the word was delivered with a forthright contemptuous amusement, which had changed not at all over the years) that hut you called a laboratory – out to the world and with your clothes on fire. The others had fled through the passage. It was too far for her to pull you that way, but pull you she did – in the opposite direction, into the wind. She has some sense after all. A few yards away, on the side the wind was coming from, there was considerable heat but little immediate danger.'

'And how did I get here?'

'I don't know. Caroline went eventually to find help, which was very difficult because of the confusion, and when she returned with some others, you had gone. Someone else must have found you in the meantime.'

'She risked her life for me.'

'Yes. She did well. I'm not sure you're really worth it!' The remark was delivered with her agreeable laugh, which disarmed it. Celia had something of her mother's asperity without the rancour.

'Is Caroline injured?'

'She has some minor burns which will soon heal. But dragging you unconscious over rough ground was almost beyond her strength. She wrecked her back. She is lying on her bed groaning. She can't even walk at the moment, but it will soon pass – or so Dr Luck tells us.'

'Will she come here?'

'Certainly. To look after you until you recover.'

'She should come soon.'

Celia looked at him reprovingly. You're not going to die on us, are you? Don't. We need you.'

'I'm sure I don't know what for. I shall be a liability. We lost everything, I presume?'

'Yes. Everything. The house was completely burned out. Like countless others,' she added. 'But you can live with us in Cottesthorpe, at least for the time being. Until you can get on again with whatever it is that you do.'

'I don't know. Chymistry I think,' answered Joseph. 'But we can contribute nothing.'

'Caroline can work in the inn. You can concentrate on recovering your health. Or you could make some gold,' she suggested with a laugh, 'as you used to.'

'I only make learned papers these days. And a mysterious form of air.'

'I like your first idea best!' was this sensible woman's opinion.

When Celia had gone, he began to think seriously about her last remark in spite of its jocular intent. If his new ideas of the nature of matter were correct, would transmutation still be possible? He thought not – if no common ground existed for the elements, then conversion could not happen.

From this conclusion, which he found rather depressing, he turned to the other of his early dreams – those dreams that he had shared with so many others over the ages – the Elixir, the cure-all. Don Hidalgo's memorable explanation of its operation, drawing analogies with ferments, was still valid. But by what magic did a ferment work? His new view had nothing to offer on this – and he realised also that, even in the language he had used in framing the question, he had fallen into the old trap. Nothing betrayed one's assumptions more clearly than words inadvertently chosen. He had used the word 'magic.' Ferments remained as mysterious as ever, but it was unnecessary – entirely inhibiting in fact – to assume that magic was involved.

Why had he lately dreamed of an army of metallic beings? Was he now contaminated by the view he had so long despised – that living things were nothing more than clever bits of mechanism, pieces of architecture, designed in an unknown office and constructed from bricks, stone, iron and dust?

The Elixir and the incorruptibility of gold had been magnificent standard-bearers for a better world. The ideal had been clear:

*... to reduce all arts (in this our age spotted and imperfect) to perfection; so that finally man might thereby understand his own nobleness and worth...*

His new view of natural philosophy had little to say about benefits to mankind or the world, still less about the perfectibility of the arts or the salvation of the soul. It was neutral. It did not understand the question. It stared uncomprehendingly back. It exercised its right to silence.

His life was directed to no useful purpose. He had become obsessed with the minutiae of the world.

For several more days he alternated between periods of semi-consciousness and a daunting clarity of mind. The only common factor was despair.

But once, lying somewhere between sleep and waking, he experienced a deep joy and he heard his own voice speaking as though from on high:

*Seeing the only wise and merciful God in these latter days hath poured out so richly his mercy and goodness to mankind, whereby we do attain more to the perfect knowledge of his son Jesus Christ and Nature...*

He awoke to a new dilemma. Once it had been possible to link Jesus Christ and Nature together in one phrase. Now, for all the nobility of the words, the coupling seemed false. One of the inner voices in this motet was singing a wrong note. The Rosicrucian manifestos were noble and uplifting works. But what actually did they mean? In his youth he had seen them as a supreme synthesis where natural philosophy, magic and religion were united. Or conflated – just pressed together. Or confused even? Should they not represent different areas of human experience, perhaps overlapping?

Who *was* Christian Rosencreutz? Had he ever existed? It seemed possible that Rosencreutz also was an invention. If Isaac Casaubon lived a year or two longer he might have turned his attention to an examination of the manifestos and from their internal evidence established the great founder of the movement as a noble fiction of the imagination of some anonymous person or persons.

He found himself walking in a great city, with wide streets and buildings of a beautiful yellow stone that seemed to emit its own sunlight. Its general aspect suggested Rome, but that building on the hill was unmistakably the Parthenon, and over here on the opposite side of market – surely that was St Paul's Cathedral. The morning was of great beauty, with a relaxed autumnal sunlight, but something was wrong. There were too many people hurrying about, in too great a haste. Most of them had crinkled faces and grey beards. Towards him in the street came an elderly man, moving as quickly as his limp would allow, but stopping every few paces to recover his breath and to look anxiously over his shoulder, as though he feared that someone was following him. Joseph stood in his path, forcing him to stop.

'Why are you in such a hurry?' he asked.

The old man tried to push past, but finding that he could not, pulled out a sheet of paper and thrust it into Joseph's face. It was headed:

**Department of the Interior and Exterior and All Regions in Between.**

And underneath it simply read:

**Everyone over the age of sixty will be shot.**
**Everyone over the age of six hundred will be shot twice**.

Apologising, Joseph stepped aside and allowed the old man to hobble away. 'Cruel,' he thought, 'but maybe it's a good idea.'

He wandered on enjoying the unseasonably bright day. St Paul's was badly blackened but was covered with workmen apparently rebuilding it in a radical style. Turning the next corner he was stopped by a man dressed in the English infantry uniform of the day and carrying a pistol, which he immediately pointed at Joseph's chest.

'When were you born?' he demanded.

Joseph looked around. A line of soldiers, clad like the first, stood at the side of the street with their muskets at their sides, as alike as identical twins, in perfect military order.

'It is not me that you're looking for,' said Joseph. 'I was born in 1614. I am fifty-two years old.'

'That is the poorest excuse I have heard this morning,' said the officer. He raised his arm and the soldiers, in one precisely executed movement, raised their guns to the firing position and took aim at Joseph.

He woke in a terrible sweat, only part of which was attributable to the nightmare.

Ah, the defection of his Generals as the fortunes of battle shifted! Rosencreutz would doubtless join them. Hermes Trismegistus had already gone – not by desertion, but deprived of his command. The writings of the Thrice Great, had been banished by Casaubon, exposed as a fraud committed by a writer from the Second or Third Century AD, who had predicted the coming of Christ. The surest form of prophecy – to forecast what has already happened! And two great authorities, Lactantius and Augustine, had been deceived by him.

Aristotle had been forced out. And with him, Ptolemy and Galen. These were great men whose work had been admired and fruitfully used for a millennium or more. Aristotle deserved the greatest respect. Galileo had indeed granted him such, in fulsome words, while chasing him with a cleaver.

Perhaps those who had defended the authority of the Ancients, sometimes by cruel and oppressive means, had an important point of view after all. 'People will be questioning the authority of the Scriptures next,' they had grumbled. At Joseph's feet, the ground began to open up, leaving a mighty chasm into whose darkness he now looked. The voice came back to him of the woman at the meeting in Bristol, requesting a better identification of the Midianites and the Ishmailites. A trivial enough matter, but the word of God, surely, should be perfect, and with all the other authorities falling around him like cracked columns, he felt the Temple beginning to sway. Was the Veil of the Temple about to be torn asunder?

Was there perhaps a sixty or six-hundred-year proclamation in effect? Or some such edict? If the authority of the Bible collapsed all would be lost, bringing with it the disintegration of moral order. A return to chaos would surely ensue, or the terrible scenes of the Apocalypse. He had a dreadful but ultimately rather ridiculous vision of the Four Horsemen charging along the main street of Cottesthorpe causing havoc.

Joseph was flying through a huge rocky desert. By him on all sides low craggy hills swept past. He seemed to be moving without effort or control. After some time – impossible to say how much time – his flight began to slow, but through no decision or action of his own. Soon he was walking through a barren waterless wilderness The stars above him shone with their customary magnificence but the familiar pattern had shifted across the sky and the constellations were set at odd angles so that Orion, for instance, was low in the sky and the mighty hunter of fearsome game looked as though he might be peering into a rabbit hole. Conversion to such modest ambitions struck Joseph as being sinister. His attention was soon directed back to the earth. From the corner of his eye he had seen something moving. Ahead of him the bald skull of an enormous man was shining in the moonlight. The giant was standing on the huge, but empty, shell of a massive turtle, possibly on several turtles stacked upon each other. He had already seen Joseph and was beckoning him, or rather was waving to him, urging him to approach in what seemed to be a quite frantic manner.

'Absolutely not!' muttered Joseph to himself and he ran as hard as he could in the opposite direction, looking over his shoulder anxiously as he went. This almost resulted in a collision with an elderly man who was standing in the middle of the path. The man was wearing an apron with telltale spots of pigment spattered over it – clearly a craftsman of some kind – a painter or engraver perhaps. He addressed Joseph in gloomy tones:

'You shouldn't worry about him. He's harmless. Just lonely and rather sad. He needs someone to talk to. He lost his job. He used to hold up the Earth. It was important work. He can't find anything comparable to replace it.'

'Someone else can console him,' said Joseph, wiping his forehead.

'Are you looking for the Father?' the stranger asked.

Joseph decided to give the more provocative of two possible answers.

'Yes,' he said, although no longer clear who the Father might be.

'You are too late. He died of despair. At least I think so. He left Heaven and wandered into Pangaea. He defied an ancient curse with dreadful consequence. As he touched the Earth, he was transformed into a stromatolite.'

'What is a stromatalite?'

'It's a kind of circular mound of rock that grows by accretion. It makes a good memorial. It's dead, but alive too.'

'Then I may not meet Him?' said Joseph.

'No. But you could make a pilgrimage to pay homage at his stromatolite. Pass the Falls of Golgoth on your left. Then it is number 524287 on the right hand side.'

'Number 524287,' said Joseph faintly. 'Is that the best they could do for Him?'

'It *is* a prime number,' said the man hopefully.

They were interrupted by the first aureate segment of the sun. The brilliant sliver crept over a mountain top, growing in size and splendour with every moment as they watched. The wild and hostile region was immediately transformed into a wonderland of black and gold, the immense long dark shadows of the mountains interpolated by the radiant red gold of the growing disc, writing a wordless book, speaking in silence, eloquent, saying nothing, saying everything.

Joseph watched in awe. 'How beautiful!' he said at last.

'Boring!' replied his companion. 'Happens every day! Always the same. It's been doing it forever and will go on doing it forever. Always the same. On and on. From eternity until now and to eternity again. Like everything else. Things interlocking or going round each other endlessly. Wheels meshing, gears grinding, levers pushing, particles colliding. Cause and effect; sand blowing, thrown against the wind, blown back in your face. Chemicals reacting, rearranging themselves, congealing into lumps, growing legs. Life devoid of life. Dust to unliving dust, to dust again. Ashes to trees again to ashes. I was wrong all my life. Urizen designed it all. But he's a stromatolite too. Number 524288, if you're interested.'

He awoke to find that depression had grown into despair. On a hill, silhouetted against an evil sky, were two crosses bearing dying thieves, with a gap in between as though another cross should have stood there. Perhaps this was the inevitable destination of all knowledge, a desert landscape from which the Creator had been banished, or which had no need for a Creator, which had existed forever for its own mysterious purposes.

He heard more and more voices.

*The tree of knowledge brushes Heaven with its branches, but has its roots in Hell.*

Yes, and perhaps its fruits also. The Medieval Church had been right in discouraging knowledge.

*God has abdicated His throne. The human race is an experiment that failed.*

The periods of despair were recurrent, but there were other times also when he ascended effortlessly – often from the greatest depths – to experience a strange and contradictory elation, almost an ecstasy. The renewal was like the obstinate pushing up of flower heads through the snow, or the apparently impossible gushing out of green growth following a forest fire, where everything around was death and devastation. Inside him was a stubborn renewal of something important, an obstinate conviction that the pursuit of knowledge must and would continue, wherever it led. It was not of itself wholly good nor wholly bad, not laudable nor contemptible, not to be condemned or condoned, but *necessary*. It was not a matter of choice. It was not a subject for morality. It was *given*. It was an inherent part of the mind and life of men and women and must continue until such time as the Earth was swallowed by some catastrophe or reached the limits of its own mortality.

Another fit of coughing shook him like a reed in the wind. All night he fought for breath while the sweat saturated his dressings. As the first light was gathering he fell into a calm sleep, was aware only of a familiar voice and a hand holding his in the deepening darkness.

\*     \*     \*     \*     \*

Before him were new colours, unheard of colours that he had never seen while waking. The night and day seemed to coexist, one shading imperceptibly into the other. All the landscapes that he had ever seen – desert, meadow, lake, mountain, river, delta, sea, island, forest, moor, swamp and dune were all represented. All time and times were there too. The skies were filled with an immense peace. Nothing could trouble such a skyscape. Here was a new Heaven and a new Earth, the two embracing on the distant horizon.

After minutes of profound stillness and utter peace, a subtle change, so slow that one could not be sure that it was really happening, began to transform the sky, like a ferment or elixir. Clouds of illuminated droplets and glistening crystals were forming from the radiant light and moving about the heavens as though stirred by an invisible spoon. The sun glanced off the drops – there were so many – making beautiful rainbow patterns like those above a waterfall. Some seemed to be assembling into linear patterns and changing into wooden spars, which gathered together close by him, but his attention was rather on the glorious lights and colours above. He watched in astonishment as the specks and shards gradually crystallised into words:

### *Everything that lives is holy*

The scene was supremely wonderful. But the words stopped forming, as though the unseen mechanism had jammed or the author had suffered a severe bout of writer's block. There followed the sounds of dispute. The atmosphere of peace and harmony had been too good to last of course. Off stage somewhere was a rising babble of voices. An argument was taking place. The message stayed there for some time while the confused noises swelled, diminished and swelled again. 'There must be a committee in progress,' thought Joseph. 'We are going to wait a long time. Or else it's the usual administrative blunder, and we will wait even longer. The amazing thing is not that we fail so often, but that anything ever gets done at all.' The words began to disintegrate into separate shards and were soon streaming away, leaving an empty sky.

He was startled suddenly by another event. He had been so preoccupied watching the sky that he had not noticed that some of the evanescent materials of the atmosphere had aggregated into spars of timber and were assembling in front of him. A chair was constructing itself a few feet away. And a figure was gradually solidifying – a figure somewhat out of context in the transfigured other-worldly scene. The figure was not sitting in the chair but was crawling about underneath it, with his definitely untransfigured bum sticking out towards Joseph. He was subjecting the legs of the chair to a searching examination as though he suspected that they had been sabotaged.

Above, there was evidence that the dispute behind the scenes had been resolved. Joseph's attention turned back to the sky, where the shafts of light were reassembling themselves into a glorious illuminated script. Another sentence was being written. He watched in amazement as the new message was fastened together as if by unseen hands. This time it seemed to be complete and read:

### *Everything that exists is holy.*

The figure had now emerged from underneath the chair. He seemed to be satisfied and had entrusted his bottom to the seat, but the effort of examination had been considerable and for several minutes he sat facing away, puffing and blowing. At last he had recovered his breath and swivelled towards Joseph. The bushy, receding hair and moustache seemed vaguely familiar, but Joseph could not think why. He feared that he was about to be put through some tough questioning. This time, however, the professor was relaxed, affable and smiling warmly.

'Good morning,' he said, 'you may not remember me...'

# GLOSSARY

| | |
|---|---|
| **Adepti** | general term for those who had special knowledge – who had *attained* or *acquired,* from Latin *adipiscor.* |
| **Alembic** | distillation vessel. |
| **Ampulla** | two-handled flask or pot. |
| **Aqua regia** | royal water, a name implying that it dissolves the noble metals. In modern times made by mixing hydrochloric and nitric acids. |
| **Argente vive** | living silver, presumably quicksilver, ie. mercury. |
| **Arminianism** | a theological movement of the $17^{th}$. Century, liberalising Calvinistic idea of election. |
| **Athanor** | self-feeding furnace. |
| **Bacchantes** | Priestesses of Bacchus. |
| **Bain-marie** | the modern water bath or double saucepan. |
| **Bartholomeaus Anglicus** | Author of a famous encylopaedia, published about 1240. |
| **Calcination** | roasting heat |
| **Calx** | The residue left by heating a metal in air. Usually an oxide in modern terms. |
| **Cassola** | vessel with perforated cover. |
| **Cibation** | Continual feeding of a crucible with fresh material. |
| **Clivers** | cleavers or goose grass, also **Galium aparine**. |
| **Crepitation** | *crackling* as in salt cast into a fire. |
| **Croll** | Oswald Crollius, 1580-1609. Advocate of Paracelsus's ideas on chemical medicines. |
| **Cucurbit** | a cylindrical (gourd shaped) vessel, usually part of an alembic. |
| **Culpeper** | Nicholas Culpeper, apothecary, who published The Complete Herbal (1649). |
| **Cyprium** | copper, cuprum, cyprium derive from the Greek *Cyprian*. Cyprus was a rich source of copper for the Ancient World. |
| **Decans** | The 10-day units into which the Ancient Egyptian year was divided, each marked by the appearance of a particular star at dawn. |
| **Decoction** | extraction in boiling water. |
| **Demiurge** | A subordinate god (Plato and Gnosticism), assisting in the ordering of the material world. |

**Diaphoretic** substance provoking sweating.
**Fama fraternitatis**
first book of the Rosicrucian Manifesto, published 1614.
**Guaiac** from the genus Guaiacum.
**Hubert** Robert Hubert was hanged for allegedly setting the Great Fire of London. To call the court's verdict 'unsafe' would be a gross understatement.
**Iatrochemists** Term associated particularly with Paracelsus and his followers, indicating the application of chemistry to medicine.
**Inceration** the act of smearing or covering with wax.
**Jesuits' Bark** from the cinchona species; containing quinine, until recent times the only effective drug for malaria.
**Kabbala** Jewish mysticism from Medieval period, involving much symbolism and numerology.
**Lactantius** AD 240-320. Christian apologist.
**Lapis lazuli** semi-precious gem containing the blue pigment, ultramarine. Used by artists in the Mediaeval and Renaissance periods.
**Marcus Graecus**
Identity not known. The Book of Fires was probably a $11^{th}$ or $12^{th}$ Century production, but, in the $17^{th}$ Century attributed to earlier times – an attempt, in part, to describe the Greek fire of the Ancient World.
**Mary the Jew** Alchemist from the Alexandrian period.
**Mendeleyev** originator of the Periodic Table of elements.
**Mercurius Dulcis**
sweet mercury or calomel. Now known as mercurous chloride. Mild and slow acting compared with the freely soluble mercury sublimate (modern mercuric chloride).
**Metoposcopy** the forerunner of $19^{th}$. Century phrenology.
**Mundification** Cleaning or purifying.
**Orpiment** Arsenic trisulphide in modern terms.
**Paropsis** a square dish
**Permanganic** the colour of potassium permanganate. Probably not known in the $17^{th}$ Century.
**Phoebus** Phoebus Apollo, the Greek sun god.
**Regulus** metallic part of ore, sinking to the bottom of the vessel, especially used in connection with antimony. The *regulus martis stellatus* appeared in a striking star pattern.
**Rosenkreuz** Christian Rosenkreuz, supposed founder of the Rosicrucian Order, described in the Fama Fraternitatis (see above).
**Sackbut** Old form of trombone.
**Scammony** prepared from the great bindweed, Calystegia sepium.
**Scutella** platter.

**Sephiroth**    the ten mystic names of God (see *Kabala*).
**Skimmington Ride**
    Procession in which the effigy of a miscreant was borne around the streets and abused by the citizens. See The Mayor of Casterbridge – but it is centuries older than Hardy.
**Stibnite**    antimony sulphide, used in Old Testament times by women as mascara.
**Sublimation**    Vapourising by heat
**Testum**    a cooking dish or lid on top of which hot coals were placed
**Theriac**    antidote to venemous bites.
**Van Helmont 1577-1644.**
    Practised alchemy but also conducted important experiments in the modern sense.
**Venter equines** literally the horse's belly or womb.

Printed in the United Kingdom
by Lightning Source UK Ltd.
126628UK00001B/55-72/A